ARK ROYAL

CHRISTOPHER G. NUTTALL

http://www.chrishanger.net
http://chrishanger.wordpress.com/
http://www.facebook.com/ChristopherGNuttall

All Comments Welcome!

IF YOU WISH FOR PEACE PREPARE FOR WAR

-Royal Navy Motto

Seventy years ago, the interstellar supercarrier *Ark Royal* was the pride of the Royal Navy. But now, her weapons are outdated and her solid-state armour nothing more than a burden on her colossal hull. She floats in permanent orbit near Earth, a dumping ground for the officers and crew the Royal Navy wishes to keep out of the public eye.

But when a deadly alien threat appears, the modern starships built by humanity are no match for the powerful alien weapons. *Ark Royal* and her mismatched crew must go on the offensive, buying time with their lives And yet, with a drunkard for a Captain, an over-ambitious first officer and a crew composed of reservists and the dregs of the service, do they have even the faintest hope of surviving…

…And returning to an Earth which may no longer be there?

Text copyright © 2014 Christopher G Nuttall

ISBN: 1502885689
ISBN 13: 9781502885685

*There's no real British space program –
and the cynic in me doubts that there ever will be.*

But I can dream.

CHAPTER ONE

"Commodore?"

Commodore Sir Theodore Smith opened his eyes and glared at his wristcom, lying where he'd left it on his bedside table. His mouth tasted foul, reminding him that he'd drunk several pints of ship-brewed rotgut before staggering into his bunk and going to bed. The ship's doctor would probably want a few words with him later; regulations might not frown on officers and crewmen drinking when they weren't on duty, but ship-brewed alcohol wasn't always healthy.

"Yes," he growled, pushing the thought aside. God, he needed a drink. "What is it?"

"There's a priority-one message from the Admiralty," Midshipwoman Lopez said. There were times when Ted wondered just who the young woman had pissed off at Portsmouth Naval Training Base. *Ark Royal* was no posting for an ambitious and capable young officer. "They request your immediate presence at Nelson Base."

Ted blinked in surprise. He'd always had the impression that Nelson Base preferred to forget that *Ark Royal* – and her drunkard of a commander – existed. They were an embarrassment, a relic of Britain's first step into interstellar power. If *Ark Royal* hadn't been famous, she would probably have been broken up for scrap or sold to a third-rate power by now. And if Ted hadn't been a drunkard, he might have been promoted to Admiral.

"I'm on my way," he said, finally. Urgent summons from the Admiralty were almost never good news. "Have my shuttle prepared."

He stumbled out of bed, then reached into his drawer and removed a stimulant tab, which he pressed against his forearm. Once, it had seemed a wise precaution; now, he honestly didn't know why he bothered. But it had paid off for him, he had to admit, as he felt the drug working its way through his body. He wouldn't go into the meeting, whatever it was, suffering from the aftermath of too much drinking.

Biting down a series of curses, he stepped into the washroom and glared at his face in the mirror. His hair had gone white years ago; his face was marred with stubble. He rapidly ran a shaver over his cheekbones and jaw, then stepped into the shower and washed himself rapidly. Outside, he pulled on the dark blue dress uniform favoured by Her Majesty's Navy, then checked his appearance in the mirror. He might not look as perfect as the men and women on the recruiting posters, he knew, but at least he looked presentable.

He left his cabin and strode through the ship towards the shuttlebay. By now, he could have found his way around his ship blindfold. Ted had spent fifty years in the British Navy and most of them had been spent on *Ark Royal*, a position that had been intended as a punishment for carelessness as a young Lieutenant. Somehow, he'd been promoted upwards until he reached Captain and then Commodore, although the ranks were partly worthless. *Ark Royal* wouldn't see action unless the Navy was desperate.

She was seventy years old, the first true interstellar carrier put into space by the British Navy – and a piece of living history. Civilians found her box-like shape ugly as hell, but Ted loved her for what she was. Over the years, keeping *Ark Royal* in something resembling fighting trim had become an obsession, one that had consumed his life. He sometimes wondered if the Navy had known what it was doing by assigning him to the carrier, or if it had been sheer luck. He pushed the thought aside as he scrambled into his shuttle and nodded to the pilot to take them to Nelson Base. No doubt the Navy had its reasons for the urgent summons.

Space was filled with activity, he realised, as the shuttle headed towards Nelson Base. There were military starships everywhere; American, Russian, Chinese, European, Japanese and several smaller nations, all frantically preparing for operations. Ted eyed them in surprise, then activated the shuttle's datanet and scanned for answers. There was nothing, beyond a general alert from the Admiralty. Ted felt his eyes narrow. The First Space Lord might have decided to call an unscheduled exercise, but that wouldn't have affected the other interstellar powers. Something was *definitely* up.

Nelson Base was a giant station, hanging in geostationary orbit over Britain. It was actually older than *Ark Royal*, although it had been extensively modified in the ninety years since it had been constructed and then activated. Ted frowned as there was a series of security checks, all of which had to be cleared before the shuttle was allowed to dock. Inside, a pair of armed Royal Marines escorted him to the First Space Lord's office. But what was going on?

"Commodore Smith," the First Space Lord said, as Ted was escorted through the hatch and into the office. "Please, have a seat."

Ted nodded. The First Space Lord had once been a classmate of his, years ago. They'd gone through Portsmouth together. Now, one of them was the most powerful uniformed officer in the service and the other... was a drunkard in command of a carrier most officers regarded as a national embarrassment. The First Space Lord had put on a little weight, he noted, but his hair was still as red as ever. Ted wondered, in a moment of insight, if his old friend dyed his hair. He'd certainly been vain when they'd been younger.

The hatch opened again, revealing a thin-faced young man wearing a Captain's uniform, but without a ship name on the jacket. Ted scowled, not liking the implications. By long tradition, the only people allowed to claim the rank of *Captain* were actual starship commanders. In some ways, it was possible to be both a Commodore and a Captain, although Ted himself was a special case. It didn't mean he drew two salaries.

"Captain Fitzwilliam," the First Space Lord said. The newcomer managed a perfect salute; Ted found himself disliking him on sight. "Be seated."

He waited for the newcomer to seat himself, then continued. "There has been an incident," he said. "The Vera Cruz colony has been attacked."

Ted frowned. War seemed the only reasonable explanation for so much military activity in Earth orbit, but Vera Cruz? If he recalled correctly, the world was on the edge of the expanding sphere of human settlement – and not really considered worth fighting over. The Mexicans had

3

won the settlement rights and started to settle the planet. But who would have attacked the planet? There wasn't anything worth taking.

"To be precise, the attack was carried out by aliens," the First Space Lord continued. "There have been three more attacks since then, although we only found out about them seven hours ago. News moves slowly along the edge of the sphere."

"Aliens?" Ted repeated. He would have sooner believed in pirates than aliens. "Are you *sure*?"

"Yes," the First Space Lord said. "We recovered little useful data from Vera Cruz, but both the Chinese mining colony orbiting IAS-73782 and the independent settlement on Maxwell's World had small starships that managed to escape the attackers. The starships that attacked the planets were completely unknown. This is the dawn of an interstellar war."

Ted swallowed. In three hundred years of expansion, ever since the Puller Drive had been invented, humanity hadn't encountered another intelligent race. The highest form of life outside Earth had been a whale-like creature on an oceanic world. Humanity, once convinced that aliens were everywhere, had slowly come to believe that they were alone in the universe.

"We do not know why the aliens attacked the colonies," the First Space Lord said. "So far, all attempts to communicate have simply been ignored. We do know that humanity is at war. The Vulcan Protocols have been activated."

"...Shit," Ted said.

The Vulcan Protocols had been a theoretical study, nothing more. They harked back to a time when alien contact and interstellar war was seen as a very real possibility. In theory, the human race – or at least the major spacefaring powers – was obliged to unite in defence of humanity, putting all grudges aside. Ted rather suspected that it wouldn't be that easy to actually make it happen in practice.

"We will, of course, hope for a diplomatic solution," the First Space Lord said. "However, we are currently preparing for the worst. How long will it take before *Ark Royal* is ready for deployment, assuming an unlimited budget and workforce?"

That was something Ted had worked on ever since he'd been promoted into the command chair, no matter how meaningless it had seemed. "Two weeks if we cut corners, four if we take it slowly," he said. "But the crew would have to be experienced."

Captain Fitzwilliam gaped at him. "*Four* weeks?"

Ted laughed. "Do you think that I spend my days engaging in rum, sodomy and the lash?"

The First Space Lord nodded. "I am pleased to hear that your time on the vessel has not been wasted," he said. "However, it is felt that someone new should take command of *Ark Royal*."

Ted felt cold ice trickling down his spine as he realised where this was leading. "Captain Fitzwilliam will assume command of *Ark Royal*," the First Space Lord informed him. "You will supervise the refitting and then…"

The ice flashed into anger. Ted had served on *Ark Royal* for forty-four years. He was familiar with every last inch of her decks – and with every new component his skeleton crew had installed over the years. Their surprise at the short time it would need to have the ship prepped for service was quite understandable…but they didn't realise that he *hadn't* spent his time drunk out of his mind. No, he'd been keeping the old girl as close to readiness as possible. They hadn't even been paying attention to the supplies he'd requisitioned over the years!

"No," he said, simply.

The First Space Lord lifted his eyebrows. It was a breach of military formality to *interrupt* one's superior, unless it was a matter of life and death.

Ted turned to face Captain Fitzwilliam, fighting to keep his voice even. "Are you familiar with the modifications we have made to our Mark-IV normal space drive? Are you aware of the problems in flying Buccaneer bombers off the flight decks? Do you understand the outdated computer cores we have not been able to replace? Do you realise that half our small craft component is actually outdated? Do you understand the limitations of our onboard weapons systems?"

He looked back at the First Space Lord. "I'm sure that Captain Fitzwilliam is a fine officer," he said, knowing that he would either secure his career or destroy it. "But he hasn't trained on *anything* remotely comparable to *Ark Royal*. There is very little standard about her, sir; her internal systems are a mixture of modern technology and outdated technology that cannot be replaced without tearing up the hull. Are you aware, for example, that we *cannot* mount a modern sensor node on the hull? When switched to active mode, they will blind her inner systems. We actually have to use sensor probes and outriders to expand our sensor range."

"That's absurd," Captain Fitzwilliam protested. "What sort of system would be designed to blind its carrier?"

"It isn't," Ted assured him. "A *modern* carrier wouldn't have a problem. *Ark Royal*, however, was designed as a solid-state entity. She was built to *survive*. We cannot replace the older systems without tearing the hull wide open, which would take far longer than four weeks. We'd be looking at nine months, at best."

He smiled at the younger man. "Still feel like you can take command of *my* ship?"

Captain Fitzwilliam's face darkened, but he held his temper. Ted was privately impressed. He had no illusions about what navy scuttlebutt said about him; it was unlikely in the extreme that any young officer would look up to him as someone to be emulated. It was rather more likely that they considered his career to be a nightmare. Someone edging towards squadron or fleet command would be horrified at the idea of spending forty-four years on the same ship. It wasn't the mark of a promising officer.

"You've made your point," the First Space Lord said. "But four weeks is a rather short time for a complete refit."

"I should have sent you flypaper reports," Ted said, remembering one of the classes they'd shared at Portsmouth. An officer, pestered for paperwork he didn't have, had started sending reports on the number of flies killed by flypaper while on deployment. The whole episode had been used as a warning of the dangers of too much bureaucracy. "Didn't anyone ever read my reports?"

He shook his head a moment later. The only ship considered less likely to go into battle was Lord Nelson's *Victory*, which was – technically – the First Space Lord's flagship. But as *Victory* was a sailing ship, it was unlikely the First Space Lord had spent any time on her since the commission. She normally served as a tourist attraction.

"I will take your word for it," the First Space Lord said. His tone suggested that if it took *longer* than four weeks to get *Ark Royal* ready for deployment, Ted could start looking for a new job. "Captain Fitzwilliam will serve as your XO."

Ted swallowed a curse – and, beside him, Captain Fitzwilliam didn't look any happier. For one of them, there would be an XO looking for a place to plant the knife; for the other, there was an effective demotion. There was only one Captain on a starship and it wouldn't be Fitzwilliam. Unless, of course, Ted failed to make good on his boast. Silently, he promised himself that he would read through Captain Fitzwilliam's file as soon as possible. He didn't even know the man's first name!

"Thank you, sir," he said, finally. "Might I enquire as to deployment plans?"

"The UN Security Council is meeting in emergency session," the First Space Lord said. he jerked a finger towards the deck – and Earth, far below. "For the moment, the Admiralty is concentrating on protecting Britannia and contributing to the defence of Earth. We assume that we will be making future deployments once the Vulcan Protocols are fully activated, but as yet we don't have any details."

Ted nodded. Britannia was Britain's largest possession, a colony world with over a billion settlers from Earth. The British Commonwealth had worked hard to both settle the planet and build up local industry, taking advantage of the latest UN environmental regulations to encourage corporations and private individuals to move to Britannia. There was no way the Government would leave the planet uncovered, even if it meant drawing ships away from Earth. Indeed, Ted had been surprised that *Ark Royal* hadn't been moved to Britannia long ago.

There were other colonies, including a handful of mining settlements and a stake on an Earth-like world that might become a second colony soon enough, but Britannia was too important to lose. The Royal Navy stationed seven of its twelve modern carriers in the system permanently, while the other five were never far away. It seemed unlikely that *anyone* could break through the defences and take the planet.

He scowled. Humanity hadn't really fought an interstellar war. Sure, there had been the skirmishes between Edo and Ghandi, or the confrontation between Washington and Confucius over a third system, but nothing that had broken out into general war. Hell, there were even agreements that Earth and the Sol System would remain neutral if war actually did break out. No one really knew how the latest military technology would work in open warfare. There were simulations and exercises, but they were never as useful as the real thing.

And now there was an alien threat. What sort of technology would *they* have?

"So far, the media has not caught wind of the threat," the First Space Lord informed him, shortly. "The Prime Minister and other world leaders has ordered a total blackout. However, I do not expect that to last long. Rumours are already flying around the datanet and it won't be long before someone breaks the blackout. It will certainly be broken when we start calling up reserves and conscripting civilians.

"Go back to your ship, taking your new XO with you," he continued. "Requisition whatever you need; I'll do my best to make sure you have it. If we're lucky, this will all blow over, but I rather doubt it."

Ted nodded in agreement. The aliens had just attacked. Unprovoked, as far as anyone knew, they'd just attacked – and not one colony, but four. It suggested either unhealthy confidence or careful observation of humanity before opening fire. Ted wouldn't have been surprised to discover that the aliens had surveyed the entire human sphere. There was enough civilian traffic moving through interstellar space to conceal a handful of alien spy ships, if the aliens showed up on sensors at all. Whatever the civilians might think, there was plenty of space between the planets to hide the entire human fleet.

They think they can win, Ted thought. He shivered at the thought. Only a fool would start a war they didn't think they could win. *What do they want?*

"Yes, sir," he said, pushing his thoughts aside. The prospect of actually taking his ship into harm's way galvanised him. "I won't let you down."

He rose to his feet and saluted, as smartly as he could. Captain Fitzwilliam – no, he'd be a *Commander* now – followed, his face blank and unreadable. Ted sighed, inwardly. Fitzwilliam would have a major chip on his shoulder after being told he would be given command – and then watching as it was snatched away from him. Ted wouldn't really *blame* him for being irked, but he couldn't afford the distraction of a sulking XO. They would have to talk and hash it out, perhaps over a drink…

No, Ted told himself, firmly. A drunkard could not take command of a ship that was going into action. *That* was plain common sense. *You are not going to drink until the war is over.*

CHAPTER
TWO

Captain James Montrose Fitzwilliam had to fight to keep his annoyance and disappointment from showing on his face as he followed his new commanding officer through the metallic corridors of Nelson Base. It had seemed so perfect. His uncle – a high-ranking officer – had known about the alert in time for James to attempt to push himself forward as *Ark Royal's* commander. A modern carrier would have required an officer with more experience – the old boy's network went only so far – but *Ark Royal* didn't have such stringent requirements. He could have taken command – and, in becoming the youngest commanding officer in the Royal Navy, ensured his swift promotion to command of a more modern starship.

But Commodore – *Captain*, he reminded himself – Smith had talked the Admiral into leaving *him* in command of *Ark Royal*. The hell of it was, James knew, was that Smith might not be too far wrong. James had served on two carriers and a frigate, but all three of them had been modern ships. *Britannia* had barely been out of the slips when he'd served as her tactical officer. But *Ark Royal* was over seventy years old. She might well be harder to command than a more modern vessel.

Resentment bubbled at the corner of his mind, muted by the grim awareness that Smith might have saved him from embarrassment – or worse. He wouldn't gain experience of serving as XO on a modern carrier if he served on *Ark Royal* – and he wouldn't gain command experience to offset the starship's age. His career might just have been frozen solid, as solid as Smith's own...and he'd done it to himself. How could he reasonably blame Smith for wanting to keep command? *He* wanted command!

They entered the shuttlebay and passed a handful of elaborate security checks before boarding the tiny ship. Smith spoke briefly to the pilot, then settled back in his chair and closed his eyes. James eyed him thoughtfully, wondering just what the older man was thinking. Relief, perhaps, that he'd retained his command? Or irritation at having a new XO thrust down his throat? But then, *Ark Royal* hadn't had an official XO since she'd been placed in the reserves. Smith had effectively been his own XO.

The shuttle quivered as it floated out of the shuttlebay and headed towards the naval reserve yards, where *Ark Royal* was waiting. James couldn't help a flicker of excitement as he leaned forward, peering out the porthole for his first glimpse of the massive carrier. Even if he wasn't going to take command, he would still be serving on her – and the first sight of a new starship was always special. Dozens of other shuttles and tiny starships floated through Earth's crowded orbital space, their sheer multitude a sign that something was badly wrong. It was only a matter of time, James knew, before the news media discovered what was going on. And then...

He swallowed, feeling a curious tension at the base of his throat. Unless it was all a big misunderstanding, they were going to be going to war – with aliens. It was a staggering thought. No one had anticipated aliens, not really. The Royal Navy had confronted Chinese and Russian starships over brief disputes over mining and settlement rights, but there had been no major shooting war since the Puller Drive had been invented. And yet...he wondered, suddenly, just why so many resources had been poured into the military. All of the major spacefaring powers had built up their navies, often at staggering cost. Had they known there *was* a potential outside threat?

But humans aren't known for being peaceable, he thought, snidely. *If we didn't keep up with our defences, our human enemies would overwhelm us.*

The shuttle quivered again as *Ark Royal* came into view. James sucked in his breath, drinking in the details; the giant carrier was larger than he'd realised...and cruder. The elegant lines of modern carriers – to say nothing of civilian starships – were missing. Instead, she was a boxy hulk, studded with weapons and sensor blisters. Four fighter launch tubes protruded out of her hull, each one wrapped in heavy armour. *Ark Royal* was as much battleship as she was carrier, he recalled from the briefing notes. The naval doctrine of her time had insisted that carriers had to be able to take damage as well as dish it out. It was one of the reasons her rate of acceleration was so slow.

"Half of the weapons have been replaced over the years," Smith said. "Our tactical system had to be modified extensively just to handle them."

James jumped. He hadn't realised Smith was watching him. The back of his neck heated as he turned to face his commanding officer, realising that he had no choice, but to do his job to the best of his ability. Connections, no matter how highly placed, wouldn't be enough to save him if his commanding officer wrote a negative review. And besides, he *had* asked for it.

"She's magnificent, sir," he said, and meant it. "How well does she handle?"

"Like a wallowing pig," Smith said. "There aren't many real improvements we could make to the drives without tearing the whole rear section apart and replacing them completely."

The shuttle altered course, allowing him to see every last detail of the carrier's hull. James had to admit that she looked good, if crude. She might have been in the reserves, but her crew hadn't been allowed to slack off... even if they had felt they'd been exiled to the ass end of nowhere. He felt an odd flicker of admiration for Smith. The man might have a reputation for drinking, yet he'd managed to keep his command in shape.

Smith keyed his terminal as the shuttle straightened out and headed towards the shuttlebay. "I'm calling the senior crew to the shuttlebay," he said, by way of explanation. "There won't be a formal welcoming party, I'm afraid, but I'll introduce you to the senior officers. You can meet the others later, once we're more organised."

"Yes, sir," James said. There were senior officers who would be furious if the formalities were ignored, but he saw Smith's point. *Ark Royal's* reserve crew didn't have the manpower to put on a display. He swallowed again as he realised the depth of his own ignorance. *Ark Royal's* crew knew far more than him about their starship's condition. "I look forward to it."

Smith smiled. The shuttle landed – there was a faint shiver as the shuttle's artificial gravity field merged with the starship's internal field – and the hatch hissed open. James rose to his feet and followed Smith out of the hatch and into the shuttlebay, looking around with considerable interest. The shuttlebay looked as crude as the starship's interior, but it was clearly kept in good shape. Two more shuttles, both partly cannibalised for spare parts, sat on the other side of the giant compartment. They looked oddly pitiful to James's eyes.

It took him a moment to realise that something was missing...and several more moments to realise what it *was*. The omnipresent background noise from the starship's drives was simply absent. James felt his eyes narrow, then realised that most of the drives and their fusion cores would have been shut down while the starship remained in the reserves. There was no point in placing further wear and tear on equipment that was effectively irreplaceable.

They stepped through the airlock and into the welcoming lounge. James saluted the flag, then straightened automatically as he saw four officers waiting for them. All four of them looked alarmingly dishevelled, as if they'd only just climbed out of their bunks. They didn't seem to have much pride in themselves, he realised grimly, and yet there was something about them that kept him from dismissing them automatically. He couldn't place his finger on it.

"Welcome aboard," Smith said. "Commander Fitzwilliam, please allow me to introduce Alan Anderson, Chief Engineer, Lieutenant Daniel Lightbridge, Helmsman, Lieutenant Commander Keith Farley, Tactical Officer and Midshipwoman Janelle Lopez."

There was a long moment as they exchanged salutes. James studied them, silently promising to read their files as soon as possible. Anderson looked tough; his left arm had been replaced with a metallic prosthetic that made no attempt to pass for natural flesh and blood. Like most senior engineering crew, James knew, he would have spent most of his career on *Ark Royal*, working his way up the ranks to Chief Engineer. Chances were that he wouldn't have a hope of another posting, even if *Ark Royal* were to be permanently decommissioned. His experience would be years out of date.

Lightbridge was a tall black man, his bald head gleaming in the cold light from overhead. He held himself so still that it seemed almost unnatural, although there was a hint of easy competence in his stance. All helmsmen, at least in James's experience, resented not being starfighter pilots and tended to put their ships through exaggerated manoeuvres purely to prove they could. *Ark Royal* probably wouldn't be able to tolerate it, he guessed, making another mental note to check the files. Just who had Lightbridge pissed off to be posted to the ancient carrier?

Keith Farley, by contrast, seemed permanently uncertain of his capabilities. The name was oddly familiar, but it took James several moments to remember a naval bulletin that had named and shamed an officer who'd managed to ram an asteroid, a feat that should have been impossible. No doubt part of the story had been missing, he decided, as he eyed Farley carefully. He should have been kicked out of the navy if he'd actually rammed an asteroid.

Midshipwomen Lopez was a surprise. She was tall and slim, with a dark complexion and long dark hair that fell down her back. Naval uniforms were far from flattering, but James couldn't help noticing the swell of her breasts and the shape of her hips. What was *she* doing on the ship? James wondered, sourly, if she was having a relationship with one of the other crewmen. Being assigned to *Ark Royal* was career death, to all intents and purposes. The thought made him scowl, bitterly. His own career might have been killed...and he'd done it to himself.

"You can meet everyone formally later," Smith said. He raised his voice, addressing his officers. "Briefing Room A, ten minutes."

James nodded and followed Smith through the starship's interior. The corridors were bare; every few metres, a hatch lay open, revealing the starship's innards. James cringed, remembering just what his first CO had said when a hatch had been left open accidentally, then realised that *Ark Royal's* crew didn't have much choice. There was so much to do and so few of them to actually do it. He was mildly surprised that there was no dust in the corridors; indeed, it seemed that the whole ship was surprisingly clean.

He paused as he heard a dull rumble echoing through the ship. "What was *that*?"

"Test cycle for Fusion Five," Smith said. "We test one of the six fusion cores each day, just to make sure that they are still operational. Losing one of them would be irritating."

"More than irritating," James said, recalling his earlier thoughts. "Could they be replaced, if necessary?".

"We'd have to have the cores built specially for *Ark Royal*," Smith said. He smirked, as if something amusing had just struck him. "Not the only such problem, of course. We couldn't get the different generations of computer cores to work together, no matter what the manufacturer claimed. In the end, we had to splice in a Chinese system we scrounged up from somewhere, just to provide a bridging system. If we have to replace the cores, we can probably improve on the design and cut out half of the cost."

James stared at him. "You have a *Chinese* computer system attached to the ship?"

"Among others," Smith said. He seemed to be enjoying James's discomfort. "As I told you, we've had to improvise."

Briefing Room A looked as though it had been reassuringly normal, once. A large table sat in the middle of the compartment, surrounded by chairs...half of which were piled high with boxes. Judging by the markings, James decided, Smith and his crew had laid claim to thousands of outdated spare parts that would otherwise have been sold to civilians or simply discarded for scrap. Probably the former, he told himself, after a moment. Even outdated military surplus would be useful for civilian starship crews.

"Find a seat," Smith said. "We'll start in a moment."

James hesitated, then took one of the handful of empty seats and watched as Midshipwoman Lopez entered, carrying a tray of mugs. There was a large bottle beside the mugs, he noticed as she put the tray down on the table, but it was completely unmarked. If it came from a still on *Ark Royal* – technically against regulations, yet he'd never served on a ship that *didn't* have a still – it might well be very strong indeed.

"Be seated," Smith ordered as his officers entered the compartment. "We have a great deal to discuss."

It seemed remarkably informal to James, but he realised – as the officers sat down and reached for their mugs - that they shared a camaraderie that bound them together, no matter how poor their grasp of naval discipline seemed to be. Smith had forged a good team, he suspected, although they had never been tested in the fire. But then, very few officers had any experience with interstellar combat. A great many officers and men were going to be tested soon.

"There have been developments," Smith said, quietly. He briefly ran through what the Admiral had told them, ending with the statement that *Ark Royal* was going to return to active service. "We have a month – perhaps less – to ready ourselves for combat."

"Aliens," Anderson repeated. "Not another race of Alien Space Bats, I hope?"

James had to smile. The Alien Space Bats had been a hoax, perpetrated by bored asteroid miners years ago, back when humanity hadn't yet left the Sol System. By the time the miners had finally confessed to the hoax, countless academics had been taken in and wasted thousands of hours trying to make contact with the enigmatic aliens. The affair had dented so many otherwise reputable careers that many scientists had refused to believe it when spacers had reported discovering non-intelligent life forms on several extra-solar worlds.

"There have been deaths," Smith said. "And it isn't just us. Every spacefaring power is bringing its military to full alert."

There was a long pause as they contemplated the end of peace. James knew that MI6 knew the strengths and weaknesses of the other human interstellar powers...but they knew nothing about the enigmatic alien threat. Unless he'd been right, he told himself, and enough people *had* known to start preparing the human race for contact. And yet...surely the secret would have leaked out by now. Humanity's governments were very poor at keeping secrets.

"We should have our new crewmen assigned to us within the week," Smith said, before anyone could start discussing the potential nature of the threat. "Once we do, I want to move ahead with a full rejuvenation of the ship." He looked over at Anderson. "We'll go with Option Alpha, I think, and concentrate on our war-fighting capabilities first."

"Understood," Anderson said, gruffly. "We will need to clear the launch bays before we can start taking on new fighters."

"It may be a while before we get them," Smith said. "They'll all have to be removed from storage and checked out before they're sent to us."

James blinked in surprise. The carrier had no fighters?

"They might send us the older models," Farley suggested. "I don't think that many of the newer carriers could handle them."

"We will check it out," Smith said. He looked from face to face. "This isn't a drill, but a real situation. We – the entire human race – are going to war with a threat of unknown power and motivation. All we really know about them is that they're hostile. I expect each and every one of you to do your duty."

"Of course, sir," Anderson said. He patted the table affectionately. "The old lady will do her duty too."

Smith smiled. "Of course she will," he agreed. He stood, then paused. "As yet, there has been no formal announcement of the situation. I imagine that will change, soon enough, but until then please don't mention it in your v-mails. It would be inconvenient to have to break you out of prison."

James had to smile at the weak joke, although he knew that Smith was right. It wouldn't be long before word got out – and, once it did, there would be panic. No wonder the Admiral had wanted to get as much done as possible before the news hit the media datanet. But something would definitely leak once the reserves were called up…

Of course it will, he thought, tartly. *The reserves haven't been called up for anything other than mandatory training in years.*

Smith waited for the officers to leave the compartment, then turned to James. "I want you to familiarise yourself as quickly as possible with the crew and our internal systems," he ordered, shortly. "Once we get the first set of reservists, I want you to handle their integration into the ship's crew. My current set of officers will have seniority, regardless of actual time served. We can't afford unpractised officers trying to take command, not now."

"Understood," James said, recognising the unspoken warning. *He* was an unpractised officer, at least on *Ark Royal*. There was no alternative, but to study the ship as quickly as possible and figure out just what improvements had been made to the original systems. "I won't let you down."

CHAPTER

THREE

"But it wasn't my fault!"

Kurt Schneider gritted his teeth as he drove away from the school, silently cursing his teenage daughter under his breath. It *was* her fault, he knew, that he had been summoned out of work early just to hear the head-teacher explain, in great detail, precisely why Penny had been summarily suspended from school for two weeks. And then – and *then* – he'd been warned that if her behaviour didn't improve, she would be permanently expelled and forced to find another school.

"It really wasn't," Penny whined. "I didn't mean to get into a fight..."

"You told your teacher that she was a right stupid cow," Kurt growled. The recording of the whole incident had been shocking. "And your head-teacher was quite right to say your behaviour was unacceptable."

"But she kept changing the rules," Penny insisted. "I..."

"Shut up," Kurt snapped, massaging his temples. It had been a long day even before the call had come from school. "When we get home, we are going to have a proper talk about your conduct."

Penny snorted, crossed her arms under her breasts and stared out the window, sulking in a pose that was as old as humanity itself. Kurt glared at her, wondering just when his sweet little daughter had become a monster, then turned his attention back to the road. If his wife hadn't thought that Polly – and her brother Percy – deserved an expensive education, they wouldn't be forced into pointless classes...and he wouldn't have to work such long hours just to keep them in school. He loved his children, really he did, but he wasn't in the mood to put up with an argument.

She didn't say a word until he finally pulled up outside the house, whereupon she jumped out of the car and flounced inside, no doubt hoping to get her side of the story over to her mother first. Kurt sighed, closing his eyes for a long moment of rest, then opened the door and climbed out of the car. Inside, he could already hear Molly shouting at her daughter. His wife didn't sound pleased at all. She'd yell at Penny...and then, Kurt knew, she'd yell at him. It was funny how his daughter became his sole responsibility whenever she was in trouble.

Sighing, he walked up the garden path and into the house. Molly stood in the kitchen, her hands on her hips, glaring menacingly at Penny, who was shouting back at her. It struck Kurt, not for the first time, that Penny was very much a younger version of her mother, complete with blonde hair and a powerful pair of lungs. Kurt sighed again, then blinked in surprise as Molly marched over to him and shoved a piece of paper into his hand. It was a printout of a email, he realised, as he unfolded it and read quickly. And it was calling him back to duty.

"You are grounded for the next two weeks," Molly snarled at Penny. "Go to your room and stay there!"

Penny didn't go quietly. Kurt heard her stamping up the stairs, then slamming the door to her bedroom hard enough to shake the house. He ignored it with the ease of long practice as he reread the sheet of paper. The Royal Navy wanted him back in the service, as soon as possible.

"Well?" Molly demanded. "What's all this about?"

Kurt gritted his teeth, again. His head was already pounding and her razor-sharp words were cutting through what remained of his composure. The message didn't leave any room for evasion, he realised dully. He was ordered to report to the nearest naval base at once or face the consequences. And those consequences could be quite serious.

"They're calling me back to the flag," he said, softly. He swallowed, then nodded. "I'll have to call my boss."

"Now see here," Molly snapped. "I thought you wouldn't have to go back on active duty..."

Kurt rubbed his forehead. They'd met when he'd been a starfighter pilot, resplendent in his dark blue uniform. But a starfighter pilot didn't earn much and, when Penny had been born, he'd resigned from the service and gone into business. The thought of getting back in a cockpit was staggering, but it had been years…he shook his head. There was no room to evade his duty. He'd signed up to the reserves and pocketed the extra cash. In exchange, he had to drop everything when his country called.

"There isn't a choice," he said, tiredly. Mentally, he catalogued what he'd need. He kept an overnight bag under the bed; he'd just have to check it, then add anything else he needed before departing. And then he'd have to hire a taxi…he couldn't take the car, not if he was going away for longer than a few hours. "We took the money, remember?"

Molly's face darkened, unpleasantly. She obsessed over the children, insisting that they received the best of everything, from food to education. Both of them had genuinely believed that Kurt would never be asked to return to duty, apart from the mandatory week of training and exercises all reservists were expected to undertake. But they'd been wrong.

"I signed the papers," Kurt reminded her, before she could explode again. "If I don't respond to the call, I could be jailed. And then there would be no one to feed the family."

Molly sniffed as he turned and walked upstairs, wincing slightly at the sound of loud and obscene music coming from Penny's room. Molly had spoilt her daughter, he told himself tiredly. There were days when he wondered if they would be called to jail to bail Penny out of trouble. If, of course, they could…it had been his fault too, he knew, but he was hardly ever there. How could he spend quality time with his family while earning enough to keep the kids in school?

Shaking his head, he walked into the bedroom and picked up his overnight bag. He checked it carefully, then slung it over his shoulder and walked back downstairs. Penny was already there, her face blotchy with tears. Kurt rolled his eyes, not bothering to conceal his reaction. Why the hell was *Penny* crying? She was probably looking forward to a few days off school.

"You'd better write to me as soon as possible," Molly said, sternly. "And this young lady" – she nodded towards Penny – "will be doing plenty of chores around the house."

Penny looked rebellious. Kurt reached out and gave her a hug, then turned to face Molly. His wife looked tired, but grimly determined. Kurt silently thanked God that he wouldn't be there to hear the coming argument. Molly would know, even if Penny didn't, just how vital it was that she stayed in the expensive school. If nothing else, they would lose the rest of the year's payments if Penny was expelled.

Walking outside, he saw a taxi moving along the street and waved, hastily. The taxi pulled up beside the curve, allowing him to climb inside. He gave the address of the nearest aerospace base – he could report in to any military base, whereupon he would be directed to his muster point – and settled back, feeling his headache slowly fade away. Being away from the children and his wife certainly seemed to make him feel better, no matter how unpleasant it sounded. Just what had he been thinking, he asked himself, when he'd married her?

You were distracted by her enormous knockers, he thought, ruefully. No, that wasn't entirely fair. Molly had been charming as well as attractive – and she could still be charming, when she wanted to be. But she spent most of her time with the kids while he was at work, which made it harder for them to relax and just be themselves. Maybe the break would do him good...but what the hell was going on? The last time he'd reported for training exercises had been seven months ago. It was way too early for another one.

There was a bleep from the taxi's radio as the music cut out, replaced by a nervous-sounding voice. "Please stay tuned for a message from the Prime Minister," it said. The cabbie swore and changed the channel, but it made no difference. Kurt leaned forward as he realised that the message was going out on all channels. "The Prime Minister will address the nation in ten minutes."

Kurt waited, impatiently, for the Prime Minister to begin to speak. Combined with the call-up, it suggested bad news. It suggested war. He didn't make a habit of following international and interplanetary affairs, but he hadn't heard anything that suggested war was on the verge of breaking out. There were bouts of trouble on colony worlds, brief disputes on Earth between smaller nations, yet nothing that should have demanded a full mobilisation...

The radio bleeped again, then a familiar voice came over the airwaves. Kurt realised, as he listened, that the Prime Minister sounded dreadfully tired. Something was definitely wrong.

"We have received news from the very edge of settled space," the Prime Minister said, in a manner that suggested he wasn't quite sure he believed his own words. "A number of human settlements have been attacked by a force of unknown origin. We do not know why these...aliens attacked us, or what they want. All we know is that they are hostile."

Kurt felt his blood run cold. *Aliens*? There had been speculation – and no shortage of movies, books and interactive games – about what might happen when humanity finally met another intelligent race. The aliens might be friendly, they might be so different that communication was next to impossible...or they might be hostile. And yet, there was no logical reason for two interstellar powers to go to war. There was no shortage of resources in space, nothing to fight over. Unless they were so completely repulsed by humanity...

He shook his head as the Prime Minister kept speaking, declaring a state of emergency and informing the country that every last military reservist was being called up at once. Kurt sighed, knowing just how many problems that would cause. His job wasn't vitally important, but there were Royal Navy reservists working for interstellar transport and colonisation corporations. Calling them all up to the colours would probably cause economic problems for the entire world. But there seemed to be no alternative.

"Aliens," the cabbie said, when the Prime Minister had finally finished speaking. "Do you believe it?"

Kurt hesitated, then nodded. "I think so," he said, reluctantly. "They wouldn't call up every last reservist if they didn't expect real trouble."

The cabbie said nothing else until they pulled up outside East Fortune Aerospace Base. Kurt got out, paid him a sizable tip and then headed towards the gates. A handful of RAF Regiment soldiers were on guard outside, fingering their weapons nervously. Kurt eyed them as he joined the queue of reservists waiting to pass through the gates, realising – again – that this was deadly serious. Inside, he reported in and then waited for orders. They were a long time in coming.

"*Ark Royal*?" He said, when the message finally popped up in his terminal. "They're reactivating the Old Lady?"

"So it would seem," the harassed dispatcher said. If Kurt had had any doubts about the seriousness of the situation, they would have been pushed aside by how desperately the military was scrambling to get everyone where they were going. No one seemed to have done any preplanning at all. "There's a shuttle for Cochrane Yards leaving in an hour; once you're there, you can join the other reservists for pickup."

"Understood," Kurt said. He cursed inwardly, remembering that he had to call his boss – and Molly. Would she be concerned about the prospect of him going to war? "Let me know when the shuttle is boarding."

————

Major Charles Parnell cursed out loud as the enemy force appeared out of nowhere, advancing towards the handful of Royal Marines with deadly intent. He'd deployed most of his men forward, leaving him and his officers dangerously exposed – precisely, he realised now, what the exercise designers had intended. He dived for cover, then lifted his rifle and started firing towards the enemy soldiers. They ducked themselves, but kept advancing.

I screwed this one up, he told himself, as he motioned for his men to fall back. There was no time to recall any of his squads, not in time to make a difference. He'd misread the situation and was about to suffer for it. The post-exercise discussions would be hellish. *I...*

His radio buzzed. "ENDEX," a voice said. "I say again, ENDEX."

Charles blinked in surprise. The exercise had barely begun! Why was it being terminated?

"Understood," he said, keying his throat mike. "ENDEX acknowledged."

He stood up and looked around. Salisbury Plain training area had been carefully designed to allow the various ground forces to practice their trade. The Royal Marines, who were regularly deployed to various colony worlds, made good use of the facilities...but now, the exercise had simply been terminated. He saw his commandos leaving cover and walking back towards the garrison, chatting to friends among the 'enemy' force. One way or another, he knew, he would never have a chance to recover from his mistake. It would be a permanent black mark on his record.

They reached the garrison, where a handful of sergeants were hastily sorting out the various units and pointing them towards their barracks. Charles spoke briefly to his Regimental Sergeant Major, then hastened down the corridor towards the briefing room. It looked as though *every* exercise had been terminated, all commanding officers gathering to be briefed together. Something was definitely wrong.

He took a seat in the briefing room and chatted briefly to the other officers, but it rapidly became clear that none of them knew what was going on. The CO entered the room, waved them back into their chairs before they could salute properly, then took his place at the front of the chamber. His face was pale, almost ashen. Had there been a natural disaster, Charles asked himself, or had terrorists struck again? He forced himself to relax. No doubt they would be given the answers soon enough.

"We have made first contact – and they're hostile," the CO said, once the doors had been sealed. "Several planets have been attacked by alien forces."

He ran through a brief outline of everything they knew, which wasn't much. Civilians had no idea how long it could take to get a message from the edge of human space to Earth, which meant that the aliens might already have invaded several more worlds. It was quite likely that several worlds along the frontier had no idea of what was going on – and the first warning they'd get would come when alien starships materialised in their skies.

"All exercises are hereby terminated," the CO continued, once he had finished outlining the bare bones of the situation. "We will be deploying within the week, ideally, either to places on Earth or Britannia. Marine units will probably be deployed to Royal Navy starships; so far, we have only the bare bones of a deployment plan. I don't think I have to tell you that all leave is cancelled."

There were some chuckles. "Sir," a wag in the back row said, "would this be a good time to take my sick leave?"

"Probably," the CO said, to general amusement. He smiled, then sobered. "We have been prepping for minor deployments, not a full-scale war. It is possible, I suppose, that the whole issue will be settled before too long, once the diplomats get to work. But we have to assume the worst. You and your men will go to war against an immensely powerful enemy with unknown motivations. We don't know who they are and we don't know what they want."

"Us, it would seem," Charles muttered.

The CO ignored him. "Prepare your men; I want everyone ready for departure within twenty-four hours. Deployment orders will be issued as soon as possible. Once the orders are issued, we will arrange transport on a priority basis. I imagine that the Marines will go first, as the Royal Navy is preparing its carriers for departure."

He paused. "Are there any questions?"

A Colonel stuck up his hand. "Are we going to be engaged in joint operations?"

"I don't know, but I assume so," the CO said. "Scuttlebutt suggests that the Prime Minister is attempting to hammer out the details of a unified command with the other interstellar powers, but it could take months before we have a clear idea of who's in ultimate command. For the moment, we will operate on the assumption that we will fight under separate national authority."

Charles scowled. Collectively, the human race had a formidable number of carriers, starfighters and smaller warships. But that strength would be diluted if they fought separately, rather than as one unified force. Unity of command would be vitally important...but, at the same time, he suspected the Royal Navy would balk at placing its ships under Chinese or Russian command. Or French, for that matter. The old rivalry between Britain and France kept popping up from time to time.

Not a problem for us, at least, he told himself. Unless British settlements were attacked, it was unlikely the ground forces would see any action. But then, they *were* prepped for starship deployments...

"See to your men," the CO ordered. "Dismissed!

Four hours later, orders finally arrived. Charles read them, wondering just what the head shed were thinking. Instead of being attached to a modern carrier, his unit would be deployed to *Ark Royal*. It looked as though someone expected the carrier to see action.

Or, he thought silently, *that they don't want us to see action.*

CHAPTER

FOUR

"Captain," Midshipwoman Lopez said, over the intercom, "the latest shuttle is approaching the shuttlebay."

Ted nodded. Three days of struggling desperately to prepare *Ark Royal* for active service had reminded him, again, of just how much paperwork the first commanding officer of any starship had to actually do. Everything had to be carefully detailed and documented, in triplicate, before the ship could leave orbit. In *Ark Royal's* case, the modifications the crew had made to keep her functional also had to be carefully noted, just to make life simpler for the bureaucrats. But they'd probably end up with headaches if they tried to follow what his crew had done.

"Understood," he said, dropping the terminal on his desk. His office was large, in theory, but several more boxes of spare parts had been stored there for the last few years. "I'm on my way."

He looked wistfully at the cabinet containing his selection of alcohol, then angrily dismissed the thought and strode out of the cabin. It was tempting, so very tempting, to take a glass…but he knew it wouldn't remain at a single glass. He'd take another, and then another, until he was blind drunk. And then the Admiral would relieve him of command, once he found out.

Two hundred crewmen, mainly borrowed from the Luna Shipyards, had already come aboard *Ark Royal* since the PM had made his announcement. They'd done wonders for the ship, but it would still be at least two weeks before they could reasonably claim to be ready for any kind of deployment. Ted marched down the corridor, noting where internal nodes had been carefully replaced with modern systems, then reminded himself to skim through the paperwork once the work was completed. They had to make sure that all of the different systems could work together before they took the starship into combat.

He nodded to Commander Fitzwilliam as he entered the shuttlebay, just in time to watch as the shuttle came into land. Fitzwilliam wasn't doing too badly, as far as Ted could tell, although he was clearly unprepared for the carrier's idiosyncrasies. But then, that would be true of almost everyone in the Royal Navy. The only way to prepare for the carrier was to serve on the carrier. Thankfully, Fitzwilliam was smart enough to listen to his subordinates, rather than lord himself over them. He understood the limitations of his own knowledge.

"Mainly starfighter pilots," Fitzwilliam said, as the shuttle's hatch opened. "They seem to think we need them more than engineers and other workers."

Ted wasn't surprised. Years of experience with the Royal Navy's bureaucracy had left him convinced that the bureaucrats knew absolutely nothing about commanding a starship. A bureaucrat had determined that *Ark Royal* needed starfighter pilots and starfighter pilots had been sent, even though there were no starfighters for them to fly. It probably helped that the starfighter pilots were almost all reservists, who really should have been called up later, once the ship was ready for them.

He waited until the pilots were lined up, then stepped forward. "Welcome aboard," he said. "I will be blunt. There are no starfighters, so we're adding you to the personnel pool right now. You will start by cleaning out your living space, then helping to prepare the launch tubes for the starfighters, once they finally arrive."

None of the pilots looked very happy at his words. Ted concealed his amusement with an effort. Pilots were often prima donnas, demanding everything from the very best of rations to having their starfighters prioritised for repair. It was a form of compensation, he had been told, for the simple fact that one hit would destroy their starfighters and kill them. But it was still incredibly annoying.

"As yet, we have no word on when we will actually deploy," he continued. "However, I will inform you as soon as we get the word."

He nodded to Fitzwilliam, who stepped forward and led the starfighter pilots towards their living quarters. Their quarters had been largely untouched since *Ark Royal* had gone into the reserves, leaving the pilots with the task of cleaning them up. It was irritating – Ted would have preferred more time to prepare – but the bureaucrats hadn't given him a choice. They'd already caused the pilots to waste two days at Cochrane.

Shaking his head, he turned and headed back towards his office. The paperwork wouldn't do itself, sadly. And besides, he needed to requisition some other equipment personally. The bureaucrats hadn't listened to Anderson when he'd made the request. But they'd listen to him.

Or so he hoped.

———

It had been nearly ten years since Kurt Schneider had set foot on a carrier – and that had been a modern carrier, for its time. *Ark Royal*, by contrast, seemed to have come out of a museum, complete with pieces of outdated equipment that should have been discarded years ago. The air smelled faintly musty as he followed the XO through a series of airlocks and into the quarters set aside for starfighter pilots. When he saw them, he couldn't help swearing out loud.

"Crap," one of the younger pilots said. She wasn't a reservist; Kurt had no idea what she'd done to be assigned to *Ark Royal*. "Dust. Dust everywhere."

"You'll have to deal with it," the XO said. "I'm afraid we don't have time to handle everything ourselves."

Kurt sighed, but nodded. Their enforced break on Cochrane had allowed him a chance to download the files on *Ark Royal* – at least the ones available to a reservist without an active clearance – and one thing had been clear. With only forty crewmen assigned to the crew, there was no way the ship could be kept in tip-top condition. It was unfortunate that they would have to clear their own living quarters first, but there was no alternative.

"A word with you, Schneider," the XO continued. "If you'll join me outside...?"

It wasn't a request, Kurt knew. He followed the XO back out of the compartment, then into a smaller compartment that was probably intended to be the CAG's office. All of the equipment that would once have been held there had been stripped out, leaving the compartment thoroughly bare. It was a minor miracle, Kurt decided, that there was even a light. The entire compartment resembled a dim cave, rather than a place to work.

"We are unlikely to receive many active duty starfighter pilots," the XO said, without preamble. "The ones we do have are the ones with... disciplinary problems. Accordingly, you are appointed Commander Air Group, at least for the moment. Is that acceptable?"

Kurt swallowed. "It's been eight years since I served in a regular unit," he said, finally. "And I was never more than squadron XO..."

"You're the best we have," the XO said. "We may get someone else, someone preferable, later on, but for the moment we have you. Suck it up and deal with it."

"Yes, sir," Kurt said. He scowled to himself. How could he be a CAG when there were no starfighters for his pilots to fly? "When are we likely to receive fighters?"

"Hopefully, within the week," the XO assured him. "But we have to prepare the launch tubes first, you see."

Kurt nodded, then turned and walked back into his quarters. He knew a couple of the other pilots from his previous service, but it seemed that the bureaucrats – in their infinite wisdom – hadn't seen fit to keep reserve units together. It wasn't too surprising, he knew; his reserve unit had been scattered over interplanetary space, with a handful of the pilots even based on Britannia rather than Earth. But it still meant that they would have to build up a working relationship faster than anyone would have preferred.

He pursed his lips, then blew a single note. The pilots looked up at him, expectantly. He looked back, wondering which of them were going to be problems. The active duty pilots might have expected to be promoted – maybe that was why some of them had transferred – despite whatever problems were concealed within their files. Normally, they would have been right too. Active duty pilots were considered one grade senior to their reserve counterparts.

"I have been appointed CAG, *pro tem*," he said, shortly. If anyone was disappointed, they'd just have to deal with it. "We should receive our starfighters within the week. However, until then, we will have to prepare the fighter tubes for launch."

There was some grumbling, but no actual dissent. Kurt allowed himself a moment of relief. They were all adults, thankfully, not little children. Or even big children like Penny and Percy, he added, in the privacy of his own thoughts.

"I know this isn't what we expected when we signed on the dotted line," he added, "but it has to be done. I'll speak privately to each of you over the coming week, so we get to know each other a little better. Once we receive our fighters, we will begin regular training. We may be able to cannibalise a simulator from Luna Base, but it won't be as good as reality."

He smiled at their expressions. Simulators were good, he had to admit, and much safer than actual training missions, but they didn't quite do *everything*. Pilots could replay the infamous trench scene in a simulator, or go buzzing through an asteroid field that didn't exist, at least outside the imaginations of science-fiction writers, yet the sense of danger was missing. A crash in a simulator was embarrassing, a crash in a real starfighter was lethal.

"Now," he said, looking around the compartment. "Time to get this mess cleared up."

He watched the other pilots as they swept up the dust, removed the protective covers from the bunks and cleaned out the showers. Most of them seemed to accept their task willingly, but a handful were grumbling under their breath as they worked. One – a girl who would have been pretty, if she hadn't been scowling all the time – looked particularly annoyed. Kurt wondered, absently, if she had a reason to be annoyed, then dismissed the thought. If she hadn't wanted to go where she was sent, she shouldn't have joined the military.

You weren't much better when you were on active duty, he reminded himself. It was an uncomfortable thought. *Were you?*

Once the room was clean – or at least cleaner – he reached for his terminal and checked the duty roster. Neither he nor his pilots had been added to it – the XO presumably hadn't gotten around to it – so he told his pilots to get a few hours of sleep before time ran out. It wouldn't be long, he was sure, before they were put back to work. But it would be just long enough to write out a message for Molly and then work out what needed to be done to get the fighter tubes ready for their new craft.

James watched the newly-appointed CAG returned to his quarters – there was no hope of a separate set of quarters for the CAG, at least not yet – then pulled his terminal off his belt and glanced down at the list of tasks. The next flight of crewmen – engineering crew this time, thankfully – were due to arrive in an hour, giving him time to inspect the tactical section before they arrived. There was already a long list of improvements and modifications that had to be made, but he knew they were nowhere near the end.

He strode back through the network of corridors – *Ark Royal* was even more internally complex than the more modern carriers – and into the tactical section. Lieutenant Commander Keith Farley was already there, issuing orders to a handful of crewmen while watching a tactical simulation on the display. There was little data on the enemy forces – at least, not yet – but *Ark Royal* had quite a few surprises for any human star-ship that got too close. The rail guns and mass drivers might be outdated, yet they packed one hell of a wallop.

"We're going to need a regular supply of projectiles," Farley informed him. "I'd like to obtain a compressor – perhaps from an asteroid mining crew – and then use that to produce new projectiles upon demand. We may be operating some distance from regular supply services."

James nodded, impressed. Mass drivers were powerful, but they burned through ammunition at a terrifying rate. It wasn't as if they were firing expensive missiles – the projectiles were nothing more than pieces of rock – yet even a carrier as large as *Ark Royal* couldn't carry an infinite supply. But a compressor would allow them to produce their own projectiles from asteroid materials, if they had time to pause to reload.

"Put in the request and I'll countersign it," he said. "There shouldn't be any problem arranging for a compressor, not when no one else would have a use for it. The only other ships that carried mass drivers were older ships from the lesser powers. "What about missiles and pulse cannons?"

"Missiles may be delayed," Farley admitted, reaching for his terminal. "Everyone and their dog wants missiles right now and we're down at the bottom of the priority list. The pulse cannons are on their way – thankfully, the other carriers already had theirs installed – and we should have them set up within the week. The real problem, of course, is going to be coordinating everything."

James winced. Modern carriers were built to *avoid* friendly fire... but *Ark Royal's* systems were less capable of separating friend from foe. Even with computers – no human mind could hope to handle the speeds involved – it was still difficult to be absolutely sure that a foe was being targeted before the opportunity vanished into nothingness. The engineering crew had promised that more modern sensors would be arranged, but they had problems interacting with the other systems. Given enough time, he suspected that Anderson would have preferred to rip everything out and start again with more modern technology. But that would have taken years.

"I'm currently working out ways to manipulate active sensor probes and passive sensor arrays to make it easier to provide full coverage," Farley added. "However, if we were flying with more modern carriers, I would suggest tapping down our own sensors and relying on theirs."

"Dangerous," James observed. "I don't think the Captain would approve."

"Me neither," Farley agreed. "It depends on just how the Admiralty intends to employ us."

James sighed. After the first briefing, there had been nothing from the Admiralty – at least nothing concerning *Ark Royal* directly. There had been security alerts, warnings that peaceniks were already starting to protest against the war, and a handful of speculative papers on just what the aliens might have in mind, but nothing more specific. The media had been crammed with even more baseless speculation, ranging from horror stories about alien atrocities to suggestions that the human race had somehow provoked the war. But no one knew anything for sure.

"I believe that depends on how quickly we get ready for active service," James said. He sighed, then looked up at the simulation. "Keep me informed of progress."

Farley nodded, then returned to his work.

James's terminal buzzed. "Sir," Midshipwomen Lopez said, "the Royal Marine shuttle is requesting permission to land."

"Oh," James said. He glanced at his chronometer, then swore. The planned schedule had called for the Marines to arrive the following day, when *Ark Royal* was ready for them. If the Marines came onboard now… they would have to help set up their own gear. The crewmen didn't have the time to handle it. "Tell them to dock, then inform the Captain. I'll meet them in the shuttlebay."

――――

"Someone seems to like us, sir," Captain Reginald Jackson said, once the XO had shown them to the barracks and departed. "Only a little dust, smelly sheets…good god, they even gave us a shower!"

Charles snorted, unable to conceal his amusement completely. Compared to some of the places his commando had slept over the years, *Ark Royal* was paradise incarnate. Marine Country was always cramped, forcing the commandos to share beds from time to time, but that wouldn't be a problem on *Ark Royal*. Only 120 Royal Marine Commandos had been assigned to the ship under his command, which meant there was plenty of room for them to spread out in the vast barracks.

"It doesn't look like they set out to welcome us," he agreed. Normally, Royal Marines and naval crewmen hazed one another mercilessly. *Ark Royal's* crew clearly hadn't had the time, even if they'd had the inclination, to prepare an unpleasant welcome for the marines. But then, there *was* a war on. Even the pettiest of naval crewmen would have thought better of continuing the rivalry when they might have to rely on the marines to save their lives. "Get the bags unpacked, then we can inspect the training facilities."

He watched his men preparing themselves, feeling a twinge of pride. The Royal Marines prided themselves on being the roughest and toughest British fighting men – a claim that was hotly disputed by other units that considered themselves equally tough – and no marine was ever allowed to wear an armoured combat suit without proving himself on the ground first. Training was harsh, unrelenting and sometimes lethal, but those who emerged from the experience were ready for anything. But they'd never seriously prepared for alien contact.

The RSM saluted, once the final bags were stowed away. "All present and correct, sir," he said. "We're ready for deployment."

Charles smiled. "Good," he said. Royal Marines served as everything from boarding parties to onboard security. If nothing else, they could be sure of doing something new every few days. Just because there was a war on there was no good reason to neglect endless training and exercises. "Let us go prepare for the war."

CHAPTER

FIVE

"Enemy fighters at three o'clock," Kurt said.

"Roger," Rose answered. "What should I do until then?"

Kurt rolled his eyes. The joke had been outdated when the military had started experimenting with jet fighters, let alone starfighters in inter-planetary space. But it was good to realise that the squadrons were coming together, even if it did mean some cheek and backtalk from his subordinates. He settled back into his chair, then watched as the enemy fighters closed in rapidly on the flight of Spitfires.

"On my mark, jink and engage," he ordered, curtly. "I don't want them anywhere near the carrier."

The enemy starfighters looked as if they weren't even bothering to try to hold a formation. A civilian pair of eyes would have thought the pilots were drunk or incompetent, but experienced starfighter pilots knew better. Predicable flight paths meant certain death for the pilots; the enemy were jinking around like mad, even as they approached *Ark Royal's* defenders. Long-range shots would almost certainly do nothing more than alarm them – and accomplish that much only if they were not experienced enough to know that the odds of being hit were almost non-existent.

Spitfires didn't *look* anything like their famous namesakes from the Battle of Britain. They were spherical craft, bristling with weapons and drive thrusters that could push them in any direction. Spacecraft didn't have to be bound by the laws governing jet aircraft in planetary atmospheres, after all. It was impossible to build a starfighter that also functioned as a jet fighter to engage targets on the ground.

"Mark," he ordered. "Now!"

The starfighters jinked, then opened fire as the enemy came into range. Kurt watched grimly as the enemy concentrated on blowing through the defending formation, instead of trying to hunt them down one by one. It suggested, part of his mind noted, that they were armed with anti-carrier missiles rather than being configured to sweep space clean of hostile starfighters. But they still carried chain guns of their own, ready to take shots at any starfighter that presented itself as a target. Kurt cursed under his breath as two of his pilots died, followed by five enemy fighters. The remainder accelerated towards *Ark Royal*, forcing the defenders to give chase.

We're rusty, he thought, sourly. Two weeks of intensive practice had allowed the pilots to recover their skills, but none of them had worked together before being assigned to *Ark Royal*. It didn't help that some of the reservists hadn't set foot on a carrier for years, let alone flown a starfighter. If they were being graded, Kurt suspected, the entire unit would have been relieved of duty and probably broken up completely. But instead they might have to face a mysterious alien foe…

The enemy starfighters didn't flinch as they flew into the teeth of Ark Royal's point defence. Instead, they launched missiles towards the carrier, then tried to break free before it was too late, scattering randomly as they fled. Kurt cursed again as four of the missiles struck home, nuclear warheads detonating against the ship's hull. Moments later, it was all over.

"End exercise," he ordered, quietly. *Ark Royal* was tough, armoured in a way no modern carrier was armoured, but even she couldn't survive four nuclear blasts in quick succession. Even a single direct hit would have been alarming; if nothing else, it would damage the network of sensors and weapons mounted on the ship's hull. "Return to base; I say again, return to base."

He didn't say anything else until they were seated in the briefing compartment with mugs of hot tea in front of them. There was no hard data on just what the enemy could do, he knew, so they'd assumed that they would be facing modern starfighters armed with the latest in drives, weapons and stealth gear. The Spitfires weren't *that* outdated – the mechanics had been able to refit them with modern sensors – but they had their limitations. And *Ark Royal's* limited sensor arrays didn't help.

"So," he said, looking around the compartment. "We lost the carrier. I think that counts as a disaster."

No one disagreed. Starfighters couldn't hope to return home without a carrier, not with their very limited life support. In theory, they could be picked up by other starships, but no one had ever tried to recover more than a handful of starfighters at once. Kurt made a mental note to recommend that such operations be practiced as soon as possible, although he suspected that the Royal Navy had other problems. Two carriers had been added to the unified defence fleet and dispatched outwards to New Russia, while most of the remainder had been assigned to Earth or Britannia. It would be months before they were ready to start experimenting with new procedures.

"The Captain will not be pleased, I imagine," he continued. "What did we do wrong?"

"Let them get past us," Rose said, sourly. She'd come very close to being taken out too. "We need another flight of starfighters closer to the carrier."

"And what would happen," another pilot asked, "if the point defence mistakes those craft for enemy fighters?"

"They end up dead," Rose pointed out, snidely. "Look; we either run the risk of letting them get within missile range of the carrier or we run the risk of letting our point defence take pot-shots at us."

Kurt snorted. He knew the ideal answer from exercises, but exercises always left out the real danger. The Royal Navy's planners fought constant battles with the bureaucrats and well-meaning politicians over the use of live weapons in exercises, even though such exercises were always more informative than simulated danger. But then, losing a pilot in an exercise would be politically dangerous. It would be used against the Navy by the politicians.

"We will have to split our forces," he said, raising his voice. Debates were often interesting and it was important that the pilots learned to speak their minds, but in the end the final responsibility stopped with

Kurt himself. Somehow, he doubted the other pilots would be allowed to join him when he faced a court martial if things went wrong. "It will mean additional risk, true, but I see no alternative."

He sighed. "We'll run another set of exercises in two hours," he added. "Go get some sleep, then assemble back here for pre-flight briefing. Any questions?"

"Yes," one of the pilots said. "When can we expect to receive more pilots?"

Kurt sighed. After the first rush to get pilots and fighters to *Ark Royal*, the bureaucrats had switched their attention to equipping the unified defence fleet, downgrading the ancient carrier to a lower priority. He couldn't really blame them, he knew, but it was still frustrating when he was responsible for the carrier's fighters. They could cram another two wings of starfighters into the launch bays without real difficulty, hopefully including some torpedo-bombers. Right now, *Ark Royal* had almost no long-range striking power, apart from the mass drivers.

"We'll get them when we get them," he said, tiredly. Someone had clearly worked out that recalling the naval reservists from interplanetary shipping lines would be economically disastrous. He would have been impressed by this display of common sense on the part of the bureaucrats if it hadn't been so irritating to have to constantly report that the fighter wings were not ready for deployment. "Go get some sleep."

He held out a hand as Rose stood up. "Hold on," he said, as the other pilots cleared the room. "I want a word with you."

Rose looked up at him crossly, then sat down again, one hand toying with her short blonde hair. She wasn't unattractive, Kurt knew, but her permanently soured expression made it harder to feel any attraction for her. Not that was a bad thing, he reminded himself hastily. He *was* a married man. Once the other pilots were gone, he closed the hatch and sat down facing her.

"You're having personal problems," he said, silently damning himself for ever agreeing to take the CAG post. He was meant to fly with the pilots as well as discipline them. A normal CAG wouldn't fly at all, except in emergencies. "And they're affecting your performance."

Rose scowled. "That's none of your bloody business," she snapped. "With all due respect, sir..."

Kurt cut her off. "You're an excellent flier when you put your mind to it, but you're being distracted," he said. There was no point in penalising her for her tone. "Either share your problems with me or put them out of your mind, for good."

"It's my boyfriend," Rose said, softly. "He's...he's been deployed with the unified defence force."

It took Kurt a moment to put it together. Her file hadn't been too clear on what she'd actually done to be sent to *Ark Royal*; indeed, the comments had been so elliptical that he hadn't been able to work them out. But if she'd been sleeping with a fellow pilot, perhaps even one in the same squadron...

He shook his head. Fraternisation between crewmembers was a dirty little secret within the Royal Navy; it wasn't meant to happen, but everyone knew someone who'd engaged in sexual relationships while on deployment. Sometimes, a commanding officer would turn a blind eye; sometimes, the happy couple would be broken up, normally by having one of them reassigned to a different starship. There was no formal regulations, but informally it depended on just how badly the relationship affected discipline.

"I'm sorry to hear that," he said, and meant it. He'd never had a relationship with another pilot, but he knew just how intense such relationships could become. "But you can't let it affect your duties."

Rose sagged. "I know that," she said, weakly. "What do you suggest I do?"

"Write him v-mails, then forget about it," Kurt said. He paused, feeling a sudden flush of embarrassment. "Remember that some v-mails may be viewed by security officers now that we're in a state of war."

He smiled at her expression. It hadn't been that long ago that a girlfriend had composed v-mails to her boyfriend in the navy, including videos of her naked and performing sexual acts with a girlfriend. Somehow – Kurt suspected treachery – the videos had been distributed through the naval communications network and then into the planetary datanet. The resulting inquiry hadn't been able to place the blame.

"I don't think I have time to be explicit," Rose said. She gave him a smile that completely transformed her face. "Thank you, sir."

Kurt dismissed her, then turned his attention to his terminal. A new v-mail from Molly had popped into the ship's datanet, allowing him to view it now he was alone. It wasn't even remotely explicit; Molly reported that Penny still wasn't doing too well at school, while Kurt's boss had warned that he might have to find a replacement if Kurt didn't return to work soon. Technically, it was illegal to sack a reservist who had been called back to the colours, but Kurt understood his boss's dilemma. He couldn't afford to pay Kurt's salary while receiving nothing in return and it might be months or years before government compensation appeared.

He shook his head, ruefully, as Molly kept outlining the problems with Penny. Their daughter was smart enough to understand just how incompetent her teacher was, according to Molly, which led her to act badly in class. But Kurt knew that there would always be incompetent assholes in the world...and many of them would be in places of power. Penny was doing herself no favours by challenging her tutor...

Shaking his head, he keyed the switch and started to record another message. Maybe another lecture from her father would help. Or maybe she'd just keep rebelling against her parents...

"I have the final set of medical reports," Midshipwoman Lopez said, once she had stepped into James's cabin and closed the hatch behind her. "Doctor Hastings requests that you make time to discuss a handful of issues with her."

"Understood," James said, as he took the datapad she offered him and glanced down at it thoughtfully. Regulations stated that every officer and crewman had to undergo a complete physical examination, but putting them off as long as possible was an old Royal Navy tradition. He'd set a good example by reporting for his own exam as soon as the doctor had configured sickbay to her liking, yet he'd still had to chase the other senior officers to force them to put time aside to see the doctor. "Take a seat."

He studied the younger woman as she sat down, resting her hands on her lap. Midshipwoman Lopez's file was curiously empty, without even the codes that might imply that there were details well above his level of access. As far as he could tell, she'd gone through the Academy – she hadn't been part of the honours class, but she'd hardly done badly – and then been assigned to *Ark Royal*. It made no sense. None of the original crew had been assigned to *Ark Royal* without screwing up at one point or another. But Midshipwoman Lopez seemed to be the exception.

Maybe she annoyed someone, he thought. But who could a Midshipwoman annoy who would assign her to *Ark Royal*? It was true that some Admirals could be hellishly vindictive, but something so blatant would only attract attention – and the old boy's network had ways to deal with Admirals who abused their positions too much.

He threw caution to the winds and asked. "Why are you here?"

"You told me you wanted the reports as soon as possible," Midshipwoman Lopez said. "I brought them to you..."

"Not now," James said. "Why are you assigned to *Ark Royal*?"

"I requested it," Midshipwoman Lopez said.

James gaped at her, unable to even *try* to control his expression. *He* had requested the assignment to *Ark Royal*, but he'd assumed that he would be her CO. If that hadn't seemed likely, he would have tried to take a position on one of the more modern carriers. Even if he hadn't been promoted to command, he would have been well-placed to take command later, once his CO moved onwards.

But someone as hopelessly junior as a midshipwoman? She would always have the shadow of *Ark Royal* looming over her, reminding her future commanding officers that she would require extensive retraining to serve on a modern starship. Maybe, just maybe, she'd assumed that she would climb the ranks on *Ark Royal*, but that would still leave her on a starship that should be sent to the breakers. Unless she'd known, somehow, that *Ark Royal* would be called back to service...

He shook his head, dismissing the thought. That was impossible.

"You requested it," he repeated. It wasn't uncommon for graduating officers to request postings...but, unless they were in the top ten places at the Academy, it was rare for a newly-minted officer to receive the post they wanted. But there would be almost no competition for slots on *Ark Royal*. "Might I ask why?"

Midshipwomen Lopez hesitated. "My maternal grandfather was the Elected King of Karees," she said, after a long moment. "The population was one of the more eccentric asteroid civilisations...until one day there was a major life support failure and the entire asteroid had to be evacuated. *Ark Royal* was the Royal Navy starship that responded to the crisis and took my grandfather and his people onboard."

James had to smile, remembering the notation in *Ark Royal's* logbook. The engineers had noted, afterwards, that the population seemed to have deliberately sabotaged their own asteroid, although no one had been able to figure out why. Some asteroids held settlements with really strange principles, including a handful who enjoyed taking risks with the life support. The discovery of the Puller Drive had sent thousands of such settlements expanding out of the solar system to places where they could enjoy true privacy.

"My grandfather ended up becoming a British citizen," Midshipwomen Lopez added. "He also willed his remaining funds to the preservation trust for *Ark Royal*. When I graduated, keeping the Old Lady going seemed a worthwhile use of my time."

"I see," James said. It was odd, but hardly a major problem. "I trust that you enjoy serving on the ship?"

"It's quite fascinating," Midshipwomen Lopez assured him. "We can't just insert components into the ship's computers and expect them to work. We often have to rewrite the computer codes or insert bridges between two separate systems that were never intended to work together. Understanding all the different links is tricky, but..."

She shrugged, her face lighting up. "I dare say I've learned more than anyone outside engineering or computer support," she added. "And we *have* kept the Old Lady ready for action."

"Or close to it," James agreed. He looked down at the reports on his desk. It would be another week before *Ark Royal* was truly ready for deployment – or as close to it as he expected they would ever become – but the crew had done an excellent job. "Thank you for coming. I have no doubt I will have more tasks for you in a few hours."

Midshipwomen Lopez rose to her feet. "Thank you, sir," she said. "I'm due in Engineering in twenty minutes."

"Go grab a mug of coffee," James said, absently. He paused as a thought occurred to him. "Was your grandfather the driving force behind the preservation society?"

"No, just one of them," Midshipwomen Lopez assured him.

James smiled as she left the compartment, remembering what he'd been told when he'd first realised that *Ark Royal* might be reactivated. There was a pressure group dedicated to keeping the Old Lady in service, even if she was just in the reserves. Why not? She was hardly the only starship to merit being kept alive. And besides, with the sudden desperate need for hulls, the Royal Navy might have good cause to be relieved they'd kept her.

Shaking his head, he picked up the terminal and went back to work.

CHAPTER
SIX

Ted had to smile when he walked into Briefing Room A, followed closely by Commander Fitzwilliam. The boxes of spare parts had been removed from the compartment and stowed away in disused cabins, allowing his senior officers to take their seats without having to worry about being careful where they sat. Midshipwomen Lopez had even managed to scrounge up some replacement chairs, although they weren't marked with *Ark Royal's* crest.

"Be seated," he ordered, shortly. "We seem to have met our deadline."

His senior crew exchanged nods. They'd worked frantically for over a month to get *Ark Royal* ready for service, a month during which there had been no further alien contact. Ted had heard that the unified defence command was talking about sending scoutships back to the attacked systems, just to see what was happening there, but as far as he knew nothing had actually come of the proposals. All he could really do was wait to see what happened, just like the civilians on Earth. Thankfully, the panic had slowly faded away as further attacks failed to materialise.

"We could still do with additional training," Wing Commander Schneider said. The CAG leaned forward, resting his elbows on the table. "The fighter wings have a very inconsistent level of practice, I'm afraid."

"Keep working on it," Ted ordered, dryly. He understood Schneider's problem, but they needed to start thinking about deployment. "We may be asked to leave at any moment."

"Which leads to an important question," Farley said. "Where *are* they?"

Ted scowled. The aliens had hit their first target over six weeks ago. By now, they should have been reaching Earth...or at least feeling their way into the heart of human space. But instead they seemed to be doing nothing, nothing at all. It made no sense. What sort of mindset would start a war, a war that had come as a complete surprise to its target, and then hold off long enough for the target to get over its shock and mobilise? Even the endless political debate over command and control was drawing to an end.

He looked up at the holographic starchart, thinking hard. The unified defence command had concluded that New Russia was the next target for the alien invaders. Fortunately, it had a growing industrial base, as well as a deeply nationalistic population that would resist when – if – the aliens tried to land. By now, twelve carriers and over a hundred smaller ships – the largest fleet humanity had ever deployed outside the Sol System – were based there, ready to meet the aliens when they arrived. But so far the aliens hadn't shown their hand.

"They may not agree with our thoughts on how to fight a war," Ted observed, finally. Who knew *how* aliens thought? For all they knew, the aliens hadn't realised they were facing an interstellar power. And yet... surely they would have known from studying the remains of the destroyed colonies. "Or maybe their drive systems are inferior to our own."

The starchart shimmered at his command, showing the known gravitational tramlines running between the targeted worlds and New Russia. Unless the alien systems were *far* inferior to humanity's systems, they should have been at New Russia within a week, hard on the heels of news of their arrival. It just didn't make sense.

"Or maybe they think they've bit off more than they can chew," Fitzwilliam offered. "The massed might of humanity is hard to bet against, isn't it?"

Ted shrugged. Interstellar carriers were an expensive investment, but once the industrial base for building them had been completed the costs tended to fall. There was no reason why the aliens couldn't have ten carriers for every one of humanity's – or far more. He gritted his teeth, wishing – yet again – that they knew something about their foe. All they really knew for sure was that the aliens were hostile.

"That isn't our concern," he said, finally. "Unless anyone has any strong objections, I intend to inform the Admiralty that *Ark Royal* will be ready for deployment at the end of the week."

No one objected, although he saw a handful of concerned expressions. He couldn't really blame them. *Ark Royal* had been sitting in the reserves for so long that she might well have problems that wouldn't become apparent until she was fully powered up. But the sooner they found out, the sooner such problems could be overcome.

Farley smiled. "Has there been any word on deployments?"

"Nothing so far," Ted said. "We may be assigned to the unified defence fleet – or we may find ourselves assigned to serve as an independent raider and head behind enemy lines."

"That would be interesting," Fitzwilliam observed. "But we don't know where to go."

"We'll find out," Ted assured him. "The scouts are already searching for enemy territory."

He looked back at the starchart. Assuming that humanity's sphere of expansion had brushed against alien territory – and assuming that the aliens had similar requirements to humanity – there were several dozen G2 stars that might possess alien-settled worlds. The scouts would still take months to sort through them, hunting for potential targets. And some of them might not come back.

If they don't, he told himself, *we would know where to look*.

"We'll do a full power-up tomorrow," he said, as he rose to his feet. "And then we will know where we stand."

———

The sound of the intercom woke him from a fitful sleep.

"Captain," Midshipwoman Lopez said, "we have picked up an emergency signal from the Admiralty. You and Commander Fitzwilliam are to report to Nelson Base at once."

Ted groaned, then reached for his chronometer. It was 0423 and he'd slept for less than five hours, after watching the final preparations for power-up in engineering. Even if he wasn't drinking, he wasn't sleeping very well. No doubt he was having too many fears about taking his ship into combat for the first time.

"Inform the Commander that I'll meet him in the shuttlebay," he ordered, as he swung his legs over the side of the bed and stood up. "Did they give any explanation?"

"No, sir," Midshipwoman Lopez said. "Just an emergency call."

Ted groaned, then fumbled through his desk drawers for a stimulant, which he swallowed before getting dressed. An emergency call was never good news, even though the last time he'd visited Nelson Base he'd managed to keep command of his ship. He eyed the bottles of rotgut with interest, then picked up the bottle of water and took a long swig. Once he was refreshed, he made his way to the shuttlebay. Commander Fitzwilliam was already there, looking disgustingly well-presented. Ted nodded to him, then led the way into the shuttlecraft. The pilot was already powering up the drive.

He said nothing to Fitzwilliam as the shuttle headed out of the shuttlebay and directly towards Nelson Base. Orbital activity didn't seem to have reached any higher a tempo than it had once the first warnings had reached Earth, but he couldn't help noticing that *Ark Royal* wasn't the only starship sending shuttles to the naval base. In fact, almost every ship was sending shuttles to its respective headquarters. Something had clearly gone very wrong, he decided, feeling a chill settling around his spine. Had the aliens attacked again?

They were greeted by a party of Royal Marines, who checked their ID implants and then pointed the two newcomers into a large briefing chamber. Dozens of other commanding officers – and a handful of subordinates – were filling into the chamber, all looking equally bemused. Ted nodded to a couple of commanders he knew, then found a seat near the stand and sat down. Fitzwilliam sat down next to him.

The First Space Lord entered a moment later and took the stand. He looked more than just tired, Ted noted; he looked badly shocked. Something had definitely gone badly wrong...he leaned forward as a Commodore called the room to attention, then dismissed the formalities with almost indecent speed.

"Four hours ago, a courier boat arrived from New Russia," the First Space Lord said, without preamble. "The system has fallen to the enemy."

It took a long moment for his words to sink in. Everyone knew just how many starships had been assigned to New Russia, along with the planet's not-inconsiderable orbital and planetary defences. The Russian government had always taken a progressive view of building up their defences, if only to ensure that the new Russian homeland remained untouched and untouchable. There were few worlds with more fixed defences…

"Analysts are working on the recordings now," the First Space Lord continued. "However, it is with a heavy heart that I must confirm the destruction of the unified defence force, including HMS *Invincible* and *Formidable*."

This time, shock swept around the compartment like a physical thing. *Invincible* and *Formidable* were – had been – the two most modern carriers in the Royal Navy. They'd both carried the most capable fighter units in the fleet, while their crews had been counted among the elite. And now they were gone.

"As of now, we must assume that New Russia is under occupation," the First Space Lord said. "Furthermore, the political unity of humanity has been badly dented."

Ted swallowed. There had been twelve carriers at New Russia; six Russian, three American, two British and one French. Between them, the smaller ships and the fixed defences, there had been almost a *million* naval personal assigned to the system. The recriminations would start soon, if they hadn't begun already. Humanity's unity could be lost before it had ever really been established.

"The Russians only had nine carriers," Fitzwilliam said, softly. "Losing six of them is going to hurt."

It would do more than that, Ted knew. The Russians had believed, perhaps rightly, that it was better to have a handful of carriers but place most of their resources into smaller ships. Right now, though, those smaller ships would be badly outmatched by the aliens. There was little hope of recovering New Russia.

He scowled, thinking through the implications. Humanity had lost the industrial base the Russians had built up over seventy years, along with losing control of gravitational tramlines leading further into human space. The aliens could jump out towards Earth, if they were so inclined, or they could alter course and pick off a number of smaller colony worlds before bringing the war to an end. There were just too many targets to be defended adequately.

If there is such a thing, he told himself, bitterly. There had been twelve carriers at New Russia...and the aliens had taken them apart. God alone knew how much damage the aliens had taken, but he couldn't help feeling that it was very limited. And, even if humanity had taken out twelve alien carriers in exchange for the human ships, no one knew how big a dent that was in alien capabilities. They might have a thousand carriers on their way to human space.

Fitzwilliam nudged him. The First Space Lord had yielded the podium to a tired-looking analyst. For once, almost every officer seemed to be paying attention, even though the officer was only a lieutenant – and not even a line officer. But they all needed to know what had happened at New Russia.

"We have only preliminary results," the analyst said. "However, they suggest that the aliens are dangerously advanced over us. In particular, their weapons and drives seem to be vastly superior."

Ted sat up, feeling cold. *Ark Royal* had been the most advanced starship of her time, but she couldn't hope to beat a modern carrier in a long-range engagement. Even a handful of such carriers would have problems winning against a more advanced foe. The original warships launched by the Royal Navy would have been rapidly wiped out by the modern ships, no matter how numerous they were. If the aliens were advanced enough, there was no amount of blood sweat and tears that would make up the difference.

"Alien fighters seem to be roughly equal to ours in terms of drives," the analyst said. "However, they posses both stealth systems and advanced energy weapons capable of seriously damaging a starship's hull. Our best guess is that they are actually modified plasma cannons, which suggests that the aliens have actually overcome the containment field problems that bedevil human researchers. An alternative is that the weapons actually induce limited fission in their targets."

Ted winced. Humanity's plasma cannons had a nasty habit of over-heating and exploding, which was why they were rarely deployed by the military. But if the aliens had cracked that problem, somehow, it would give them a decisive advantage. For one, all of their starfighters would pack the punch of a torpedo-bomber. They'd have genuine duel-role starfighters.

"They also managed to get much closer to our carriers without being detected than we believed possible," the analyst added. "Indeed, our first thought was that the alien starfighters had managed to make an in-system FTL jump. If we hadn't been so convinced that was impossible, we might not have realised that they merely remained hidden until they were very close to our ships. We are currently looking for ways to break their stealth systems, but so far we have come up with nothing.

"Worse, it seems likely that they have a better FTL system than ourselves," he concluded. He pointed to a starchart, then focused it on the New Russia system. "Their appearance within the system didn't correspond to any known tramline. It seems that they jumped from a star we would consider outside normal tramline range. This suggests that our strategic maps of human space may be badly outdated."

Ted exchanged a long look with Fitzwilliam as the information sank in. Normally, the tramlines rarely stretched past five light years. It still took time to move from system to system...but if the aliens had access to weaker tramlines, they might well be able to evade the human defences and outmanoeuvre the human starships. It could give them a potentially decisive advantage.

To add to the other ones they have, he thought, grimly. They'd been wrong; the aliens hadn't been reluctant to attack further, they'd just waited until humanity had offered them a tempting target. And then they'd attacked, wiping out a colossal force and shattering humanity's unity. The loss of New Russia alone was a serious blow.

"We have prepared recordings of the battle for you," the First Space Lord said. "I advise you to watch carefully, as the recordings will not be released until the PM has addressed the nation."

"Good idea," Fitzwilliam muttered. "There will be panic if this gets out."

Ted didn't bother to disagree. Everyone *knew* that carriers were the most powerful starships in existence. Losing one alone would be a disaster, losing twelve...even if only two of them had been British, would seem catastrophic. And, if the aliens really did have a decisive technological advantage, it might not be long before Earth itself was targeted.

He leaned forward as the main display lit up, showing the New Russia system as a tactical display. The alien fleet – fifteen carrier-sized starships, forty smaller craft – jumped into the system, well away from any known tramline. Ted wondered, absently, if the aliens were actually trying to trick the human analysts. They had enough stealth technology to hide their fleet until the moment they chose to show themselves. Why not try to intimidate humanity into surrender?

But those plasma weapons weren't illusions, he thought, numbly. *They were real.*

Humanity's fleet assembled, blocking the alien advance. Messages were sent, offering talks...only to be ignored. Humanity's starfighters had advanced forward, ready to engage the enemy...until the moment the enemy starfighters had appeared, between the human starfighters and their carriers. They had to have passed through the swarm of human fighters, completely undetected. Ignoring the suddenly frantic starfighters, the aliens threw themselves at the human carriers. Powerful blasts of plasma fire tore into their hulls, burning through flimsy armour and wrecking havoc inside the ships. One by one, humanity's ships were rapidly torn apart.

The battle wasn't completely one sided, he noted. Human weapons could and did kill enemy fighters, but there were just too many of them. The humans were overwhelmed and destroyed before they could reorganised their formation, allowing the alien starships to advance forward to engage New Russia itself. And then the recording came to an end.

"We will be rethinking our plans in light of this development," the First Space Lord said, with admirable understatement. "I don't think I need to explain just how serious this situation is, do I?"

No one disagreed.

Ted stared down at his hands, wondering briefly why he hadn't taken early retirement. It wasn't as if the navy wanted to keep him. And he could have been on the ground, instead of standing on the command deck of a carrier. But the navy was his life. And he knew his duty.

I volunteered to place myself between Britain and war, he reminded himself. And yet he'd never really faced the prospect of his own death in wartime. Accidents had accounted for more naval deaths over the past decades than enemy action. *I don't get to back out because it might have become dangerous.*

"Dismissed, gentlemen," the First Space Lord said. "Captain Smith, if you and Commander Fitzwilliam will remain behind..."

"Yes, sir," Ted said.

He waited until the massive compartment was almost empty, then followed the First Space Lord through a guarded airlock into a tactical planning centre. A handful of analysts were seated at terminals, working their way through the data from New Russia. He looked at one of the screens and saw an alien carrier, a fragile-looking craft. But they hadn't needed heavy armour to rip New Russia's defences apart.

"Take a seat," the First Space Lord ordered. "We have a mission for you."

CHAPTER

SEVEN

"A mission," Ted repeated. "What do you want us to do?"

"The important detail, I think, is that the modern carriers simply lacked the armour to stand up to alien weapons," the First Space Lord said. "That, combined with their stealth systems, gave them a definite advantage over the united fleet, allowing them to tear us apart."

His voice was curiously flat. Ted realised, not entirely to his surprise, that the First Space Lord was too tired to really *feel* the deaths...and grasp the full magnitude of what it meant for the war. If humanity's unarmoured ships were easy prey for alien fighters, the war was within shouting distance of being lost along with the carriers. Once the carriers were gone, humanity wouldn't even be able to continue the war.

Understanding clicked. "*Ark Royal* might be able to stand up to them," he said. He found himself fighting to hold back the urge to giggle in a decidedly-unmilitary manner. "We still have *our* armour."

"Indeed," the First Space Lord agreed. "*Ark Royal* might be able to survive where more modern carriers would have real problems."

He tapped a switch, activating the star chart. "We are still studying the records, of course, but it seems to me that the aliens managed to jump over nine light years to New Russia, judging by their appearance. If this is the case, they have a major advantage over us. In particular, they will be able to avoid all of our blocking forces and reach Earth directly."

Ted nodded. Earth possessed over seventy percent of humanity's industrial base, population and fixed defences. It wouldn't go down easily, but if Sol were to be lost the human race might as well set off and try to escape in a ragtag fleet of starships, hoping they could evade the enemy long enough to rebuild and return to restart the war. But the odds would be against a successful escape.

"I believe that the aliens will attempt to jump here" – the First Space Lord tapped another star – "and use it as a waypoint on their road to Earth. There's nothing there, apart from a handful of tiny mining stations and independent settlements. The aliens will have no trouble destroying them – or simply ignoring the settlers completely. I want *Ark Royal* in position to intercept the enemy fleet."

"And then…what?" Ted asked. "We would be massively outgunned."

"Delay them, force them back on their heels," the First Space Lord said, grimly. "Their carriers don't appear to be any stronger than ours – and you have mass drivers and other projectile weapons. I intend to attach a squadron of missile frigates too, once they're worked up and ready for deployment. If you can give them a bloody nose…"

Ted saw the logic, even though it still seemed chancy. It might well be a suicide mission, yet he could understand why the First Space Lord would want to keep the fighting as far from Earth as possible. Between the political shockwaves and the panic that was likely to result, once the news finally broke, Earth would be in no state to defend itself.

Commander Fitzwilliam studied the map for a long moment. "What happened to New Russia?"

"We don't know," the First Space Lord confessed. "But we're not optimistic."

"They might have wiped out most of the population," Ted said, softly. New Russia wasn't anything like as developed as Earth, but it would still be easy for the aliens to wipe out the settlements from orbit. "Or they might have destroyed the orbital defences and moved onwards."

"We don't know," the First Space Lord repeated.

He looked up, meeting Smith's eyes. "I confess I had my doubts about *Ark Royal*," he admitted, keeping his voice so quiet that Smith had to strain to hear him. "The ship seemed a waste of resources, nothing more than a dumping ground for crew we couldn't be bothered to sack. Now… she might be our salvation."

Ted swallowed. *Ark Royal* was effectively unique, the only carrier with such heavy armour – let alone primitive weapons. It would take years to modify the yards to produce new armoured ships, unless the boffins came up with a new form of ablative armour that could be rapidly applied to the modern carriers. If *Ark Royal* were to be lost…but there was no alternative, at least as far as he could see. The carrier was the only effective weapon humanity had.

"Thank you, sir," he said, finally.

"You are to depart within two days," the First Space Lord added. He picked a datachip off his desk and passed it to Ted, who took it carefully. "Your crew can send the usual messages, but make sure they know that they *will* be vetted and censored, if necessary. We don't want to panic the civilians."

"Understood," Ted said. "Will any other ships be joining us?"

"It depends on international affairs," the First Space Lord said. "Right now, they're still stunned. They have to get through the recrimination stage before they start thinking what to actually *do* about the situation."

Ted nodded. It had been bare hours since the news had reached Earth. By now, world leaders would have been briefed and were struggling to come to terms with the news from New Russia. It wouldn't be long before the news leaked out, not with so many people already aware of it. And then there would be panic…

"Thank you, sir," he said, again. "We won't let you down."

———

James mentally replayed everything he'd seen and heard in the briefing as the shuttle carried them back to *Ark Royal*. If he'd managed to get himself assigned to one of the modern carriers, he told himself, he might well have ensured his own death. The details of the battle suggested, very strongly, that there were no actual survivors. He'd known friends and family who had served in the unified defence fleet. Those people were dead…or alien prisoners, POWs trapped light years from friendly territory. Would the aliens even bother to take prisoners? There was no way to know.

"Call the senior officers for a briefing," Captain Smith ordered, as soon as the shuttle had landed in the shuttlebay. "And then put the entire ship under a communications barrier. I don't want anyone sending a message home, not yet."

James nodded and started to work, grateful for the distraction. He hadn't woken any of the other senior officers when they'd left the ship – the watch crew were the only ones awake – but he could see to that now. Once he'd woken them, he contacted the communications department and ordered them to hold all personal messages. The only ones allowed out of the ship would be priority messages from the senior crew.

"The war situation has taken a turn for the worse," Captain Smith said, as soon as the senior officers had gathered in the briefing room. "New Russia has fallen to the enemy."

He ran through everything they'd been told, then showed the images from the battle. The senior officers stared in disbelief; by any reasonable standard, the battle had been hellishly short. Humanity didn't have much experience at space warfare, but simulations suggested that battles should take longer.

"Their starfighters seem to be less capable than ours, excepting the stealth and their weapons," Schneider observed, finally. "Their stealth systems can't be perfect or they would use them all the time."

James couldn't disagree. He'd watched enough bad movies where the enemy weapons fire had seemed to come out of nowhere to know that it was a viable tactic, if the technology could be made to work. But the aliens had deactivated their stealth before engaging the human carriers, even though keeping it would have given them a decisive advantage. No, the systems couldn't be perfect…unless, of course, the aliens thought that going in without stealth was honourable. But who knew how aliens might think?

"We will study all of the records during the trip," the Captain said. "Our orders are to engage the enemy in this system."

He ran through their orders and the rationale behind them. "I know that these orders are a gamble," he added, "but I see no alternative. We will power up our systems this afternoon, then leave tomorrow. Prior to then, I want all section heads to brief their subordinates, then remind them to write wills and record final messages. Please *also* remind them that the censors will have a look at them first."

James had to smile. The crew wasn't stupid, they'd know better than to say anything too revealing. But there were plenty of messages they could send that shouldn't be shared any further, certainly not with a bureaucratic asshole just looking for something he could use to pretend he was doing something useful.

"If there is anything else you need," he concluded, "I want you to request it by the end of the day. We should have priority shipping for anything we want – as long as we can get it before our departure time. If not… it will just have to wait for us."

There was a long pause. "Dismissed!"

James lifted an eyebrow as Schneider caught his eye, then nodded and waited for the room to clear before speaking to the CAG. "Yes?"

"Sir, one of my pilots had a…friend on *Formidable*," Schneider said. "She probably won't be the only one to have someone missing, perhaps dead. Do you want me to talk to her?"

James hesitated. As XO, it was his duty to see to it…but Schneider was definitely closer to his pilots. And besides, she almost certainly wasn't the only one to have a friend on the destroyed ships.

"Yes, please," he said, finally. He'd have to check the records, but they rarely showed anything more than relatives. Someone might hear about their dead friend from the general ship-wide announcement. "And if you feel she needs further counselling, please inform me."

Schneider nodded and left the briefing room. James watched him go, then reached for his terminal. There would have been to be a general announcement before they powered up the drives for the first time…after praying desperately for success. James knew far too well just how tricky it would be to replace the fusion cores if they failed – it would take months, at the very least.

And by then humanity could very well have lost the war.

———

Kurt had to admit that, after a great deal of grumbling, his pilots had managed to sort out the squadron bunking in a suitable manner. Their quarters had been cleaned, new bedding had been installed and there were even a small collection of reading devices, although the latter had barely been touched between endless exercises and napping. Once they'd set up a working simulator, he'd kept his pilots too busy to do anything else.

There were no barriers offering any form of privacy, even when male and female pilots were sharing the same territory. Body modesty was rare among naval crewmen – and besides, pilots were not supposed to show any untoward interest in one another. Kurt had known that relationships happened a long time before he met Rose – and he'd actually had second thoughts about allowing mixed quarters – but he trusted her to behave herself. But now...

He leaned forward and tapped her on the shoulder. Like most active-duty naval crewmen, she had long since mastered the art of snapping awake when called, which gave her an advantage over the reservists. *They* had to relearn the art. Kurt was ruefully aware that if an active-duty pilot had been assigned as CAG, there might well have been a mutiny in short order. Reservists wouldn't take kindly to being treated as active-duty pilots, most of whom were young enough to get by on only a few hours of sleep a day.

"Sir?" Rose asked, looking up at him. "What's happened?"

"Grab your robe and come with me," Kurt ordered. He glanced at the other bunks, where the remainder of the squadron were still sleeping. "Quietly."

He felt his cheeks heat with embarrassment as she rolled off her bunk, revealing that she was wearing an undershirt and panties...and not much else. The swell of her breasts was instantly noticeable, while her long legs were perfect, strongly muscled and very pale. Irked, he looked away and paced out of the compartment. She joined him a moment later and followed him down to the room he'd turned into a makeshift office. He felt a moment of sympathy for her, all unaware of just how sharply her life had changed, then started to speak.

"*Formidable* has been destroyed," he said, softly. It still seemed unreal to him, even though he'd seen the records. "As far as we know, she went up with all hands."

Rose stared at him. For a long moment, it was clear, she didn't believe what she was hearing.

"I'm sorry," he said. He wondered, briefly, if he'd made a mistake. "I thought you should know..."

"He can't be dead," Rose said. "He..."

Kurt understood. She would find it hard to come to terms with the news. Rose wasn't listed as one of her boyfriend's relatives; she wasn't, technically, entitled to a visit from officers bearing the bad tidings. She wouldn't have heard the truth until the entire navy was told about the disaster. And there wouldn't be any support for her...would there be any support for anyone? It had been a long time since the Royal Navy had lost so many crewmen in a single battle. Even the catastrophic life support failure on HMS *Impervious*, fifteen years ago, had only killed seventeen crewmen.

But the Battle of New Russia had killed nearly seven *thousand* officers and men. Two carriers, twenty-two support ships and over seven hundred starfighters. By any pre-war standard, the losses had been disastrous. And they were far from over.

"He shouldn't have died," Rose said. Her entire body was shaking. "I...he can't be dead."

Kurt reached out and drew her into a hug, feeling her shake against him as she broke down. She'd genuinely loved her boyfriend; she'd accepted the assignment to *Ark Royal*, at least in part, because she wasn't willing to give him up. But now...he was gone. Or, at best, an alien POW. Did the aliens take prisoners? Human history showed a wide range of possible treatment of prisoners, everything from reasonably nice camps to outright torture and enslavement. What would the aliens consider acceptable?

He tried to push the thought aside as she sobbed. Would Molly sob, he asked himself, if *Ark Royal* were to be destroyed? If Kurt himself were to die? Or would she force her feelings aside and carry on, for Penny and Percy if no one else? What sort of help would be extended towards a widowed woman when there would be thousands of others in the same boat?

"I'm sorry," Rose said. There was a flat tone in her voice he didn't like at all. "I won't be a problem for you and..."

"No, you won't," Kurt said, wishing he knew more about how to talk to someone who'd lost a lover in battle. "You'll get your chance to exact revenge."

Rose looked up, her face blotchy and weepy. "Are you sure?"

"We're going to engage the enemy," Kurt assured her. He knew it wouldn't be easy – and he wasn't sure if he should be telling her at all, at least until the Captain made a formal announcement – but she needed to know. "I think we'll be leaving in a day or two."

"*Formidable* is gone," Rose said, bitterly. "What chance do *we* stand?"

"We will see," Kurt said. There was no point in telling her, now, about the carrier's armour - and how it might make a major difference in the next engagement. He held her for a long moment, then gently let her go. "I want you to take the next few hours off..."

"No," Rose said. She shook her head firmly, then stood upright. If her face hadn't been stained with tears, it would have been convincing. "I can't show weakness."

"Then I don't want to see any problems from you," Kurt said, changing his mind. If she felt it would be better to throw herself into her work, he would let her do it and hope to hell it was the right thing to do. "And we will be starting very early this morning."

He pushed her gently towards the chair, then smiled. "There's a wash-room through there," he said, indicating the hatch at the rear of the room. "Wash yourself, then stay here for a couple of hours if you need to. I won't be using the room."

"Thank you," Rose said.

She didn't look any better, Kurt decided. Perhaps he should call the doctor and ask her to take a look at Rose. But he knew she'd hate it. Doctors, particularly psychologists, were despised by pilots. And how could the pilots be blamed when psychologists tended to have no understanding of their lives, but banned them from flying whenever they thought there was cause for concern. But now there *was* cause for concern.

Loyalty warred with prudence. Loyalty won.

"I shall speak to you again before we go flying," he said, finally. If she still seemed off, he would make her see the doctor, no matter what happened. "Until then, take care of yourself."

Shaking his head, he walked out of the compartment and down towards the flight deck. There was a spare simulator there, one he could use to review the records from New Russia. He didn't know if he would find anything, just by replaying them time and time again, but there was no harm in looking. Besides, Rose wasn't the only one who wanted revenge. Kurt wanted to make the aliens pay too.

CHAPTER

EIGHT

A civilian, Ted knew, would not have been impressed with *Ark Royal's* bridge. The modern Royal Navy had wasted time making bridges look photogenic – naval crewmen joked that the consoles had explosive charges underneath so they could be detonated on cue – but that hadn't been a concern for *Ark Royal's* designers. The bridge was nothing more than a collection of consoles, organised around a large command chair and a holographic display system. There wasn't even a chair for the XO, who would be based in the CIC. If something happened to the bridge, the CIC could take over.

He sat down and looked from console to console. They were a curious mishmash of systems; thankfully, all of them were British rather than produced outside the British Commonwealth. The engineers had worked them all together, but they had never really been tested in combat; now, Ted knew, they would find out just how well their jury-rigged modifications had actually worked. He sucked in his breath as he activated his console and checked the situation reports flowing up from the various departmental heads. Everyone claimed to be ready for departure.

"Begin power-up sequence," he ordered.

A low hum ran through the ship as all six fusion cores powered up together. All of them had been tested, one by one, but there had been no need to power them all up while they'd drifted in the reserves. Now... he watched the readings, silently praying that everything would work properly without problems. In theory, they could operate with four fusion cores, but he didn't want to try it in practice. If nothing else, there would be no redundancy if one of the cores failed during battle.

Or was destroyed, he thought, remembering how effectively the alien weapons had sliced the modern carriers apart. *What if we're wrong about how effective our armour will be?*

The thought made him scowl. Someone had released the recordings of the battle onto the planetary datanet, provoking panic. There had been riots in a dozen British cities, riots which had sucked away the attention of the military, making it harder for them to prepare for a possible invasion. If *Ark Royal* couldn't delay the aliens long enough to prepare additional defences, Earth itself might be invaded sooner rather than later. And who knew how the aliens would treat humanity's homeworld?

He pushed the thought aside as Anderson called him. "All six fusion cores are optimal, Captain," the Chief Engineer said. "Power curves are steady; I recommend we proceed with full power-up."

Ted took another breath. "Do it," he ordered. "Now."

Ark Royal hadn't needed more than a tenth of the output of one fusion core to keep her essential systems running while she'd been in the reserves. The power requirements were minimal; Ted knew he could have reduced them still further, if he hadn't wanted to keep the starship in something resembling fighting trim. Now...inch by inch, his starship was coming to life around him. Section after section responded to the call and came online; sensors activated, sweeping space for hostile threats, while weapons systems prepared themselves to fire on potential targets.

"We have four sections that need urgent replacement," Anderson said. Red lights blinked up briefly in the status display, then faded away. "I don't think our work was up to scratch. I've dispatched repair crews now."

"Good," Ted said. He wasn't too surprised. Given *Ark Royal's* age and the number of different components that had been worked into her hull, he'd expected more than a few minor problems when they powered up for the first time. "Are we ready for deployment?"

"Main drive system; online, ready to go," Anderson said. "Puller Drive; online, ready to go."

There was a long pause as Ted closed his eyes, feeling his ship coming to life around him. In the reserves, she had felt as if she were sleeping. Now...power was thrumming through her hull, her drives, weapons and sensors were online and her starfighters were ready to deploy. The oldest starship still in service, anywhere, was ready and raring to go.

He smiled. "Contact Nelson Base," he ordered. "Inform them that *Ark Royal* is ready for deployment."

"Aye, sir," Lieutenant Annie Davidson said. The communications officer had not been best pleased to be assigned to *Ark Royal*, once she'd been called from the reserves, but she'd started to change her mind after hearing about the loss of two modern carriers. At least *Ark Royal* was capable of taking a beating and remaining functional. "Message sent."

Ted nodded. Hardly anyone, apart from the First Space Lord and his staff, knew about *Ark Royal's* mission. To everyone else, she was just another ancient starship, pressed into service to fight a dangerously powerful foe. Just like one of the civilian ships hastily being fitted with pop-guns, according to one reporter who'd been embedded on Nelson Base. Ted had been offended for his command, but the truth had to remain concealed. The reporter could be made to eat his own words later.

"They're ordering us to proceed to our destination at once," Annie said, after several minutes had gone by. "There's a classified data package for you, sir."

"Forward it to my console," Ted ordered. He looked over at Lightbridge. The helmsman was looking keenly determined, staring down at his console as if he expected to have to react within a split second. "Have you calculated an appropriate jump point?"

"Aye, sir," Lightbridge said. "We can reach our destination in two jumps."

"Then take us to the jump point, best possible speed," Ted ordered. "But do not activate the Puller Drive without my specific authorisation."

He settled back in his command chair and watched the updates from engineering as the crew scurried around, fixing the problems that had become apparent. If there was a real problem, he knew, they would have to hold position in the Sol System so that it could be fixed...but, thankfully, it didn't look as though there was any need to wait. The engineering crew had the tools and spare parts to replace the useless or burned out components. Anderson and his staff had spent the last two weeks scrounging up everything they could and stuffing every last compartment in the ship with spare parts. *Ark Royal* could, in theory, operate for several years without needing outside supplies.

"The computer cores are holding together, thankfully," Anderson said. "I was worried they would object when we actually started to move."

"I know," Ted said. "Keep monitoring their progress."

He scowled, knowing how tricky that was likely to be. The different generations of computer systems had never been designed to work together, let alone the ones that came from outside the Commonwealth. In hindsight, he suspected, the human race might have good reason to regret not establishing a few common standards for technology. Right now, a British carrier couldn't be repaired with spare parts from a Chinese carrier. If the human race managed to remain united – and without unity, they were surely going to lose the war – that was going to have to be fixed.

Assuming we trusted them not to play games, he thought. The Admiralty hadn't objected to *Ark Royal's* crew using begged or scrounged Chinese components, but he'd always assumed that his superiors hadn't bothered to read his reports. His crew had always checked the systems carefully, yet it was quite possible that they'd missed something dangerous, something the Chinese could use to manipulate the carrier to their advantage. Would they try anything like that when the human race needed to remain united?

The starship quivered again as the main drives came to life, pushing her forward towards the jump point. *Ark Royal* handled badly, compared to a frigate or a starfighters, but there was a reassuring firmness around her actions that more modern carriers lacked. Or was that just his imagination, after seeing so many powerful ships torn apart with terrifying speed? No wonder the civilians were panicking – along with quite a few politicians. The Battle of New Russia had lasted barely ten minutes, most of which had been spent getting into position.

"Power curves remain nominal," Anderson said. "The main drive system is functional, sir."

"Glad to hear it," Ted said, dryly. If the drive had failed, they'd know about it already. "Repeat the standard tests on the Puller Drive, if you please."

"Yes, sir," Anderson said.

Ted tapped his console, accessing the data package as *Ark Royal* continued to move towards the jump point. Every analyst in space had been working over the recordings from New Russia, drawing what conclusions they could. Much of the data wasn't *new*, not entirely to Ted's surprise, but there were some interesting suggestions. One of them suggested that the alien ships could be tracked with a little careful effort. Another insisted that the alien starfighters weren't really effective dogfighters at all.

Not that it matters, Ted thought. *They're designed to break through to our carriers and rip them apart.*

There was relatively little data on the alien capital ships, he noted, mostly consisting of uninformed speculation. No one was even sure where the carriers launched their fighters; unlike human craft, the fighter launch tubes appeared to be worked solidly into their hulls. It was an interesting design, he had to admit, suggesting that they weren't too worried about having their carriers targeted. Did they have a good reason to be confident?

They have energy weapons on their starfighters, he thought, sourly. *Their hulls might be bristling with energy weapons too.*

"Sir," Lightbridge said, breaking into his thoughts, "we have reached the jump point."

"Power up the Puller Drive," Ted ordered. He couldn't help feeling the old thrill of jumping out of the Sol System, even though it had been years since he'd been on an interstellar starship. "And then sound the alert."

Another quiver ran through the ship, followed by a low hooting that warned all non-essential crew to brace themselves for the jump. Most spacers grew used to it fairly quickly, but there were always a handful who couldn't take the jump without throwing up or even being rendered comatose. Over a hundred years of FTL travel hadn't yielded any way to identify such people before they took their first jump, although it manifested very quickly. Back at the Academy, British spacers were taken through a jump within the first six months of their training. If they reacted badly, they were assigned to in-system positions only.

Like Ark Royal, he thought, grimly. His crew included a few people who couldn't take the jump, but were desperately needed to keep the starship functional. It was something the Admiralty had overlooked at the time. Ted and Commander Fitzwilliam had dealt with the problem by ordering all such personnel to sickbay before the jump, but they knew it was only a temporary solution. The crewmen would have to be relieved of duty sooner rather than later.

"Puller drive online," Lightbridge said.

"All systems check out properly," Anderson added. "The drive is in full working order."

And thank god for that, Ted thought. The Puller Drive had never seemed very important, not compared to all the other systems that had to be kept operational for *Ark Royal* to remain on the books. And it couldn't really be replaced without chopping open the hull, which would take months. He keyed his console, checking the power curves for himself. For something that was surprisingly simple, the Puller Drive was a colossal power hog.

"Good," Ted said. He looked around the bridge, feeling a hint of pride in his crew. They'd practiced endlessly over the last two weeks, but this was *real*. "Jump!"

The Puller Drive wasn't – technically – a drive at all. Over a century ago, Professor Wang had discovered the existence of gravitational tramlines running between stars and planets – and then worked out a system for exploiting them. If the Puller Drive was triggered at the right place along the tramline, the ship would jump instantly from one star system to the next...providing the tramline was strong enough to allow it. There were stars it was possible to jump to, but not possible to jump back along the same tramline. A black hole, Wang had warned, might be impossible to escape. Its sheer mass would bend the tramlines out of shape. Fortunately, there were none within human space.

For a long moment, the universe seemed to darken...and then snap back to normal. Ted let out a breath he hadn't realised he was holding, then glanced down at his console. The Puller Drive was cycling down, all power curves still nominal. Ted allowed himself a tight smile. His ship might be old, but she was still fully functional and ready for action.

"Jump completed, sir," Lightbridge reported. "No problems detected." "Take us to the next tramline," Ted ordered.

Jumping along a tramline was instantaneous – or close enough to instant to make it impossible to provide a precise estimate of how long it took. Moving from tramline to tramline, on the other hand, could take hours. Ted wasn't blind to the implications of the aliens having a Puller Drive that allowed longer jumps; they might easily outflank humanity's defenders and then attack Earth, just as the First Space Lord had predicted. They might need to spend a few years mopping up afterwards, but the loss of Earth would cost humanity the war.

"Picking up a signal from Terra Nova," Annie said. "They're requesting our IFF. And they sound a little jumpy."

"I'm not surprised," Ted said. *Ark Royal* looked different enough from a modern carrier to be alarmingly unfamiliar to long-range sensors. They might well mistake her for an alien ship. "Shoot them a copy of our IFF, then inform them that we are proceeding to the next tramline."

He sighed. Terra Nova had been the first planet humanity had settled, with each and every ethnic, racial or religious group being offered an enclave. It hadn't worked out very well; none of the interstellar powers felt inclined to invest in it, while the smaller powers didn't have the resources to turn the planet into a success. Ironically, it turned out that human groups were perfectly capable of getting along provided there was some distance between them. Several light years seemed about perfect.

And Terra Nova is practically defenceless, he thought, grimly. None of the bigger powers would risk political unrest by devoting starships to defending a world many civilians regarded as a barbarous backwater. There were only a handful of starships in the system, none of which were modern and several of which were older than *Ark Royal*. It wouldn't take the aliens long to overwhelm them and take the system. If, of course, they were inclined to bother.

Just how much did the aliens *know* about humanity? There was no way to know what they might have recovered from Vera Cruz – an intact navigational database would have told them the location of each and every settled planet in human space – but there could be no doubt about what they could have recovered from New Russia. It was unlikely in the extreme that the Russians would have managed to destroy all of their files before the aliens landed...no, they had to assume the worst. The aliens knew where to find their targets.

But what *else* did they know? If they had time to go through everything on New Russia, they probably knew just how vital Earth was to the unified defence force. And then...

"Captain," Lightbridge said, "we are approaching the second tramline."

Ted pushed his morbid thoughts aside. "Understood," he said. "Power up the Puller Drive, then jump us to our next destination."

He forced himself to remain calm as the universe darkened once again, before snapping back to normal. This time, there were no major settlements in the system. The early survey parties had found nothing of interest, beyond a handful of comets, and nothing had turned up since to make the system more interesting. But that didn't stop it being useful. Four different tramlines ran through the system, allowing it to serve as a transfer point for interstellar shipping. The corporation that had laid claim to the system did a roaring trade in supplies, including some that were technically illegal elsewhere. None of the major interstellar powers wanted to intervene, not when it might have provoked a major confrontation.

"Transit completed, sir," Lightbridge said.

"Very good," Ted agreed. "Take us to the next tramline."

He looked back down at his console, reading the updates from the departmental heads. There didn't seem to be any major problems, thankfully, which meant that they were as close to being ready for action as they were ever likely to get. But if the First Space Lord was wrong...*Ark Royal* might miss out on the war entirely, then find herself forced to flee. Rumour had it that some ships were already taking colonists – and a small industrial base – well away from the aliens. But rumour was unreliable at the best of times.

They'd have real problems maintaining that technological base, he thought. *Or of choosing the colonists, when the time came to leave.*

Tapping a switch, he brought up the First Space Lord's modified chart, showing the tramlines he believed the aliens could use. Ted saw his logic, but the whole conclusion rested on a dangerous gamble. What if the aliens had tricked the human observers? Or what if their tech was vastly more advanced than anyone had realised? Hell, what if they'd managed to escape the tramlines entirely?

We'd be dead, he thought. Escaping the tramlines was the holy grail of human gravitational research. *If that happens, the war will be lost completely...*

Shaking his head, he brought up another piece of analysis, but rapidly realised that it was worse than useless. There was no hard data on the aliens, so speculations on their psychology and motivation were pointless.

We know they want to kill us, he thought, dryly. *That's the important detail. Everything else is immaterial.*

CHAPTER
NINE

No one had bothered to give the system a name, not even the miners who had flocked to the asteroid cluster when a survey party had discovered that the asteroids were rich in raw materials. The brief wave of interest in the system hadn't lasted past the discovery of other sources in more habitable systems, leaving a handful of miners and settlers making a living from selling what they mined at low cost. According to the database, most of the settlers really wanted to isolate themselves from the rest of the human race.

It was hard to escape the feeling, James decided, that they had succeeded. If *Ark Royal* hadn't known the settlements were there, it was quite possible that they would have been overlooked. They were really nothing more than a handful of mined-out asteroids, closed ecosystems powered by solar collectors. There wasn't much room for expansion, he knew, but they could maintain their position for hundreds of years before they had to make some hard choices. By then, human space would have changed so radically that who knew what sort of society would greet them, if they chose to return home?

Ark Royal hung near the tramline to Earth – or where the tramline would be, if the Old Lady's drive had been able to use it. Predicting where the aliens might go was easy enough, assuming that the First Space Lord's calculations had been correct. There was certainly nothing else to interest the aliens; the settlements weren't worth the effort of destroying them, assuming that the aliens weren't bent on total genocide. But if they were wrong...

He looked up at the display, seeing a handful of fast-attack frigates hanging close to the massive carrier. They'd arrived the day after *Ark Royal*, bringing updates from Earth, including records from a Russian starship that had remained concealed and watched as the aliens landed on New Russia. Apparently, the aliens had bombarded the planetary defence centres, but otherwise ignored the human population. James couldn't decide if that was a good or bad thing. It was good, because it suggested that the aliens weren't bent on genocide after all, yet it was also bad because it prevented contact between humans and aliens. There was no hope of opening a dialogue that might result in peace talks.

Not that they have to worry, he thought, grimly. *As long as they're winning, they can dictate terms to us and we will have to bend over and take them.*

"Captain on the deck," the duty officer said.

James turned to see Captain Smith entering the CIC. The Captain looked galvanised, but – like the rest of his crew – he was clearly worried about what they were doing in the unnamed system. If they were wrong about the alien plans, they were quite likely to discover it the hard way, when they finally returned to Earth and found it under alien occupation. James was merely relieved that the Captain hadn't started to drink again. If he did, James would have to relieve him of command...which would almost certainly doom James's career too.

"Captain," he said. "We have finished deploying the decoys."

The Captain nodded. They'd hashed out the possibilities endlessly, but one thing had been clear from the start. They would have to lure the aliens to their position, not gamble on the aliens appearing right next to them. Any planetary system, even one orbiting an insignificant red dwarf, was so vast that the odds against them being in the right place were staggeringly high. But if the aliens thought they had a valid set of targets...

"Activate them," the Captain ordered. "And hope that they fool the aliens."

James nodded. The drones were the most advanced decoys produced by human technology, but no one knew what the aliens would make of them. If their sensor technology was advanced enough, they would probably realise that the decoys weren't *real* carriers and give them a wide berth. Or maybe they would assume that the decoys were nothing more than a bluff.

He keyed a switch, activating the drones. Sensor ghosts appeared briefly on the display, showing the location of five modern carriers. Even knowing that the images weren't real, *Ark Royal's* sensor crews had difficulty separating the illusions from reality. Hopefully, the aliens wouldn't question what they saw.

"They won't see any starfighters," he warned. "Or, rather, they won't see *enough* starfighters."

The Captain shrugged. *Ark Royal* carried four wings of starfighters; a modern carrier could carry ten, along with a small armada of smaller craft. There was no way their four wings could pretend to be the fighters attached to five modern carriers, but if they were lucky the aliens would assume that the remaining fighters hadn't been launched. Or maybe they would think that the human carriers were trying to retreat…

James made a face. There were too many flaws in the plan for him to be entirely comfortable with it.

Idiot, he told himself. *If you'd taken command, you would have to grapple with the same problems yourself.*

An alarm sounded, making him jump. "Sir," Farley said, "we just picked up a warning signal from the sensor drones. Seven enemy carriers and forty smaller ships have just jumped into the system."

"Show me," the Captain ordered. Red icons appeared on the display, surrounded by lines projecting their course and speed. They were heading towards the predicted tramline. "It appears we have company."

"Yes, sir," James said, feeling cold ice running down the back of his spine. The aliens had chopped through twelve modern carriers…what if they were wrong about *Ark Royal's* armour? Or what if they were right…and they were still overwhelmed anyway. "I think they saw the drones."

On the display, the alien craft altered course. "No fighters," the Captain noted. "Or are they there and we can't see them?"

James shrugged. A human CO might keep his pilots in the launch tubes as long as possible, giving them what protection he could, but who knew how the aliens thought?

The Captain keyed his terminal. "Red alert," he said, "I say again, red alert. All hands to battlestations."

A low drumbeat echoed through the ship, bringing the crew to full readiness. "I'm going to the bridge," the Captain added. "We're about to find out the truth for ourselves."

James nodded, then turned back to the display.

———

"Get your ass in gear," Kurt snapped, as the pilots ran for their starfighters. "Into the cockpits, now! Move, damn it!"

He scrambled up the ladder into his own cockpit, then hastily keyed the switch to bring his fighter to full power. They'd been sitting in the ready room when the alert had sounded; if he'd had his druthers, half of the formation would have been on combat space patrol at all times. But he understood the Captain's logic, even if he didn't like it. They didn't dare let the aliens seem something that suggested the decoy carriers weren't real.

"Ready for launch," he said, once he'd strapped himself into the cockpit. "Check in, by the numbers."

One by one, the pilots sounded off. Nothing had gone wrong, thankfully; he'd seen several deployments when starfighters had suffered failures that had forced the crews to hold them back long enough to be fixed. Pilots hated it when that happened, but Kurt suspected that it was better than suffering a catastrophic failure while in interplanetary space. He checked in with the CIC as soon as all of the pilots had reported in, then braced himself for the launch. It always felt like a roller coaster, despite the best compensators the Royal Navy could produce.

He forgot his concerns as soon as he was blasted out of the tube into interstellar space. The stars burned brightly around him, illuminating the darkened shape of the carrier. There was no way they could see the alien craft with the naked eye, but their carriers were showing up clearly on his display. The starfighters, on the other hand, weren't showing up at all. He gritted his teeth, realised just how dangerous the alien stealth systems could be. If their sensors were unreliable, the aliens could just snipe the human craft out of visual range, picking them off one by one.

"Additional sensor drones are being launched," the XO said. "If the aliens can't maintain their stealth when they go to full power..."

And if they can, we're dead, Kurt thought. He looked back at the alien carriers on the display, trying to estimate how long it would take the alien starfighters to enter engagement range. But there just wasn't enough hard data to make a realistic guess.

"Alpha and Beta, with me," he ordered. "Delta and Gamma, remain to cover the Old Lady."

He listened to the acknowledgements, then gunned the starfighter's thrusters, forcing it forward. Ahead of them, the alien carriers grew larger on the display.

———

Ted wanted a drink, desperately. Something to give him a little courage and determination, something to keep him going as seven massive alien carriers bore down on his command. It was clear that the aliens had been fooled by the decoys – it was the only explanation that made sense – and yet, he knew all too well that they had the firepower to deal with the illusionary ships. He *needed* a drink...

He forced the thought aside as he watched his starfighters advancing towards the enemy, fighters taking the lead while the bombers followed afterwards, waiting for their chance to launch their missiles at the enemy ships. The aliens had a definite unfair advantage, he decided; their starfighters could switch roles effortlessly, while the human craft were easy to separate out, isolating the ones that posed a definite threat to the enemy ships. He had no doubt that the aliens intended to take advantage of their technology as much as possible. It was what he would have done.

"Picking up some odd distortion as the drones advance forward," Farley said. The tactical officer was staring down at his console, puzzled. "We might be able to provide rough locations for the alien fighters."

"We need something more precise," Ted said. They could detonate a string of nukes...but if they weren't careful, they'd risk damaging their own starfighters too. "Can you get a lock on them we can use to..."

He broke off as new red icons blinked into existence. Despite himself, he couldn't help a flicker of admiration for the alien technology...and the pilots of the alien starfighters. Flying so close to their target was ballsy, all right, even if they knew they were effectively invisible. But now they could be seen...he watched as Gamma wing altered course, swinging up to confront the alien craft, while Delta wing remained behind to shield the carrier's hull. So far, their planning seemed to have paid off.

"Clear to engage," he ordered, as the alien starfighters accelerated forward. Their power curves were definitely less capable than human starfighters...and there was a curious elegance about them that seemed oddly impractical. Or maybe they genuinely *could* operate within a planetary atmosphere. "I say again, clear to engage."

"They're coming right towards us now," Commander Fitzwilliam said, through the intercom. "They must have realised that the other carriers are decoys."

"Looks that way," Ted agreed. "Deactivate the drones. We can recover them after the battle."

He scowled as the alien craft came closer, showing no hint of surprise when the dummy carriers vanished from the screens. Yes, they'd definitely seen through the deception...he tried, quickly, to work out *when* they'd seen through it, but it was impossible to say for sure. He pushed the thought aside, gritting his teeth. The whole theory about his ship's armour was about to be put to the test.

The alien starfighters didn't bother to do more than fire a handful of shots at the human starfighters as they roared past them, concentrating instead on *Ark Royal*. Ted watched, feeling a moment of relief as four alien starfighters vanished from the display, picked off by his ships, then braced himself as they came into engagement range. This was where they'd torn the more advanced carriers apart...a handful of them fell to the carrier's point defence, but the remainder kept boring in. He watched, mentally praying desperately to a god he wasn't sure he believed in, as the alien weapons flared to life...and slammed into the carrier's armour.

"No major damage," Anderson reported. The Chief Engineer sounded as relieved as Ted felt. "I say again, no major damage."

"Continue firing," Ted ordered, as Delta wing chased the alien starfighters over the carrier's hull. "Drive them away from us."

He glanced down at the reports, sighing in relief. *Ark Royal's* armour *could* take the alien blasts...but it wouldn't stop the alien starfighters from disarming and blinding the carrier by picking off her weapons and sensors. One by one, the alien craft fell back towards their own carriers, clearly rethinking their task. Behind them, Gamma wing gave chase while Delta wing remained with *Ark Royal*.

"Lock mass drivers on target," he ordered. The alien carriers were coming into effective range, although – unlike powered missiles – the mass drivers were nothing more than ballistic weapons. "Prepare to fire."

What, he asked himself absently, would a mass driver do to a modern carrier? Assuming a direct hit, it would rip the carrier apart from end to end. It made him wonder if there had been a quiet agreement among the various interstellar powers to ban mass drivers from starships, even though they were effective weapons. If there was, it wouldn't last much longer, not if the theories were correct. The aliens were about to be kissed.

"Weapons locked on target," Farley reported. "Ready to fire."

Ted smiled. "Fire," he ordered.

Projectiles launched from mass drivers couldn't alter course, allowing them to be evaded fairly easily if the target saw them coming. But they made up for that by being immensely destructive if they did hit, as well as fast enough to give the targets relatively little warning of their arrival. The aliens clearly didn't see them coming in time; one carrier was smashed amidships by a projectile, while another, clearly badly damaged, limped out of formation and started to retreat.

"Two direct hits," Farley said. On the display, the first alien carrier disintegrated in a series of tearing explosions. "The mass driver is reloading."

"Fire as soon as possible," Ted ordered. The mass driver took too long to reload, another problem that would have to be solved before the end of the war. "Target an untouched alien ship."

The aliens seemed uncertain of what to do, he realised, as he watched their formation spread apart. They clearly hadn't expected the mass driver, but now they'd seen it they were taking precautions, making it harder to guarantee a direct hit. And mass drivers *needed* direct hits to be effective…

"Take us towards them," he ordered. *Ark Royal* was large and intimidating and she'd just handed out the worst beating the aliens had taken in the war. If they were lucky, the aliens might just break off…but he wasn't sure he *wanted* them to break off. He wanted revenge for the dead crewmen who'd died at New Russia. "Order our escorts to open fire."

The alien starfighters altered course, then swept back towards *Ark Royal*. Ted watched grimly as he realised what the aliens had in mind. Take out the mass driver, take out the missile tubes…and *Ark Royal* would be practically defenceless. He barked orders as the alien craft closed in, blowing through the defending starfighters, only to run straight into the teeth of the carrier's point defence. They weren't even trying to stealth themselves.

The stealth system must have a huge power requirement, he decided, as the starfighters lanced down and opened fire. Again, the armour deflected most of it, but a number of weapons and sensors were blown off the hull. Absently, he wondered what would happen if the aliens kept firing into where the weapons had been. There were additional layers of armour under the primary hull, but they weren't as thick as the first line of defence.

"Firing," Farley reported. There was a long pause as five solid projectiles raced towards their targets. "One hit; three more picked off by the aliens."

One solid miss, Ted noted. He cursed under his breath. The aliens had thought of using counter-battery fire – and, unlike most offensive weapons, mass drivers were vulnerable to defensive fire. It was simple enough to predict their courses and take them out before it was too late. Given time, the human race might manage to build enough mass driver-armed ships to render that a moot point, but God alone knew what the aliens would improvise as a countermeasure. Or were they incapable of innovation? It didn't seem likely.

They're not stupid, he told himself. Dealing with a stupid enemy would be easier – but a stupid enemy could never have built those ships. *Whatever else they are, they're not stupid.*

He scowled. He *really* needed a drink.

"Lock missiles on target, then open fire," he ordered, instead. On the display, the alien carriers had started to reverse course, tacitly abandoning the battlefield. But it would take them at least ten minutes to reach a usable tramline. He'd be able to use that time to hammer their ships into scrap metal. "And continue firing with the mass drivers until we run out of projectiles."

"Aye, sir," Farley said. "Opening fire…now."

On the display, *Ark Royal* and her escorts went to rapid fire. Moments later, the enemy point defence came to life, spewing out blasts of plasma fire like machine gun bursts…

Ted gritted his teeth. If they shot their magazines dry, the aliens could still win. This was going to hurt…

CHAPTER
TEN

Kurt had expected, he realised now, the alien carrier to look rather like human carriers, which tended to follow the same basic design. *Ark Royal* was the only real exception and then only because her designers hadn't known as much about designing starships as their successors. But the aliens, it was clear, had their own aesthetics. Their carriers were giant spheres, seemingly completely unarmed. And yet, when the human starfighters came within range, bursts of plasma fire swept out towards them from hidden gun ports.

"Evasive action," he snapped, yanking his starfighter away from a burst of light that almost ripped him apart. The aliens, it seemed, didn't have to worry about running out of ammunition. Nor were they inclined to hold back some of their starfighters to provide a combat space patrol. "Let the bombers go in to launch missiles."

He watched, grimly, as the bombers launched their missiles. The aliens, realising the threat, focused all of their attention on the nuclear-tipped warheads, wiping all but one of them out before they stuck the alien hull. One missile made it through and detonated, significantly damaging the alien carrier. It drifted out of formation, then exploded in a shockingly powerful blast. Kurt wondered, absently, just what the aliens used for a power source.

Antimatter would have killed us all, he guessed, as he led the fighters back towards the carrier. Nearly a third of the bombers had been wiped out, while the remainder had shot their missiles. The aliens had a definite advantage...he hoped, silently, that the human race managed to improve their own directed-energy weapons or plasma cannons. Without them, they were always going to be at a disadvantage.

The alien starfighters lanced back towards the human craft, intent on killing them before they could return to *Ark Royal* and rearm. Kurt barked orders, then led his craft through the enemy formation, firing madly at brief targets. Two alien craft died, the remainder fell back and let the humans escape. Behind them, *Ark Royal* and her escorts were approaching rapidly, launching a steady stream of missiles. Another alien carrier, already badly damaged, exploded into a ball of expanding plasma, leaving the remainder to escape as best as they could. The alien escorts were already putting themselves between the carriers and *Ark Royal*.

Brave of them, he conceded, reluctantly. *They're safeguarding the carriers at the cost of their own lives.*

He watched grimly as the bombers returned to *Ark Royal*, then turned his starfighters to cover the carrier as she advanced on the alien craft.

———

"Sir, the bombers are reloading."

Ted nodded, thinking hard. The bombers had lost nearly a third of their number, a staggeringly high loss rate even if they *had* taken out a single alien carrier. And the aliens were in full retreat. But he didn't want to let them escape, if it were possible to stop them.

"Order them to launch again once they have reloaded," he ordered. "And then..."

He broke off as a red light flashed up on the display. "Sir, *Amati* is gone," Farley snapped. "They just blew her apart!"

Ted stared down at the display. There was nothing left of the missile frigate save an expanding cloud of atoms. "What happened?"

"Unsure," Farley said, after a moment. "I think...I think they have a short-range plasma weapon of staggering power."

It would have to be, Ted realised. A mass driver would have been noticeable – and logically the aliens would have fired it at *Ark*

Royal, rather than one of the smaller craft. And, whatever it was had to be short-ranged or *Ark Royal* would have been blown apart by now.

"Hold the range open," he ordered, thinking hard. What *was* the minimum range? He keyed his console. "Analysis; I want to know what happened and why."

There was a long pause. "Our best guess is that they have an intensely powerful plasma system," the analyst said, finally. She sounded unhappy; analysts were rarely called upon to provide data during a battle. Or at least they hadn't been. That too was going to change. "I think they couldn't maintain containment for very long, sir. Once the field fails, the blast would simply come apart."

And be harmless, Ted thought. One by one, the alien escorts were slowing their retreat, threatening to bring the human ships into range. If he wasn't careful, he would wind up impaling himself on their weapons.

"Thank you," he said. Unlike a mass driver, the alien weapon's plasma would move at the speed of light. There would be no warning before it struck home...and it was clearly an order of magnitude more powerful than the weapons mounted on alien starfighters. "Will our armour be able to handle it?"

"Unknown, sir," the analyst said. "However, the weapon did manage to take out a frigate. We have to assume the worst."

Ted closed the channel, then looked over at Farley. "Target missiles and mass drivers on the alien escorts," he ordered. He was effectively letting the alien carriers go – they were picking up speed at a surprising rate – but there was no alternative. If nothing else, the aliens had taken a very definite bloody nose after trying to outflank Earth's defences. "The bombers are to attempt to engage the alien carriers."

He settled back in his command chair and watched as the range continued to open. The alien ships were in full retreat, not even trying to send their own starfighters to engage *Ark Royal* and her escorts. Ted allowed himself a moment of pleasure at their discomfort, then glanced down at the reports from engineering. The damaged weapons and sensors wouldn't take too long to repair, thankfully. They could give chase if their FTL drive had been equal to the alien system.

"Captain," Farley said, "they're approaching the tramline."

Ted sighed. By any standards, they had won a naval victory…but they still had no idea just how powerful the aliens actually were. It was impossible to tell if they'd degraded the enemy fleet by ten percent, one percent or point one percent. The only sign that the aliens might not be as strong as they had feared was that they'd sent only a handful of carriers through the back door. But they might well have been attempting to secure their lines of communication before launching the main thrust towards Earth.

"Recall the fighters," he ordered, softly. "Let them go."

Five minutes later, the aliens flickered out and vanished.

———

It was against regulations, but Kurt couldn't help flipping his starfighter over in a loop-the-loop before guiding the tiny craft into the recovery bay. Outside, the maintenance crews were going crazy, cheering the fighter pilots as they cracked open their cockpits and jumped out onto the deck. Kurt found himself being kissed by several women and two men before he finally managed to disentangle himself and bellow for order. Slowly, quiet fell over the recovery bay.

"We won," he said.

The sound of cheering almost deafened him. They'd all seen the images from New Russia, they'd all feared that their first engagement would be their last. But they'd adapted, reacted and overcome. The aliens would be back, he was sure, but they'd given them a bloody nose that would make them rethink their plans for overrunning human space.

"We will go over everything that happened tomorrow," he continued. There was a chorus of good-natured groans, entirely understandably, but no one objected out loud. "For the moment, eat, drink and be merry…and any of you who turn up drunk will regret it for the rest of a very short and miserable career."

He smiled at their expressions. It hadn't been uncommon for pilots to drink, sometimes heavily, despite regulations. Clearly, that was something that hadn't changed since he'd transferred to the reserves. But this was wartime and he was damned if he was going to be kind and sympathetic to any of his pilots who ended up drunk. There were treatments to force someone to sober up within moments and he would use them, if necessary.

"Make sure you get some sleep too," he added. "We don't know when the aliens will come back."

That got their attention, as he'd expected. The aliens might just take a few hours to rethink their plans, then go back on the offensive. They would need a special weapon to take out *Ark Royal*, but that wouldn't be too hard for them. A mass driver would be quite effective, or a simple set of nuclear torpedoes. There was no way they didn't have nukes, not if they had plasma cannons and an improved FTL system. Hell, they might even have something *more* effective, once they realised the potentials of their own system.

"And well done, all of you," he concluded.

He turned and walked out of the bay, remembering the days when he'd been a simple pilot and could participate in after-action parties. But, as CAG, he wasn't supposed to be condoning any of it. It wasn't fair...he shook his head, annoyed at himself. The world was not fair. Just ask the crews of *Formidable* and *Invincible*.

"Kurt," a voice called. He turned to see Rose following him. "Do you have a moment?"

Kurt lifted an eyebrow, but nodded, allowing her to follow him into his office. The analysts hadn't wasted any time, he noted; there was a complete copy of all of the sensor records on his terminal, just waiting for his input. The battle would be dissected over the coming days and weeks until every last micron of data was wrung from the records and used to plan humanity's next move. But, for the moment, all Kurt wanted to do was sleep.

"You should be at the party I'm not meant to know about," he said. "Why did you come here?"

"I killed five of them," Rose said. "Do you think I killed enough?"

It took Kurt a moment to understand what she meant. "I think we've only just begun," he said. "Three enemy carriers were destroyed, one more was badly damaged..."

"But she managed to escape," Rose pointed out. "We could have taken her intact otherwise..."

Kurt nodded. Humanity was known for solving technical problems – now they knew what the aliens could do, human researchers would be trying to duplicate it – but he had to admit that recovering samples of alien technology would speed the whole process up considerably. But somehow he doubted the aliens would allow their technology to be captured so easily, not by a potentially deadly enemy. Human systems were rigged to prevent them falling into enemy hands.

"Maybe we could have," Kurt agreed, finally. He gave her a long look. "Are you going to stop now?"

Rose blinked owlishly at him. "What do you mean?"

"Do you feel that five aliens are enough," Kurt asked, "or do you mean to keep killing them until the war comes to an end?"

"Keep killing them," Rose snapped. She sounded more than a little annoyed by his comment. "I don't think that any number of the bastards can make up for him."

Kurt scowled. Rose bothered him, even though she was hardly the worst of his problem children. It was easy to imagine her putting her desire for revenge ahead of sound tactics and careful planning – to say nothing of the overall objective. He understood the desire for revenge, even shared it, but he also knew that he had to put his own problems to one side and concentrate on his duty.

"Relax now," he ordered, softly. "And remember that there will be other battles."

"There will be," Rose agreed. She grinned, suddenly. "We gave them a fright, didn't we?"

Kurt nodded.

"And we showed those fools back on Earth that we can kick butt with the best of them," Rose said, her grin widening into a smile. "Thank you, sir."

She gave him a peck on the cheek, then walked out of the compartment before Kurt could say a word. He stared at her, one finger touching the spot where she'd kissed him, then shook his head in disbelief. Rose… wasn't anywhere close to stable. But then, few pilots were.

"Damn it," he muttered. He closed the hatch, then keyed his terminal. There was just time to record a v-mail to Molly before he went back to the pilot quarters for some sleep. "What's gotten into her now?"

He waited till the recording light came on, then started to speak. "Hi, Molly, I don't know quite when you will get this message, but I think you'll get it before I return home. We won a battle..."

When he was finished, he saved the message, uploaded it to the communications network and then went to get some sleep.

———

Ted sat in his cabin, eying the bottle on his desk. It was finest Scotch, a present from an old friend upon his promotion to Commodore; Ted had been saving it for a special occasion. Now, with an alien fleet in full retreat and his ship thoroughly vindicated, it seemed as good an occasion as any. But he wasn't sure he could ensure that he stuck to just one glass...

He'd won, he knew. The Royal Navy might call him a drunkard, the other commanding officers might question his qualifications, but none of them could deny that he'd won a battle against a powerful and seemingly overwhelming foe. Everyone had seen the recordings of New Russia by now, everyone knew that humanity's very future hung in the balance. But he'd pulled off a victory and, in doing so, altered the course of the war. Or so he hoped.

It was worthy of a drink. Wasn't it?

He should know better, he told himself. Hundreds of thousands of naval crewmen experimented with drink...and, as a general rule, most of them learned to control the impulse or simply give it up. But Ted hadn't really learned, which was why he'd been assigned to *Ark Royal* as a mere Lieutenant-Commander. The Royal Navy had preferred to move him to a dead-end assignment rather than have him dishonourably dismissed from the service – or even quietly retire him when his first enlistment ended. There were days when he'd wondered just what his superior officers had been thinking. Had they been too lazy to do the paperwork for early retirement or had they questioned the wisdom of forcibly retiring someone who'd earned a knighthood through saving lives as a young Lieutenant?

The bottle glimmered faintly under the cabin light. It was worth over three hundred pounds, he knew; his friend had been making a point as well as presenting Ted with a gift. Part of him wanted to tear the bottle's cap off and take a swig, part of him knew that he didn't dare indulge. *Ark Royal* was no longer orbiting a beacon in the Earth-Moon system, but facing a dangerous alien threat. The bastards could be back at any moment.

And he could lose his command. No one really cared if a reservist commander drank, not when there was no real danger to his crew. But now…his XO wanted his post and had friends in high places. Fitzwilliam hadn't done anything overt to stab Ted in the back, yet Ted knew the younger man was ambitious…and all of the arguments he'd used to convince the First Space Lord to let Ted remain in command had become less and less effective as Fitzwilliam learned more about the ancient carrier. Hell, he *would* be a good commander, Ted knew. The younger man had an optimism about him that Ted had long since lost.

But Ted had no intention of surrendering his command. It would be the first step towards early – enforced – retirement. There was no way he would be allowed to take command of a modern carrier, even an escort ship. He'd be lucky if he was assigned to an asteroid mining facility in the middle of nowhere. Humanity's only winner or not, he would be lucky to be allowed to keep his rank. The Royal Navy would have its doubts about giving a modern starship to a known drunkard.

Angrily, he lashed out. The bottle plummeted from the desk and struck the deck, shattering on impact. Glass and alcohol splashed everywhere. Ted swore out loud, then stood upright and reached for a towel. There was no point in ordering Midshipwomen Lopez or another junior crewman to clear up the mess. Besides, he was more than a little ashamed of his own weakness. It was something he had to tackle on his own. Once the mess was cleared, he dumped the towel into the recycler, glass and all. It would at least serve a useful purpose when it was broken down for raw material.

His intercom buzzed. "Captain," Fitzwilliam said. For an absurd moment, Ted wondered if someone outside the cabin had heard the bottle break, or smelled the Scotch through the airlock. "The Marines are ready to start sifting through the debris, while *Primrose* is ready to return to Earth."

Ted grunted. "Tell them to make best possible speed," he ordered. The frigate would carry the news of the victory to Earth. "And tell them that we will return to Earth within four days unless they have other orders for us."

He scowled up at the star chart. The aliens definitely had a more advanced FTL drive than humanity's. That was a given, now. If they used it aggressively, they might even be able to jump directly to Earth. And there wouldn't be any real warning before they arrived. Once *Ark Royal* returned to Earth, they might not be allowed to leave, even though they were ideally suited to raiding behind enemy lines.

Damn it, he thought, as he turned on the air conditioning to get rid of the smell. *We've won one battle, but not the war. Not yet.*

CHAPTER
ELEVEN

The remains of the alien craft were almost invisible in the darkness of interplanetary space.

"I'm not picking up very much, beyond chunks of molten metal," Corporal Henderson reported. "I don't think we're going to find anything we can reverse-engineer."

"At least not immediately," Charles said. The Royal Marines had a multitude of roles when they weren't actually serving as ground or space troopers. One of them was conducting the preliminary post-battle search for intelligence. Marines, in theory, were trained to recognise danger, something that couldn't always be said of civilian researchers. "The ship was smashed to rubble."

He shrugged. There were no shortage of stories where a piece of alien technology was captured the first day, reverse-engineered the second and then used to produce a vastly-improved human version the third. It had never struck him as particularly realistic. He knew it could take months to reverse-engineer something produced by the Russians or Chinese – and *they* were human. How long might it take to deduce the operating principles of a piece of completely alien technology?

Maybe not that long, he told himself. *Their technology can't be that different from ours. The laws of science will work the same for them, won't they?*

He glanced down at the scanner as the tiny shuttle nosed its way through the debris cloud. Automated systems were already picking up samples of alien metal, although the first sweeps suggested that alien hullmetal wasn't anything uncommon. The researchers might speculate endlessly on new elements or previously undiscovered composites, but that was rather less than likely. Or so Charles assumed. If they started believing that there was something about alien technology that would be forever beyond humanity's reach, they would always accept their own inferiority.

There was a ping from the console. "Picking up traces of biological matter," Henderson said. "Sir?"

"Get it swept up by the drones," Charles ordered, forcing down the surge of excitement he felt. Despite himself, he desperately wanted to know what the aliens *looked* like – and what they called themselves. Humanity had no name for them. But while he had seen bodies survive seemingly devastating explosions, he didn't want to raise false hopes. They might have found nothing more than blood and ashes. "Then send them into quarantine."

"Yes, sir," Henderson said. He looked up, suddenly. "Will they catch colds and die?"

Charles shrugged. The human race had discovered thirty Earth-like worlds – and seventy worlds that could be terraformed, although it was such a colossal investment that few were prepared to make the effort – but none of them had possessed a viral life form that was actually dangerous to humanity. As far as anyone knew, Earth was the only world that had produced an intelligent race...well, as far as anyone had known. Unless the aliens were actually humans from a prehistoric space-based civilisation – and that seemed absurd – it was clear that there was more than one world that had given birth to an intelligent race.

"I doubt it," he said, finally. "Chances are that their biology will be so different from ours that our diseases will do little to them – and vice versa."

Unless someone deliberately engineers a killing disease, he thought, grimly. The Royal Marines had been involved in the suppression of genetically-engineered diseases – there had been several attempts to commit genocide using tailored viruses – and, despite all the international treaties, the world had come alarmingly close to disaster more than once. *Maybe we will take the gloves off when the aliens push us to the wall.*

He looked down at Henderson, realising – not for the first time – just how young the Corporal actually was. Charles had fifteen years in the Royal Marines, Henderson was barely out of training. He'd never seen any real action, not down on the ground. And Royal Marines rarely won plaudits for serving on starships that went into combat. They were tasked to serve as groundpounders or space troopers, not starship officers.

The console pinged again. "Got something else, sir," Henderson said. "This one's a bit bigger."

Charles nodded. "Send the drones after it," he ordered. "Then run the live feed through the screens here."

He looked over at the console as the drones closed in on their target, reporting a steady increase in the density of biological material as they made their way through space. Slowly, something humanoid came into view, illuminated by the lights mounted on the drones. It was damaged, perhaps badly, but it was definitely far from human. Charles felt a chill running down his spine as he gazed into the face of an alien.

There had been no shortage of speculation, he knew, about what the aliens might actually be like. The general assumption had been that the aliens were too alien to realise that war was unnecessary; after all, everyone in academia knew that cooperation was the way forward, not wasteful war. Charles had read speculation that ranged from giant spiders, complete with insect mentalities, to robots that had killed their creators and gone on a rampage across the universe, but the academics had been wrong. The proof was drifting right in front of him.

The alien was humanoid, as far as he could tell, although it – he, perhaps – had clearly lost a leg. His skin was thick and leathery, almost like a humanoid elephant; his eyes were dark and shadowy. There were no clothes, although with skin like that, he realised, the alien wouldn't really need protection from the elements. The remainder of the alien body was damaged, broken and bleeding in a dozen places. It was very clearly dead.

Charles swallowed, then spoke. "Contact the ship," he ordered. "We've found a body."

He watched as the drones pulled back, waiting for the EVA specialists to arrive. The body would be bagged up, then transported back to the carrier and placed on ice. No one would be allowed to see it, let alone touch it, until they'd taken it safely back to Earth, where it would be examined in a sealed facility. He was fairly sure that alien bugs wouldn't be lethal to humanity, but there was no point in taking chances. Besides, everyone and his aunt would want to see the body.

"It doesn't look friendly," Henderson commented. The normally bouncy young man – there were a handful of sharp remarks about the need for discipline in his file – sounded subdued, almost terrified. "Do you think they're all helplessly evil?"

Charles looked down at the screen. The alien *did* look unfriendly, he had to admit; his jaws were filled with sharp teeth, set in a permanent grimace. But that meant nothing, he knew; the alien might easily be smiling instead, or merely screaming in agony as his body froze to death. Besides, he'd seen plenty of humans who had looked dangerous – or merely unpleasant – only to discover that looks could be deceiving.

"I think you shouldn't judge someone by their looks," he said, dryly. "Unless they're pointing a gun at you, of course."

He wondered, briefly, what the various human-alien friendship protest groups would make of it. There had been no shortage of idiots willing to believe that the human race had started the war, perhaps by settling a world the aliens had already claimed…although, if that was the case, why hadn't they made contact rather than simply opened fire? Somehow, he doubted the human race would have been stubborn if the aliens explained that they'd gotten to Vera Cruz first. And, even if they had removed the humans by force, why carry on to attack New Russia? And then start an advance on Earth?

There was no way to know. Human morality might mean nothing to the aliens – and there were dozens of human groups with their own versions of morality. Maybe the aliens thought that exterminating every other form of life was a holy duty or maybe they considered themselves the masters of the universe, with everyone else battered into slavery. Charles could imagine a dozen motives for the attack that were heartless and cruel, but not unprecedented. Hell, maybe there was an alien emperor who wanted to start a war in the hopes it would distract attention from problems at home.

He watched, grimly, as the alien was bagged up, then returned his attention to sweeping through the remainder of the debris field. Any hopes he might have had for recovering alien technology seemed as unlikely as ever; the largest chunk of debris they found was nothing more than a piece of alien hull. Several of the other searchers picked up alien bodies, including one that seemed almost completely intact. They were bagged up and returned to the carrier too.

The intercom buzzed. "Return to the Old Lady," the XO ordered, flatly. "We're going back to Earth."

———

"I had a preliminary look at the pieces of debris," Anderson reported, "but most of them are too badly battered to be understandable."

Ted nodded, sharing a long look with his XO. He hadn't really expected any ground-shaking discoveries, apart from the alien bodies, but it was still disappointing. It would have been nice to recover an alien plasma weapon intact so it could be reverse-engineered…

He shook his head, dismissing the thought. "What can you tell us about the alien ships?"

"Their hulls are actually stronger than one of our modern carriers, but weaker than *Ark Royal's* armour," Anderson said. "There's nothing particularly…*alien* about the composite they use, it's merely something that might prove more resistant to plasma blasts. I think we can place it into production ourselves in short order, although it would still take months – more likely years – before we could sheath all of the modern carriers in alien-derived armour."

"They might want to start building new carriers from scratch," Fitzwilliam observed. "And battleships too."

Ted nodded. Mass drivers had been the most effective weapon humanity had found, so far, and he could see the value in producing hundreds of mass driver-armed starships. If *Ark Royal's* limited system had been able to wreck havoc, an entire fleet of such starships would be unstoppable. Hell, they could just start by rigging mass drivers onto the hulls of escort ships, then produce a more formal design later.

"It takes upwards of a year to produce a modern carrier – longer, of course, to produce something like the Old Lady," Anderson reminded him, stroking the desk absently with one hand. "New carriers will be required, eventually, but it will be quicker to modify the ones we have."

"The Admiralty can decide that," Ted said. He keyed a switch, accessing a secure data store and displaying the images of the alien bodies. "The face of the enemy, gentlemen."

He smiled at their reactions to the alien face. In proper lighting, he couldn't help thinking of a amphibious creature. The alien might be equally at home in and out of the water, he decided; their leathery skin and the absence of any protective garment suggested that they were actually tougher than humans. It seemed odd to consider a starship crew that were completely naked – even if they had no nudity taboo, surely they would need protection against accidents – but maybe it worked for them. There was nothing that suggested the alien's sex, at least as far as he could tell.

"Ugly bastards," Farley said, finally. "And tough too."

"Very tough," Doctor Jeanette Hastings agreed. She leaned forward. "As per regulations, I transferred the bodies into storage tubes rather than attempting to study them myself. However, I can tell you, just from a visual inspection, that the aliens are definitely tough – and probably faster than they look. Judging from the shape of their eyes, they're used to a darker environment than humanity; they're probably far more capable of seeing in the dark without technological aid."

Fitzwilliam smiled. "What gender are they?"

"Impossible to tell without an autopsy," Jeanette said. "I was unable to locate anything resembling either a penis or a vagina through visual inspection. They look humanoid, but they don't have to breed like humans. They could lay eggs, for example, or they might have a biological caste system and the bodies we've recovered belong to a caste that doesn't breed."

She shrugged. "I did take a look at some of the recovered blood," she added. "They're biologically incompatible with us, so any dreams of cross-racial hybrids will remain just that – dreams."

Ted rolled his eyes. If there was one great disadvantage to the planetary datanet that linked Earth together, it was that it allowed hundreds of kooks to feel that they were not alone. One pressure group, in particular, believed that the aliens wanted to mate with human women to produce pointy-eared hybrids. The fact that this was biologically impossible – humans couldn't produce offspring with their closest relatives in the animal kingdom, let alone creatures from a completely different biological system – never seemed to have crossed their minds.

"Glad to hear it," he said, dryly. He looked around the table. "We will proceed back to Earth within the hour, bearing the recovered bodies with us. Should we consider leaving teams behind to continue the search?"

"We've inspected most of the debris," Anderson said. "I don't feel that there will be any important discoveries made from the remainder, sir. Most of it is just pieces of alien hull; anything that might be useful has been firmly melted down into scrap metal. I suspect that Earth will dispatch a post-battle assessment team to check out the remainder anyway."

"They probably will," Ted agreed. He suspected that the other interstellar powers would send their own teams. Britain gaining access to alien bodies – and technology – might upset the balance of power. Or it would have, if anything they found wasn't shared. With a powerful alien race breathing down their necks, it was unlikely that the Admiralty would see fit to classify the recovered bodies and data. "Overall...do we have any better idea of where to look for the alien homeworld?"

Anderson and Jeanette exchanged glances, then Anderson shook his head. "I doubt it," he said. "It's possible that *something* might turn up, once the post-battle teams arrive in the system, but it's unlikely."

Ted had his doubts. The security officers had gone through *Ark Royal* and discovered an alarming amount of data – unsecured data – that could point the aliens towards Earth. He knew the computer cores were designed to wipe themselves, then melt down into puddles of molten liquid, but books and diaries were far less secure. But how many of them would be comprehensible to the aliens?

He stood. "Inform your departmental heads that they have all performed brilliantly," he ordered, as they rose to their feet. "We have good reason to be proud of what we have done today. Dismissed."

Fitzwilliam waited for the room to clear, then walked over to stand beside his commander. "I have a report on repairs," he said, quietly. "We can fix up the damage within a day or two, even without outside help."

"I know," Ted said. *Ark Royal* had been designed for long-duration cruises, after all. "But we do have to return to Earth."

He wondered, briefly, what the Admiralty would make of the victory. On one hand, it was a stunning reversal of fortunes; on the other, it implied that there was only one starship capable of standing up to the aliens. But then…there was no reason why mass drivers and other weapons couldn't be deployed to defend Earth very quickly. Hell, after the first reports of the battle had made it back to humanity's homeworld, preparations had probably already started.

"Understood, sir," Fitzwilliam said.

"Go to the bridge, then lay in a course," Ted ordered. "I'll join you before we leave the system."

He closed his eyes as soon as the XO left, leaving him alone. The victory hadn't come cheaply, he knew, even though the aliens had suffered worse by an order of magnitude. Thirty-two starfighter pilots dead, ninety-two officers and men on the destroyed frigate…*that* weapon was going to be a major problem. It was quite possible that a close-range duel with one of the alien craft would be impossible.

And they'd all died under his command.

Angrily, he pushed the guilt aside and opened his eyes. A naval career, even one spent on an isolated asteroid mining station, always carried the risk of a violent death. No one joined the navy believing it to be *safe*. Hell, space was *never* safe. The civilian death rate was actually higher than the navy's, although civilian starships tended to operate far closer to the margins than naval starships. He knew that to be true. But somehow it didn't make his task any easier.

Gritting his teeth, he strode out of the Briefing Room and marched towards the bridge, almost tripping over several boxes of spare parts someone had stowed in the passageway. He made a mental note to discuss it with his XO. As important as it was to cram the ship to the gunwales with spare parts, it was equally important not to impede the crew from rushing to battle stations when the alarm sounded.

"Captain," Fitzwilliam said, when he stepped through the airlock. "Our course is laid in, ready to go."

Ted took his command chair and nodded. "Take us home," he ordered. It felt good to say it, even though part of him worried over the reaction from the Admiralty. Would they have expected him to destroy the entire alien force? "Best possible speed."

He smiled to himself, wanly. A week ago, crewmen assigned to *Ark Royal* had been mocked by their fellows. The Old Lady was ancient, a relic of a bygone era…there had been several fights, which had been broken up by the local police. But who, he asked himself, would be laughing now? The Old Lady had more than proved herself in combat.

Good, he thought, patting his command chair. *Now we just have to win the war.*

CHAPTER

TWELVE

Ted had never set foot in Westminster Abbey. Not as a schoolchild, not as a tourist and not as a naval officer. But now...he settled uncomfortably on his seat, wishing desperately for drink, as the service for the dead droned on. The Admiralty had surrendered to the political desire to honour the dead in Westminster Abbey...he shook his head, cursing the politicians under his breath. Surely, the dead deserved better than this farce of a ceremony.

He looked around, feeling oddly out of place among the brass. It seemed that every officer above the rank of Commodore had been summoned to the Abbey, along with thousands of politicians, celebrities and reporters. The latter were baying for blood – or newsworthy quotes – outside the Abbey, calling out to everyone they saw for something they could record and put on the datanet. Ted would have preferred to face the aliens again, rather than the reporters. At least the aliens would only have killed him, rather than dissecting his career, reputation and appearance.

It took nearly an hour before the service finally came to an end. By that time, Ted was praying desperately for something – anything – to break the monotony. Everyone from the Prime Minister to the First Space Lord seemed to have something to say, even though most of it consisted of useless platitudes. Ted wished he could make his escape as soon as the end came, but he knew better. There was a reception being held immediately after for *Ark Royal's* senior officers. It would be hellish.

He glanced down at his terminal as the PM left the Abbey, followed by a stream of senior officers. There was a security alert at the top; apparently, thousands of additional reporters were pressing against the police barricades, even though they all had access to the live feed from within the Abbey. But that wouldn't be the same, Ted knew, as catching someone in the act of doing something embarrassing. Or recording something that could be taken out of context and then turned into a weapon. It struck him, not for the first time, that it had probably been reporters who had arranged for a ban on duelling. They would have found themselves challenged repeatedly, otherwise.

Outside, the baying of the reporters grew louder as he followed the First Space Lord out of the Abbey and down towards a set of white cars. They shouted and screamed, begging for him to turn and look at them, or answer their questions, no matter how absurd they were. Ted kept his face as expressionless as possible, sighing in relief the moment he climbed into the car and shut the door. After having his character alternatively praised and assassinated, he would be happy if he never saw any reporter ever again.

"The politicians needed soothing and so did the general public," the First Space Lord said, once he'd run a bug detector over the car. Technically, bugging government or military facilities was illegal, but that didn't stop the media. "They were really quite upset."

Ted nodded. It had been two days since *Ark Royal* had returned to Earth and the public had gone wild. Everyone had *known* that the aliens were invincible...until *Ark Royal* proved otherwise. Certainly, quite a few armchair admirals had complained about the decision to abandon the backdoor system after the battle, but the Admiralty had understood. The aliens might easily come back with more firepower...or simply pick another star to use as a waypoint on the way to Earth.

"It's a farce, sir," he said. He cursed himself a moment later. Normally, he would never have been so expressive in front of a superior officer. "My people deserved better."

"They always do," the First Space Lord said. He smiled as the car came to a halt in front of a large building, protected by a row of policemen. "Enjoy the reception, Captain. You're the hero of the hour."

Ted sighed, inwardly. He was the highest-ranking officer from the carrier...but most of the guests would be higher-ranking still. Every naval officer – and probably a few army officers – had tried hard to wrangle invitations. His crewmen would be hopelessly junior to the officers they were supposed to chitchat with, promising a day of awkward chatter and embarrassing silences. But it had to be endured.

"Thank you, sir," he said, unconvincingly.

Inside, a band was playing, hundreds of senior officers were already milling about…and there was a large table full of expensive booze. Ted stared, wondering just how many thousands of pounds had been spent on the wine alone, then reached for a glass before stopping himself. He couldn't afford to get drunk, not now. Instead, he took a glass of orange juice and looked around for someone he could actually talk to. But there was no one, apart from the Japanese Naval Attaché. And he was known to be the most frightful bore.

Sighing, Ted walked over to greet him anyway. It had been two years since they'd last met, when the Japanese officer had managed to convince the Royal Navy to give him a tour of *Ark Royal*. Ted had wondered, in all seriousness, if the Japanese Navy intended to build their own armoured carriers, but nothing had ever materialised. Under the circumstances, he decided, that seemed something of a pity.

"Congratulations on your victory," the Japanese officer said. "I wish to hear all about it."

———

James had grown up in an aristocratic family, although he liked to think that he had made it into the navy on his own abilities. As boring as aristocratic parties could be – and the reception was organised on the same principles – they were also an excellent chance to network. He took a glass of water this time – getting tipsy could still be embarrassing, if not disastrous – and moved from person to person, keeping an eye on the other crewmen as he did. Not all of them had any experience in parties and the last thing he wanted was to have to get them out of trouble.

"Ah, I hear you did well for yourself after all," a voice said. "Good show!"

James turned to see his Uncle Winchester, a retired naval officer of fifty years experience. The grizzled old man had been one of the prime influences on his life, James had to admit, although he hadn't listened to everything the older man had taught him. Trying to force his way into command of *Ark Royal* was something certain to annoy Uncle Winchester... and the fact it had blown up in James's face certain to amuse him.

"Yes, Uncle," he said, remembering the models of carriers and escort vessels his uncle had given him as a child. Some of them had been remarkably impractical, others prospective designs for future naval development. Uncle Winchester, if he recalled correctly, had actually had a hand in developing the modern carriers the aliens had torn apart. "I have learnt a great deal from Captain Smith."

"Glad to hear it," Uncle Winchester said. He placed a hand on James's arm, half-pushing him towards a side room. "You have to learn to walk before you can run."

The sound of the band cut off the moment the door closed. James hesitated, then turned to face his uncle. The side rooms were often used for backroom dealing between people who could never be seen together in public, although there was no reason he couldn't speak to his uncle anywhere. But then another door opened and the First Space Lord entered the room.

"Be seated," the First Space Lord ordered, shortly. "We don't have much time."

James swallowed and obeyed, feeling suddenly very unsure of his own ground. He'd used the Old Boys Network to push the First Space Lord into promoting him, only to discover that his pressure only went so far. In hindsight, he knew, Captain Smith had been entirely correct to point out that James was hardly ready for command of a modern carrier, let alone an ancient ship held together by improvised fixes and scrounged spare parts. But it would be years, he suspected, before he was ever allowed to forget that he'd tried to snatch command out of the hands of his current CO.

"I need to ask you a question," the First Space Lord continued, once he'd taken a seat facing James. Uncle Winchester sat to the side, his eyes never leaving James's face. "Is Captain Smith suitable for command?"

James stared at him, unable to keep his shock off his face. Asking an XO to comment on his Captain's fitness for command was a severe breach of naval etiquette. If the CO found out, it would shatter the trust between him and his XO, trust that had already been weakened by James's attempt to snatch command for himself. There *were* situations when an XO could legally relieve the Captain of command, but they tended to result in the XO's career coming to a screeching halt. If the Admiralty had their doubts, they should have sent in an investigative officer.

He realised, suddenly, just how poor the Admiralty's position actually *was*. They'd found it impossible to push a knighted officer into early requirement, so they'd given him *Ark Royal* and left him to his own devices. Instead of drinking himself to death, Smith had kept *Ark Royal* functional; the starship had barely needed a month of intensive work to return to full combat-worthy status. And then Smith had pulled off a victory that had made him the world's man of the hour. The media was already comparing him to Drake, Nelson, Cunningham and Singh. If the Admiralty had wanted to relieve him of command, they would have to explain it to the media…and to politicians, eager to make political hay at the Admiralty's expense.

Smith had been lucky, James knew, feeling an odd flicker of amusement. The reporters had dug up some of his file, including his drinking problem, but they'd spun it into a morality tale about a hero overcoming his issues and defending Britain against outside attack. And it wasn't just Britain either. Smith was a hero right across the world. Maybe, just maybe, the media would sour, but until then Smith was politically untouchable. The consequences of relieving him could be dire.

Uncle Winchester coughed. "I feel, Farnham, that the boy is confused."

James flushed, brightly. "I'm not twelve any longer, uncle!"

"Learn to keep your face under control," Uncle Winchester lectured, sternly. He looked over at the First Space Lord. "This is an invidious line of questioning, Farnham."

"You know better, I think," the First Space Lord said. "Commander Fitzwilliam, I do need an answer."

James winced. If he answered the question, it could utterly destroy his professional reputation. No one would ever trust him again. They'd think of him as a sneak, a coward who didn't even have the nerve to stand up and relieve his CO of command. But if he didn't answer the question, it could impact his career too. The First Space Lord had no shortage of places to assign officers who had annoyed him. It was darkly amusing to realise that *Ark Royal* had once been one of those places.

"It won't go any further," Uncle Winchester assured him. "Will it?"

"No," the First Space Lord said.

James gathered himself. "Since I have served on *Ark Royal*, the Captain has not – to my knowledge – touched a drop of alcohol," he said, firmly. "Furthermore, he has handled my education in the carrier's mechanics, the integration of the new crewmembers and our first real deployment with exceptional skill. He has, after all, had years to think of the best way to refit his ship for combat. And he *has* successfully pulled off our first real victory."

The First Space Lord looked unconvinced. "But he could backslide at any moment..."

"I have seen nothing to indicate that he will," James said, sharply. It crossed his mind, a second too late, that he had interrupted the senior uniformed officer in the entire navy, but he forced the thought to one side. "My ambitions aside, there is no good reason to relieve him of command."

He wondered, absently, just what the First Space Lord had in mind. There were ways to put someone on the beach while seemingly rewarding them. It was why, he suspected, there were so many Admirals in the Royal Navy. Not all of them were assigned to fleet or squadron commands – or naval bases. Smith's promotion to Admiral would be greeted with raptures by the media, who wouldn't recognise that he was being promoted into obscurity.

Or maybe they would, he thought. *By now, they expect Captain Smith to take command of the next unified defence force.*

"I expect you to keep a close eye on him," the First Space Lord said. "How does he work with the crew?"

"Fatherly, rather than dictatorial," James said. He'd served under a CO who'd been a tyrant, although he'd had the advantage of not caring about James's family. James had actually found that somewhat refreshing. "He's friendly and caring...it helps, it think, that most of his senior crew served together on *Ark Royal* while she was in the reserves. They've had plenty of time to build up a relationship."

The First Space Lord leaned forward. "No improper relationships?"

James scowled. If the Captain had *any* relationships – or relations – away from *Ark Royal*, James had never seen anything of them. But then, the Captain hadn't taken any leave for *years*, according to his file. Had he simply become an introverted hermit on *Ark Royal*? Or had he formed a relationship with one of the supply crewwomen? Or crewmen?

"Not to the best of my knowledge," he said. He braced himself, then pushed forward. "Permission to speak freely, sir?"

"Granted," the First Space Lord said.

"I rather thought we were," Uncle Winchester said.

James ignored him. "Sir, with all due respect, this whole conversation is dreadfully improper," he said. "I should not be asked to...pass judgement on my commanding officer, certainly not outside a formal Board of Inquiry. In any case, while I admit I had concerns about the Captain's drinking, I have seen no evidence that he has returned to his old habits in the seven weeks I have served under his command.

"Furthermore, he is perhaps the most experienced officer we could hope to have with the older weapons that won us a victory," he continued. "Most newer officers, including myself, were trained to serve on modern carriers, not solid masses of metal like *Ark Royal*. But those carriers are nothing more than targets for the alien starfighters. We need him, sir. We shouldn't be planning to stick a knife in his back."

The First Space Lord's expression darkened for a long moment. James wondered if he'd gone too far, then reminded himself that at least he still had his pride. And besides, Uncle Winchester would defend him, if necessary. He still recalled the older man ticking off his aunt for assuming that James and his brothers had ruined her prize flowerbed.

"I concede your point," the First Space Lord said, finally. "However, there are...issues with Captain Smith. I shall be expecting you to watch him closely and take whatever action seems appropriate if the Captain slides back into drunkenness."

He stood and marched out of the room. James watched him go, then turned to look at his uncle. "Farnham always was too political," Uncle Winchester muttered. "But at such high attitude, politics and war are always intermingled. He's better than most at running interference between politicians and naval officers."

"Yes, uncle," James agreed.

Uncle Winchester stood. "Go back to the party, keep an eye on your junior officers and try to have fun," he advised. "Or go find a debutante and have some fun with her. You'll be back in space soon enough."

James nodded. The schedule had insisted that *Ark Royal's* crewmen return to her immediately after the party. He didn't really blame the organisers, not when the media were already laying siege to the building. One careless word in the wrong pair of ears could trigger a political earthquake.

"Thank you, uncle," he said, sourly. He couldn't escape the feeling of being used – without even being given a reward for his service. "And… can I avoid this from happening again?"

Uncle Winchester reached out and grabbed James's shoulder. "The family gives you an advantage over your less…wellborn comrades," he said. "You have automatic entrance to places like Sandhurst or the Luna Academy, if you wish to take advantage of it. But the price comes in upholding the system of government…and serving as part of backchannel discussions, if necessary. And if you fail the family, or refuse to pay your dues, the results will be unpleasant."

James nodded. Automatic entrance was one thing, automatic graduation was quite another. There was no way he would be allowed to pass through the Academy without actually being qualified, something that Uncle Winchester – among others – had hammered into his head while he was still packing his first regulation suitcase. It hadn't really dawned on him that there was another price for access to the Old Boys Network. But the network had always been good at entangling people before it demanded payment. Hell, one didn't even have to be an aristocrat to engage in a little mutual back-scratching.

He returned to the party and noted, to his relief, that nothing seemed to have gone spectacularly wrong. Most of the drinks were being claimed by senior officers, he couldn't help noticing; the Captain, thankfully, had restricted himself to juice and water. Absently, James wondered if he should tell the Captain what had happened, before deciding that it would be a bad idea. No one would trust him if he did. All he could do was watch his Captain's back…

…And pray to God that his faith in his CO was not misplaced.

CHAPTER

THIRTEEN

"I've told everyone at school that you're a pilot and they're dead excited. How many BEMs did you kill?"

Kurt smiled at his son's enthusiasm. Percy had never quite believed that his father – his staid harassed investment banker father – was also a starfighter pilot, not until Kurt had been featured on the local news. Kurt was privately rather annoyed by how easily the media had gotten access to his files – they'd even dug up a set of photos taken when he'd first served on a carrier – but it had definitely improved his relationship with his son.

"I killed seven enemy starfighters," he said, shortly. "Thirteen more and I will make ace."

"That's great," Percy said, grinning from ear to ear. "I…"

He was pushed out of the screen by Penny, who looked sulky. "Madam Cowpat is still being a pain," she said. "Why do I have to put up with her again?"

Kurt sighed. "Just put up with her," he ordered. Not that he could really blame Penny for disliking her teacher. It was clear that Madam Capet was far from ideal as a French teacher, but for some reason the school couldn't sack her or even convince her to shape up. "You'll move onto the next teacher soon."

"The only French words I know are rude ones," Penny continued. "You should demand your money back."

"What you get out of school depends on what you put into it," Kurt said. Had *he* been so blatantly disrespectful to his teachers as a child? Probably. "And if Madam Capet is so completely unsuitable, we can arrange some private tutoring during the summer holidays."

Penny's face fell. She'd been talking about joining her friends on a visit to the moon...although Kurt had privately resolved to forbid it even before the war had started restricting civilian spaceflight. No teenage girl wanted to spend her summer holidays with a private tutor...hell, Kurt wasn't even sure if he *could* afford a private tutor. His boss wasn't legally allowed to fire him for being recalled to active service, but Kurt suspected that it was only a matter of time before the penny-pinching bastard started reducing Kurt's salary. But if Penny needed it...

"You two nip off downstairs," Molly ordered, her face appearing in the screen. She sat down in front of the monitor as the two teenagers left the room, closing the door behind them. "When are you coming home?"

Kurt blinked at her tone. "I don't know," he confessed. "The war has only just begun."

"I'm being driven crazy by these two," Molly said, ignoring him. "Penny is fighting with one of her friends, while Percy is talking about joining the Royal Navy. I expect you to put that out of his mind."

"Why?" Kurt asked. "He won't be able to sign up for another two years, at the very earliest..."

"I won't have my son risking his life," Molly snapped, interrupting him. "He will not be allowed to throw his life away."

Kurt felt his head start to pound. "Your *husband* is already risking his life," he remarked, sharply. "What about me?"

"If it were up to me," Molly said, "you wouldn't have gone at all."

She sighed, rubbing her own forehead. "Suzie's father is one of those damned peaceniks," she added. "She gave Penny a very hard time and now the girls aren't talking to one another."

It took Kurt a moment to place the name. One of Penny's friends, a young girl on the verge of womanhood, so much so that he felt like a dirty old man whenever he looked at her. She hadn't struck him as particularly malicious, although teenagers could often be very unpleasant to one another one moment and then make up the next. If her father was indeed a peacenik...

"I'm sorry to hear that," he said. "Tell Penny to ignore the silly girl."

Molly gave him a sardonic look. "And were you so easily able to ignore taunts when you were a child?"

Kurt scowled, recognising her point.

"They're just driving me mad," Molly added. "I almost slapped Penny this morning, after she started to throw a tantrum. Please...when are you coming home?"

"I don't know," Kurt admitted. "I..."

"You're a goddamned hero," Molly snapped. "Can't they gave you a few days of leave?"

"All leaves have been cancelled," Kurt reminded her. "We aren't allowed to leave our posts..."

"And yet they let you down to London," Molly thundered. "How many girls did you eye there?"

Kurt gritted his teeth. "Molly..."

A window flashed up on the display, warning him that his session was about to expire. "Molly, I will be back as soon as I can," he promised. "But I don't get to choose my timing..."

The session expired. He swore out loud as the screen went blank, then stood up and left the privacy cubicle. He'd have to write out an email or record a v-mail...and then hope that she was in a forgiving mood. Molly bore grudges for eternity, digging them up at the worst possible moment and rubbing them in his face. The last thing he wanted was her screaming at the children because of him, not when the family was already under so much stress. It was one of the reasons most junior naval personnel were not advised to marry. A military family could be torn apart by constant separations and not having any real control over their own lives.

"You don't look well, sir," Rose said, as he entered their quarters. "Bad news from home?"

Kurt sighed. "What do you say to a teenage girl who keeps picking fights with her teacher and who fell out with her best friend, purely because her father is a starfighter pilot?"

"My father would probably have yelled at me for an hour," Rose said, after a moment. "But I had to work desperately just to meet the requirements to enter the Academy. What's her problem with the teacher?"

"She isn't very good," Kurt sighed. "Once, she was proctoring an exam and she changed the examination papers, midway through the session."

Rose blinked. "Is that even permissible?"

"She seems to have gotten away with it," Kurt observed. "I think she was the one who wrote the exam too."

"I see," Rose said. "It strikes me that you could file a formal complaint..."

"It was a little hard to do it when Penny got in so much trouble," Kurt admitted. It had smacked of blaming the victim. Kurt's father had been a firm believer in not trying to hide behind excuses, no matter how accurate they were. "But I suppose you're right."

"Tell your daughter to concentrate on her book studies if the teacher is such a bitch," Rose added. "And then promise her a reward if she passes and a punishment if she fails."

"It's hard to punish her these days," Kurt confessed. "I'm here, Molly spends half of her time at work...the kids have just too much leeway to get into trouble."

"They do get better," Rose assured him. She stood and headed towards the hatch. "Good luck, sir."

Kurt scowled after her, then picked up his terminal and started to write, feeling the age-old frustration bubbling up within him. Molly was a wonderful person, really she was, but when she got the bit between her teeth she was almost intolerable. The kids could drive her to the edge of a screaming fit – and, when it wasn't the kids, it was everything from money to how much time she could spend with her husband. He couldn't even remember the last time they'd had sex.

He finished writing the message, then scrolled through the message log. As always, a handful of messages had arrived in the buffer while the carrier was on deployment, held at Earth until they returned home. Half of them were untraceable spam – spammers could be fined a pound for every unwanted message, but the bastards were very good at remaining untraced – but the remainder were various messages from the press and other organisations. Some of them wanted interviews, some of them wanted permission to interview his children for background news – he wrote back categorically denying permission – and a couple invited him and his pilots to Sin City.

They'd love it, he thought. Even now, two hundred years after settlement, the moon was still a patchwork quilt of tiny settlements, with no overall authority. Sin City prided itself on allowing anything, as long as the money was there, from whores to gambling and illicit VR simulations. Rumour had it that travellers could get *anything* there, as long as they had the money. And discretion was part of the package.

It was tempting, he had to admit, if he could convince the XO to let them go. The pilots needed some reward for their efforts, something more than the respect of their formally sneering peers and mentions in dispatches. But at the same time...he had no interest in gambling or semi-legal VR games. If he went, he'd want to see a whore...

...And that would be betraying Molly.

Part of his mind insisted that wouldn't be a bad thing. Their relationship had changed; they were no longer the horny teenagers who'd fallen into bed together. Molly was too tired for sex most of the time and, in all honesty, investment banking had killed Kurt's fire too. It wouldn't hurt her if he went to Sin City for a few hours of pleasure with a whore. The rest of his mind insisted that it would be disastrous. Molly hadn't given him permission to sleep with anyone else; she'd be heartbroken – or at least very angry – if he cheated on her.

"Damn it," he muttered out loud. Starfighter pilots chased women like there was no tomorrow...because, quite often, there was at least the *prospect* of there being no tomorrow. Now, after the aliens had sliced apart the defences of New Russia, it was quite likely that the rest of the starfighter pilots would die too, along with the other officers and men. He'd been horny as hell when he'd been an active duty pilot...and now he was such a pilot again. "What the hell do I do?"

He found himself unsure of what to say. He didn't have to go to Sin City; it would be simple enough to arrange the trip, if there were pilots who would want to go. Besides, there *was* a war on. It was quite likely that permission would be refused. He could claim that he'd asked the XO and been turned down.

And what, he asked himself, *is the difference between that and your reluctance to suggest to the headteacher that Madam Capet be held to account?*

Angrily, he reread the message. There was no official flight from the Royal Navy's yards to Sin City, not when the Luna settlement had such a bad reputation. But there were plenty of ways to reach the settlement from Armstrong City or Baxter Base. They could go...

Irked, he forwarded the message to the XO – let him handle it – then started to write out a new message to Penny. Maybe he could talk some sense into her. Or maybe she would just do whatever the hell she felt like, anyway. At her age, listening to authority was an overrated pastime. But one day, he feared, she would go too far. For all the money parents like him invested in private school, there were still some pupils who ended up in prison before they were even old enough to legally drink.

And then he started to write another letter to Percy.

———

"I suggest we insert a handful of additional rail guns here and here," Anderson said, tapping the paper schematics. James wasn't sure why the ancient engineer insisted on using paper, rather than holograms, but it certainly added novelty to the experience. "We lost the guns here fairly quickly, which could have been disastrous. It certainly will be next time."

James nodded. He'd reviewed the recordings of the battle during the long trudge back to Earth and one thing had become immediately clear. They'd surprised the aliens, surprised them badly. But that wouldn't last. The aliens would realise their own weaknesses, then adapt, react and overcome, just like humanity. By then, humanity had to be ready to close the gap.

The aliens might not be able to break *Ark Royal's* armour – although the destruction of one of the frigates suggested that only applied to starfighter weapons – but they could certainly sweep her weapons and sensors off the hull. If that happened, the carrier would be blind as well as defenceless, waiting helplessly for the alien capital ships to come into range and open fire. So far, there was no proof that the aliens had any form of projectile weapon – either ballistic or powered – but that would certainly change. Humanity *definitely* had to take the lead.

"I won't disagree with you," he said. He looked down at the paper sheets, puzzling them out. "Can we operate the rail-guns there, though?"

"We'd have to run a few extra power lines," Anderson said. "It would be simple enough to link them into the turrets we already have, but if we lost them…well, we'd lose the entire subsection. It will only take a few days if we have help from naval crewmen here."

"That won't be a problem," James said. After the battle, *Ark Royal* had been granted absolute priority over every other starship in the system. Indeed, they'd even been able to convince the other powers to make contributions of older spare parts for the ship. "Can you do it without putting us out of action?"

"Easily," Anderson assured him. "We will be able to spring back into battle within seconds."

James allowed himself a moment of relief. No one really knew how the aliens would react to the bloody nose they'd received, but it was quite possible that they would launch an all-out attack on Earth. Careful analysis of the ship's sensor records had revealed that the aliens could probably access at least a dozen new tramlines that would lead them directly to Sol. Three of them, in addition to the unnamed star system, were so completely isolated that there would be no warning before the aliens advanced on Earth.

Beats them being free of the tramlines, I suppose, he thought. *If they were, we would be screwed.*

"Make it so, then," James ordered. The Chief Engineer rolled up his papers, then headed towards the hatch. "Send in Midshipwoman Lopez on your way out."

The hatch opened and the Chief Engineer stepped through. Moments later, Midshipwoman Lopez entered and closed the door behind her. She looked tired, James noted, which wasn't too surprising. When she wasn't tending to her duties, she was helping the senior officers with their paperwork and refusing requests for interviews from the media.

"Sir," she said. James hadn't told her why he'd asked her to report to his cabin, something that was rarely good news. "What can I do for you?"

"I want you to understand something first," James said, silently damning himself. He had no right to keep an eye on his commanding officer, let alone involve a young and defenceless officer in his activities. "If what I am about to say makes you feel uncomfortable in any way, you are free to leave and forget about it, as long as you keep your mouth shut."

The young woman's eyes narrowed. James winced, inwardly. Clearly, she suspected that her superior was about to make an indecent proposal. Which was true enough, James had to admit, even if it wasn't quite the proposal she thought was coming.

"The Captain, as you know, used to have a problem with drinking," he said. "Do you think he still has a problem?"

Midshipwoman Lopez looked thoroughly uncomfortable. "I believe," she said, after a moment, "that he has largely stopped drinking. However, I do not monitor his alcoholic intake."

"No, you wouldn't," James nodded. He did his best to avoid sounding threatening or disapproving. "I need you to let me know if you have good reason to believe that this has changed."

There was a long pause. "Sir," she said, "you seem to be expecting me to spy on the Captain."

James didn't bother to try to deny it. That *was* precisely what he was asking. But it opened up a whole new can of worms. Captains had a right to privacy – they were the only officers onboard ship with a reasonable expectation of privacy – and he was asking a young officer to betray that. It would destroy her career far more thoroughly than anything the Captain could do to *him*.

"The Captain is under a great deal of stress," he said, instead. "That will only get worse as the media frenzy grows stronger – and it will. I need to know if the Captain returns to his old habits. If you tell me, it won't go any further. And I'm sorry."

"If I see such evidence, I will let you know," Midshipwoman Lopez said, clearly biting off several words that would probably have earned her instant demotion. Not that James could really blame her for anything she called him, at least in the privacy of her own head. Her tart voice was almost painful. "May I leave?"

In a way, James realised, she'd lost her virginity. Everyone liked to think of the navy as a band of brothers...and it was, to some extent. But there was also treachery, backstabbing and a certain amount of one-upmanship. Perhaps the war would change that, James hoped, or perhaps it would just make it worse.

He shook his head. All he could do was monitor the Captain and hope that nothing showed up that would force him to take action.

"You may," he said. "And thank you."

"Really?" She asked, as she turned and headed towards the hatch. "For what?"

CHAPTER
FOURTEEN

Ted couldn't help feeling a little amusement at how the officers on Nelson Base reacted when he and Fitzwilliam walked through the hatch. Once, they would have either ignored him or snickered at him behind his back. What could they say to a drunkard who had somehow lucked into keeping his command, even if his command was only a starship the Royal Navy used as a dumping ground for its problem children? But now, after his victory, they fell over themselves to shake his hand. Even the Marines seemed impressed.

He rolled his eyes as the First Space Lord's latest assistant showed him into a small compartment, where the First Space Lord and a couple of junior officers were waiting for him. One of them was wearing the unmarked uniform favoured by the Intelligence Corps, the other was wearing the too-neat uniform of a PR officer. Ted sighed, inwardly; he'd hoped to avoid Public Relations as much as possible. It might be important to keep civilian morale up, but he hated giving interviews even to friendly reporters.

"Please, be seated," the First Space Lord said. This time, it was clear, they wouldn't be visiting the main briefing compartment. "We have a great deal to discuss."

Ted kept his face expressionless as he sat down and rested his hands in his lap. A private discussion meant another deployment, he hoped; he couldn't help feeling that the alternatives were worse. Perhaps they wanted him to go on a speaking tour, reassuring the public that all was well with the war. But, even after he'd stopped drinking, he was hardly as photogenic as the actor who'd played Dan Dare in the 2123 remake of the classic space opera. And no one would be reassured if they saw his service record.

The First Space Lord nodded to the Intelligence Corps officer. "Commander Steenblik?"

Steenblik nodded, then tapped a switch, activating the holographic processor. Ted studied him with some interest. Like most Intelligence Corps officers, there was a blandness about him that would have left him almost unnoticed, at least when compared to line officers. And yet he knew better than to underestimate the sandy-haired young man. The Intelligence Corps recruited only the smartest of officers, men and women willing to work behind the scenes to ensure that the Royal Navy got the intelligence it needed, when it needed it. They'd failed to predict the arrival of the aliens, admittedly, but no one else had done any better.

Unless the conspiracy theories are actually true, Ted thought, as he looked up at the display. *If someone did know, that might explain our military build-up...*

"The face of the enemy," Commander Steenblik said, as an alien face appeared in front of them. "This is the most intact body we have, although it is quite badly damaged in several places. By comparing this body with the others, we have been able to put together a comprehensive picture of what the aliens actually *look* like. However, we still have plenty of unanswered questions about their biology, let alone their society."

He smiled, rather humourlessly. "Despite being humanoid, they are completely unrelated to humanity," he continued. "Although we believe that they and we can share the same worlds, the food we found in their stomachs – they have two separate stomachs – would be poisonous to us. We don't think they can eat our foodstuffs. Their diseases will probably not affect us and vice-versa."

"So no hope of any human-alien hybrids to end the war," Fitzwilliam said, dryly. He nodded towards the holographic alien. "What sex is it?"

"Male, we think," Steenblik said. "We've identified organs that seem to serve the role of testes, but the penis seems to be completely retractable...in truth, it will be several months before we can say anything with confidence. All the remaining bodies seem to share the same sexual characteristics, so we are assuming that they're all male. However, I must caution you that we could be completely wrong. We have very little experience with alien biology."

"Assuming you're right," Ted said, "what does this say about them?"

"Nothing for certain," Steenblik warned. "They may be as sexually restrictive as some of our darker societies or we may simply have failed to recover any female bodies. Statistically, two-thirds of the Royal Navy is composed of men, while certain units are male-only – the Marines, for example. We simply don't know enough to be able to say anything about their society from what little we pulled from the bodies.

"One thing we are fairly sure about is that they need water more than we do," he continued, rotating the image so they could see the leathery skin. "This might explain the high concentration of water droplets in the wreckage; the aliens need a moist atmosphere to survive. Their eyesight may be better than ours, their bodies slightly weaker...although, again, we have no way to be sure. The alien bodies we recovered may well be atypical."

Ted nodded, studying the alien. It was ugly as sin, he decided, although the aliens probably felt the same way about humanity. Was that the cause of the war? Had the aliens looked at humanity and decided that they were too ugly to live? Or maybe just that humans were inherently inferior and needed to be knocked down and out before they posed a threat to the alien civilisation?

Or maybe they're just nasty bastards, he thought. But there was no way to know.

Fitzwilliam coughed. "Can they speak to us?"

"I think they would have real problems speaking English understandably, given the shape of their mouths," Steenblik admitted. "But they would probably have no difficulty constructing a voder that would allow them to speak to us. We're currently working on producing something similar, although – as we have no samples of the alien language – it's all mainly guesswork."

"There was an attempt to use the First Contact package at New Russia," the First Space Lord said. "The aliens didn't respond."

Ted frowned. The First Contact package had been dreamed up in the days when humanity expected to discover a new intelligent race at every new star. It was, in theory, simple to understand, at least for a race that understood enough scientific laws to make it into space. By law, every starship carried a copy, just in case they encountered an alien starship, but it had never really been tested. No one knew just how well it would work when aliens were encountered for the first time.

Not well, he decided. For all he knew, the aliens had interpreted the package as a challenge to do battle. *Or maybe they just couldn't understand what they were hearing.*

"We have also learned a great deal about alien technology from the battle," Steenblik said, tapping a switch. The image of the alien vanished. "Their stealth systems, as we believed, are incredibly power-intensive, to the point that the aliens seem unable to use them and fire at the same time. They may also be unable to switch them on and off at will, which is fortunate. If they could, we would be in real trouble."

Ted snorted. "You mean we're not now?"

"Worse trouble, then," Steenblik amended. "It's possible – although we don't know for sure – that their stealth systems actually impede their sensors and drives. We've been looking closely at the records of the battle and it's clear that the aliens were slightly out of place when they dropped their stealth and attacked. They may well be unable to see where they're going while under stealth. We also picked up faint hints that their drives *are* detectable at very close range; we're currently programming drones to provide targeting, allowing the alien fighters to be wiped out before they can drop their stealth systems and attack."

"That would be useful," Ted agreed. He leaned forward. "Is there anything unusual about the alien hulls?"

"Their composites are not much different from our own," Steenblik admitted. "There are some unusual points – the aliens seem to have turned their outer hulls into giant superconductors – but that would be well within our capabilities, if we had the need to duplicate it. We're not sure why..."

"I bet I know," Fitzwilliam said. "It's part of their point defence system."

Ted grimaced, remembering watching as his starfighters were blown out of space, their missiles picked off before they could reach their targets. Casualties had been high, even though the human starfighter pilots had been ready for the aliens this time. The only consolation was that there was no shortage of replacements. *Ark Royal* had moved from a dumping ground to a prime opportunity for glory and promotion. Assuming, of course, that the newcomers survived the war.

"That's one theory," Steenblik agreed. "However, we don't know for sure. Another possibility is that it's related to their FTL drive; so far, we don't even have a theory for how they're able to use tramlines we cannot even begin to access."

He shrugged. "A full report has been uploaded to the secure datanet..."

"And shared with our allies," the First Space Lord said. "It was decided at the very highest levels" – he nodded towards a picture of the Prime Minister – "that our intelligence was best shared with the remainder of humanity."

Ted lifted his eyebrows, surprised. He didn't disagree with the logic – like it or not, the whole human race had to remain united – but he was impressed that the decision had been taken so quickly. But then, there wasn't anything in their findings that would allow the Americans or the Chinese to reverse-engineer any alien tech ahead of Britain. The hell of it was that the human race *needed* someone to do just that.

The First Space Lord pressed his fingertips together as he sat back in his chair. Ted sucked in a breath, knowing that this was it. His superior was about to explain precisely why they'd been called to Nelson Base.

"So far, the aliens have made no further attempt at outflanking the defences," the First Space Lord said. "They certainly have not attempted to attack Earth. However, we fear that this is just a matter of time. *Ark Royal* might be tricky to duplicate within a year, but we can improve our defences, start producing vast numbers of mass drivers and take other steps to make Earth less vulnerable. And we got very lucky when *Ark Royal* was in place to intercept the aliens."

Ted couldn't disagree. The First Space Lord had gambled and won, but the aliens would be more careful next time. And they would probably start working on their own countermeasures against *Ark Royal* and her non-existent sisters. Even if they couldn't build nukes for themselves, which he strongly doubted, they could certainly recover them from New Russia. Unless the Russians *had* managed to fire off all their weapons before the aliens landed...

The First Space Lord took control of the display. "There was a great deal of arguing about the best way to proceed," he continued. "However, the upshot of it was that *Ark Royal* was best employed in raiding New Russia, along with a couple of dozen older ships from minor powers. If there is a chance to strike some blows against the aliens, we should take them."

Ted wondered, absently, just what deals had been struck to convince the Royal Navy to take the risk. The aliens had to know which tramlines the human race would need to use to reach New Russia, which meant that those systems would probably be heavily defended. There *had* been some political disputes between Britain and Russia over the years. Perhaps the Russians on Earth had offered to settle those in Britain's favour in exchange for the raid. Or perhaps the Admiralty had reasoned that knocking the aliens back on their heels would help win time to pre-pare Earth's defences.

"I would be delighted if you kicked the aliens off New Russia com-pletely," the First Space Lord continued, "but I doubt it would be pos-sible. Instead, your orders are to give the aliens a nasty surprise and then attempt to make contact with any surviving humans on New Russia. The Russians have provided a contact team, which will actually land on the planet's surface – if it seems possible. They've agreed that the final deci-sion will be up to you."

"Brave of them," Fitzwilliam said.

Ted couldn't disagree. The aliens might well have exterminated most of the planet's population from orbit…or simply taken control of the high orbitals and ignored the human population. But flying a shuttle through the alien positions would be tricky, almost suicidal. It was possible, he supposed, that the aliens could be decoyed away, but after the aliens had been fooled by the sensor decoys he'd deployed they'd be more careful about what they believed to be real.

"Precisely how you reach New Russia and engage the enemy will be your choice, of course," the First Space Lord said. "However, we would like you to carry out the mission within the month."

"That would give us time to outflank any alien pickets," Ted mused. There were several tramlines that led through a series of useless or underdeveloped star systems, systems he suspected the aliens would probably ignore. But it wouldn't take more than a single stroke of bad luck for the aliens to get a fix on their position and scramble to attack. "As long as you didn't mind us taking the long road."

The First Space Lord smiled. Traditionally, the Admiralty issued its orders and expected its subordinates to come up with their own operational plans. It made sense, Ted knew; there was no way to micromanage military operations across interstellar distances. The situation might change between a system CO sending a request for orders and receiving a response from the Admiralty, leaving the orders already out of date. But given how badly shocked everyone had been by the war, it wasn't impossible for the Admiralty to start issuing orders that tried to cover every little detail.

He was a CO himself, Ted remembered. *He knows better than to try to micromanage.*

"There is a catch," the First Space Lord added.

Ted scowled, inwardly. There was *always* a catch.

"You'll be taking a handful of embedded reporters with you," the First Space Lord said. "I'm afraid it isn't negotiable."

"Reporters," Ted repeated.

"Reporters," the First Space Lord confirmed. "I will expect you to show them every courtesy."

Ted felt his scowl deepening. The last time he'd had to deal with reporters had been before his assignment to *Ark Royal,* when he'd been a mere Lieutenant. His CO at the time had told him that it was a perfect opportunity to broaden his mind and learn how to handle newcomers, something that Ted had clung to until he'd actually *met* the reporters. After that, he'd been convinced he'd somehow offended his Captain and the assignment was actually a non-too-subtle punishment.

"This is actually quite important," the First Space Lord said. "Have you been following the mood on Earth?"

Ted shook his head. The First Space Lord nodded to the PR officer, who stepped forward.

"The public mood started out as wary, but confident," the officer said. His nametag read Abramczyk. "After New Russia, it crashed right down and we had a whole series of riots led by people who thought that the entire world was about to come to an end. Then you pulled off your victory and the public mood started climbing upwards again."

"Panicky civilians," Fitzwilliam said.

"The average civilian knows nothing about the realities of naval combat," Abramczyk reminded him. "They assume that the aliens can reach us in seconds and act on that assumption. The decision to try to cover up some of the details of New Russia didn't really help, as it was poorly done and the truth leaked out. Having reporters on your ship may be a big step forwards towards rebuilding the public's trust."

Ted didn't – quite – sneer. "Sir," he said, addressing the First Space Lord, "is that *important*?"

The First Space Lord didn't seem annoyed by the question. "Right now, the government is in a very weak position," he said. "A number of MPs are threatening to desert – or are facing the risk of having their seats challenged in recall elections. If they lose their seats, we may face a reformed government that wants peace with the aliens, peace at any price. And Britain isn't the only country having problems. Both Russia and America may face political disasters in the next few months."

"The aliens timed their attacks well," Ted observed.

"Indeed they did," the First Space Lord said.

Fitzwilliam looked over at Commander Steenblik. "Coincidence?"

"We don't know," Steenblik admitted. "It's quite possible that they were watching us for years before finally starting the war. There were all of those reports about unknown starships being detected on long-range sensors…"

The First Space Lord cleared his throat. "You'll take the reporters and like it," he growled, addressing Ted. "You'll have them bound by the War Powers Act, even the foreigners, so you can put them in irons if they really make a nuisance of themselves. But it is vitally important that we regain the public's trust."

Ted sighed. "Very well, sir," he said. He had a vision of the reporters walking through his ship, harassing his crew. "I shall have them assigned quarters onboard *Ark Royal*. However, I will not tolerate my crew being harassed."

"That is understandable," the First Space Lord said. "You will have the power to deal with them, if necessary."

Ted sighed, again. The War Powers Act *did* give commanding officers considerable leeway to deal with reporters and other subhuman forms of life, but it was subject to review. He *could* put a reporter in irons...and, if the Admiralty found it politically embarrassing, they could renounce him after the war.

"Understood, sir," he said. "We'll do our very best."

CHAPTER
FIFTEEN

The Captain, James decided, as he waited in the shuttlebay, must have realised that James had been speaking to the First Space Lord behind the Captain's back. It was the only explanation, he felt, for why the Captain had given *him* the assignment for babysitting the reporters, even though there were more junior officers – including Lieutenant Abramczyk – who could have handled the task. But then, he had to admit, he certainly deserved some kind of punishment for breaking the Captain's trust. Having to deal with reporters was definitely cruel and unusual punishment.

He shifted uncomfortably inside his dress uniform as the shuttle settled slowly onto the deck, a dull clunk echoing round the shuttlebay as it landed. The PR staffers always looked photogenic, something that had puzzled James until he'd realised that they were trying to impress reporters too ignorant or stupid to know that a clean uniform wasn't always the sign of a competent officer. James had served under one commanding officer who had insisted that his senior officers always wear their dress uniforms, even though regulations only required them for special occasions. He wondered what had happened to that CO as the shuttle's hatch opened, revealing the reporters.

They weren't a prepossessing bunch, he decided, as they stumbled out onto the deck. A couple wore clothes that looked military, at least when seen from a distance, and several more wore khaki jackets that would have been better suited to embedding with the ground forces, rather than the

Royal Navy. The remainder wore a wide variety of civilian clothes, ranging from simple tracksuits to low-cut shirts and miniskirts that would be sure to draw attention from the ship's crew. A less professional bunch, James decided, would be hard to find. Even the entertainers who made their way from starship to starship looked more professional.

He stepped forward, pasting a smile on his face. His family had taught him how to face the press, although none of their training had covered this exact scenario. The downside of being born into the aristocracy, he'd been told time and time again, was that everything you did was considered newsworthy. You could fart in bed, his grandfather had told him, and someone would consider it news. And while one set of reporters would consider an aristocrat someone to admire, another set would consider him someone to tear down at all costs. Being in the navy, he'd thought, would preserve him from their particular brand of savagery. Clearly, he'd been wrong.

"Welcome onboard *Ark Royal*," he said, as he surveyed the reporters. Several of them carried cameras and other forms of recording equipment; he'd have to make sure that none of it interfered with the ship's systems. "If you'll come with me...?"

He led them through a maze of corridors and into a small briefing compartment. Two junior crewmen had spent the day transferring all of the boxes of spare parts out of the compartment, just so he could brief the reporters. He scowled inwardly at the waste of time it represented, even though he knew that neither he nor Captain Smith had been offered a choice. The reporters had to be humoured, at least until they crossed the line so badly that no one could argue when the Captain threw them into the brig.

"Please, be seated," he said, wondering idly which of them would make the first complaint. The overweight man pretending to be a naval officer or the blonde-haired girl who looked thinner than a plastic doll? James had seen *children* with more meat on their bones than her. "We have a great deal to get through and not much time."

The reporters should have been briefed on Nelson Base, but James had already privately resolved to run through everything again, anyway. It wouldn't be the first time, Lieutenant Abramczyk had warned him, where a PR officer on a base had neglected to tell the reporters what they needed to hear, fearing that it would destroy his career. James hadn't been surprised at all to hear it. Reporters, in his experience, were rarely smart enough to realise that the military's rules and regulations existed for a reason.

"How many of you," he asked, "have embedded on a military starship before?"

A handful of hands – four in all – went up. James sighed, inwardly. At least they weren't *all* virgins. It wasn't a reassuring thought. Even modern carriers suffered their fair share of accidents when new crewmembers moved in…and some of those accidents were lethal. The reporters were even less prepared for *Ark Royal* than James himself.

"Right," he said. "This is a military starship – and a very dangerous environment. Cabins have been assigned to you; I strongly recommend that you remain in your cabins unless you have an escort. If you choose to leave your cabins, bear in mind that there are some parts of the ship that are completely off-limits without prior permission and an escort. Those locations are detailed in your briefing notes."

He paused. "I understand that you will want interviews with crewmen," he added. "Such interviews will be arranged upon request. I advise you not to interfere with crewmen as they go about their duties, or to attempt to force them to be interviewed."

"But you'll have a chance to brief those you let speak to us," one of the older reporters objected. "We want unprepared interviews."

James tried not to roll his eyes. If the reporter had suspected that every one of the prepared interviewees would toe the party line, he shouldn't have said it out loud. Or was he laying the groundwork for attacking the navy if the interviews didn't turn up anything he wanted? Or was he simply an idiot?

"None of them will be briefed ahead of time," James said. He shook his head, then pressed onwards. "All of your reports will be viewed by the PR staff before they are transmitted home. Certain pieces of information, outlined in your briefing notes, are not supposed to be included in public reports. If you include them, you will be placed in the brig and left there until we return to Earth, whereupon you will be handed over to the police."

"The aliens can't intercept our news broadcasts," another reporter objected. "Those rules are designed to protect the government, not humanity."

"That's as may be," James said, feeling his head start to pound. Perhaps the Captain had something he could drink to relieve his feelings. He'd sooner face a mob of aliens stark naked than reporters. No doubt he would be made to look really ugly when the reporters started releasing their reports. "The point is that operational security cannot be violated without consequences."

He ran through the rest of the notes – a short primer on how to behave on the ship – and then led them to their cabins. Originally, the cabins had been intended for an Admiral and his staff; they were the largest cabins on the ship. Even three or four reporters to a compartment was better than the junior crewmen received, deep in the bowels of the ship. But the complaining started almost at once.

What exactly did they expect? James asked himself. *A massive compartment for each of them, alone? With a bath and a dressing room and...*

He shook his head, then smiled at them, humourlessly. "You can return to Earth if you like," he said. "The shuttle will still be in the bay for another hour or two. If you don't like the quarters, you can return to Earth. However, there is no guarantee of receiving another embedded post."

It was interesting, he decided, as the complaints faded away, just to see who was doing the complaining. None of the prior embeds had complained, even slightly. James made a mental note to glance at their files. The newcomers were the ones who complained loudest at the prospect of sharing quarters. James could understand a desire for privacy, but anyone who wanted privacy shouldn't bother to join the navy. He'd seen his first crewmates naked more times than he cared to remember.

"You are welcome to join the senior crew in the mess for dinner," James lied, smoothly. "If, of course, you do not wish to join the junior crew instead."

He smiled at their reactions. Had they expected room service? The Captain was the only person on the ship who was allowed to eat meals in his cabin – even Admirals had to eat in the wardroom with their staff. But the reporters seemed to think they should be allowed to eat apart from the crew.

His smile grew wider. Just wait until they encountered naval food.

———

Ted looked up at the holographic display, silently cursing the First Space Lord under his breath. Being granted an international rank – a honour held by only a handful of officers, only one other of them British – came with an additional salary, but it also came with new and unpleasant responsibilities. The twenty-seven starships currently assembled around *Ark Royal* represented eight different navies, only three of them solid British allies. The remainder were deeply suspicious of the combined defence command's decision to assign them to the deep-space raiding mission.

They had reason to be suspicious, Ted decided, as he surveyed the ships. Most of them were younger than *Ark Royal*, but hadn't been updated as thoroughly as the massive carrier. Their heavy armour would give them an advantage against alien starfighters – although probably not the giant plasma weapon the aliens had used in the previous battle – but their drives and weapons were heavily outdated. *Ark Royal* was a lumbering brute of a ship, yet a handful of the smaller ships weren't even capable of keeping pace with her. If it had been up to him, Ted knew, most of them would have been broken down into spare parts and replaced with more modern ships.

The only real advantage, he knew, was the older weapons they carried. Unlike the newer designs, they had the fittings for mass drivers and adding them onto their hulls hadn't taken more than a few days. Ted hadn't been too surprised to discover that several governments had stockpiled mass drivers, despite the unspoken agreement against deploying them. The older ships also carried additional missile racks, all of which might come in handy when they faced the aliens for the second time. But they were still critically low in starfighters.

Ted sighed, then looked down at the latest update from the Admiralty. No one seemed disposed to cut loose a modern carrier, not even one of the freighters that had been hastily reconfigured into a makeshift starfighter platform. Not that *that* was entirely unwelcome, he decided; the makeshift platforms had been constructed so rapidly, with so much improvising, that they could barely launch a single squadron of fighters and then only at a terrifyingly slow rate. But with modern carriers suddenly very vulnerable, it was hard to blame the Admiralty – and its foreign counterparts – for clutching at straws.

He needed a drink. Desperately.

The door chimed. "Come."

Commander Fitzwilliam strode into the cabin, looking like a man in desperate need of a drink. Ted knew precisely how he felt. Passing the reporters over to Commander Fitzwilliam had been a mean trick, but Ted was damned if he was wasting any of his own time on the reporters. Besides, he had to speak with his new subordinates, reassure them as much as possible that he had no intention of wasting their lives, then plan their deployment to New Russia. The direct route, he'd already decided, was out.

"The reporters are settled in their cabins," Commander Fitzwilliam said, taking the chair Ted indicated. "They're already grumbling about the arrangements."

Ted shrugged. It was hard to care, not when most of his pre-*Ark Royal* career had been spent in shared cabins and wardrooms.

"Some of them might have had prior relationships," he said, after a moment. "They can change their sleeping places, if they wish."

"They're reporters," James agreed. There were stories about how reporters sometimes behaved while on deployment. Most of them were probably nonsense, but Ted was old enough to know the more outrageous the story, the greater the chance there was a kernel of truth in it somewhere. "If they want to have foursomes and tell themselves they're being daring to have them on a military ship…"

Ted snorted. "I've spoken to our new allies," he said. "We're going to be going the long way around."

He tapped the control, bringing up the planned route. It would take them by a couple of human settlements, but otherwise the star systems in question were largely useless. No commercial pilot would sign off on such a course – it would burn up too much of their power cells – yet Ted didn't have to worry about that, not during wartime. If they were lucky, it would allow them to evade enemy pickets until they actually reached New Russia.

And if we're not lucky, he told himself darkly, *we could find ourselves in some real trouble.*

He looked up at the tramlines. Human-accessible tramlines were marked in green, but prospective alien tramlines, marked in red, ran through them like an infestation. Given a stroke of luck, the aliens could see them coming and set up an ambush…or simply prepare the defences of New Russia. So far, they hadn't shown much interest in other human worlds in the same direction, but that was probably because the worlds were effectively worthless from a military point of view. Whatever they had in mind for humanity could wait until after the end of the war.

"Understandable," Commander Fitzwilliam agreed. "But I wish we knew more about what was happening at New Russia itself."

Ted nodded. So far, according to the Admiralty, the Russians had tried to slip a handful of ships into the system. But none of them had reported back. The aliens were clearly *very* good at locating intruders and picking them off before they could get back to the tramlines.

"Me too," he said. "Me too."

———

Kurt strode into the briefing room…and stopped, in surprise, when he saw some of his pilots gathered around a blonde girl who looked too thin to be real. One of the reporters, he realised, remembering that some of them had requested permission to attend the briefings. Sighing, Kurt walked to the podium and whistled, loudly. A little shamefaced, his pilots turned back to face him.

"I see you've met our new friend," he said, softly. "However, I'm going to have to tell you to put her out of your minds. We have a great deal to cover and not much time."

He scowled from face to face until he had their attention, then continued. "First, a warm welcome to the newcomers, who have *finally* arrived. Not their fault, I hasten to add, but we're having to reorganise the squadrons while en route to our target and that's going to be a pain in the butt.

The new squadron rosters are posted on the datanet; I've appointed brevet squadron leaders from the more experienced pilots to take command."

There was a long pause. "Seniority alone was not counted," he added. None of the newcomers had any experience facing the alien starfighters. "If any of you have a problem with it, go tell the XO you want to spend the rest of the cruise in the brig and save me some time."

He met Rose's eyes briefly. He'd spoken to her already, telling her that she would be one of the new squadron leaders. Thankfully, she'd accepted the challenge without demur. Ted wasn't sure if she was completely reliable, but she did have experience and she needed something to focus on, beside her desire for revenge.

"We have updated simulations based on our previous encounter with the aliens," Kurt continued, in a calmer tone. "After this meeting, we will go straight into them and spend the next few hours practicing, practicing and practicing. If there are problems, I would prefer to discover them in the simulator rather than actual flying. We will continue simulations even when we're on the way, apart from one squadron that will maintain a permanent CSP around the flotilla. The aliens may surprise us at any moment."

The pilots didn't look happy at the reminder. Kurt couldn't really blame them. One squadron wasn't really enough to provide cover for the flotilla, even if the flotilla was armed with rail guns and improved sensor programs that should give the aliens a nasty shock. Ideally, the other pilots would be able to rush from the simulators to their starfighters within minutes, but even their best timing wasn't ideal. When they got closer to New Russia, they'd have to abandon the simulators and remain on combat launch alert.

He made a show of glancing at his watch. "We start simulating in five minutes," he said, raising his voice. "Anyone not there when I arrive will be buying the drinks."

The room emptied, rapidly. Kurt allowed himself a smile as he saw the reporter's bemusement. The pilots might have allowed themselves to chat her up, but not when their wallets were on the line. Kurt hadn't been joking when he'd told them that any latecomers would be buying the drinks, next time the pilots went on leave. The costs could easily reach a few hundred pounds.

"You can watch, if you like," Kurt said, "but do not interrupt."

The reporter looked up at him. Up close, she was so emaciated that Kurt seriously considered dragging her to the doctor and asking for a check-up.

"I won't interrupt," she assured him. "But can I ask for an interview later?"

Kurt met her eyes. There were tiny flecks of gold in them, hidden recording systems that would record everything she saw. Kurt had seen similar systems used by investment bankers, although their systems were different. He wondered, absently, just how the reporter found time to review everything she recorded.

"Maybe," he said. "But it depends on my schedule."

CHAPTER
SIXTEEN

"All ships have reported in, Captain," Lieutenant Annie Davidson reported. "They're ready to depart."

Ted nodded. *Ark Royal* had been designed as a command ship, but her fleet command systems had been removed long ago. Refitting the ship with a modern system had taken two days of hard work, which hadn't left much time for practicing operational manoeuvres. They could still simulate operations, but it wasn't the same.

"Then signal the Admiralty," he ordered. "Inform them that we are ready to depart."

A dull quiver ran through the ship as her drives powered up. Ted allowed himself a tight smile, then checked the ship's status display. Everything seemed to be optimal, although he wasn't entirely confident about how well the newer systems had integrated with the older systems.

"The Admiralty wishes us luck," Annie said. "They've cleared us to depart."

"Good," Ted said. He looked over at the helmsman. "Take us out."

Ark Royal quivered again as she moved forward, advancing towards the tramline. Ted watched the other starships fanning out around the carrier – unlike *Ark Royal*, they were nimble even if they did have other problems – and then looked back at the orbital display. Earth was heavily defended – the various spacefaring powers had managed to rig up orbital platforms to launch starfighters, as well as modifying civilian mass drivers to serve as weapons – but it was impossible to tell just how long the defences would stand against a determined alien attack. Besides, the aliens could do considerable damage by staying out of range of Earth's defenders and attacking installations across the solar system.

"Tramline in two hours, forty minutes," Lieutenant Daniel Lightbridge reported. "We're clear of the Earth-Moon defence perimeter."

Ted nodded, settling back into his command chair. He wouldn't relax at all, he knew, until they were on their way home. Three weeks of travel to reach their destination…a great deal could happen in three weeks. What if the aliens managed to block their retreat? Or…New Russia wasn't the youngest full-fledged colony world in the human sphere, but the tramlines further away from New Russia and Vera Cruz had never been truly explored. The alien homeworld might be lurking at the far end of one of those tramlines…

…*Or it might be much further away*, Ted thought, grimly. *Their improved Puller Drive might give them far more range than we believe possible.*

He shook his head. There was nothing in the detailed reports, half of which were nothing more than guesswork, that even gave a *hint* at the alien motives. Some of the scientists believed that it was nothing more than an accident, others – more cynical – pointed out that humanity had developed plenty of bastards who'd started wars to increase their own power, spread their religion, steal natural resources or simply for fun. But there was no way to know. Humanity's visions of aliens ranged between inhuman monsters to incredibly advanced creatures who would share the secrets of the universe. Right now, it was looking like the former was actually correct.

"Inform me when we enter the tramline," he ordered. "Until then, clear the CAG to commence his exercises."

"Aye, sir," Lightbridge said.

There had been a dispute between James and the reporters over the question of their right to step onto the bridge. James had ruled – and the Captain had backed him up – that the bridge was closed to the reporters at all times, except by prior arrangement. The reporters had contacted the Admiralty and whined, with the net result that the Admiralty insisted they should have access to the CIC when *Ark Royal* wasn't actually in combat or undergoing combat exercises. James was already planning a series of exercises that would work the crew to death while keeping a careful eye on the reporters. Thankfully, he *had* managed to insist that only four reporters could enter the compartment at a time.

"It isn't very impressive," one of the reporters – the inhumanly thin girl – muttered. "I was expecting more."

James wanted to roll his eyes. "This isn't a movie set," he said, trying to keep the sarcasm out of his voice. "Every one of these consoles is designed to be useful, not explode at the drop of a hat."

He tapped a switch, bringing up the display. "As you can see, the flotilla is currently accompanying us…"

Somehow, he made it through the rest of the hour without losing his temper. The handful of experienced reporters seemed to know what they were doing, even the reporter who had embedded with 16 Air Assault Brigade during the raid on Lovell Base on Mars, but the inexperienced reporters kept asking the same silly questions, over and over again. And the unimpressive CIC didn't seem to help. Absently, he wondered if the Royal Navy shouldn't produce a Potemkin starship for the reporters, with more attention paid to aesthetics rather than actual fighting power. Maybe they could share the costs with the other spacefaring powers. None of them enjoyed particularly respectful reporters.

He was still in a grumpy mood when he walked down to his cabin for the first interview. All of the reporters had wanted to interview him – and the Captain and everyone else on the ship – but he'd managed to insist on choosing his own interviewer. He'd picked one of the experienced reporters, a man who'd actually *been* a carrier tech before retraining as a journalist. His reports held a genuine flavour of someone who had actually been on a carrier as more than just a visitor, although there were hints that he thought he could do better. At least, James considered, he had some reason for thinking so. Most of the others would get themselves killed if they were allowed to roam the carrier unescorted.

"Commander," the reporter said. Marcus Yang was tall, a his face a mixture of Chinese and English features, but there was a reassuring competence in his attitude that James appreciated more than he cared to admit. "Thank you for the interview."

James snorted as he sat down and waved the reporter to the other chair. If it had been up to him, there would be no interviews at all…particularly not with the reporters who'd gained their places on account of their looks, rather than general competence. He reminded himself, sharply, that they might not be fools. Good looks didn't always equal stupidity. One of the female reporters might prefer to be underestimated by her prey.

"You're welcome," he said. It was a lie and he knew Yang *knew* it was a lie. "But I'm afraid time is at a premium."

"I won't take too much of your time," Yang said. "How did you wind up on *Ark Royal*?"

"The navy assigned me," James said. It was true enough, if certain details were excluded from consideration. He'd worked hard to insert himself into the carrier's chain of command, prior to discovering her true condition. "I went willingly."

"So it would seem," Yang mused. He changed the subject with suspicious haste. "What do *you* believe the aliens actually want?"

"I believe that it would be a mistake to speculate without data," James said, firmly. He wasn't sure just how much data the reporters had access to, although he would have been surprised if none of the reports had leaked. "We simply know nothing about their culture, their society or what they actually want from us."

Yang smiled. "You don't have a theory?"

"No," James said, not altogether truthfully. He had his theories, but none of them had any real weight. "Maybe they just think we're ugly as sin."

Yang's smile grew wider. "What would you say to the suggestion that top brass in the various spacefaring nations knew that the aliens existed a long time before they actually revealed themselves?"

James hesitated, remembering his private theories. It was certainly odd to realise just how much time and effort – to say nothing of money – had been poured into the various space navies over the last century. But if the Admiralty – and the politicians - had known about the aliens for so long, the secret would almost certainly have leaked. Keeping it a secret would have required paying off or co-opting so many people that it would have made a significant dent in the navy's budget.

"I would say that it seems unlikely," he said. He made a mental note to record a message for Uncle Winchester. None of the briefing notes had covered this eventuality. If there was any truth to the suggestion at all, he wanted to know about it. "The governments of this world are not good at keeping secrets."

Yang smiled, rather ruthlessly. "That happens to be true," he agreed. "Do you happen to think the Captain is suitable for command?"

James sat upright, sharply. "What?"

"Captain Smith was hitting the bottle pretty hard," Yang observed. "It's right there on his service record. No one made any attempt to hide it. Do you think the Captain is suitable for command?"

"Get out," James ordered. It was a poor reaction, as he admitted to himself a moment later, but he was damned if he was allowing this line of questioning to continue. And to think he'd thought that Yang was one of the *reasonable* reporters!

Yang rose to his feet, but didn't leave the room. "Off the record," he said. "What do you think?"

It had been bad enough, James knew, when the First Space Lord had been asking him to watch the Captain. At least the First Space Lord was a superior officer, not a damned reporter. How had Yang even gained access to the Captain's service record? Had it been allowed to slip into his hands deliberately? If someone felt that Captain Smith was a poor Captain, they might have hoped the media would bring pressure to bear against him.

But Captain Smith was a hero…

James shook his head. If there was one lesson the aristocracy had learned and learned well, it was that the media could turn on their previous darling and savage him ruthlessly.

"I think that Captain Smith has won the first and *only* victory against the aliens," he snapped, finally. "And I think you should bear that in mind."

He watched Yang leave his quarters, then reached for his terminal. There was an hour to go before they crossed the tramline and started their cruise, more than long enough for him to contact Uncle Winchester and explain what had happened. There would be no time for a reply, but it didn't matter. If Yang decided to express his doubts…if he did have doubts. It struck James that Yang hadn't really expressed any feelings of his own.

Idiot, he thought, recalling other pieces of advice from the past. *When you tangle with the press, you never come out ahead in the long run.*

———

Kurt wiped sweat from his brow as he clambered out of his starfighter and half-walked, half-staggered towards the wardroom. Behind him, he heard the sound of the launch bay crew moving the starfighter back into the launch tubes, replacing the power cells as they moved. The sound faded away as he stepped through the airlock, then into the wardroom. Luckily, the wardroom was one of the places barred to reporters by prior arrangement.

He stripped off his flight suit and dropped it in the basket, then strode into the shower to wash away the sweat. Water ran down, cleansing his body; he closed his eyes and allowed it to run over his face. He heard the door opening again behind him, but ignored it. Moments later, several other bodies joined him in the shower.

Opening his eyes, he smiled to see that none of the younger pilots looked any better than he felt. It had been a *hard* exercise, with everyone pushed to the limit. Rose had designed it, partly to make it clear to her subordinates that she was more experienced than them, but Kurt suspected that he would have to have a few words with her about overdoing it. A pair of experienced pilots had come alarmingly close to disaster.

"Get some rest," he advised, as he stepped out of the shower and towelled himself off. "We will be going back to the simulators in the morning."

Walking back into the wardroom, he pulled on his shipsuit and headed towards the door. It opened a moment before he reached it, revealing Rose and a handful of her new subordinates, chatting together with surprising enthusiasm. The exercise must have comprehensively broken the ice, he decided. It helped that she'd been a squadron flyer until her sudden promotion after the first battle.

"I need a word with you after you've showered," he said, catching Rose's arm. "Meet me in my office."

He let her go and walked past her, into the small office. A quick check of the terminal revealed messages from both Percy and Penny, but nothing from Molly. Feeling an odd spurt of confusion and alarm, he opened the first message from Percy and discovered, to his surprise, that Molly had hired an older girl to take care of the kids. Percy seemed enthused about this development, which puzzled Kurt until he placed the caretaker's name and remembered just how pretty she was. Penny, on the other hand, complained long and loudly about having an older girl watching her at all times. Apparently, the older girl had made the mistake of believing Molly's instructions. Kurt's daughter had found herself going through her homework again and again until the babysitter – Penny seemed to believe that the older girl was her babysitter, which she found *very* insulting – was satisfied.

Kurt gritted his teeth, then started to record a message. It was hard to blame Molly for hiring help – and besides, it sounded as though the new girl was doing an excellent job. Penny would just have to get used to being supervised, at least until she started working up to the standards Kurt expected. Kurt finished his message by promising a reward, as Rose had suggested, then recorded a second one for Percy. At least his son seemed happy with the situation.

At least until it gets embarrassing, Kurt thought, remembering his own youth. A girl more than three or four years older than he'd been would never have given him a second glance. Percy would waste time trying to impress her, then either do something stupid or get over his crush. Kurt briefly considered trying to warn him, before deciding that it was pointless. His father had tried and Kurt hadn't listened. It was astonishing just how smart the old man had become in the years between Kurt reaching his teenage years and growing out of them.

There was a tap on the door, which opened to reveal Rose. She looked cleaner, Kurt was relieved to see, but she still looked pleased with herself. Kurt waved her to a chair, then spun his own chair around to face her. Rose sat down, looking past him to see the monitor.

"Did you hear anything from your daughter?"

"She's complaining about the girl Molly has hired as a…*babysitter*," Kurt said, loading his voice with as much disdain as a teenage girl could cram into an otherwise innocuous word. "I need to speak to you about the exercise."

Rose looked thoughtful. "Pushed it a little far, did I?"

"A little," Kurt agreed, dryly. "You do realise we have reporters on this ship, don't you?"

"I believe I might have noticed," Rose said, equally dryly. "One of them wanted me to pose on a starfighter in my underwear."

Kurt blinked at her. "Why...?"

"I think he saw *The Horniness of Khan* once too many times," Rose said. "I told him he couldn't afford my rates."

Kurt rolled his eyes. That movie had been giving starfighter pilots giggling fits for years, despite the basement production values. Clearly, no one cared about the lack of special effects if the pilots were all attractive women, particularly women who went through everything from group sex to bondage and spanking. He briefly considered demanding the reporter's name, then decided it was pointless if Rose didn't want to make an official complaint.

"Glad to hear it," he said, instead. "I would prefer not to watch our pilots die in exercises in front of a group of lusty reporters."

"Understood," Rose said.

Kurt sighed. He understood her need to prove herself, but it was a major headache when they were on their way to the war. Maybe, now she'd done it, she could ease off.

"They may start asking for interviews," he added. The XO had issued additional orders concerning the reporters. "When they do, I expect you to refuse unless you have prior permission."

"He did ask me some questions," Rose admitted. Her face crinkled up into a droll smile that made her look pretty after all. "Most of them were really fucking stupid."

"Why," Kurt asked, "am I not surprised?"

He glanced at his monitor, then smiled at her. "Go get some sleep," he ordered. The timer showed seven minutes until their first jump away from Earth. "Tomorrow, we will be starting more intensive simulations. And I will expect your pilots to be on the ball."

Rose left, grinning. Kurt watched her go, then turned back to his paperwork. The bureaucrats, it seemed, didn't realise there was a war on. Instead of making time for further exercises, they insisted he submit updated copies of his forms prior to departure. At least they weren't nagging him for another will, thankfully. He disliked the thought of writing out – again – what he wanted to happen to his estate if he died. Molly would acquire most of it, while Penny and Percy would both get the remainder. There was no one else he wanted to mention in his will.

He hoped, desperately, that Molly would send him a message. But, by the time they jumped out of the Sol System, no message had come.

CHAPTER
SEVENTEEN

The days started to blur together as *Ark Royal* made her elliptic journey towards New Russia. Ted ran endless drills, testing the new starships along with *Ark Royal's* new crewmen, while keeping a wary eye out for trouble. The handful of human colony worlds they passed signalled briefly, but received no reply. Ted had strict orders to maintain radio silence, even if they weren't trying to hide completely. Privately, he suspected that someone at the Admiralty was trying to have their cake and eat it too. They wanted to reassure the defenceless worlds that there was still a human space navy, but avoid revealing any compromising details, just in case.

Two weeks into the passage, he finally hosted a dinner for the reporters and a handful of senior officers. None of the reporters seemed particularly impressed by the food, although the more experienced ones kept their complaints down to a minimum. The Royal Navy certainly *could* have produced tastier food for its crewmen, but senior officers – it was commonly joked – preferred the standard rations in order to keep their crews hopping mad, ready to take it out on the enemy. Ted knew there were some stored rations intended for Admirals; he'd briefly considered sharing them with the reporters before dismissing the idea and insisting they ate the standard fare. Let them get a taste of the *real* naval experience.

As always, most of their questions were either absurd or unanswerable. Ted had no intention of discussing his non-existent love life with anyone, particularly reporters, and he had great difficulty in believing that anyone would be actually interested. Nor did he have any real idea what awaited them at New Russia. The aliens might have started to build the system up into a springboard for attacking Earth...or they might have started to settle the world with their own colonists...or they might simply have reduced the surface of the planet to radioactive ash. Ted had no way of knowing and no intention of allowing himself to develop preconceptions that could easily blind him to the truth.

"I'm surprised that you're not serving wine," one of the reporters observed. "Or is this a dry ship?"

"We're going into combat," Ted reminded him, keeping his expression blank. Was that question a jab at him or was it a wild coincidence? "I do not feel that drunken crewmen would help our chances."

He exchanged glances with Fitzwilliam, who scowled. There was no way to know the motives behind the question. It was quite possible, he admitted to himself, that the reporter wanted something alcoholic himself. They had brought a bottle or two each, according to the crewmen who had helped them unpack, but hardly enough for them to even get a pleasant buzz after the first few days. But Ted had no intention of serving anything alcoholic anywhere he was in command. He didn't need the temptation himself.

"But we're not crewmen," another reporter objected. "And there isn't much to do onboard ship."

Ted grinned, openly. Nothing to do? There was never any shortage of work to be done, even on a modern carrier. There were exercises and drills, spare parts to be inventoried...the crewmen could work from dawn till dusk and never get anywhere near finished. And then there was the ever-present rounds of basic maintenance. God alone knew what would happen if they skipped a few sections, but Ted had a very good idea. It would come back to haunt them at the worst possible time.

But he supposed that wasn't entirely true of the reporters. Only a handful of crewmen would speak to them openly, while the senior officers had been carefully briefed on what they could and couldn't say. The reporters were denied access to all of the *interesting* parts of the ship, leaving them wandering the corridors, chatting to crewmen in the mess or lurking in their cabins, accessing and viewing entertainment programs the Admiralty deemed appropriate for its crewmen. It was a shame they couldn't be put to work, Ted knew, but he wouldn't have trusted them to replace even the simplest plug-and-play component.

"That's the nature of wartime," he said, instead of pointing out that the crewmen had a great deal to do. "Long days, weeks and even months of boredom, broken only by moments of terror. When we reach New Russia, I assure you that you won't be bored."

The reporters didn't seem too happy at the reminder. They'd started out with the assumption that *Ark Royal* was effectively invincible, an assumption Fitzwilliam had dispelled when he'd shown them the damage inflicted by the aliens during the first battle. The next time, Ted knew, the aliens would be ready for them. *Ark Royal* was tough as nails, but a handful of nukes would crack her armour or – if they detonated inside her hull – vaporise her outright.

"True, Captain," Yang said. "Will we be permitted to observe the battle from the bridge?"

"Perhaps not," Ted said. "We have a secondary bridge that you can use as an observation point."

He had to smile at their puzzlement. *Ark Royal* had been deliberately over-engineered, with almost every department provided with its own backup. The secondary bridge had never been reactivated completely – the CIC provided a secondary nexus of control and if it were to be taken out the entire ship would be lost with it – but it would let the reporters feel important as they watched the holographic displays. And it would keep them out of his and his XO's hair.

"It seems that you have too many bridges on this ship," Yang observed. "Did the designers overdo it?"

Ted smirked. "This isn't a civilian ship," he reminded him. As if the reporter could be in any doubt! "We don't have time to wait for help if we run into trouble."

He looked up as Midshipwomen Lopez entered, pushing a trolley in front of her. Two of the younger reporters actually helped to pile up the dirty plates for disposal, something that puzzled Ted – good manners were not something he associated with reporters – until he realised that they were trying to impress the young lady. So far, there had been no actual trouble, but Fitzwilliam had quietly told him that several of the reporters had tried to lure crewmen and women into their bunks. Ted had no objections, as long as it was a willing liaison, but some of the reporters he'd met didn't seem to know the meaning of the word *no*.

The terrifyingly thin young reporter looked over at him, nervously. "Are we going to run into trouble?"

"We're looking for it," Yang said, before Ted could say a word. They exchanged glances of mutual understanding. Yang, whatever his faults, was an experienced embed. If the other reporter had any qualifications for her position, Ted had no idea what they were. "This isn't a pleasure cruise, you know."

The reporter's face seemed to colour, very slightly. Ted couldn't help wondering just how much work she'd had done on her body; her face was unnaturally pale as well as thin. There were no shortage of humans who modified themselves to cope with the dictates of fashion or to live on marginally habitable worlds, but the reporter seemed to have taken it to an extreme.

"I know," she said, finally. It was almost a whisper. "I know."

Ted shrugged, inwardly. He'd suffered through four years at the Academy, plenty of time to come to terms with his own mortality. The Royal Navy's highest losses – before the aliens had arrived – hadn't come from combat, but training exercises and simple shoddy maintenance. Each student had been told, time and time again, that they couldn't afford to take their eyes off the ball, not even for a second. Some of the horror stories had been exaggerated, but they'd still sunk in. Death was always a constant threat for young crewmen.

But the reporter had grown up in a safe world, where there had been no real danger. She was lucky, Ted knew, but she was also ignorant. Did she honestly believe, he asked himself, that her reporter ID would save her from alien missiles? The aliens hadn't bothered to check ID cards before opening fire in previous battles. They would hardly start now. Or had she accepted the theoretical danger and only just realised that it was *real*?

Midshipwomen Lopez departed, then returned with another trolley two minutes later. This one held small bowls of rice pudding, flavoured with spices and fruits the galley staff had scrounged up during the celebrations on Earth. Ted waited until each of the reporters had a bowl in front of them, then motioned for them to start eating. This time, it tasted better than he recalled. Clearly, having a famous starship making the requests helped ensure they got the very best of foods.

Smiling to himself, he finished his bowl and then nodded to Farley, the junior crewman present. Farley tapped his knife against his glass for attention, then stood.

"Ladies and gentlemen," he said. "I give you God, the King and the United Kingdom."

The reporters drank, some more enthusiastically than others. Fruit juice was common on earth, but rare on interstellar starships. Ted wondered, absently, just which of the reporters considered themselves neutral observers, then dismissed the thought. In his experience, there was no such thing as a neutral reporter. There were those who kidded themselves that they were being unbiased and those who were so prejudiced against the military that they swallowed the enemy's story, hook, line and stinker.

Good thing the aliens don't seem to care about our reporters, he thought. *If they did, they could probably split the defensive alliance in half, just by telling us what we wanted to hear.*

He rose to his feet. "Thank you for coming," he said. The toast marked the end of the formal dinner. "As you will appreciate, my staff and I have work to do. But you are welcome to remain here as long as you like."

Fitzwilliam followed him as he strode out of the private mess. "Captain," he said, once the airlock was closed. "I didn't realise that they would be so awful as a group."

"They wanted to outnumber us," Ted snapped. He didn't really blame his XO for the dinner; hell, he'd heard stories of far less pleasant dinners with reporters and other unwelcome guests. "And they wanted to do something other than sit in their cabins."

He shook his head, then jerked a hand towards the bulkhead. "Don't you just wish you could put them all down there?"

Fitzwilliam nodded in understanding. The star system they were travelling through had a barely-habitable world that was coming out of an ice age. Judging the world useless for conventional settlement, humanity had turned it into a penal colony. Criminals deemed utterly unredeemable were loaded into one-shot transport capsules, given a small quantity of food and supplies, then shot down into the planet's atmosphere. If they lived or died...no one on Earth gave a damn. The sociologists claimed that they would form a united society within two to three hundred years, but Ted had his doubts. A society built on criminals who should have been executed would be very far from stable.

"Yes, sir," he said. "It would be pleasant, wouldn't it?"

Ted smiled, then turned to head towards his cabin. "I'm going to get a nap," he said. He needed a shower too, just to wash the reporters off his skin. "Take command when shift changes, then ping me. I've got paperwork to do."

"You really should consider coming with us."

Major Charles Parnell shrugged. The seven-man Russian commando team had largely kept themselves to themselves during the first two weeks of the voyage, even though they'd been given quarters – barracks – right next to the Royal Marines. Now, their leader had finally condescended to speak to the British CO, even though he clearly had his doubts about the wisdom of talking to anyone. But they did have to coordinate their deployment with *Ark Royal*.

"It might be interesting," he agreed. "But we have other orders."

The Russian – the only name he'd given anyone was Ivan, which Charles suspected was a false name – snorted, rudely. He was a terrifyingly big man, his skin bulging with implanted weapons and combat systems. There had been no attempt to make him look normal, something that impressed and alarmed Charles in equal measure. Even the most capable cyborgs in British service still looked *human*.

"We have ours too," Ivan said. "We have to get down to the surface before they react to our presence."

"We understand," Charles said. It was going to be tricky, even if the alien sensors were no better than human sensors. Entering a planet's atmosphere would leave a trail a blind man could spot. The aliens could simply track them to their destination or intercept them in flight. "You will have all the support we can muster."

Ivan grunted. "Perhaps you should shoot those reporters out of missile tubes," he grated. He muttered a handful of Russian words Charles recognised, then slipped back to English. "They are pains in the buttocks."

"You never spoke a truer word," Charles said. Royal Marines were discouraged from talking to the press, which hadn't stopped the assholes from badgering him and his men for interviews. It wasn't as if they had anything useful to say – or even anything newsworthy. "I will speak to the XO and ask him to tell them to leave you and your men alone."

Ivan muttered something in Russian about Siberia and the proper punishment for inquisitive reporters, then tapped the display. "The main body of settlement on New Russia is here," he said, pointing to the main continent. "We intend to land here."

Charles gave him a surprised look. Royal Marines were no strangers to long route marches, but Ivan was talking about walking several thousand miles to the settlements. It would take weeks, even for the fittest soldiers in the human sphere. He found himself eying the cyborg implants, wondering if they were far more capable than he had assumed. But there was no way to know.

"There is a hidden military facility not too far from our planned landing zone," Ivan explained, reluctantly. "The planetary government will have relocated there, as planned, in the wake of the battle. We will make contact with them, then proceed to gain a full report of conditions on the ground."

"That makes sense," Charles agreed. He wondered, absently, if the Russians would ever have told anyone about the facility without being pressed, then decided it didn't matter. It wasn't as if British secrets were shared openly either, although he knew that the other human powers had parsed them out. "How do you plan to get down to the surface?"

There was a long awkward pause, long enough to make Charles wonder if the Russians really *did* have a plan – or if they were merely playing it by ear.

"That," Ivan admitted finally, "is where we need your help."

———

Ted had been right, he knew, when he'd told the reporters that military service was mostly boredom, broken by moments of screaming terror. Knowing was half the battle, as the saying went, yet it wasn't that much help. In a sense, he realised now, he'd been spoilt by spending most of his career as the commander of a starship held in the reserves. It had been simple enough to arrange for bottles of booze to be shipped to him from Earth or even made a brief visit to Sin City or another Luna settlement. The Admiralty had paid so little attention to *Ark Royal* that he could have turned her into a spacefaring gambling palace and they would never have noticed.

But now, alone and isolated, Ted couldn't help feeling the urge for a drink. It mocked him, reminding him that he hadn't been able to work up the determination to smash his remaining bottles of alcohol…or even to do more than insist that Anderson dismantled his still. He could pour himself a drink, the voice at the back of his head insisted; he could pour himself a drink and take a swig and no one would ever know.

But it wouldn't stop at one glass, he told himself, savagely. *Would it?*

It wouldn't, he knew. Once, he had finished one or two bottles of Anderson's rotgut every day. In hindsight, it was a minor miracle he hadn't managed to invalidate himself out of the Royal Navy. It wasn't uncommon for ship-made alcohol to be effectively poison, if the brewer didn't know what he was doing. If the Admiralty had been paying enough attention to realise that he was drinking himself to death…

They knew, his thoughts reminded him. Someone had made note of his drunkenness and reported it to the Admiralty. It had even been in his personal file. *They just didn't care.*

Angrily, he paced over to the bunk and lay down, pulling the blankets over his head. He felt too keyed up to sleep, too tired to remain awake. There were pills he could take, he knew, but they tended to have unfortunate side-effects. Instead, he closed his eyes and forced himself to mentally recite the regulations governing waste disposal on starships. It was an old trick he'd learned at the Academy. The tutors had sworn blind that it beat counting sheep. Slowly, he fell asleep…

And then the alarms went off.

Ted jerked out of bed as red lights flashed. "Red Alert," Fitzwilliam's voice said. "I say again, Red Alert. This is not a drill. All hands to battlestations. Captain to the bridge."

Cursing, his blood running cold, Ted keyed his bedside console. "Report," he snapped. "What's happening?"

"Incoming alien starfighters," Fitzwilliam reported. There was a grim note to his voice that belayed any hope that it might be a sadistic drill. "We're under attack!"

CHAPTER
EIGHTEEN

James had privately expected to run into trouble long before they reached New Russia. The aliens weren't fools, whatever else could be said about them, and they would have to suspect that some kind of counter-attack would be mounted as soon as possible. Indeed, given the care the aliens had taken in mounting their invasion, it was unlikely that they would fail to seal the backdoor. Or, at least, to hide picket ships in human systems.

"I'm picking up forty-seven alien starfighters, advancing towards us on attack vector," Farley reported. "They're not even *trying* to stealth themselves."

"Maybe it's a diversion," James said. Where *was* the Captain? He'd said he was on his way. "Launch all starfighters, then order four squadrons to remain close to the flotilla and provide cover."

He looked up as the Captain strode onto the bridge. The older man looked tired, but not drunk or zonked out of awareness. James let out a sigh of relief he hadn't realised he was holding, then rose to his feet and surrendered the command chair to his commander. The Captain took it, nodded to him and then checked the tactical display. A second flight of alien starfighters was just coming into sensor range.

"Alter course," the Captain ordered. "Bring us about to face the threat, then launch a shell of recon drones. I want to know where those starfighters came from."

"They must have a carrier somewhere within the system," James muttered. "Unless they set up a hidden base."

The Captain nodded. "Seems an odd place to hide a carrier," he said. "Unless they saw us coming and deliberately set up an ambush. Why not? We did it to them earlier."

James looked down at the display, silently weighing up the potential vectors. Just how much endurance did the alien starfighters have? There was no way to know, which meant any estimates of the location of their carrier were nothing more than guesses at best. For all they knew, the alien starfighters could travel for hours before needing to replenish their supplies.

"If they found us here, they have to know where we're going," James mused. "They could have ambushed us at New Russia instead."

"True," the Captain agreed. On the display, the first squadron of alien starfighters was breaking up, skimming along the edge of the flotilla. "Go to the CIC and take command there. If we lose the bridge..."

James nodded and left the compartment. Outside, much to his astonishment, he ran into a pair of reporters. Were they actually trying to sneak onto the bridge during a battle?

"Get back to your quarters," he snapped. There was no point in trying to show them to the secondary bridge, not now. "Get back there or the Marines will escort you to the brig."

The reporters hesitated, then fled.

———

Kurt gritted his teeth as the starfighter was blasted out of the launch tube and into interplanetary space. He checked the display briefly to make sure that the entire wing had launched from the carrier, then refocused his systems on the alien starfighters. They seemed to be dodging and dancing at the edge of weapons range, rather than pressing the offensive against the human ships. It made no sense to him until he realised that they were trying to get hard sensor locks of their own, pinning down the human ships.

"Alpha squadron, with me," he ordered, visions of an alien mass driver running through his head. *Ark Royal* was tough, but not *that* tough. "We need to drive those bastards away from the carrier."

He heard the acknowledgements as he led the flight towards the alien starfighters. As before, they didn't seem as capable as his own starfighters, although that might not make a difference if there was enough of them. The aliens hesitated, then ducked back towards the second flight of their starfighters, concentrating their forces. Moments later, they turned and raced towards the outer edge of the flotilla. Kurt switched his targeting systems to full power, then gunned his engine and roared towards them. At such speeds, they entered firing range within seconds.

"Two targets down," Alpha Three reported. The computers had to handle the firing. No human mind could handle an engagement at such speeds. "One more broke off. I might have winged him."

Kurt doubted it. Unless the alien starfighters were much tougher than they seemed, the merest kiss from a starfighter-mounted railgun would be enough to shatter them beyond repair. Maybe the alien pilot had had a technical fault that had forced him to pull out and return to his carrier. Kurt quickly checked the scanner, hoping to track the alien craft, but found nothing. The alien had managed to evade before any of the humans could get a lock on him.

He yanked the fighter around and followed the aliens as they fell on the older starships like wolves on sheep, although *these* sheep were hardly defenceless. A number of alien starfighters were picked off before they opened fire, but their weapons proved devastatingly effective. They'd learned, Kurt noted absently, as he closed the range and opened fire; they were going after weapons and sensor blisters, rather than trying to simply punch through the hull.

"Clever bastards," Rose observed. She'd clearly made the same observation. "Two more wings of alien starfighters have just come into view."

Kurt swore. Were there *two* enemy carriers out there? Or had the aliens hidden a base somewhere within the system? He took a moment to link into the live feed from the drones, but saw nothing. Logically, if the aliens could stealth their starfighters, why not a carrier?

"Keep the bastards away from the ships," he ordered. Two ancient frigates were already effectively useless, their lost weapons making them easy prey for successive wings of alien starfighters. "Alpha and Beta, fall in with me; Delta and Gamma, cover the ships."

And hope it isn't a trap, he thought, as he turned and accelerated back towards the incoming alien starfighters. They'd have a few moments to tear a hole in their formation before the aliens blew past them...unless, of course, they decided to stop and dogfight instead. They might well realise that wearing down *Ark Royal's* fighters would be a highly effective tactic...

"They should have sent another carrier with us," one of the pilots commented.

"As you were," Kurt said, sharply. He agreed, but there was no time for a discussion. "Take them at a run."

———

Ted watched, grimly, as the alien starfighters blew through the defending starfighters and lanced towards their targets. They didn't seem to be going after *Ark Royal* in particular, which was odd...and a reversal of military doctrine, at least as the aliens seemed to understand it. He considered the problem as the flotilla closed up, the smaller ships linking their point defence systems together to give the aliens a nasty surprise, then decided that the aliens probably wanted to weaken his defences before going after the carrier. It was the only answer that seemed to make sense.

"Launch a second shell of recon drones," he ordered. He'd wondered if he was looking at a diversion, but the aliens definitely seemed to be coming from the same direction. "Send them out along the path taken by the alien starfighters."

He looked back down at the display, silently calculating vectors. But there were just too many unknown variables for the analysts to say anything for sure. No matter how he looked at it, it was clear that the aliens had put some effort into their ambush. But did they know that the flotilla was heading for New Russia? They had to know...unless they assumed that Ted intended to attack the alien homeworlds...

A thought struck him and he pulled up the tramline chart, thinking hard. The aliens had been careful – targeting a world that could pose a danger while ignoring ones that didn't – but Vera Cruz hadn't posed a danger. It had been nothing more than an isolated stage-one colony world...and its founders didn't have the resources to turn it into a centre of industrial production. Had the aliens merely wanted to test their weapons against a defenceless target or had they something else in mind? All they'd done, as far as Ted could tell, was give the human race a month's warning, time to gather the defensive force that had been destroyed at New Russia. Had *that* been the objective?

He shook his head. Any plan with too many moving pieces was a plan that was likely to go spectacularly wrong. *That* had been hammered into his head at the Academy. Logically, the aliens would have learnt the same lesson during their expansion into space. And that meant...

...What if Vera Cruz was right next to an alien system?

Shaking his head, he pushed the thought aside as a new set of icons appeared on the display.

"One alien carrier, previously unknown design," Fitzwilliam's voice said. "Judging by her size, she can deploy more starfighters than any of our carriers."

"Take us towards her," Ted ordered. He switched back to the system display and smiled to himself. Unless the aliens retreated at once, they wouldn't be able to find a tramline to escape before the humans overran their position. "And ready the mass drivers."

He studied the live feed from the drones, silently considering what he was seeing. The alien carrier looked fragile, somehow, compared to *Ark Royal*. But then, so did a modern human carrier. Once they got a solid lock on her hull, she was dead. He watched the mass drivers powering up, ready to unleash a shotgun blast of ballistic projectiles that would be enough to damage the alien ship, even destroy her if they scored a direct hit. On the display, the alien ship launched another wing of starfighters, then started to pull back. Ted wasn't too surprised.

Quickly, he considered his options. He could launch bombers after her, knowing that the tiny ships could definitely catch up with the alien ship. But the alien ship bristled with point defence and he didn't dare lose too many bombers, not unless he intended to return to Earth with his tail between his legs. He could cut loose a handful of frigates and send *them* after the carrier, escorted by a couple of starfighter squadrons...it seemed the best option.

Reaching for his console, he began to issue orders.

———

"You heard the Captain," Kurt said, as five of the frigates moved out of formation and started to advance on the alien carrier. "Alpha and Beta will cover the frigates."

The alien starfighters seemed to recognise the threat at the same moment. They broke away from their previous engagements and streaked towards the frigates, aiming blasts of plasma fire at their weapons and drives. One of the frigates staggered out of formation as a lucky hit totalled its drive systems, the others continued towards the alien carrier, which seemed to be picking up speed alarmingly fast. No match for a frigate, Kurt noted absently, but faster than any human carrier. All their calculations had been based on flawed data.

He shot a brief burst of fire at one of the alien starfighters, then threw his starfighter into an evasive pattern as two alien craft swooped down on him. His first target evaded his fire and continued attacking the frigates, only to be picked off by a burst of railgun fire from the lead starship. Kurt allowed himself a smile, then yanked his craft around and blew one of his pursuers into flaming vapour. The other broke off and headed back towards his carrier.

"They're pulling back," Rose said, in surprise. "Where do they think they're going?"

"One of their tramlines," Kurt said, as the frigates picked up speed desperately. Warning lights flashed on his display as *Ark Royal* unleashed a blast of shotgun pellets from her mass drivers, but somehow he doubted they would score a hit. The aliens, aware of the danger, were randomly altering course as they struggled towards the tramline. "I think we're going to lose her."

Four minutes later, he swore out loud as the alien craft crossed the edge of the tramline, recovered her remaining fighters and vanished. There was a brief gravimetric pulse, indicating a successful transit, then nothing. The aliens had taken advantage of their technology to escape. He looked down at his display, wondering if there were any alien starfighters that hadn't been recovered in time to allow them to escape, but saw nothing. The battlefield was empty of hostile ships.

"Return to the barn," he ordered. "Beta will remain on CSP. Everyone else, land and snatch a mug of tea. The bastards will be back."

———

"Their drive gives them an advantage," James nodded, looking up at the display. It was easy to tell where the aliens had gone, but impossible to stop them. There was a tramline that ran from the alien destination to New Russia, which meant that the aliens in New Russia would have at least a day's warning that *Ark Royal* was on her way. "Tell the boffins we need a comparable system ourselves."

The Captain snorted. "I don't think it's that easy to duplicate an alien system," he said, over the intercom. "We still don't even have a theory for how they do it."

James nodded ruefully, running his hand through his hair. By any reasonable standard, they'd won another victory...but it could lead to their defeat. The aliens had lost more starfighters, yet they'd managed to damage a handful of frigates *and* alert their superiors that a human formation was approaching New Russia. He found himself seriously considering advising the Captain to abort the mission. No one would object if the Captain chose to safeguard his ship – the one victorious ship in the Royal Navy –rather than launching a direct assault on a world that would be ready for them, by the time they finally arrived.

"We need to build those battleships," the Captain added. "If we had more mobile firepower, we might be able to give the aliens a nasty surprise."

"True," James agreed. "A battleship would be very useful."

He smiled. To give the Royal Navy's designers their due credit, they had started updating *Ark Royal's* schematics...and then outlining a battleship concept that would be crammed with mass drivers, rail guns and armoured so heavily that the alien weapons wouldn't have a hope of breaking through into the vulnerable innards. But it would take at least a year, once the designs were finalised, to put them into production... assuming that nothing went wrong.

And the war doesn't come to a screeching halt before we complete them,
he added, in the privacy of his own thoughts. *The aliens aren't going to stop
innovating either.*

"Captain," he said slowly, "should we consider withdrawing?"

The Captain hesitated. "I think we should do what repairs we can,
then I will make the final decision," he said. "Two of the frigates may have
to be sent back to Earth."

Which would be very unlucky for them, James knew, if the aliens had
started trying to block their escape route. Given their FTL drives, they
could put a small squadron of lighter starships within all of the potential
human systems…and then intercept the human ships before they even
realised they were under attack. But the alternative was abandoning them
in the penal system or simply scuttling them now, before the aliens could
recover the ships.

"I'll see to it," James said. "Should we spare any other ships to act as escorts?"

The Captain shook his head. "We can't spare anything, not now," he
said. He grinned, suddenly. "And you can brief the reporters yourself."

James sighed. "Yes, sir," he said. "But they will want an interview with
you too."

"I'm going to be very busy," the Captain said. He smirked, although
there was no malice in his expression. "You'll have to handle them."

"Yes, sir," James said, again.

He closed the channel, then procrastinated by checking the damage
reports from the ships the aliens had targeted. They'd definitely learnt
from experience, he told himself; they'd targeted weapons, rather than
the armoured hulls. But it was an effective tactic, he had to admit, and
one that could be repeated time and time again. There might be a second
attack in the next system, which would have the additional disadvantage
of convincing the aliens that New Russia was the target…

As if they were in any doubt, he thought, sourly.

———

Kurt ordered his squadron to wait in the ready room until he was reasonably confident that the aliens weren't about to put in another attack

immediately, then reminded the pilots to make sure they staggered their showers and meals. If the aliens *did* return, they'd need to drop everything and return to the fray. Starfighter pilots were used to snatching sleep where they could – constant exercises saw to that - but this was different. This time, they might be snapped awake and flung out into space to do battle with the aliens once again.

Shaking his head, he reached for a terminal and began to type out a message for his family. If the damaged frigates were sent back to Earth, they could carry the messages…although he knew the censors would see them before they were uploaded into the planetary datanet. He was midway through writing the message when another message popped up in his inbox. It was from one of the reporters, asking for an interview. Judging by the curses he could hear around the ready room, he wasn't the only one to get such a message.

"Tell them you're still on duty," he advised. Honestly, the constant demands for interviews were getting beyond a joke. "And then remember that you *are* on duty."

CHAPTER
NINETEEN

"Captain," Farley said. "The two frigates have crossed the tramline and vanished."

"Good," Ted said. The frigates, assuming they made it, carried both letters from his crewmen and his theory that Vera Cruz was near an alien homeworld. Whatever happened, the Admiralty would have a chance to consider the possibilities. "Resume course."

"Aye, sir," Lightbridge said. A dull quiver ran through the ship as the carrier resumed her slow plod towards New Russia, accompanied by the remainder of the flotilla. "Course underway."

"Launch a second shell of recon drones," Ted added. "I want to know about the faintest hint of an alien presence."

He looked up at the display. The aliens, damn them, would know their rough course and speed. Assuming their commanders reacted at once – an assumption he dared not reject – they could have another carrier in place to intercept the flotilla long before they reached New Russia. But there was a chance they could sneak through...

"Drones away," Farley said. "Passive sensors...online."

Ted nodded. Passive sensors were nowhere near as capable as active sensors, but at least they didn't radiate any betraying emissions for alien sensors to detect. Using active sensors would have betrayed their position to the aliens, while the aliens themselves might remain undetected until it was far too late to avoid another ambush. There were times, Ted knew, when he might want to advertise his presence, but not in what might as well be unfriendly space.

He rose to his feet. "You have the bridge," he said, addressing Farley. "I'll be in my office."

"Aye, sir," Farley said. "I have the bridge."

Ted strode through the airlock and sagged, almost as soon as the airlock hissed closed behind him. The weight of command had never felt so heavy, not even when he'd first assumed command of the carrier... although, to be fair, no one had ever seriously expected *Ark Royal* to resume active service as anything more than a museum piece. Now...a mistake on his part could cost humanity the war. What if the attack on New Russia was a total disaster?

He'd thought, seriously, about abandoning the mission and withdrawing the way they'd come. It wouldn't have been a cowardly decision, he knew; there were strong reasons to favour a withdrawal and a return to Earth. He knew that there would be people who would say otherwise, who would accuse him of being a coward, yet he knew he had the moral stubbornness to proceed anyway. But they had to knock the aliens back on their heels and New Russia was the only reasonable target...at least until they found an alien homeworld they could target.

There was a chime. He looked up, then keyed the switch that opened the hatch, allowing Midshipwomen Lopez to step into the office. Annoyingly, she looked as fresh as ever, despite the brief and violent battle. Ted rubbed his forehead, wondering if he was losing his hair at a faster rate now he was going back into action, then dismissed the thought.

"Commander Fitzwilliam ordered me to bring you tea and cake," she said, as she placed the tray down on his desk. Ted blinked in surprise, then looked up at her. There was nothing, but earnestness in her eyes. "He also said you should get some sleep."

Ted grunted. It would be three days before they reached New Russia – three days, which would give the aliens ample time to prepare a surprise. He'd planned their approach to bring them into the system as far from the primary star as possible, but he was still uncomfortably aware that the aliens might well detect their arrival and come swarming. Just what were they *doing* in the system, anyway? There were no shortage of theories, yet there was no hard data.

"Thank you," he said, wondering why Fitzwilliam hadn't suggested it in person. It wasn't as if their relationship was *that* tense. "Was there anything else he wanted to say?"

"Apparently, one of the reporters wants to talk to you," Midshipwomen Lopez said. "But I believe the XO has headed her off at the pass."

"Understood," Ted said. "Tell him that I will speak to *one* reporter tomorrow."

He rolled his eyes. No doubt the reporters wanted reassurance from the command staff that they hadn't been in any real danger. He wondered, absently, if they'd believe the truth, that the aliens had been the ones who had decided the tempo of operations. If they'd pressed the offensive…it was odd, when he thought about it. The aliens had shown an odd sensitivity to losses.

Or maybe they were just scared of us, he thought. By any standard, *Ark Royal* had hammered the aliens badly in the last encounter. *It would be comforting to believe that was true…*

Midshipwomen Lopez poured him a mug of tea, then turned and left the office. Ted took a sip and realised, to his surprise, that the tea was actually real, rather than the processed seeds used to fuel the endless supplies of tea in the mess. Someone – he suspected Fitzwilliam – had had them shipped onboard, then donated them to Lopez with orders to use them to make the Captain's personal tea. He hesitated, then took another sip of tea and started to read through the reports from the smaller ships. Thankfully, the smaller navies hadn't developed the unfortunate tendency to be absurdly verbose, unlike the larger navies.

Unwilling to go further than he absolutely had to from the bridge, he walked over to the sofa, lay down and closed his eyes. He had been more exhausted than he'd realised, for the next thing he knew was his timer bleeping frantically, reminding him that it was time to take his next shift on the bridge. He pulled himself to his feet, hastily undressed and jumped into the shower, then washed himself clean before pulling on the same uniform. It felt slightly unclean against his flesh, but there was no time to get a new one.

He stepped onto the bridge and glanced at the status display. The carrier was still following the planned course, without any alien presence in sight. Ted prayed, silently, that it stayed that way, although he knew that, with a little care, an alien ship could be shadowing them at a distance and remain unseen. The only real risk lay in trying to follow them through a tramline...

Sighing, he sat down and started to read through the next set of reports.

———

"So," Yang said. "Just how much danger were we in?"

James briefly considered telling him that they'd come within a hairsbreadth of being killed – the inhumanly-thin reporter was right next to him, looking so pale he could almost see her bones under her skin – but decided it would be cruel. Besides, Yang probably had the experience to know that he would be lying.

"The aliens probed our defences, then broke off," he said, shortly. Yang might understand the real implications, but he had no intention of spelling them out for his partner. "They didn't come near the carrier."

"Odd choice of tactics," Yang said. "Modern-day doctrine dictates the immediate destruction of the enemy's carriers."

James couldn't disagree. The vast majority of space navies – and God knew there was no sign the aliens disagreed – had poured resources into carriers, rather than fixed defences. It gave them a flexibility, the admirals had concluded, that orbital battlestations couldn't hope to match – and besides, orbital battlestations were sitting ducks. It was no surprise that the aliens had gone after humanity's carriers during the Battle of New Russia; they'd known that destroying the carriers would eventually give them the victory. And they'd been right.

"True enough," he said. "But the aliens might well have discovered who we are and backed off."

"Or they have plans for a future ambush," Yang said, with evident pleasure. His partner whimpered. "They might be ready for us."

"It's a possibility," James agreed, shortly. The Captain had planned their entry to minimise the chances of detection, but the aliens – assuming they knew how humanity's drives worked – might well manage to catch their arrival anyway. "But we have to press on anyway."

The thin reporter looked up. "You mean to fly right into a trap?"

James shook his head, reflecting privately that the reporter wasn't as stupid as she looked.

"It is a trap," she insisted. "Why else would they back off and let us go?"

"They would not have been able to assign too many ships to guarding all of the possible angles of approach," James said, as patiently as he could. "I don't think they expected an armoured carrier and a small fleet of armoured warships. The smart thing to do was to back off, which they did."

The reporter sighed. James found himself studying her, privately reflecting – again – that perhaps he should send her to sickbay. She was so inhumanly thin...it crossed his mind to wonder if she was actually *human*, before dismissing the thought with all the contempt it deserved. Having her body extensively modified to allow her to survive with so little meat on her bones was stupid, but it didn't make her inhuman. Unless she was an alien spy...

He smirked at the thought. Humanity's first depictions of aliens had been little more than humans in rubber suits. It hadn't been until computer technology had allowed the creation of computer-generated monsters that truly inhuman monsters had been depicted on the big screen. But the first *real* aliens humanity had encountered had been humanoid... the theorists that suggested that different worlds, faced with the same problems, would find the same answers, might have been right after all. And yet...somehow, he doubted they could pose as human.

But was it unbelievable that some humans would turn traitor? The aliens had taken prisoners, they assumed; they'd certainly captured a handful of human colony worlds. It would be easy enough, he knew, to convince some of their captives to serve them instead. If they happened to take an entire family prisoner, they could threaten the children to force the adults to comply. Why, if humans could be so unpleasant to their fellow humans, could they expect the aliens to be any better? And yet, there was no reason to assume that the aliens hadn't already started building up spy networks long before Vera Cruz.

James scowled. If suspicions were directed at everyone who might just have come into contact with the aliens, somewhere along the edge of explored space...

The reporter coughed. "Is there a problem, Commander?"

"I'm not sure," James said. He made a mental note to write down his suspicions, although he was fairly sure MI5 would already have considered the possibilities. But the last thing humanity needed was a witch hunt for alien spies. "Are you having second thoughts about being on this ship?"

The reporter coloured, very slightly. "I was told it would make my career," she said, miserably. "And that I would be safe."

James had to fight to keep himself from giggling. What manner of idiot would believe that a military starship going into action was *safe*? But maybe it did make sense, in a weird kind of way. Embedded journalists like Yang went into action beside military units, even taking up weapons and opening fire if necessary. Other journalists remained behind the lines, donned clean uniforms and told themselves that they were being daring. And, having close access to cameras for 'live' reporting, tended to shape the media environment the way they wanted it to go.

"It may well make your career," James said, although he didn't have the slightest idea of why anyone would have thought that too. "But it will not, I'm afraid, be safe."

Yang stood. "If you don't mind, Commander, I have to go file a report," he said. "Can I leave Barbie in your capable hands?"

James blinked in surprise. Yang knew perfectly well there was no way to file a report, not until they returned to Earth or sent another ship back in their place. It puzzled him until he looked at Barbie – so that was her name – and realised that she was on the verge of crying. He scowled at Yang's retreating back, then wondered just who had wanted to be rid of her. Maybe she was too silly to be considered an asset even in the most liberal mainstream media outlet...

Or maybe someone made her boss send her away, James thought, ruefully. From what he'd heard, media outlets were driven by feuds and jealousies that made the aristocracy look calm and reasonable. *She seduced someone and her rival exacted a little revenge...*

"It isn't safe at all," he confirmed. "But the Old Lady is a tough little ship. She'll survive."

Barbie – absently, he wondered if that was just a media name – reached out and gave him a hug. James hesitated, then returned the hug, feeling her body pressing against his. She felt odd, almost childish, to the touch. The feeling was disturbing on a very primal level, so he pushed her away as soon as he decently could. Up close, her body seemed almost too thin to be sexual. According to her file, she was in her mid-twenties. He would have questioned if she was barely entering her teens.

"Thank you," she said. She stepped backwards and turned, allowing him to see her buttocks. They too were thin, thin enough to be almost unrecognisable. "I'll hold you to it."

James rolled his eyes as she walked out of the compartment, leaving him alone. If *Ark Royal* were to be destroyed, James would die beside her... and the rest of the crew. Perhaps, just perhaps, they could evacuate...no, that wasn't likely to happen. Even if they did, they would be exploding outwards into alien-controlled territory. Would the aliens ignore the lifepods, fire on them or take their crews prisoner? There was no way to know.

"Idiot," he muttered.

―――――

"This isn't a plan," Charles objected, when he looked at the finished operational outline. "I think this is guaranteed suicide."

Ivan's face didn't change, but there was a definite hint of amusement in his eyes. "I always knew you British were soft," he said. "This plan is bound to succeed."

Charles gave him a sharp look. "Because it's so absurd that no one in their right mind would expect it?"

"Precisely," Ivan said. "We go anywhere and do anything to complete the mission."

That, Charles knew, was true. The Russian Special Forces were known for pushing themselves to the limit, just like the other such units around the world. And, unlike the more open powers, the Russians had fewer qualms about taking terrifying risks to complete the mission. Their performance in the Third Afghanistan War alone had marked their operators as being men to watch, even before they'd started bending the letter of international agreements on cyborg soldiers.

"We have to break into the system first," Charles said, after a long moment. "And if we do that, we have to assault the planetary defences too…"

"They won't have time to install anything heavier than a handful of automated platforms," Ivan said, confidently. He shrugged, an exaggerated gesture that seemed to make up for his frozen features. "We know the risks, Major, and we know we have to break into the system first. Should that fail, we will consider alternatives. But, for the moment, this is our best option."

"I will consult with the Captain," Charles said, flatly. "He will have the final say…unless you wish to insert your shuttle into the system on your own?"

"Maybe as a last resort," Ivan said. He looked down at the plan, then passed Charles a copy. "I would advise you not to share it with anyone, but I don't think it matters here."

Charles snorted. Three months ago, the concept of having Russian SF forces on *Ark Royal* would have been utterly absurd. Even though the carrier was in the reserves, the Admiralty would have had kittens at the thought…unless they decided to sell the carrier. But that would have alienated a pressure group that would have brought an immense political storm down on their heads. Now…working with the Russians – and a handful of smaller navies – might mean the difference between victory and defeat.

"I'll show it to the Captain alone," he said. "He will have the final say, as I said."

He understood Ivan's impatience to act. New Russia and millions of Russian civilians were under enemy occupation – if, of course, they were still alive. The aliens could have butchered them all by now. If Charles could feel the urge to hurry up and get stuck into an enemy that had casually wiped out two British carriers and thousands of crewmen, Ivan would feel far worse. But they had to be careful. *Ark Royal* was effectively irreplaceable. Did the enemy realise that was true?

"Good," Ivan growled. He didn't look happy, but at least he'd conceded the point. "See to it, please."

Charles nodded, then checked the terminal. Two days to the tramline that would lead them directly to New Russia. Two days...to lay their plans and hope, desperately, that the aliens weren't in position to intercept them. And if it went wrong...

We'll have to fight our way out, he thought. There was no way he was surrendering his men to enemy POW camps...assuming, of course, the aliens didn't simply execute surrendered prisoners on sight. At least *Ark Royal* had some experience at fighting her way out of enemy traps.

He shook his head. Surrender, it seemed, wasn't really an option.

CHAPTER
TWENTY

"*Kiev* is in position, sir."

Ted nodded, one eye glancing down at the status display. The entire ship was at battlestations, every gun charged and ready to engage enemy targets, every starfighter ready to launch at a moment's notice. Ahead of them, the invisible gravimetric tramline shimmered on the display, waiting for them to trigger the Puller Drive and be catapulted into the New Russia System.

"Order her to jump in five minutes," he said. The Russian frigate had requested – demanded – the right to make the first jump into enemy-held territory. Ted had his doubts, but *someone* had to take the risk and jump. "And then recheck our stealth systems."

He scowled at the thought, pushing down the mad impulse that called for a drink. *Ark Royal* had been carefully rigged for silent running, but compared to the alien stealth systems humanity's systems were a sick joke. All it would take was a brief failure and the aliens would know precisely where they were. The moment they launched starfighters, he knew, they might as well surrender all attempts to remain hidden. And the aliens might just, if they caught a tiny break, track them from a distance without tipping their hand.

"All systems are operational," Farley said. The tactical officer sounded grimly professional, without the doubts that afflicted his commanding officer. "They won't see us coming."

"Let us hope not," Ted grunted. He looked over at the screen showing Fitzwilliam's face. "XO?"

"All decks report ready, sir," the XO said. He sounded rather less confident than Farley. They'd been through as many possible scenarios as they could, but it was impossible to escape the simple fact that the aliens knew they were coming. It was quite possible that they'd rigged a proper ambush at New Russia, just waiting for *Ark Royal* to stick her head in the noose. "We're as ready as we will ever be."

Ted smiled, rather sadistically. "And the reporters?"

"In the secondary bridge, under supervision," Fitzwilliam assured him. "They're terrified, sir."

Good to hear it, Ted thought. The reporters were pests in human form – if, of course, reporters could be considered human. At least the experienced ones knew better than to assume that they weren't going into danger. The doctor had even told him that three of the reporters had requested sleeping pills, just to help them rest at nights. Clearly, the inexperienced reporters should have spent more time considering the implications of a deep-strike mission before it was too late to refuse the assignment.

He pushed the thought aside as the counter reached zero. *Kiev* vanished from the display, flickering out of one star system and into another. The usable section of the tramline was entire light-hours long – it was unlikely that the aliens had managed to mass their ships in the right position to catch the flotilla as soon as it arrived – but he had to be wary. It was quite possible that the aliens had made some accurate guesses about where his ships intended to arrive and positioned themselves accordingly.

What if the frigate never returned? They'd discussed all of the possibilities, finally coming to the conclusion that they would need to back off and seek another tramline into the New Russia System. It would be inconvenient, to say the least; they'd be risking another encounter with alien starships, all the while drawing no closer to completing their mission. Maybe, if that happened, they would be better off withdrawing and returning to Earth...

There was a *ping* from the console as the frigate snapped back into existence.

Ted let out a sigh of relief, then leaned forward. "Get me a full data download," he said, addressing Farley. "Now!"

He watched as the data scrolled up on his screen. *Kiev* was one of the most modern starships in the Russian Navy – and, with her mission set in stone, various other powers had contributed their own sensor systems for her part of the operation. As far as she could tell, there were no alien starships within sensor range – or, for that matter, any human signals coming from New Russia. The only detectable signals seemed to be alien; they'd been recorded for analysis, but so far the automated systems couldn't make head or tails of them.

Not too surprising, Ted thought. The Royal Navy encrypted radio transmissions as a matter of course – they preferred laser communicators, which were effectively beyond interception – and there was no reason to assume the aliens thought differently. Even if they didn't, they still spoke an alien tongue that wouldn't be anything like English. *Deciphering their language will take years.*

"Looks clear," his XO said, finally. His voice hardened. "Unless it's a trap, of course."

Ted nodded. The aliens might not want to distribute starships randomly around the stars surrounding New Russia – they'd run the risk of being overwhelmed by a locally superior human force – but they wouldn't want to abandon New Russia without a fight. Leaving the door open could be nothing more than an attempt to lure *Ark Royal* into the system, with the aliens waiting until they were deep inside before springing the trap. But there was no way to avoid the risk. If they backed off entirely, they might as well surrender New Russia for good.

"Signal the flotilla," he ordered. He couldn't push his doubts out of his mind, but he had to proceed anyway. "We will advance to the tramline and jump."

Moments later, *Ark Royal* shuddered as her drives came online, propelling her onwards towards the tramline…and destiny.

———

The flight suits were supposed to be the most comfortable outfits in the Royal Navy, Kurt had been told. With inserted computer systems, each one cost upwards of a hundred thousand pounds, a price tag that never failed to make civilians sputter in horror. They were sup-posed to be comfortable...so why did he feel sweat trickling down his back?

Your first real combat jump, he told himself. The starfighter pilots were on alert, crammed into their craft and braced for immediate launch...if they ran into an alien ambush. He couldn't help thinking of the possible disasters waiting for them. What if the aliens had an ambush waiting for them that would blow *Ark Royal* away before she launched her fighters? Or what if...he tried to push the thought out of his mind, but it mocked him. He felt helplessly vulnerable. Outside, even in his fragile fighter, he would have a chance. Inside, he knew that he could die before the fighters were launched into space.

"All hands, prepare for jump," the XO's voice said. "I say again, all hands prepare for jump."

Kurt braced himself, feeling tension running down his spine. All of the pilots probably felt the same way. Combat jumps were rare, even in exercises; now, they were performing one for real. If something went wrong...angrily, he forced himself to think about the series of v-mails he had recorded for his children. Of course, if the entire flotilla was wiped out, they would never receive them. It was one of the reasons the Admiralty insisted on all naval personnel recording farewell messages and rewriting their wills prior to departure.

He wondered, absently, what they would think of him after he died. Would they think of him as a hero or a man who had abandoned his family to play starfighter pilot? He hadn't had a choice, yet it might not matter. Part of Kurt still resented his father for dying, even though the old man hadn't had a choice either. Would Penny and Percy understand why he'd had to go or would they resent him for dying? God knew it wasn't as through the family could claim a proper pension from his former employers. He wouldn't be old enough to qualify for the company's pen-sion scheme, if he died today. And the Royal Navy pension wouldn't be enough for the family.

Molly will hate me, he thought, morosely. And why not? Without his income, the kids would have to be transferred to a free school. Their education would suffer quite badly, he knew; he had no faith at all in government-run schools. And Penny would fall in with an even worse crowd than she had at her private school. But she'd probably be pleased. At least she wouldn't have to put up with Madame Capet any longer.

"Seconds to go," Rose said, her voice breaking into his thoughts. She sounded suspiciously eager to come to blows with the aliens. "I love you all, guys."

Kurt rolled his eyes as the other pilots made their replies, some of them dreadfully obscene, then cleared his throat loudly. "Maintain radio silence," he reminded them. It was unlikely that the alien sensors were good enough to pick up the tiny bursts from the starfighters, at least while they were in their launch tubes, but he didn't want to take chances. "And do *try* to be professional out there."

"Ten seconds to jump," the XO said. "All hands, brace for jump. I say again, all hands brace for jump."

Understood, Kurt thought. He braced himself as best as he could. *Five seconds to go...*

———

Charles, wearing full shipboard armour, watched as the Royal Marines braced themselves for the jump. They were all brave men – no one joined the Royal Marines without being ready for anything – but none of them *liked* the idea of being helpless as their starship jumped into potential danger. On the ground, they were lions; in space, they fretted over the prospect of being wiped out by a random missile strike. If *Ark Royal* came under heavy attack, there was little they could do beyond assisting the damage control teams.

"Five seconds," Sergeant Fred Miles said, softly. "Here we go."

Charles gritted his teeth as he felt the strange sensation of the jump building up around them, a feeling that defied analysis. The scientists swore backwards and forwards that no one should feel anything, but there was still a vaguely unpleasant feeling as the starship made its jump. Perhaps it was just a product of their imagination, the scientists had observed, a reflection of their awareness that something had changed. And yet...even when someone was unaware of the exact timing of the jump, they still felt the effects.

"Yes," he muttered, as the sensation faded away. "Here we go."

———

Ted had half-expected to see missiles or plasma bolts screeching towards them as soon as they materialised, even though *Kiev* hadn't detected any alien starships within sensor range. Instead, nothing greeted *Ark Royal* as she flickered back into existence, all hands braced for immediate attack. Ted gazed down at the screen and saw nothing, apart from the gravimetric signatures of the tramline and the system's planets. The aliens seemed to have missed their arrival completely.

"All clear," Farley said. He sounded doubtful. "But they could be lurking under stealth and we'd never know about it."

"True," Ted agreed. As long as they remained in the tramline, they could jump out again at the first sign of an alien threat, but they couldn't remain in the tramline indefinitely. "Launch the first set of recon platforms, followed by the drones. I want them established according to the operational plan."

He paused, then took a gamble. "And see if you can link into the Russian deep-space surveillance platforms," he added. "Use the command codes the Russians provided."

"Chancy," Fitzwilliam muttered. "The aliens might well have destroyed it."

Ted couldn't disagree. Like most interstellar powers, the Russians had established a sensor network to watch for illicit activity in their home system. Unlike multinational systems like Terra Nova, the Russians owned the entire New Russia System and refused to allow anyone else to establish settlements within their territory. It was easy enough to hide from such a system, but not without restricting one's activity to the bare minimum. Besides, there were enough unclaimed systems for hidden colonies to establish themselves without the risk of being obliterated by the Russians.

The seconds ticked away as the passive sensors began to pick up traces of alien activity. A handful of signals seemed to be emitting from the direction of New Russia itself, while another handful seemed to be coming from the asteroid cloud surrounding the system's larger gas giant. Ted wondered, absently, if the aliens had managed to capture the system's cloudscoop intact, before deciding it didn't matter. It wasn't as if a cloudscoop was a difficult device to construct.

"I picked up a low-level query from the Russian system," Farley reported. "They took their time."

"Too long," Fitzwilliam said. "What do they want?"

"More codes," Farley said. He looked up, alarmed. "Sir, we don't *have* any other codes."

Ted frowned. It was understandable that it had taken several minutes for the Russian system to respond. The closest platform was several light minutes from the tramline, while the automated systems would have to decide if it was worth taking the risk of responding to the signal. But to ask for other codes...? It made no sense...unless, of course, there were a handful of Russians still hiding out in the asteroid fields, watching the aliens from afar.

"Check with Ivan," Ted ordered. If the codes they had were insufficient, did they dare risk sending a signal in clear? And would the Russians believe them if they did? "If not, we will have to do without the Russian platforms."

There was a long pause. "Ivan thinks that the system has been reprogrammed by one of his people," Fitzwilliam reported. "It was apparently a security precaution. He suggests sending a message in Russian."

Ted frowned. "Ask him to record one," he ordered. He looked back down at the display. If it was a trap...they were about to spring it. "And then transmit it."

He felt his frown deepening as the message flickered down the laser link. No human starship could remain on alert indefinitely, not outside the fevered imagination of movie producers and politicians without military experience. His crew either needed to get into battle or relax, yet he didn't dare risk either. Knowing Murphy's habit of showing up at the worst possible time, they'd have their pants down around their ankles when the aliens finally launched their ambush. But if they were waiting for *Ark Royal* to move...

"Picking up a response," Farley said. "They're sending us a detailed data dump."

"Run it through the standard security precautions, then pass it to the isolated analyst system," Ted ordered. It was unlikely in the extreme that the aliens could produce a virus capable of attacking *Ark Royal's* computers – and, if they did, it wouldn't be any use against more modern carriers – but there was no point in taking chances. Besides, *human* opponents might well have worked out ways to attack the ship's systems. "And then order one-half of our crews to stand down."

"Understood," Fitzwilliam said. "Will you be resting yourself, Captain?"

"No," Ted said. He couldn't relax…and if he left the bridge, he might give into the temptation to take a drink or two. Or, if he took a pill, Fitzwilliam might have to command *Ark Royal* and the flotilla when the aliens finally attacked. *That* would look awful on his service record. "But you are to take a nap in your quarters."

An hour ticked by slowly as the recon platforms inched their way into the inner system, towards the looming presence of New Russia. The handful of orbital stations the Russians had built to make transhipment easier were gone, not entirely to Ted's surprise. Stalin, the larger of the two moons, had once held a large-sized mining colony. That too was gone, leaving only a scar on the lunar surface. Judging by the size of the blast, the aliens definitely did have nukes – and were prepared to use them too. There was nothing else, as far as he knew, that could produce such damage.

"Interesting that they didn't want to capture the facility," Farley mused. "They don't build their starships out of unobtainium or anything unknown to us. The Russians mined for materials to build starships here. Why wouldn't the aliens want it for themselves?"

Ted shrugged. "Maybe they don't intend to *keep* New Russia," he suggested. "As long as we don't know where their homeworlds are, they can just keep dancing around us, defying us to catch and crush their fleets. Eventually, they'd grind us down to the point where they can launch an invasion and occupy our remaining worlds."

He scowled at the thought. While they were crawling towards New Russia, the aliens might well have launched their fleets towards Britannia, Washington, Ghandi or even Confucius, targeting humanity's shipyards and industrial nodes away from Earth. The thought of Britannia being ravaged by the aliens was horrifying – and he knew the other spacefaring powers would feel the same. They'd invested literally trillions of pounds in the out-system colonisation program.

The console chimed. "Sir," Farley said, "we've found the alien fleet."

"Show me," Ted ordered.

One by one, the alien fleet came into view. It wasn't in orbit around New Russia – apart from a handful of frigate-sized craft that seemed to be in low orbit – but lurking some distance from the planet. Ted puzzled over it for a long moment, then decided that the aliens were clearly preparing an offensive. As alien as their craft were, they seemed to fall into roles comparable to humanity's fleets.

"Fourteen carriers, of two different types," Farley said. "Fifty-two smaller craft, mainly frigate-sized, and thirty-five freighters. The latter seem to be transhipping supplies to the carriers."

Ted cursed their luck. If they'd arrived in time to take advantage of the alien distraction...he shook his head. They'd just have to work with what they had.

"Keep expanding the recon network," he ordered. A direct assault on the alien fleet would be suicidal, but there were always options. "And then let me see what happened when the system fell."

CHAPTER
TWENTY ONE

"It doesn't look too different from Earth," Barbie said.

James rolled his eyes. New Russia was Earth-like, right down to an ecosystem that could support human settlement, even if it hadn't produced any form of intelligent life form. The existence of worlds like New Russia had once been used to confirm the theory that humanity was alone in the universe, the sole race to pass through the bottlenecks that led to intelligence and spacefaring status. That theory, he suspected, wouldn't be heard in the future. God alone knew how many other intelligent races there were out there.

"Yes," he said. None of the reporters struck him as particularly intelligent, but Barbie took the cake. "It is, in fact, a remarkably habitable world."

He allowed himself a moment of relief as his terminal buzzed, calling him back to the CIC. Leaving the reporters in the tender care of the PR officers, he stepped through the airlock and walked down the corridor to the CIC. The Marines on duty nodded as he walked past them, keeping their weapons in plain view. James rather doubted the aliens would try to board the carrier, but the Marines could and did keep the reporters away from the CIC. They didn't want to be interrupted by stupid questions in the middle of a battle.

Inside, a holographic representation of New Russia floated in the centre of the giant compartment, surrounded by a handful of red icons. The alien formation looked oddly familiar; James realised, with a sudden flicker of relief, that it was a formation designed to provide total coverage of the planet below. They hadn't obliterated the Russian population, thankfully. Their formation allowed them to keep the humans under control.

"They've taken out the spaceports and a handful of military bases," the analyst muttered, as he worked his way through the tidal wave of incoming data. "But there doesn't seem to be much damage to any of the cities."

"For which we should be grateful," the Captain said. "Is there an alien presence on the surface?"

"Not that we can pick up from this distance," the analyst reported. "We are picking up a handful of alien radio transmissions, but they're all located several hundred miles from the nearest city."

James frowned, studying the holographic planet. "They might be establishing settlements of their own," he said. "But surely they'd want to keep a close watch on the human settlements."

"Surely," the Captain agreed. "Assuming, of course, that they think like us."

He looked over at the analyst. "Are there any signs they're occupying the major cities?"

"No, but we would need to move the recon platforms into low orbit to be sure," the analyst said. "We can't pick up individual humans or aliens at this distance."

The Captain nodded to James, then led the way into a side office. "It looks like we will have to go with Plan Gamma," he said, once they were alone. "Do you have any disagreements?"

James hesitated, then shook his head. Plan Gamma made no attempt to liberate the planet, instead merely raiding the alien positions before beating a hasty retreat. Ivan and his team of commandos could try to make it down to the planet's surface while the aliens swarmed around, giving chase to the impudent human carrier…. and then linking into the recon network to upload messages to the next human formation to raid the system. It should work perfectly.

He shook his head again, sourly. The aliens had some technology that humanity hadn't been able to duplicate. If they had yet another surprise, something that tipped the balance in their favour, they might be able to win the coming battle. James already knew they didn't dare come within hitting range of an alien frigate. Small as they were, their plasma cannons could do real damage.

"Then we will launch our unpowered missiles towards the planetary occupation forces and use the mass drivers to target their fleet," the Captain said. "They won't see the first attack coming, I hope, but after that..."

James scowled. War was a democracy, he knew. The enemy got a vote too.

"Tell the Russians to prepare for launch," the Captain added. "We will start operations" – he checked his chronometer – "one hour from now."

———

Ted felt the seconds ticking away one by one as he reviewed the data they'd pulled from the Russian network. The last Earth had seen of the Battle of New Russia – when the recording starship had made its escape – the aliens had been ripping the defending fleet to shreds. But there was more. Some of the Russian starships had made a final stand, fighting desperately to protect their adopted homeworld. Others had withdrawn into the outer reaches of the system to prepare for the day they could return to New Russia in triumph.

They hadn't been willing to commit themselves, Ted discovered, not entirely to his surprise. By any reasonable standard, *Ark Royal* was badly outnumbered and outgunned, leaving the Russians convinced that they had to make a hit and run attack, rather than chasing the aliens out of the system. But they had agreed to record the course of the battle, just so Earth would know what had happened. It was the most Ted could reasonably expect of them.

"Sir," Farley said. "The mass drivers are ready to open fire."

Ted smiled. One of the little realities of interplanetary combat that civilians were persistently unable to grasp was that an object, once in motion, *remained* in motion. There was no need for a rocket engine to push the object forward, not like there would be in a planetary atmosphere. The mass driver projectiles would keep going until they ran into something...which, in interplanetary space, wasn't too likely to happen. It was one of the reasons humanity had shied away from using mass drivers as weapons. One could be fired at a starship in orbit and miss, hitting the planet instead with terrifying force.

"Good," he said. Fourteen of the escorting frigates had their own mass drivers, ready to add their fire to *Ark Royal's* own. The targeting wouldn't be precisely accurate, but hundreds of solid projectiles would be rocketing through space occupied by the alien formation. Unless, of course, the aliens decided to move before the projectiles reached them. "You may fire at will."

The display changed as the first stream of projectiles launched from the giant carrier, rocketing away at a fair percentage of the speed of light. Ted silently calculated the odds against the aliens spotting them in advance, then silently prayed that the aliens didn't have a piece of technology that shattered humanity's preconceptions. The search for a FTL sensor had been one of the holy grails of human technology for so long that most naval officers had come to believe it was impossible. But they'd believed the same of long-range FTL tramlines.

"Projectiles away, sir," Farley said. On the display, the frigates were launching their own projectiles. "Impact projected in two hours, forty minutes."

"Continue firing until we have drained our magazines to thirty percent," Ted ordered. He was tempted to throw everything he had at the aliens, but he knew the value of keeping a reserve. It was unlikely that *all* of the alien craft would be destroyed by the bombardment. "Launch the unpowered missiles."

He gritted his teeth. It went against the grain to launch unpowered missiles – they had many of the risks of using mass drivers, without some of the advantages – but there was no choice. Unlike the alien fleet, the starships they had covering the planet seemed to alter course randomly, as if they knew they were being observed. The missiles, when they went active, would be able to alter their courses to bring them to bear on the alien ships. None of the mass driver projectiles could be so flexible.

But they're also expensive, he thought, thinking wistfully of the battleship designs he'd seen during the extensive debriefings following their first encounter with the alien forces. *Given a few years, we will have entire starships crammed with mass drivers...and lose some of the flexibility in having missiles.*

The stream of projectiles came to an end. "We've reached thirty percent of our stockpiles," Farley reported. "Holding fire."

"Good," Ted muttered. He raised his voice, fighting the urge to whisper. "Take us out on the pre-planned course."

The downside of ballistic projectiles was that they didn't change course. Given a few moments, the aliens could easily project their course backwards and locate *Ark Royal*. But, once they'd moved, the aliens would be wasting their effort...or so he hoped.

He shook his head. Now, all they had to do was wait...and see how the aliens reacted. He tried to form a mental picture of their entire fleet smashed, like bugs, but he knew it wasn't likely to happen. They'd be lucky if they crippled or destroyed more than a carrier or two. "And the Russians?"

"They're on their way," Farley confirmed.

Poor brave stupid idiots, Ted thought. The odds against the Russians making it to the surface were staggering – and that assumed that the diversionary plan worked perfectly. If it didn't...somehow, Ted doubted the aliens would just ignore a mystery heat trail burning through the planet's atmosphere. A single plasma blast would vaporise the Russian commandos, along with their fancy suits and re-entry gear.

He shook his head. All they could do now was wait.

———

"So the attack is underway," Yang said. "The aliens have no idea we're here?"

"So it would seem," James agreed. Yang, at least, understood some of the implications. And he was smart enough not to demand immediate results. Space was big and – he glanced at the timer – there would still be several hours before they knew what, if anything, they'd hit. "They certainly haven't ambushed us, even when we moved away from the tramline."

That had been hair-raising for the naval personal, although he'd been fairly sure that few of the reporters had understood just how much the danger was increasing. The aliens wouldn't launch an attack while the flotilla was nesting within the tramline, if only because the humans ships would simply trigger their drives and jump out. No, he knew, they'd wait until the humans were well away from any means of escape before attacking. But no attack had materialised. Had the aliens thought *Ark Royal* wasn't going to New Russia after all? Or was the main body of their fleet off trashing Britannia, Washington…or Earth?

It was one of his private nightmares. *Ark Royal* might attack New Russia, she might even drive the aliens *away* from New Russia…and then return home to discover that the aliens had torn Earth apart. Maybe the human race knew, now, that the aliens weren't invincible. They still packed one hell of a punch.

Barbie caught his arm. "It's so *slow*," she protested. "Why didn't you go closer before opening fire?"

James swallowed the response that came to mind. "The aliens might have detected us," he said, instead. The problem with modern depictions of space combat, he knew, was that they were *fast*. Instead of long hours of boredom, there were hours of constant excitement. "We decided to fire from extreme range instead."

"But they could move," Barbie said, slowly. "They might not be there when your shots arrive."

"That's true," James said, in some surprise. He wouldn't have expected Barbie to reason *that* much out; hell, he was mildly surprised she could even tie her own shoelaces. "But it's a risk we have to take."

He sighed, inwardly, as the reporters turned back to look at the display. Civilian politicians wanted to minimise risk as much as possible, but military officers knew that some risks just had to be accepted. Besides, it wasn't as if the projectiles cost anything. A few hours alongside an asteroid and the carrier could replenish its stockpiles without particular difficulty.

None of the reporters looked very good, he noted, with a certain amount of malice. They'd been up since *Ark Royal* had entered the system, remaining awake out of fear of missing something interesting. Hell, even James and the Captain had made time for catnaps, while the starfighter pilots had each spent an hour in the sleep machines. They'd regret it later,

James suspected, but it would keep them alert for the moment. But the reporters...it didn't even seem to have occurred to them that they *all* had access to the datanet. If they missed something personally, they could review it before *Ark Royal* returned to Earth.

A chime sounded. He looked up at the display, worried. Four new red icons had entered the system from an unexpected direction.

"Four ships, unknown class," Farley reported. "Temporary designation; Alien-Six. All ships are heading towards the planet."

James nodded, studying the alien vessels. They were larger than frigates, but smaller than *Ark Royal* or any other known carrier design, human or alien. Humanity hadn't been too keen on the idea of producing giant starships, apart from the carriers, believing them to be easy targets. But now...humanity was working on its battleship design and the aliens, it seemed, had larger warships of their own. Judging from the power curves, the ships might be battlecruisers or something similar.

Barbie coughed. "Are they hunting us?"

"I don't think so," James said, as reassuringly as he could. Personally, he suspected the aliens were readying themselves to launch an attack on another human world. *Ark Royal* might have closed one backdoor, but there were plenty of others. An attack on another major colony world – even if it wasn't Earth – would place the human alliance under considerable strain. "I think they're preparing the invasion."

He concealed his amusement at her expression, then glanced at the timer again. The minutes were ticking away, but there was still another hour before the projectiles passed through the alien position. If the aliens moved, they would have fired all of those projectiles for nothing. And the Russians were still drifting through space, heading towards New Russia... they'd be dead before they even knew they were under attack.

Poor bastards, he thought.

———

"Hurry up and wait," Rose chanted. "Hurry up and wait."

Kurt sighed. They'd had the opportunity for a shower, as well as a quick nap in the sleep machine, but none of them felt very good. Spending hours in the cockpit out in space was one thing – it was easy to forget that they *were* in a tiny starfighter when surrounded by the vastness of interstellar space – yet spending them in the cockpit while in the launch tubes was quite another. He couldn't really blame Rose for being antsy. The tension of their first combat jump had faded away, replaced by a tedium that gnawed at their combat readiness.

He clicked onto the private channel and called her. "Behave yourself," he said, sternly. Had *he* been such a handful when he'd been a mere pilot? Rose was supposed to be setting a good example for her new subordinates. "There is a war on, even if we are not allowed to fight it just yet."

Rose snorted, rudely. "At this rate," she pointed out, "we will be in no condition to fight when the shit hits the fan."

"Hey, you want to complain, go join the reporters," Kurt said. "Failing that, shut up and put up."

There was no reply, leaving him alone with his thoughts. Rose was right, unfortunately; the longer they remained psyched up to launch, the less ready they'd be to fight when they actually blasted out of the launch tubes and faced the aliens. But there was no way to avoid it, unless they gambled on remaining in the ready rooms...but, given how quickly a situation could move from controlled to a desperate battle for survival, they couldn't rely on being able to launch in time.

"Sorry," Rose said, finally.

Kurt understood. She *was* young, without the maturity that came with age and greater experience. But then, few of the Royal Navy's starfighter pilots had any real combat experience...not until now. Kurt suspected that a few years of heavy fighting would rapidly separate the true pilots from the men and women who had signed up merely to wear the uniform. Rose, he decided, would be a true pilot with a little more seasoning.

But, for the moment, she just had to learn to...hurry up and wait.

"Don't worry about it," he said, kindly. He checked the timer. Twenty minutes until the shower of rocks cascaded through where the aliens were...or had been. Twenty minutes until the aliens knew that they were under attack. *Ark Royal* and her flotilla had changed position, of course, but the aliens would still have a rough idea of where they were. "Just stay alert."

He sighed. It was definitely easier said than done.

———

Ted looked up at the display, mentally ticking off the last few minutes before the projectiles flashed through the alien-occupied position. Behind them, a handful of recon platforms and drones were already manoeuvring closer, hoping to provide an accurate record of just what happened when the projectiles hit home. It would be risky – the aliens would start looking for the platforms as soon as they knew what had hit them – but he needed to know just how badly hammered the aliens had been.

"One minute," Farley said.

Ted braced himself. If they'd had more ships, with more projectiles, they could have swept more of space for alien targets. But they had to work with what they had. He cautioned himself not to get too optimistic; the projectiles and the alien carriers were tiny, in the grand scheme of things. It was entirely possible that all they'd do was alert the aliens that they were being watched, without hitting a single target.

"Thirty seconds," Farley added. He counted down the last few seconds. "Ten...five...contact!"

CHAPTER
TWENTY TWO

The recon platform had no name, nor did it want one. It was nothing more than a cluster of passive sensors, a handful of gas jets and a single laser communicator, governed by the most advanced automated systems the human race had been able to produce. There was no such thing as a true AI, at least not yet, but the controlling systems were capable of reacting to almost anything. Now, it opened its passive sensors to their full extent – taking the risk of having them blinded – and watched as the invisible projectiles smashed into the alien fleet.

Four smaller alien craft and a carrier were hit at once, all four damaged beyond repair. The remaining carriers brought up their active sensors and started sweeping space for threats, then opened fire with their point defence. Lacking any armour or means to evade incoming fire, the remaining projectiles started to vanish, one by one. The recon platform noted that the aliens took several shots to destroy each projectile, but they were definitely capable of putting out enough firepower to do it. Unbothered by human emotional reactions, the recon platform observed the destruction of another alien carrier, followed by the loss of dozens of other projectiles. Hundreds of alien starfighters swarmed free, advancing rapidly outwards to locate and destroy other projectiles. Behind them, the starships brought up their drives and started to fan out rapidly.

Faithfully, unaware of its impending destruction, the recon platform reported everything to its mothership.

Ivan had no doubts. Like the rest of his team, their emotional reactions had been minimised by the surgeons who had turned them into cyborg commandos. It was a must, he'd been told when he no longer had the emotional capability to react to what they'd done to him; they didn't dare allow their cyborgs to keep the full range of human emotions. The horror ordinary humans would feel at losing their genitals and being turned into inhuman monsters was nothing more than a minor notion to the cyborgs.

Hours of drifting through space in an unpowered shuttlecraft didn't bother him either. Yes, he knew – intellectually – that the alien sensor grids might locate his shuttlecraft and blow it out of space, vaporising it so completely that they wouldn't have a chance to test their capabilities for operating in space without a spacesuit. But it was merely an abstract concept to him. They had a mission and they would complete it or die trying.

There was no need to talk. All six cyborgs were linked together through low-power radio signals, allowing them to share thoughts and concepts without needing to open their mouths. Indeed, as they'd grown closer and closer together, they had stopped talking to others, apart from when it was strictly necessary. Ordinary humans, even Russians, feared the cyborgs, they knew. It wasn't something that bothered them. The cyborgs existed to serve as front-line commandos, nothing else. If ordinary humans were scared of them, so much the better.

Now, they prepared themselves as the unpowered missiles went active, coming online and lancing after the alien craft. The alien frigates didn't seem surprised to come under attack; they merely altered course and started to open fire with their point defence. Half of the missiles kept targeting the frigates anyway, the remainder altered course and headed down towards the planet. Assuming the odd radio signals were actually alien settlements, the cyborgs had decided when they were planning the operation, the aliens would have to concentrate on preventing the missiles from punching through the atmosphere. Unless they had radically good sensors, they would have no way to tell that the missiles carried no warheads. They'd be forced to assume nukes – or worse.

The concept of unleashing nuclear fire on alien civilians didn't bother the cyborgs. They'd had emotional reactions engineered out of them. Ivan had watched, dispassionately, as his fellow cyborgs had waged murderous war on the enemies of Mother Russia. The fact that those enemies included subversives who were, technically speaking, Russian themselves didn't bother him either. If they chose to defy the government's orders, they deserved all they got. It had been programmed into him on the day of his rebirth.

There were times when he wondered who he'd been before he'd entered the cyborg program and turned into a monstrous amalgamation of flesh and metal. Memories of another life sometimes flickered through his dreams, suggesting that once he'd been something other than a cyborg. But the dreams were nothing more than illusions, he'd been told. It wasn't something to concern himself with, not when there was no shortage of work to do.

At precisely the right moment, the cyborgs uploaded the final set of commands into the shuttle, triggering a series of explosive bolts. Wrapped in protective orbs, they plunged out of the shuttle and rocked down towards the planet's atmosphere, surrounded by the pieces of the shuttle. To human sensors, at least, it would look as through the shuttle had broken up in flight, perhaps after launching the missiles that had bedevilled the alien frigates. But if it failed…

Ivan had no doubts. He'd done all he could. Now, all he could do was wait and drop through the planet's atmosphere. And if they failed, they failed.

It was all the same to the cyborgs.

———

"Two alien carriers destroyed, nine smaller ships picked off," Farley reported. He nodded to the display, which was swarming with red icons. "I think we made them mad."

Ted smiled. "Pull us back towards the tramline," he ordered, as the alien sensors started to sweep through space for a hint of the flotilla's presence. If they managed to get out of the system before the aliens got a clear lock on them, the aliens would waste hours searching for a flotilla that had already departed. Or maybe they'd just blame everything on the Russian stragglers in the outer system. "What about the Russian commandos?"

"They made it into the atmosphere," Farley said, checking the live feed from one of the probes. "Other than that…we don't know."

Ted silently wished them good luck, then turned his attention back to the swarming alien fighters. The aliens seemed determined to ramp up their sensors to the point where human sensors would significantly damage themselves, although their ships showed no traces of the problems human sensors would rapidly develop. Behind the sensor sweeps, swarms of starfighters were advancing forwards, heading towards the human tramlines. Someone, Ted realised, was thinking ahead. The tramlines were the only way out of the system and blocking them was the quickest way to prevent Ark Royal from escaping.

"Accelerate towards Tramline Three," he ordered. The alien starfighters would get there first, but he was quite prepared to bet that Ark Royal could blast her way through them even without the help of the flotilla. "Launch a second set of drones towards the alien ships and…"

The display flared red for a long chilling moment, then faded back to black. "They swept us with a high-power radar," Farley reported. Long minutes passed as they waited to see if the aliens would lock on, then the display turned red again. This time, it stayed that way. "They've got a solid fix on our location."

Ted swore, although he'd expected it from the moment the aliens had started powering up their sensors. Ark Royal might have been impossible to separate from an asteroid if she'd been lying doggo, but a carrier moving at high speed was instantly recognisable. On the display, a swarm of alien starfighters turned and gave chase, followed by the smaller ships.

"Order our starfighters to prepare to launch," Ted ordered. "Go active; ramp up our own sensors as much as possible. There's no point in trying to hide any longer."

"I guess we poked the hornet's nest," Fitzwilliam said, from the CIC. "Mass drivers are unlikely to score hits at this range."

Ted nodded. The alien ships were accelerating forwards, but they were also altering their courses randomly, making it impossible to predict their location in time to fire at them with the mass drivers. Besides, with a swarm of starfighters covering their asses, it was unlikely that any projectiles would get through and do some real damage. Shotgunning them might have an effect, but not enough to make the expenditure worthwhile.

"The newcomers are also on their way," Farley noted. "They're pulling quite a high clip."

"Fast buggers," Fitzwilliam's voice said. "I don't think we could match them."

"True," Ted agreed. The alien carriers didn't seem to have a better acceleration rate that a modern human carrier – which still gave them an edge over *Ark Royal* – but the alien battlecruisers definitely had the highest acceleration rate ever recorded. It would be tricky for a human ship to match it, at least without heavy reengineering. But it was clear that they were going to have to do just that, sooner rather than later. "Calculate prospective intercept vectors."

He ran through them in his head, then checked them against the computer. The larger alien ships were unlikely to run them down until they crossed the tramline, but the smaller fighters would definitely try to slow them down. Even if they hadn't improved their weaponry, Ted knew he couldn't rule out the prospect of a lucky shot…or, for that matter, the simple destruction of his ship's ability to shoot back. Once they'd stripped *Ark Royal* of her defences, they would allow the bigger ships to catch up and blow his carrier apart.

"Enemy fighters will enter intercept range in ten minutes," Farley warned.

And if they had mass drivers, they would have used them by now, Ted told himself. He hoped, desperately, that he was right. A single direct hit with a mass driver would smash his ship like an eggshell.

"Launch fighters at the seven minute mark," Ted ordered. That should give his pilots enough time to launch and get into intercept position. "Hold the bombers for the moment."

Silently, he cursed the decision not to build any more *Ark Royal*-class carriers…or even makeshift escort carriers. He didn't have the starfighters to cover both his hull *and* escort the bombers to their targets, while the aliens – with their multirole fighters – had no trouble doing both. Maybe he should have pleaded with the Admiralty to assign additional modern carriers to the flotilla…but he knew they would have refused. The modern carriers, once the queens of space, were now too vulnerable to be easily risked.

"Aye, sir," Farley said. "Fighters are primed now."

"Use one of the drones to try to raise the planet," Ted ordered. If the Russians had any form of passive sensors left in orbit – or even simple ground-based telescopes – they'd know that *someone* was attacking the occupation force. And there was definitely no point in trying to hide now. "Transmit the pre-recorded message and wait for a reply."

Until the drone is destroyed, he thought, absently. The planners might not have realised it, but the moment the drone started transmitting its signal, the aliens would know precisely where it was lurking. They'd send a starfighter to vaporise it within minutes. But at least the Russians on the ground, assuming they still have a radio receiver, would know that they weren't alone.

But they'd also know that the human raiders had retreated.

He shook his head, absently. There was no alternative. The Russians would know, at least, that the rest of human space remained free…and that the aliens were far from invincible. And they would have hope…

———

To an unprepared civilian, the tactical display was a indecipherable mixture of red and green lights, dancing around in seemingly random patterns. The fact that most of his fellow reporters couldn't understand what they were seeing, Marcus Yang suspected, was all that was stopping them from panicking. Marcus, who *could* read it, could tell that a formidable alien force was giving chase, bent on destroying the imprudent carrier that had given them a bloody nose.

He settled back, watching – with some private amusement – the reactions shown by his fellow reporters. Barbie seemed shocked at the carnage, even though it was minuscule compared to the Battle of New Russia. No, the *first* Battle of New Russia, he corrected himself. One way or another, this was definitely the second. Other reporters seemed almost pleased. They knew that humanity hitting back would make for high ratings...assuming, of course, they survived the experience.

Barbie looked over at him, her too-wide eyes disturbingly inhuman in the darkened compartment. "What is happening now?"

Marcus hesitated, then made a deliberate decision to be kind. "We're withdrawing from the system," he said, which was true enough. If, of course, a few of the details – such as an onrushing alien fleet – were left out. "You'll have time to file your story soon enough."

Barbie gave him a pitiful glare. "How can you be so calm?"

Marcus shrugged. "Whatever happens, happens," he said. Being an embed in ground forces had taught him that bullets, IEDs and mortar shells were no respecters of press credentials. Nor were insurgents, as a general rule, and they tended to be savvy enough to check which reporters they'd kidnapped before deciding what to do with them. Some reporters had been released with exclusive interviews, others had been brutally raped, tortured and then murdered. "There's nothing I can do about it, so why worry?"

He smiled at her. The display kept them curiously disconnected from reality, but that would change when the aliens started hammering at *Ark Royal's* hull. And they would, he was sure; this time, the aliens had enough firepower to just punch their way through the carrier's defenders.

"You may as well relax too," he added. "There's nothing you can do to help or hinder operations."

———

"Launch fighters," Ted ordered.

"Aye, sir," Farley said. He pressed a switch on his console. "Fighters launching, now."

———

Kurt winced as the starfighter rocketed out the launch tube and into open space, followed rapidly by the rest of his pilots. Ahead of them, one cluster of alien fighters rested on the tramline; behind them, a colossal cloud of alien starfighters was catching up rapidly with the flotilla. There were so many of them that the sensors seemed to be having problems picking individual starfighters out of the cloud. Kurt had never seen so many starfighters outside exercises and flying displays for the King's birthday.

"Wonderful," Rose said. She sounded better, now they were in open space with an enemy force bearing down on them. They could take their frustration out on the enemy pilots. "I make it twenty enemy fighters each. We'll all be aces by the time this is done."

"True," Kurt agreed. "Alpha and Beta squadrons; break up the enemy formation. Delta and Gamma, mind the carrier."

The starfighters rocketed forwards, slipping past the frigates moving into intercept positions. Kurt scowled at them, hoping and praying that the IFF systems worked perfectly, even though he feared they wouldn't. It was bad enough with British systems alone, but when several other nations were involved...he gritted his teeth. In hindsight, the strongest argument against there being any foreknowledge of the alien attack was that there had been no attempt to ensure that all human technology was compatible.

But if someone had tried, he thought, *would it have been accepted*?

He pushed the thought aside as his squadron raced towards the alien craft at a staggering closing speed. Quickly, he flipped his weapons on to automatic – he'd have to gamble that the computers didn't accidentally take a shot at an allied starfighter – then braced himself, keeping his starfighter on a random course. It seemed only seconds before the guns started chattering away, spitting out tiny balls of metal towards the alien fighters. Kurt saw a handful of icons vanish from the display, only to be replaced instantly by other alien craft. *His* starfighters weren't replaced so quickly...

"Alpha-five and Alpha-seven are gone," Alpha-nine reported. Kurt hadn't even *seen* Alpha-seven die. "Alpha-three is disabled..."

Lucky bastard, Kurt thought. A fluke, a million-to-one shot that had damaged a starfighter, rather than destroying it outright. Behind him, the alien starfighters disengaged and roared towards the flotilla. Cursing, he yanked his starfighter around and gave chase, while Delta and Gamma squadrons rose up to cover the carrier. There were so many alien starfighters that some of them were almost certain to get through.

———

"Incoming starfighters," Farley reported. "Weapons range in thirty seconds."

"Open fire as soon as they enter effective weapons range," Ted ordered. The alien starfighters were ducking and weaving past the frigates, refusing to engage them. It made sense, Ted knew; if they could cripple *Ark Royal*, the frigates were unlikely to make any difference to the balance of power. Still, he would have preferred the aliens to show tactical inflexibility rather than a limited degree of imagination. "Fire at will."

He braced himself as the starfighters roared down on the carrier, scorching her hull with plasma bolts. It looked like random fire – it *was* random fire, he knew – but it had a very definite purpose. The aliens didn't have to target precisely to do damage…and, for them, spraying and praying was actually a viable tactic. Piece by piece, the damage mounted…

The carrier shuddered, slightly.

"Report," Ted snapped.

"One of the aliens crashed into our hull," Anderson said. "No major damage, sir."

But the minor damage was steadily mounting up, Ted knew. One of the mass drivers was already crippled and would need a week of repair before it was ready to use again. Other weapons and sensor blisters had already been destroyed, crippling the carrier's ability to defend herself.

"Captain," Farley snapped. Ted heard a hint of panic in his voice. "New contacts!"

Ted swung around and stared at the display. A new series of red icons had appeared, right in front of them…and blocking their escape route from the system.

They were trapped.

CHAPTER
TWENTY THREE

For a moment, Ted's tired mind refused to believe his eyes. How the hell had the aliens managed to get a force in position to come through the tramline and block their escape? If the aliens had a way to communicate at FTL speeds, without sending ships through the tramlines, humanity was thoroughly screwed. There was no way to move inside the alien decision-making loop when the alien leadership could follow events at the front from hundreds of light years away.

Or was it just sheer luck? The aliens had known that the flotilla was poking around; they might have stationed a fleet in the system, then ordered it to move after *Ark Royal* once the alien fleet at New Russia came under attack. It would work...and it would have the advantage of confusing their enemies. Ted pushed the thought aside for later contemplation as the aliens started to deploy. He could attack the newcomers – he would have to attack the newcomers, if he wanted to use that tramline – and yet the force in to pursuit would catch up and overwhelm the flotilla. If he turned back to fight them, he would still be overwhelmed.

His mind worked frantically, searching for a solution. There was no way they could break contact and hide, not with the aliens close enough to track them even if they shut down all systems and pretended to be a hole in space. The aliens would have a rough idea of where they were, allowing them to sweep space until they stumbled over the lurking carrier. And *that* assumed they managed to break contact for a few seconds in the first place. Nor could the other tramlines be reached...

He pulled up the in-system display and contemplated it. New Russia had five human-usable tramlines, three of which led to other human settlements. The aliens would have blockaded them by now, placing smaller forces in position to intercept anything that came through the tramlines – or *Ark Royal*, if she attempted to make it out. One more – the one he had intended to use – was also thoroughly blockaded, but the other...? He looked down at the reports from the drones and frowned. They might just be able to make it.

It could be a trap, he knew. Maybe it led to a red giant, utterly useless to anyone save astronomers who wanted to study, but it was still odd for the aliens to leave it uncovered. But it did make a certain kind of sense. The aliens didn't have unlimited numbers of ships, so they covered the most important targets, assuming that Tramline Five wouldn't be used by a human counterattack. They might well be right, Ted considered. Tramline Five led *away* from the core of human space and Earth. At the very least, *Ark Royal* was committing herself and her fleet to several months away from human contact.

"Set course for Tramline Five," he ordered. "Maximum speed."

He gritted his teeth. On the display, the alien starfighters were swooping back for another engagement. They'd already stripped *Ark Royal* of a handful of point defence weapons; now, they were taking advantage of the carrier's blind spots to get closer to the hull and take out other targets. His own starfighters were chasing them down, at the risk of being accidentally picked off themselves by the carrier's point defence. If the battering continued, the aliens would eventually render the carrier completely defenceless.

"Target the alien carriers with missiles," he ordered, "then launch decoys. Confuse them as long as possible."

"Aye, sir," Farley said.

Ted forced himself to remain calm and composed on the outside, even through part of him wanted to panic and the rest of him wanted a drink. The crew couldn't see their commander panicking, not when they knew they were in deep shit. He cursed inwardly as one of the frigates vanished, even as the remainder opened fire. A second salvo of missiles headed towards the newcomers, forcing them to look to their own defence. Farley hastily reprogrammed some of the missiles to take out incoming alien starfighters, using the nukes to sweep space clean. The aliens rapidly adapted and spread out, refusing to allow the humans to pick them off again.

He felt a dull tremor running through the carrier as she altered course, heading up and away from the system plane towards Tramline Five. For a long moment, the combination of ECM drones and nuclear explosions seemed to confuse the aliens, but it didn't last long enough for Ark Royal to break contact. The ECM crews took advantage of the brief pause to launch additional drones, giving the aliens several possible targets to engage. Ted would take whatever distraction he could get, but he knew it wouldn't last very long. Ark Royal was the only target shooting back at the aliens, after all.

"Order the flotilla to cover our back," he added. He'd started the operation with twenty-four frigates. Now, he had eighteen, several of which had taken heavy damage. But it would be a great deal worse, he knew, when the aliens got into weapons range. "And deploy the modified nukes, both types."

One of the brighter eggheads on Earth had speculated that the alien plasma cannons used magnetic fields to keep the bursts of superheated plasma under control. So far, duplicating the technique had proven beyond humanity's technology, but the egghead had gone on to suggest that an EMP might successfully disrupt the containment field, causing the aliens to lose control of their weapons. There might even be an explosion, the egghead had predicted, when the containment field failed. At the very least, the EMP would cripple the alien ability to keep firing.

Ted had his doubts. Humans had been building EMP-shielding into their technology since the day they'd first realised the potentially devastating effects of an electromagnetic pulse. The first use of EMP-weapons in war had only underlined the dangers, forcing the development of countermeasures forward at terrifying speed. Surely, the aliens would have gone through their own period of using nukes...but the egghead had doubted that the aliens *could* shield their magnetic containment fields. Now...Ted braced himself. The concept was about to the put to the test.

"Nukes away, sir," Farley said. Unpowered, the missiles would slip through the cloud of alien starfighters...unless they got very unlucky and actually struck an alien ship directly. "Time to detonation, seven minutes."

Ted nodded. The alien frigates were closing in rapidly, threatening to bring their plasma weapons to bear on humanity's frigates. No matter the sheer weight of armour wrapped about the ships, Ted knew, the human frigates were doomed if the aliens entered firing range. He wondered, absently, how long it would take the eggheads to come up with a directed energy weapon humans could use, one that worked better than point defence lasers. Even a small level of armour could provide protection against the lasers.

The display flared red, suddenly. "The enemy got a clear shot at *Rio*," Farley reported. "She's badly damaged, sir..."

Another icon flared red, then vanished. "She's gone," Farley said.

Ted winced. Another human frigate, a crew of thirty men and women, gone in an instant. But there was no time to mourn. A moment later, the analysts started twittering for his attention. He hesitated, then keyed the switch to hear what they had to say. They seemed to believe that the aliens had fired at extreme range, damaging *Rio* rather than destroying her outright. It had been the secondary damage that had killed the ship. Under the circumstances, Ted found it hard to care about the difference. The ship was still dead.

"Nukes detonating now," Farley said, sharply. "EMPs...underway."

"Good," Ted said. If the EMPs failed, they'd just wasted a handful of nukes for nothing. "Let me know..."

One of the alien craft flared white on the display, then vanished. Others seemed to stagger briefly, the sensors picking up odd flickers of energy on their hulls. The remainder stepped down their drives, allowing the distance between them and their prey to widen. Ted laughed as he realised that, for once, the eggheads had got something right. The destroyed ship must have been on the verge of unleashing a full blast of plasma itself, only to lose containment as the EMP detonated.

"Deploy the second set of nukes," Ted ordered. On the display, the alien starfighters seemed to be pulling back, sweeping empty space rather than going after human targets. It looked odd, almost as if they were giving up the chase...it took him a long moment to realise that they were looking for other nukes. "Then launch powered missiles towards the alien starfighters."

"Aye, sir," Farley said.

———

Kurt felt sweat trickling down his back as he pulled his starfighter around and fired a burst of pellets towards a retreating alien fighter. They missed; he swore venomously as warning lights blinked up on the display, reminding him that he was critically low on ammunition. The aliens, damn them, could keep firing indefinitely, but the humans needed to reload... he glanced at the shared datanet and swore again. He was by no means the only pilot who needed to reload his weapons.

"Beta, return to the hanger and rearm," he ordered. His pilots needed a nap, a shower and some food, perhaps not in that order, but they weren't going to get it. *Ark Royal* had won a breathing space, yet he knew better than to think it would last long enough for anything other than a quick reloading session. "Alpha; hold position and wait."

The fighting seemed to die down as the aliens continued their withdrawal, clearly taking the time necessary to work out what had happened to their frigate and devise countermeasures. Kurt busied himself by supervising the reloading process, then devising a potential attack pattern of his own. If nukes could strip an enemy craft of its point defence – and it looked like they could – he could use a nuke to clear the way for the bombers. But it would only work, he realised numbly, if the aliens were actually charging up their weapons when the nuke detonated. Or were their weapons *always* charged? The records suggested, very strongly, that the aliens could discharge plasma bursts from all over their hull.

He felt his entire body aching as he returned his fighter to the hanger, then waited impatiently as the ground crew hastily reloaded his guns. They'd drilled, time and time again, until it took no longer than five minutes to reload and prepare for a second launch, but it was always different when they were under fire. At least the aliens still seemed to be keeping their distance, although both of their formations were starting to merge into one. It didn't *look* as though they had a third force in position to cut the humans off...

"I'm getting too old for this shit," he muttered. "I should have volunteered for the home defence squadrons."

"And then you would never have your pretty uniform mussed," Rose said, sardonically. "And all the pretty girls would know you for a coward."

Kurt cursed – he was too tired to remember that everything he said was broadcast to the rest of the squadron – as the other pilots added their comments. Most of them seemed to agree that being assigned to a home defence squadron was the same as being sentenced to a very slow death, even though it was quite likely that the home defence squadrons would last longer. But then, there had always been a tendency to undervalue such squadrons. They might not have been assigned to carriers, but that didn't make them cowards. Hell, Kurt honestly had never met a pilot who hadn't applied to serve on a carrier. It was always more exciting than being assigned to a home defence squadron.

"You ask me, sir," another pilot put in, "it's the same in starfighters as it is in fucking."

Kurt rolled his eyes. "Really?"

"Of course, sir," the pilot said. "You get into your bird and take her to heaven, twice a day."

There was a long pause. "I seem to recall," Rose said, sweetly, "that both of your last two girlfriends ended up together."

"*Hey,*" the pilot protested.

"They must have bonded over the trauma of dating you," Rose added. "I think they were planning to get married, the last I heard."

Kurt smiled, although he knew there was little true humour in the situation. They knew, they all knew, that death was likely to claim them soon enough. Joking around was their way of dealing with it. But, at the end of the day, it wasn't likely to matter. He spared a thought for his children – and Molly, no matter how much they argued – and gripped his stick as the starfighter was hurled back into space. The aliens were resuming the attack.

———

"They took out the powered missiles, sir," Farley reported. "But the unpowered warheads are in position."

Ted nodded. "Activate them as soon as the enemy come within range, keyed to detonate at the first possible moment," he ordered. On the display, the aliens had reorganised their squadrons, their starfighters zooming ahead, coming in for the kill. The brief pause in combat hadn't been anything like enough for the damage control parties to perform anything other than brief repairs. "And then move our starfighters to cover our hull."

He held his breath as the alien starfighters roared past the missiles, ignoring them completely. Instead, they rocketed down towards *Ark Royal*...he muttered orders, sending his starfighters out to engage them before they could slip into one of the new blind spots, then watched as the enemy carriers closed in on the hidden missiles.

"Detonation," Farley snapped.

Ted allowed himself a smirk as the first warhead detonated, channelling all of its power into a laser beam that slashed into the alien hull. *Ark Royal* would have taken most of the blow on her armour, but the aliens hadn't seen fit to wrap their carriers in layers of protective shielding. The blast tore into one of the carriers, sending it rolling out of formation. Behind it, the alien frigates and battlecruisers spread out, searching for new threats. Now, Ted knew, they could no longer rely on their point defence to take out human missiles before they became dangerous.

He looked back at the in-system display, hastily weighing their chances. If they could last another thirty minutes, they could reach Tramline Five...but the aliens would follow them through the jump. He briefly considered attempting to mine the exit point, yet he knew that it would be a chancy operation. The aliens might not run into one of the contact nukes as they exited the tramline. Instead...

"Engineering," he said, "I want you to prepare to eject as much debris as possible, as soon as we hop through the tramline."

"Understood," Anderson said. "You propose to trick them into believing that we destroyed ourselves?"

"Yes," Ted said. If a Puller Drive was badly damaged, it wasn't unknown for a starship to arrive at her destination star system in pieces. *Ark Royal* was nowhere near that badly damaged, but it was unlikely the aliens knew that. And, if the explosion seemed big enough, it might well have swallowed the other ships too. "Let them think us gone."

"We don't have enough debris to pull it off," Anderson said. "But we could probably create the illusion on *this* side of the tramline, if you don't mind losing the ECM drones."

Ted smirked. Each ECM drone cost upwards of a billion pounds apiece and he was sure to face some hard questions from the beancounters when they returned to Earth, but the alternative was losing *Ark Royal* herself. No, he decided, shaking his head. The bureaucrats could go hang. If they wanted to complain, they could do it afterwards, when at least he would have brought his ship home.

"See to it," he ordered.

The alien attack grew more savage as the human ships crawled closer and closer to Tramline Five. Thankfully, the alien capital ships seemed to be keeping their distance, but the starfighters pressed the attack time and time again. Ted watched, grimly, as two of his starfighters were lost because the pilots were too tired to focus properly on what they were doing. Between tiredness and the aliens, he might lose a third of his starfighters before they even managed to make it out of the cursed system.

Finally, Anderson called him. "Everything is in order, sir," he said. "I recommend having the starfighters docked to our hull when we make the jump. And that we fire missiles and mass drivers at the aliens to keep them occupied."

Ted nodded. "Do it," he ordered Farley. Ahead of them, Tramline Five blinked on the display. "Launch the drones as soon as we reach the outer edge of the tramline."

The alien starfighters pulled back as the missiles were launched, leaving the carrier alone as they engaged the missiles. Oddly, they didn't seem to care about the mass driver-launched projectiles, although they might simply have calculated that there was little chance of the projectiles hitting anything important. Ted gripped the side of his command chair as the drones went to work, skilfully creating a false image that should confuse the aliens long enough for them to jump…

"Jumping…*now*," Lightbridge said.

Space seemed to twist around the massive carrier as she jumped through the tramline. Behind them, the drones created the illusion of the carrier's sudden destruction, caught in a gravimetric fold that smashed her and her comrades into rubble. The aliens would want to believe it, Ted knew. But would they?

"Jump completed," Lightbridge said. "No enemy contacts detected."

"Activate full stealth protocol," Ted ordered. The advantage of hitting the tramline at speed was that there was no way to predict their vector on the other side. Even their arrival point could be dangerously random. "I don't want a single *hint* of betraying emissions to reach their sensors."

And then pray, he added, in the privacy of his own thoughts. If the aliens caught them with drives, weapons and sensors stepped down, they were dead.

CHAPTER
TWENTY FOUR

Kurt guided his starfighter into the landing bay then sagged, barely able to move. He was utterly exhausted. Part of him just wanted to close his eyes and sleep, even though he knew he had to move. The aliens could be on them at any moment. Somehow, he managed to open the hatch and stumble out onto the deck. None of his fellow pilots, even the younger ones, looked much better.

"All hands," the intercom blared, "rig for silent running. I say again, rig for silent running."

"Crap," Kurt muttered. They were *all* exhausted – and yet, at least one squadron would have to remain on alert. He looked up, then keyed his communicator. "Move the bomber pilots to the spare fighters and prime them for immediate launch."

Shouldn't be trying to combine CAG duties with flying duties, he mocked himself, as he led the way through the airlock and into the ready room. He knew he was right; the CAG should remain separate from his squadrons, not leading them into battle. But there just weren't enough pilots onboard for him to refuse to fly a starfighter. And he didn't *want* to stand on his rights and refuse to fly. There was a reason CAGs weren't always taken seriously unless they flew every so often.

His fingers refused to cooperate properly as he wrestled with his flight suit. It took several minutes to remove it and leave it on the deck as he stumbled into the shower and gasped as icy cold water washed over his body. Behind him, the other pilots stumbled in, too tired to indulge in the laughing and joking they would normally have used to break the tension. He caught a glimpse of a female pilot's breasts, then forced himself to look away, damning himself for staring. It was a breakdown in discipline his squadron could ill afford.

Somehow, he managed to make it out of the shower and over to the sleep machines. Using them was never pleasant – they would need to catch up on natural sleep sooner rather than later – but there was no choice. A natural sleep couldn't be broken so easily, even if it did mean less wear and tear on their mood. Issuing a quick flurry of orders, he climbed into one of the machines and pulled the hatch down over his head. Moments later, he was asleep.

———

Someone – the file refused to say who – had named the red star Barong. Ted puzzled over it for a long moment, then decided it didn't matter. Barong had nothing to interest anyone, apart from a pair of tramlines that led to New Russia and Vera Cruz. Even the handful of asteroids and comets weren't particularly interesting. There was barely enough of them to sustain a very tiny settlement.

"No sign of pursuit," Farley reported. "I…"

He broke off as red icons appeared on the display. "Contact," he snapped. The mood on the bridge sank rapidly. "Four frigate-sized craft, Captain."

Ted swore. He'd known better than to think they'd fool the aliens for long, but he had hoped…and now those hopes had been shattered. But the aliens had come through the tramline at some distance from them, enough – he prayed desperately – for them to overlook the carrier when they started searching in earnest. If they *did* start searching in earnest…

"Keep a sharp eye on them," he ordered. It was possible that the aliens would merely maintain a watch for several hours, then pull back. Or that they would go doggo themselves and wait for the carrier to reveal herself. "Alert me if they start probing space near us."

He silently ran through the vectors in his mind. *Ark Royal* might have been unpowered, but she was still moving away from the tramline at a considerable speed. Given enough time, they might make it far enough from the alien craft to be able to manoeuvre without being detected, although it would take days. He shook his head. Days of rest, recuperation and repair work sounded very good right now.

"Understood, sir," Farley said. He sounded tired, utterly exhausted. "So far, they're just holding position."

Ted scowled, trying to put himself in his enemy's shoes. What would *he* think, if he thought he'd seen the carrier he was chasing accidentally destroy herself? Would he suspect a trap or would he gloat over his victory and return to preparing the invasion of human space? Ted knew, naturally, that it *was* a trick. It was hard to imagine what the enemy would do when he knew that…and that the enemy was thoroughly alien. Who knew *what* would seem to make sense to them?

"Then we will do nothing," he said. He shrugged. There was no shortage of repair work that had to be done. The point defence network had to be repaired, the mass drivers had to be reloaded…he smiled, thinking of the asteroids drifting in orbit around the dull red star. A few days of intensive mining and processing and they'd have more than enough projectiles to rebuild their stockpiles. "Contact the other ships. I want a complete breakdown of their status."

He sighed as he leaned back in his chair. "And then switch out the Alpha shift completely," he added. "Tell everyone that I want them to get at least a few hours of rest."

His earpiece buzzed, two minutes later. "Captain," Fitzwilliam said. "Might I advise you to get some rest too?"

Ted shook his head, then remembered that his XO couldn't see him. "No," he said. Rest sounded a very good idea right now, but he knew his duty. "I have to stay on the bridge."

"Captain," Fitzwilliam said, "you've been in command for the last twenty hours. You need some rest. As your XO, I must *insist* on it."

"You must *insist*," Ted repeated. It was true; one of the duties of the XO was to point out when the Captain was overworking himself. The duty was laid down in naval regulations, but it made for some awkward conversations. Ted had never heard of any other XO actually carrying out the duty. But then, it wasn't the sort of thing that would be recorded in starship logbooks. "And yourself?"

"I snatched a nap before we launched the attack," Fitzwilliam reminded him. "I'll take the next few hours on the bridge, then you can relieve me."

Ted sighed and gave up. "Very well," he said. "You take the bridge. I'll be in my office."

He looked back at the display as the channel closed. The alien ships were still holding position, watching and waiting. If they started to search...but they weren't moving. Every moment they delayed, he knew, *Ark Royal's* chances of escape grew much stronger. But realistically...all they would have to do was blockade the two tramlines and prevent the carrier from leaving the system. If, of course, they thought the carrier was still intact.

The hatch opened, revealing Fitzwilliam. Ted took a moment of petty pleasure in noting that the XO looked tired and exhausted himself, then rose to his feet and surrendered the bridge to his subordinate. The XO eyed him for a long moment, clearly concerned, then nodded towards the office hatch. Tiredly, Ted left the bridge and stepped into his office, then noticed that his terminal was blinking. The list of dead officers and men – mainly starfighter pilots – was waiting for him.

Ted glanced at it, then cursed under his breath. He knew he should feel something – anything – for the dead, but he was too tired to let their loss affect him. Instead, he sat down on the sofa, then lay down and closed his eyes. Sleep overwhelmed him seconds later.

"It'll take us at least four days to close all the blind spots," Anderson said. "The bastards did a damn good job of peeling away our defences."

James sighed, rubbing his forehead. His head hurt, but he didn't dare take anything for it, not even a simple painkiller. The last thing he needed was to have his judgement impaired any further. Even as it was, he was deeply worried about accidentally doing something that would alert the aliens to their position. The carrier was in no state to fight off a renewed offensive.

The Chief Engineer was right, he knew. *Ark Royal* had lost enough of her point defence to make her hellishly vulnerable, although none of the internal systems and power conduits had actually been destroyed. Given time, the damage could be repaired, while the destroyed weapons could be replaced from the stockpiles they'd taken onboard before they'd departed from Earth. But would they have the time?

"Start work as soon as possible, but remember we have to remain undetected," he ordered. Ideally, he would have preferred to wait a week, long enough to place quite some distance between themselves and the alien craft even without the main drives. But if the aliens caught them now, they wouldn't have a hope of fighting back long enough to reach the other tramline. "I don't want a single betraying emission."

Anderson gave him an offended look. "My crew are not amateurs," he said, crossly. "They know what they're doing."

James opened his mouth to deliver a stinging rebuke, then realised that the engineer was as exhausted as everyone else. "Get some sleep first," he said, instead. "Your second can handle the work."

"I don't trust anyone to work on the Old Lady without supervision," Anderson said, flatly. "With your permission...?"

"Keep me informed," James said. Four days of work, all of which had to be undertaken without emitting a single betraying pulse of energy that would bring the aliens down on them like a hammer. It wasn't going to be easy. "And don't hesitate to conscript others if you need more hands."

He sighed, remembering one of the stories passed down from his illustrious ancestors. One particular Fitzwilliam had shocked his aristocratic relatives by taking command of a submarine, rather than an aircraft carrier or a battleship, during the war against Adolf Hitler and the Nazis. That Fitzwilliam had once spent several days being hunted by German ships after a mission into the Baltic Sea had gone badly wrong. James hadn't understood how his ancestor had felt, not until now. Detection would mean almost certain death.

His console chimed. "Commander," Midshipwomen Lopez said, "the reporters would like to speak with you at your earliest convenience."

James bit down the response that came to mind. "Tell them that I will speak with them as soon as it is *convenient*," he said. "And until then, they should go back to their cabins and get some sleep. It will not be *convenient* for at least a day."

And longer, if I can swing it, he thought, inwardly. As XO, it was his duty to supervise the repair work, check the revised duty rosters and generally take as much of the burden of day-to-day administration as possible upon himself. If he was lucky, that should take more than just one day... and it was all urgent. Some of it, he knew, could be reasonably put aside until they returned to friendly space, but the rest was quite important. The reporters might have to wait several days for an interview.

He wondered, absently, what they'd thought of the battle. Despite the battering the carrier's weapons and sensors had taken, there hadn't been much actual *evidence* of combat apart from the view on the display. If even hardened naval officers could become detached from the realities of space combat, what might happen to reporters who didn't really comprehend what they were seeing. No doubt their reports, when they were finally filed, would consist of nothing more than poorly-written nonsense. They'd probably been disappointed when their consoles had failed to explode.

The hours ticked past, one by one. James watched the aliens warily, but they refused to move or do anything other than just wait by the tramline. Were they more patient than humans, as a general rule, or simply too unimaginative to do anything other than follow orders? But wouldn't that mean that their superiors had imaginations? The Royal Navy taught its officers to use their best judgement, taking the initiative wherever possible, yet other space navies had different ideas. James had watched a Russian exercise from a distance and he'd been struck by how little freedom the Russian junior officers had, compared to their British counterparts.

Puzzling over it, he brought up the recordings of the battle and went through them, piece by piece. The analysts were already working on the records, but he wanted to see the raw data. It was clear, he decided, that the aliens were preparing their next operation, although there was no way to deduce the target. But *Ark Royal* had shocked them badly. They'd be wiser to reconsider whatever attack plan they'd had in mind.

But what *did* they have in mind?

Human tactical doctrine called for pushing the attack as hard as possible, right into the teeth of enemy fortifications. If the human race lost its industrial base, defeat was certain, all the more so as no one had any idea where the aliens were located. A deep-strike mission couldn't be mounted without a target, unless they were prepared to spend months – if not years – exploring stars almost at random. But the aliens…they'd hit a handful of small colonies, then New Russia, then they'd launched a probing attack that had been smacked back…

He shook his head. Had *Ark Royal* shocked them so badly that they'd call a halt, long enough to reconsider their tactics?

Pushing the thought out of his mind, he called Midshipwomen Lopez. "Make sure the Captain gets something to eat," he ordered. The entire crew needed food as well as rest; he'd already had food distributed to crews at their stations, even though it was technically against regulations. But then, the bureaucrats had never imagined having to fight for more than a few brief hours. Hell, they probably hadn't imagined ever having to fight at all. "And then get some sleep yourself."

"Aye, sir," the young woman said.

Two hours later, when the Captain returned to the bridge, he looked refreshed. James allowed himself a moment of relief, then gratefully headed back to his cabin. He needed sleep too – and some time to think. One conclusion was inescapable. They had exchanged one trap for another.

And, unless the aliens got very careless, there was little hope of escape.

––––––

Kurt felt thick-headed as he opened his eyes and glanced up at the timer. Six hours. Six hours of sleep in a sleep machine. He could have scored six hours of natural sleep and woken up feeling better, if still rather shattered by the experience. Annoyed, he opened the hatch and sat upright, silently grateful that he hadn't bothered to dress before climbing into the sleep machine. He'd have to put himself on report later, he knew, but it made it easier to climb back into the shower. A quick check revealed that the aliens hadn't come anywhere near them while he'd been resting in enforced sleep.

Shaking his head, he finished washing himself, pulled on a robe and made his way down to his office. The list of slain pilots was waiting for him, demanding immediate attention. As CAG, it was his duty to write a brief note to their next-of-kin, telling them how and why their relatives had died. But it was a duty he couldn't bring himself to handle, not now. Instead, he called up the pilot rosters and rapidly reworked the squadrons. The bomber pilots would have to be permanently assigned to fighters, he decided. There was no reason to keep them in reserve if their normal craft couldn't be deployed against the aliens.

He looked up as the hatch opened, revealing Rose. She managed to look disgustingly alert, he noticed, as she stepped through the hatch and sat down on the spare chair. The dressing gown clung to her body in a number of enticing places...embarrassed, he looked away. He was almost old enough to be her father.

"They're still out there," she said, quietly. "They could find us at any moment."

Kurt nodded. He would have preferred to be flying against the enemy or even running away, not drifting through space praying that the aliens wouldn't notice them. But he knew there was no real alternative. If the aliens realised where they were, they would bring overwhelming force to bear against *Ark Royal*. The carrier would fight hard, but she would be eventually overwhelmed.

"You did well," Rose added, rising to her feet. "Very well."

She tugged at her belt. It fell free, allowing the dressing gown to fall open. Kurt stared, hypnotised by the sight of her breasts bobbing free. Her pink nipples seemed to twitch, demanding his attention. Suddenly, it was very hard to breathe.

A hundred objections ran through his mind. He was a married man – but it was unlikely he would ever see his wife and children again. He was old enough to be her father – and yet she'd chosen him. He was...her hands tugged at his robe, pulling it right open. Somehow, almost of their own volition, his hands reached for her breasts, then slipped down to her buttocks. All objections fled as he pulled her closer to him, feeling his penis already standing to attention...

Afterwards, he couldn't help feeling regret, even a little guilty. He had betrayed Molly, broken the wedding vows that he'd made in good faith. Their relationship might be dented, yet it was not gone. But he knew what had driven Rose, just as it had driven him to accept her offer. The desire not to die without feeling a fellow human's touch, one last time.

He looked up at the display and shivered. The alien ships were still there.

Waiting.

CHAPTER
TWENTY FIVE

"We could probably get to the asteroids," Charles said. "We're experienced in such matters."

The XO shook his head. Three days of drifting in space hadn't convinced the aliens that *Ark Royal* was dead. Their ships remained on the tramline to New Russia, watching and waiting for the humans to show themselves. And, in the meantime, the stress was starting to take its toll on the crew.

"Too risky," he said, finally. "We can't risk detection."

"Understood," Charles said, ruefully. Mining asteroids wasn't something his men had signed up to do, but it would make a break from assisting with repairs and watching the reporters like hawks. God knew that the reporters were still trying to make their way into secure compartments, despite being told – time and time again – that they were not allowed to enter without permission and an escort. "But we will have to mine the asteroids sooner or later."

He nodded to the XO, then headed back to the barracks. Inside, he saw a handful of Marines wrestling and two more trying to catch up on their sleep. Rolling his eyes, he barked for quiet and issued orders. Another counter-boarding drill would keep his men out of mischief for a few hours. After that...

Better here than on New Russia, he thought. He'd gone through the sensor records carefully, but he had no idea if the Russians had made it to the surface or not. Instead, all he could do was pray that they'd made it – and that their fellow countrymen were prepared to meet them.

Shaking his head, he started to organise the drill. Everything else would have to wait until they returned home – or the aliens caught up with them again.

———

"There are only two known tramlines in this system," Ted said, studying the display. "Four more, if the assumptions about alien capabilities are accurate."

There was no disagreement from his senior crew. Barong – the crew were already muttering that the star should have been named Boring – was uninteresting, only really useful in times of peace, when a convoy could shave a few hours off the voyage to Vera Cruz. The Russians might have been able to stake a claim in later years, or perhaps someone would set up an independent trading facility and try to charge passage fees for anyone making their way through the system. They'd have to be careful, Ted knew. It wasn't as if Barong was important enough to force people to pay. They could simply detour around the system if necessary.

"Going back to New Russia would be extremely dangerous," Ted added. "They will certainly have ramped up their sensor networks – and there are those ships patrolling the edge of the tramline. We may well jump straight into a trap. This time, they'll be ready for us – and we are already short on starfighters and projectiles."

He looked over at Anderson, who shrugged. "Unless the first survey of this system was rushed – and there is some evidence to suggest it was – there's no hope of finding materials we can use to make additional nukes," he said. "The asteroids appear to be bog-standard pieces of rock and metal, not rare elements."

"Pity," Fitzwilliam observed. "We taught them respect for our weapons, didn't we?"

"Yes," Ted said. "But that will make them all the more determined to prevent us from returning to human space."

He wondered, idly, if *Ark Royal* was the only starship carrying the modified weapons. It didn't seem likely. The Admiralty might well have outfitted other ships with the weapons – if there was one thing humanity had in abundance, it was nukes – and if the aliens launched another attack, they'd get a nasty surprise. But the aliens would still be hopping mad over the attack on New Russia.

"I have decided, therefore, that we will proceed down the tramline to Vera Cruz," he added. "From there, we will jump into unexplored space and work our way around to a point where we can return to human space."

"Captain," Fitzwilliam said slowly, "that will add several months to our travel time – at best."

"It will," Ted agreed. It was the XO's job to play devil's advocate, no matter how annoying it could be. "However, does anyone feel that we have a realistic chance of sneaking back into the New Russia system without being detected?"

There was a long pause. No one spoke.

"Our orders are to return home and report in," Ted continued. "However, right now, taking the direct route home is a form of suicide. Therefore, we will take the long route home – and, in addition, worry the aliens by probing the edge of their space."

He smiled at their reactions, then explained his reasoning. The attack on New Russia made sense, the attack on Vera Cruz and the other colonies did not. Logically, the aliens should have saved their strength…unless there was a strong reason to remove the human presence on those worlds. The only answer that made sense to him was that the aliens had colony worlds within one or two jumps of Vera Cruz.

They might have encountered one of our survey ships, he thought. Survey ships set out for years at a time, rarely heading home early unless they discovered something truly spectacular. No one would notice if one of the ships was several years overdue, allowing the aliens plenty of time to dissect her and her crew. And they would have no trouble pulling a complete astronomical chart of the human sphere from her computers.

The thought made him scowl. Whatever the outcome of the war, procedures would have to be carefully revised in the face of First Contact. The survey ships would have to be escorted, their computers would need to be rigged for immediate destruction if another alien contact went bad and their crews would have to be outfitted with suicide implants. It would probably take years to devise the new protocols. God knew the first set, as inadequate as they were, had taken almost a decade of scrabbling before there was a version all of the interstellar powers could accept.

"We might run into stronger alien forces," Fitzwilliam pointed out, finally. "They might well try to trap us."

"They might," Ted agreed. "The alternative is staying here, in hiding. Unless someone's invented a much better FTL drive...?"

He smiled, then looked around the compartment. "Barring discovery, we will power up our drives two days from now and start inching towards the tramline," he continued, bringing up the main display. "Should the aliens catch wind of us, we will throw caution to the winds and flee for Vera Cruz."

"If they do," Anderson observed, "they will almost certainly run us down."

Ted nodded. No matter how hard *Ark Royal* and her escorts struggled, the faster alien ships and their starfighters definitely would overtake her if it came down to a straight chase. Ideally, he wanted to get to the tramline without being detected at all. But it might not be possible...

He shook his head. If they were lucky, they would escape without further harassment. But if they weren't lucky, they would just have to fight.

———

James couldn't help feeling enthused about the Captain's plan, even though he knew that it was staggeringly risky. But if he'd wanted to avoid risk, he would have taken that slot in the Admiralty he'd been offered when he'd been promoted to Commander. It would have made him nothing more than a tea boy – one had to be a Commodore to gain attention at the Admiralty – but it would have been safe. Instead, he'd attempted to gain a promotion that would ensure he'd see combat.

How careless of me, he thought, as he strode through the starship's passageway. He smirked at the thought. *If I'd known where I was going, I might have applied to a modern carrier instead.*

Another piece of carelessness, he knew, was failing to keep himself occupied to the point where he could decline the chance to meet the reporters with a clear conscience. Most of the work he had to do had either been delegated to subordinates – he'd hated being micromanaged as a junior officer and saw no reason to torment his subordinates, now he'd been promoted – or simply placed to one side. There was no point in writing out endless reports if no one was ever going to see them. And the only other duty that needed attention, sooner rather than later, was ticking off a handful of couples who had bent the rules on relationships onboard ship.

He pushed that thought aside as he stepped into the modified briefing compartment. The reporters were sitting down, looking pale and worn. It had taken several days, but the implications of their current location had finally dawned on them. Their ship was going to have to run the gauntlet back to human space…or make a long detour through space that might well be occupied by an alien colony or two. James found it hard to feel any sympathy. They should have known the job was dangerous, he told himself once again, when they took it.

"Commander," Yang said. "Is the story true?"

James smiled. "Which one?" He asked. Like all ships, rumour spread through *Ark Royal* at the speed of light. "The one about the Engineer, the Helmsman and the Navigator?"

Yang scowled at him. "That we're trapped here, in this system," he snapped. "Are we trapped?"

"Not precisely," James said. He didn't want to discuss any specifics with them. It was absurd to think they might betray the ship to the aliens, but still…"We just have to run the gauntlet on our way out."

Barbie looked up at him, nervously. "Do…do we need to use the tramlines at all?"

James stared at her in absolute disbelief. "Do we *need* to use the tramlines?"

"The nearest stars aren't that far from here," Barbie said, carefully. "Surely we could just make our way to them without using the tramlines…"

"No," James said, crossly. "Let me see."

He ticked off points on his fingers as he spoke. "The closest star system to us that isn't New Russia is three light years away," he said. He knew he sounded disdainful, he just didn't care. "Placed in context, that means it takes three years for *light* to reach it. Assuming we work the drive to the bone, we should be able to make a third of light speed, if we don't mind the risk of burning out the system in the middle of the interstellar desert. It will take us roughly nine *years* to reach this star."

Barbie's face twisted, but James wasn't finished. "There's nothing to slow us down in interplanetary space," he added, "so we would just keep going if the drive burnt out. That would send us rocketing through the system at a sizable rate, making it impossible for us to stop. Nor could anyone catch up with us long enough to offload the crew. If we didn't run into the star, we'd just fly through and carry on to the *next* star system.

"All of this *assumes*, of course, that the food supplies don't run out. We produce only a limited amount of supplies in the hydroponic bays, as we tore half of them out to store weapons and spare parts. I estimate that we would run out of foodstuffs within two years, at the very latest. In order to get part of the crew through the voyage, the remainder would have to be eliminated, their bodies fed into the recycling system to nourish the rest of us."

Barbie blanched. "You'd have us eating human flesh?"

"Oh, it would be the only way to survive," James assured her. The fact that the food processors *could* turn human flesh into something safe to eat was a closely-guarded secret, one devised by bureaucrats intent on ensuring that the crews always had something to keep them going. So far, no one had ever had to *use* the systems. "But I'm afraid that's not the end of it.

"Nine years. Think about it. Nine *years*. The aliens could win the war by then; we might arrive at our destination only to discover an alien fleet waiting for us. Or perhaps humanity would have won the war. The universe would have moved on and we would be hopelessly out of date."

"That's enough," Yang said, sharply.

James smiled, then shrugged. "We will do our very best to get you all home," he said, wondering just how much of his lecture would make it into the final reports. Somehow, he suspected the detail about potential cannibalism would be erased by the censors before it was broadcast to the British public. "And I suggest that you relax and let us work."

"We will," Yang said, finally. He gave James a look that promised future trouble. "And thank you for your candour."

Yang didn't seem amused. James smiled to himself, wondering if Yang was interested in Barbie. Why not? Whatever usual restrictions the reporters had on their behaviour – assuming that there were any restrictions – would have faded when they'd finally realised that they were trapped. Anyone with even a small amount of experience would be able to tell that *Ark Royal* had escaped by the skin of her teeth. And, the next time, their jury-rigged repairs might not stand up to what the aliens handed out.

James shrugged. If they made it home, they would be heroes and Yang's superiors would see no profit in hammering James – or Captain Smith. And if they didn't make it home, the whole episode was thoroughly irrelevant. There wouldn't even be a messenger buoy left behind to mark their passage.

Maybe we should leave one here, James thought, making a mental note to suggest it to the Captain. *The Russians will know where we went, even if they can't know what happened afterwards. If humanity wins the war, sooner or later they will come looking for us...*

———

Kurt stared down at his screen, trying to compose a message. Silent running was strange for the pilots; half of them remained in their cockpits, ready for immediate launch, while the other half tried to relax. But it was so hard to relax, knowing that the alert might sound at any moment. Alien passive sensors were watching for them even now.

He cursed his own weakness as he angrily banished the half-written message from his screen, rather than bothering to save it for a later rewrite. Sleeping with Rose had been a mistake, of that he was sure. He'd known that right after the first time, which hadn't been enough to stop himself from doing it twice more. Everyone knew that Rose, as the new senior squadron leader, was expected to coordinate her plans with her superior officer's plans. No one would raise eyebrows at them spending time together, let alone disturb them. And no one would realise that they'd spent more time fucking like wild animals than actually doing their work...

You should be ashamed of yourself, he told himself. He *was* ashamed, he knew, no matter how hard he tried to deny it. Just not ashamed enough.

Angrily, he stood up and headed for the hatch, thinking hard. Relationships between officers of different ranks were forbidden, as were relationships between starfighter pilots who happened to share the same wardroom. Sure, there were times when such rules might be ignored – if *Ark Royal* never made it home, there would be no reason to care about regulations – but somehow he doubted this was one of those times.

He stepped through the hatch, recognising and cursing his own weakness. As CAG, it was his duty to send Rose into danger, time and time again. He would have to do it until she ran out of luck and died…or until *he* died, whereupon Rose would be promoted into his shoes. But now… he didn't *want* to send her into danger. She wasn't just a pilot to him any longer, she was far more than that. Or did she think that he was nothing more than a convenient leman for her? He didn't have to fly beside her, he wasn't likely to brag about his conquest…

Women, he thought, ruefully. *Can't live with them, can't live without them.*

But what was he going to do?

Sooner or later, he knew, someone would find out. They would walk into his office and see him screwing Rose while she was bent over the desk, or even see them exchanging warm glances and draw the right conclusions. There were few secrets in the wardroom; pilots knew each other so well that they would probably deduce the truth from a moment of carelessness. And then? Kurt didn't want to *think* about what could happen next.

Normally, you would be transferred, a mocking voice at the back of his head pointed out, sardonically. *Or she would be transferred…but she's already been transferred once, hasn't she? What sort of reputation will she get if she transfers again?*

And no one will blame you…

Kurt nodded to himself as he passed a small group of crewmen carrying a box of spare parts in the other direction. Rose's file might not be too detailed, but the world of starfighter pilots loved its rumours. One transfer might go unnoticed, a second would be all-too-noticeable… unless, of course, there was a valid excuse.

He shouldn't touch her again, he knew. But he knew that all of his resolve would melt when she met him again, soon enough.

His communicator buzzed. "CAG," the XO said, "report to Briefing Compartment A. I say again, report to Briefing Compartment A."

Kurt's blood ran cold. Did the XO know?

"Understood," he said, bracing himself. He couldn't afford to walk into the compartment looking guilty. The XO, the general disciplinarian on the ship, would notice and start wondering why. "I'm on my way."

CHAPTER
TWENTY SIX

"They haven't moved at all, sir," Farley said. "I think they're drones."

Ted gave him a sharp look. "Are you sure?"

"...No," Farley admitted. "But it's been five days and they haven't moved, not once."

"It's possible," Ted considered. Humanity had used ECM drones against the aliens with some success. There was no reason why the aliens couldn't use ECM drones themselves. It even made a certain kind of sense. Rather than tie up several starships hunting for a carrier that might already have been destroyed, the aliens could leave a handful of drones in place and rely on their presence to keep the carrier intimidated. "But we will not take the risk."

He looked over at the helmsman. "Signal the fleet," he ordered. "We will proceed to Tramline Two in ten minutes."

A dull quiver ran through the carrier as her drives slowly came to life. If there was an alien fleet lying doggo, Ted knew, they might well pick up the carrier's emissions, even if they were rigged for silent running. But the alternative was staying where they were for months, even years, while the war raged on countless light years away. No, they had to take the chance, he told himself. And at least they'd had time to do more repairs.

Score one for the Old Lady's designers, he thought. All military starships were modular, despite the best efforts of some of their designers, but *Ark Royal* was more modular than any modern carrier. Replacing the damaged or destroyed weapons hadn't taken more than a few days, although their supplies of spare parts had been stripped to the bone. *We could launch a long-range raid into enemy territory with only a handful of ships in support.*

"All systems online," Anderson reported. The Chief Engineer sounded tired, but happy. Ted and Fitzwilliam had practically dragged him into a sleep machine, just to ensure that the engineer got a few hours rest before the carrier started to move. "Our repairs are looking good, Captain."

"I knew they would be," Ted assured him. The other advantage of commanding the older carrier was that it's technology was well understood by its users. There was nothing radically new on her hull, nor would there ever be. "And our weapons?"

"Powered up, ready to engage targets," Fitzwilliam said. "Our starfighters are ready to launch; point defence crews are standing by."

Just in case there is a prowling enemy carrier, Ted thought. "Excellent," he said, instead. "And the fleet?"

"Ready to go," Fitzwilliam assured him. "*Kiev* is ready to carry out her duty."

Ted settled back in his command chair. "Then take us out," he ordered. "Inform *Kiev* that she may make the jump as soon as we reach the tramline."

Long hours ticked by as *Ark Royal* and her accompanying ships crawled across the useless system, every passive sensor primed for the faintest hint of an enemy presence. Ted forced himself to stay alert, reminding himself that the enemy could be anywhere. If they'd been fooled, all well and good…but if they hadn't been fooled, they could just be biding their time. Why bother sweeping vast reaches of empty space for the carrier when they could just wait for the carrier to show itself?

"The enemy ships haven't moved at all," Farley reported. "Either they haven't seen us or they're definitely drones."

Ted scowled. One disadvantage of widening the distance between them and the enemy ships – or drones – was that it took time to see what the enemy were doing…and, by then, the enemy might have started to do something different. The enemy ships were helpfully identifying themselves, which added some credence to Farley's theory that they were actually drones. No manned starship would identify itself so openly to a stealthed enemy. But there was no way to know for sure.

He shook his head. "We remain in silent running," he said. He'd never seen a drone that could jump through the tramlines, but the aliens might well have devised one. They might be automated, yet they could still alert the aliens at New Russia if the humans threatened to return. "Concentrate on Tramline Two."

There was a long pause as the small fleet crawled closer to the tramline. "No enemy ships detected," Farley said, finally. "But if they're in stealth…"

Ted nodded in understanding. A single enemy ship could be lying doggo…he forced the thought aside as he studied the console, reminding himself that they were committed. He couldn't keep his ship in the useless system indefinitely, nor could they hope to fight their way past the aliens at New Russia. They'd already come alarmingly close to trapping and destroying *Ark Royal* once.

"Prime our passive sensors," he ordered. "Then order *Kiev* to pass through the tramline."

On the display, there was a brief gravimetric flicker as *Kiev* vanished from the dull system, jumping directly to Vera Cruz. Ted watched, half-expecting an alien fleet to appear at any moment, but nothing happened. Cold suspicion prickled at the corner of his mind. The aliens seemed to have left the backdoor open, which meant…what? Did they believe the humans to be destroyed or were they setting up a trap further into unexplored space?

Kiev returned in another flicker of displaced gravity. "They're transmitting now," Farley reported. The display changed, showing the Vera Cruz system. "No enemy starships detected."

Ted frowned. If he'd overrun an alien-settled planet, he would have been sure to leave at least one picket in the system, just in case. But the aliens knew that Vera Cruz had never been very important…at least not as far as the pre-war human sphere had been concerned. If the system had been richer, it would probably have been snapped up by the stronger interstellar powers. Mexico wasn't a microstate, but it couldn't compete with any of the major powers…

"Take us through the tramline," he ordered, running one final check on his ship's systems as he spoke. They were ready for anything. "Now."

Space twisted around them as they vanished from the useless system and reappeared in Vera Cruz, where the war had begun. Ted stared at the display, half-expecting to see a wave of missiles lancing towards them, followed by clouds of alien starfighters, but saw nothing. A chill ran down his spine as he realised that the entire system was as dark and silent as the grave. There might be no one left alive on Vera Cruz, he realised, and there had never been any settlements established off-world. The aliens had seen, destroyed and moved on.

"No contacts detected," Farley reported.

"Launch two drones," Ted ordered. Vera Cruz's other tramline, the unexplored one, rested at the other side of the star. They'd take hours to reach it, no matter what else happened. "If there is *any* alien presence in the system, anything at all, I want to know about it."

He waited until they were well away from the tramline, then keyed his console. "Alpha Shift, get some rest," he ordered. As always, it was a nightmare deciding when he and his senior officers could rest. "Beta Shift will take command."

Given their location, it would be several hours before they learnt anything from Vera Cruz itself. Passing command over to Fitzwilliam – with a muttered order for him to take some rest himself in a few hours, Ted stepped back into his office and lay down on the sofa. Sleep overwhelmed him within seconds and he fell into darkness.

———

Piece by piece, the display built up a picture of the Vera Cruz system. James knew, from the files, that the system had never been considered particularly interesting, lacking even a large asteroid belt or a gas giant. Without them, it was unlikely that Vera Cruz would ever develop into a major industrial node. But the Mexicans hadn't cared, he knew; they'd merely wanted to establish themselves as an interstellar power. They'd invested billions of pounds in setting up the infrastructure to take thousands of colonists…

And then lost it all, James thought, sourly. For Britain – or any of the other major interstellar powers – such a disaster would be bad enough, but for the Mexicans it would be catastrophic. Somehow, he doubted that they'd insured themselves…and even if they had, there would be years of legal wrangling before anything was paid. No insurance company had offered a policy against alien attack, prior to First Contact. It was probably covered under Acts of God.

The aliens, it was clear, hadn't been particularly interested in the system either. There was no hint that they'd surveyed the handful of asteroids in the system or landed a settlement on Vera Cruz. It was an empty world, now that the humans had been exterminated; logically, the aliens could have taken it for themselves. But maybe they had good reason to hold off on landing colonists, he decided. After thousands of humans had been slaughtered, it was unlikely that the human race wouldn't retaliate against alien settlers.

Landing colonists on New Russia makes sense, he told himself. *Human shields. We couldn't bombard the planet without killing millions of Russians.*

He scowled. If there was one thing the human race had relearned over the past two centuries, it was that such tactics couldn't be tolerated. Showing weakness, even an understandable reluctance to accidentally kill friendly civilians, only encouraged the terrorists and insurgents who had fought and died fighting the civilised world. They were evil, of that James had no doubt, but were the aliens? Were they deliberately using the population of New Russia as shields or…or were they utterly unaware of what they were doing?

It seemed impossible, but the aliens weren't human. They might be humanoid, yet their thinking might be very different. It was possible that they regarded themselves as completely expendable, let alone human captives and civilians. Or that they were willing to leave human civilians alone as long as the civilians did as they were told. But the silence from Vera Cruz suggested that the entire planet was dead.

Unless they've decided not to risk using radio, he told himself. But he wasn't optimistic.

"One of the drones is entering orbit now," the sensor officer reported. "It's still picking up no trace of alien starships."

"Put the live feed on the display," James ordered. "Let's see what happened here."

The drone wasn't as advanced as an orbital recon platform, not like the systems that kept Earth's surface under 24/7 surveillance. But it was advanced enough to pick out the remains of the colony…and note the places that had once been human settlements. Now, they were nothing more than blackened ruins. Even the handful of farms, carefully primed to feed the main body of colonists when they finally arrived, had been destroyed. One of the analysts dug up the original files from Vera Cruz and placed them on the display, next to the images from the drones. It was all too clear just how badly the settlement had been hammered by the aliens.

"Interesting," Major Parnell said, through the intercom.

James jumped. He hadn't realised that the Royal Marine was watching the live feed from the drones…which was stupid, he rebuked himself. The Royal Marines would be very interested in alien conduct on the ground.

"Yes," he agreed, sardonically. "Why?"

Parnell didn't respond to the sarcasm in his tone. "There should be much more devastation," he said, instead. "If the aliens took out the colony from orbit, there should be nothing more than a giant crater in the ground. Instead…they seem to have raided the surface rather than simply destroyed it."

James hesitated. As a junior officer, he had watched targets on Earth being destroyed from orbit…and he had to admit that Parnell had a point. The aliens could have dropped a handful of kinetic strikes and obliterated the colony from orbit, but the evidence suggested otherwise.

"Point," he agreed, finally. He shivered as he studied the images of the settlement, the old file showing a standard colony arrangement, the newer ones showing destroyed buildings and…he cursed as he realised what was missing. "There's no bodies."

"No," Parnell agreed. There was no hint of triumph or amusement in his tone. "Sir, I believe we should attempt to determine what precisely happened to the settlers."

"You want to go down to the surface," James said, slowly. "Are you completely out of your mind?"

"This is the first chance anyone has had to examine the remains of an alien attack," Parnell pointed out, smoothly. "I don't think we can pass it up."

James considered it, rapidly. The Captain would have to make the final decision, of course, but Parnell was right. There *were* strong reasons to make a quick examination of the remains of the colony. On the other hand, however, if the aliens returned in force the carrier might have to withdraw rapidly, leaving the Marines completely alone. The aliens would send troops down to the surface to finish them off…or simply leave them to fend for themselves.

"I will advise the Captain that we should make the attempt," he said. They would certainly need to mine some raw materials from the handful of asteroids in the system. It wasn't something they had dared in the last system, not when there were a handful of alien ships – or drones – hanging around the tramline. "I suggest that you prepare your men."

He smiled as an evil thought struck him. "Could you take one of the reporters too?"

"One of the experienced embeds," Parnell said. Surprisingly, he didn't try to argue. But then, the Royal Marines had plenty of experience dealing with embedded reporters. "Not one of the newcomers."

James sighed. The thought of abandoning the reporters on Vera Cruz was hellishly tempting.

"Understood," he said, instead. He checked the timer and decided the Captain needed a few more hours of sleep. "Prepare your men. You'll have to move quickly once the Captain gives permission for you to go."

———

Marcus Yang had been sleeping when his terminal buzzed, dragging him out of an uneasy sleep. But at least he'd been able to sleep, he told himself; several of his fellow reporters had requested drugs from sickbay to help them sleep after they'd realised that the carrier was trapped for the foreseeable future. Lacking any real training, some of them had even started to panic…Marcus privately suspected that half of his fellows were on the verge of nervous breakdowns. Very few of them had truly understood the dangers of serving on a carrier until it was too late.

He pulled himself off the bunk and stood up, reaching for his tunic and pulling it on over his nightclothes. The other reporters in the compartment stirred, but didn't awaken, thankfully. Marcus smiled at them, then walked out of the hatch and down towards the briefing compartment put aside for the reporters. None of the others had realised – at least, not yet – that it wasn't *the* briefing compartment. It was merely a piece of window-dressing to impress them.

Inside, he blinked in surprise as he came face-to-face with a Royal Marine, wearing full battledress. It was hard to be sure, but the man looked to be around thirty, with a rough-hewn face that bore the marks of a lifetime in the service. He wore no rank stripes – they were uncommon on active service, where the enemy could use them to identify the commanding officers – but he had an air of authority that marked him as a senior officer. Marcus nodded politely to him, then waited. His experience told him that explanations would be presented soon enough.

"We're going down to the planet," the Marine said, finally. "Do you wish to accompany us?"

Marcus swallowed, nervously. The carrier wasn't going to enter orbit, unless the Captain had changed his mind. There would be several hours in a cramped shuttle, hopelessly vulnerable if the aliens returned to the system or merely if they'd left a few surprises in orbit for anyone who wanted to inspect the destroyed colony. But it would be a chance to get some *real* recordings, ones that would be exclusive to himself. He could dictate his own terms to his superiors, when – if – they returned to Earth.

"I do," he said, finally.

The Marine smiled. "Then come with me," he said. "There's no time to alert your fellows."

Because they will all want to come, Marcus thought.

"I understand," he said, out loud. "Let's go."

———

Ted, feeling much refreshed after seven hours of sleep, inspected the deployment plan carefully, then nodded. "Good luck," he said. The Marines would take at least an hour to reach the planet, then they'd have at least nine hours on the ground while *Ark Royal* mined for raw materials…unless the aliens returned. "We'll be waiting for you."

He settled back into his command chair, silently banishing Fitzwilliam to his cabin for a rest himself. It was nice of his XO to make sure that his

Captain had a few extra hours of sleep, but it was also impractical. They both needed to be fully alert at all times…which was a joke, he knew. No military officer could remain permanently on alert.

Maybe we should have two Captains and two XOs, he thought. *One pair to sleep, one pair to command…and switch every few hours.*

He shook his head. There would be arguments over which of the Captains was really in command. Shared authority, military officers knew, was diluted authority, asking for trouble when the two officers disagreed. Somehow, he doubted the Admiralty would consider it a good idea.

But war will throw other changes at us, he told himself. All of the peacetime protocols would be burnt away by the fires of war. *We won't be the same again.*

CHAPTER
TWENTY SEVEN

Seen from a distance, Charles decided, Vera Cruz didn't look too different from Earth. Like most settled worlds, it was an orb glowing with green and blue light, mostly blue. There were no hints from orbit that humans had trod on its surface, but then there wouldn't be any hints on any such world, apart from Earth. The giant orbital towers – and a handful of other human constructions – were the only things large enough to be visible to the naked eye from orbit.

He allowed himself a moment of relief as the shuttle finally reached orbit and started to fall into the planet's atmosphere. An hour of being crammed into his battlesuit inside a tiny shuttle didn't please him, even though there was no realistic alternative. Most of his accompanying squad had retreated into playing music or watching movies through their suit systems, even though the latter was frowned upon by senior officers. Charles was experienced enough not to blame them for wanting the distraction. Promising trainees had had to be removed from the program after discovering that they couldn't endure more than a few minutes of isolation in the suits.

The reporter seemed to be bearing up well, he decided, as the shuttle started to shake violently. There was no hope of hiding their existence any longer, so the pilot was trying to get them down on the ground as quickly as possible. Charles sucked in a breath as gravity started to catch at them, yanking the Marines around as the shuttle dropped lower and lower. As always, he had to fight to keep himself from throwing up. The suit's systems would take care of it, he knew, yet it was never pleasant – and he would have to buy the drinks when the regiment next went on leave. It was the simplest way, they'd found, to discourage Marines from being sick in their suits.

There was a final series of shuddering motions that tore at the shuttle, then there was a final crash and silence. Charles staggered to his feet as the hatch opened, revealing the destroyed settlement right in front of them. The Marines gathered themselves and advanced outwards, weapons at the ready as they swept for potential threats. But nothing materialised to greet them.

The settlement was very basic; a handful of prefabricated buildings making up the centre of town, surrounded by a hundred houses and makeshift shacks built from local wood and stone. Shipping anything across interstellar distances was expensive, Charles knew; it made economic sense to start using local materials as soon as possible, even if some folks whined about pillaging natural resources on newly-discovered worlds. Besides, stone and wood were much easier to replace or rebuild than anything that had been dragged across dozens of light years from Earth.

It had once been a well-developed settlement, he knew. Now, it was a ruin. The metal buildings were melted, while the more natural constructions were burned-out ruins. His suit's HUD identified some of the buildings – transit barracks, a schoolroom, the governor's residence – but it was impossible to link the names with the destroyed buildings. The Marines spread out slowly, eying the blackened ruins as if they expected them to spring to life with hostile soldiers, yet nothing happened. They were completely alone.

"Check the buildings," Charles ordered.

He knew he should remain with the shuttle, where he could coordinate the operation, but he couldn't keep himself from inspecting the schoolroom. Inside, it was a mess. The desks and chairs had been burned to ashes, while the small collection of electronic teaching aids were missing. There were no sign of any bodies. On the ground, he thought he saw a handful of tiny footprints, but he knew they could just be his imagination.

"They took the teaching aids," he said, out loud. "What could they learn from *those*?"

"They could learn our language, for a start," Sergeant Miles said. "One of my girlfriends used to say that a student could begin with no knowledge of English and master it through using one of those aids. I dare say the aliens are smarter than schoolchildren."

Charles nodded as he backed out of the schoolroom. "What else could they learn?"

"Depends what modules were loaded in," Miles admitted. "They're produced in America, so the basics of English reading and writing are a given. Then there could be modules covering everything from basic human history to specialised Mexican history. Science and maths, farming instructions...this is a colony world, sir. They'll have loaded as many modules as they could into the system."

"I see," Charles said. He hesitated, thinking hard. "They could speak to us."

"They could," Miles agreed. "And they could speak to the POWs, if they have any POWs from this colony."

Charles nodded. The aliens might not be able to speak English properly – he agreed with the analysts that the shape of their mouths would probably prevent it – but they were definitely advanced enough to produce some kind of voder. Hell, he was fairly sure that Marine battlesuits could be adapted to produce sounds the aliens could understand. But if the aliens could talk to humans, but chose not to...what did that mean? Somehow, he doubted it boded well for the future.

"Hey," Yang said. The reporter sounded unsteady; he'd been sick twice in the flight, according to the subroutine monitoring his suit. "Do you think the aliens took prisoners from here?"

"There are no bodies," Charles said. "That suggests that the aliens took prisoners or destroyed the bodies...or there were survivors, who returned long enough to bury the bodies and then retreat. But there's no sign of any survivors."

He looked towards the forested hills in the distance. If there were survivors, it was unlikely they would risk showing themselves. They might not realise that the shuttle that had landed by the settlement was human. Instead, they might remain in hiding, convinced that the aliens had started to hunt them down again. He shook his head in bitter disbelief.

No one had thought to come up with protocols for alien attack, certainly not on Vera Cruz. And that whole lack of preparation was biting them on the behind.

The remainder of the settlement was as uninformative as the schoolroom. All electronic devices seemed to have been looted, along with the bodies…and the remainder of the settlement had been scorched. Looking at the damage, Charles couldn't help wondering if the aliens had used grenades to destroy all traces of their presence, once they'd swept the colony and killed or captured the inhabitants. But they could have obliterated the entire colony from orbit, once they'd withdrawn. It made no sense.

Yang cleared his throat. "Shouldn't we try looking for survivors in the countryside?"

Charles snorted. "There's twenty-two of us," he pointed out. "We don't even begin to have the manpower to search even a small part of the countryside. All we can do is sweep the settlement and hope any survivors decide to show themselves."

He took one last look around the settlement, then called his Marines back to the shuttle. "We'll leave a message behind," he added. It was risky – if the aliens found it, they would realise that someone had been on the planet's surface – but one he knew had to be taken. If there were survivors, at least they would know they hadn't been abandoned. "They will know we were here."

"Sir," one of his Marines said. "What will happen to the planet? I mean, once the war is won?"

"I have no idea," Charles said. The Mexicans held clear title…assuming they could hang onto it while they struggled to pay their debts. But if the Captain was right and there was an alien world only one or two jumps from Vera Cruz, it was unlikely that the other interstellar powers would allow the Mexicans to keep the planet. They'd want to ship in reinforcements and planetary defences, then monitor the aliens indefinitely. "Why do you ask?"

"It's a beautiful world," the Marine said. "I could apply for settlement here."

"But very vulnerable," Charles said. It wasn't uncommon for ex-soldiers, particularly SF operators, to be headhunted by colony world settlement corporations. Their training and experience made them good at keeping law and order on the frontier. "The aliens might be right next door."

He took one final look into the distance, then cracked open his helmet. The air of Vera Cruz flooded in, a damp warmth tinged with smoke. He wondered, suddenly, if this desolation was the fate the aliens had in mind for Earth…then pushed the thought aside as he resealed his helmet and motioned for the Marines to return to the shuttle. They'd inspect one of the farms, but he wasn't hopeful. The colonists had been taken too badly by surprise to organise a resistance.

"Let's go," he said.

———

Marcus wanted to crack open his own helmet as the shuttle made the brief hop from the settlement to one of the nearer farms, but he didn't quite dare. Who knew *what* might be present in the planet's atmosphere? The Marines had booster shots that made them immune to almost every known disease, yet such broad-spectrum vaccines were rare outside the military. He forced himself to breathe through his mouth as the shuttle landed again, hitting the ground so hard he was sure they'd crashed, then followed the Marines out of the shuttle.

There was a farmhouse at one end of the field, a comfortable-looking building his briefing had identified as a *Hacienda*. Once, it had been intact; now, it's walls were blackened and it was completely deserted, just like the buildings in the main settlement. Marcus remained outside as the Marines swept through the building, hunting for survivors or hints that someone, somewhere, was still alive. But they found nothing.

"Hey," one of the Marines called. "I found a body!"

Marcus joined the general stampede towards the muddy ditch. A body lay at the bottom of the mud, clearly in an advanced state of decomposition. It was impossible to tell if it was male or female, young or old. One of the Marine stepped down into the ditch and took a DNA sample for later checking against the Mexican colony records. Marcus wondered, absently, if the body had been abandoned because no one knew it was there…or if no one had survived to come back and bury it. There was no way to tell.

"Female," the Marine grunted. The suits could run basic checks, although without the records it was impossible to positively identify the body. "Around thirty years old, but too much damage to be sure."

Poor bitch, Marcus thought. He'd seen horror before – he'd *filmed* horror for the jaded audiences in the civilised world – but this was something new. His imagination filled in all manner of scenarios. Maybe she'd been the proud owner of the farmhouse, running from the alien monsters that had destroyed her world; maybe she'd been the daughter of the farmhouse owner, trying to sneak around the aliens when they attacked. Or maybe she'd been a servant…there was no way to know. Her face would be broadcast all over the datanets, probably with a story composed to drum up support for the war, but she would never know it. God alone knew what had happened to the others.

"Leave the body here," Major Parnell ordered. "We're not equipped to take her with us."

The Marines worked rapidly, digging a hole in the ground that would make a suitable grave. Marcus wanted to argue, wanted to point out that they could take her bones home, but he knew it would be futile. For all they knew, the aliens had left the body behind as a deliberate trap, although he privately considered it unlikely. The insurgents the civilised world fought regularly had a nasty habit of doing just that, but would the aliens understand the human urge to take care of dead bodies? It was quite possible that the aliens left their dead bodies to rot where they fell…or that they ate their own flesh and blood. There were so many fictional aliens invented by humans that he liked to think that they were ready for anything.

There was a pause when the body was placed into the makeshift grave. "Do you know what to say over her body?" One of the Marines asked. "She would be Catholic, wouldn't she?"

"Perhaps," Parnell said. He stepped forward, composing himself. "My father was Isolated Catholic, but he never taught me prayers for the dead."

He hesitated. "We do not know this girl's name, our lord, and we do not know why or how she died," he added. "But we ask that you take her in your loving arms and lead her to a better world than the one that killed her. Amen."

The words sounded vaguely silly, Marcus thought, but there was a sincerity around them that outshone the prayers offered in Westminster Abbey. He made a mental note to ensure that the video of the brief ceremony was accidentally deleted. Someone would be bound to complain that the service hadn't been right, forcing the Royal Navy to waste time on rebuttals – at best. At worst, Major Parnell and his men might be punished, despite meaning well. No, it was better that the recording be destroyed forever.

"We'll leave another message here," Major Parnell said, as they headed back towards the shuttle. "But I'm not hopeful."

Marcus couldn't disagree. The aliens had systematically captured or killed every human on the planet – and they'd either taken or destroyed the bodies. Either way, he decided, it didn't bode well.

———

"No survivors," Ted said, looking down at the images from Vera Cruz. "None at all."

"There might be a handful hidden in the countryside," Major Parnell offered. The Marine didn't *look* tired, but there was a weariness around him that made Ted want to send him straight to bed. "We have no idea just how capable the aliens are on the ground or what sort of surveillance systems they will deploy."

Ted nodded. Human surveillance was good, but it could be jammed or disrupted by a well-prepared enemy. There was no way to know what the aliens might deploy on the ground, yet it was unlikely anything they had was far inferior to humanity's systems. They certainly didn't dare assume otherwise.

"Surely the colonists would have seen them coming," Fitzwilliam said. He looked up at Major Parnell. "Could your men have caught all of the colonists if you dropped from orbit?"

"If we were trying to drop in on their heads, we'd do a paraglide from the shuttles," Parnell said. "Or we could risk a straight drop through the planet's atmosphere, although I'd hate to try that against any kind of ground-based defences. Still, Vera Cruz had no defences at all. The colonists might even have assumed the aliens were human visitors until it was too late."

Ted barely heard him. "The colonists might have been taken as prisoners," he mused. "Do we *know*?"

"No, sir," Parnell said. "We know nothing for sure. The bodies could easily have been carried some distance from the colony and buried – or simply vaporised. We don't *know* the aliens took prisoners. But if I was waging war on a newly-discovered alien race, I'd sure as hell want prisoners to study."

"Assuming they think like us," Fitzwilliam mused.

"They can't be that different," Parnell said. "Even if they are homicidal monsters who find humans irredeemably ugly, surely they would want to know how to kill us."

Ted shuddered. Human doctors and scientists without morals had performed chilling experiments on helpless test subjects, after carefully deeming them to be subhuman and thus not worthy of any legal protection. The aliens wouldn't even have to wonder if the humans deserved legal protection; they'd just start experimenting at will. After all, humans had happily carried out experiments on non-human creatures before even *starting* to reach into interstellar space.

"I think they've already mastered the art of killing humans," Fitzwilliam said, sardonically. "Just ask the crews of *Formidable* and *Invincible*."

"It doesn't matter," Ted said. The concept of humans being used as alien test subjects – or even being kept in POW camps – was horrifying, but there was nothing they could do about it for the moment. "XO, how do we stand with the loading?"

Fitzwilliam glanced down at his terminal. "A few more hours to take on raw material, then compress it down into suitable projectiles," he said. "Assuming we don't get interrupted, we should be ready to make the next jump in a day or two."

"Which will also give the crew a chance to rest," Ted said. Not that they dared relax completely. The aliens had to suspect that *Ark Royal* needed to replenish her stocks of raw materials. If they were watching… he shuddered and put the thought out of his mind. Doing nothing might have been safer, but it was also futile. "We'll jump through the unexplored tramline tomorrow, then. I feel rather exposed out here."

"My men can return to inspect the remaining settlements," Parnell offered. "Or even to try low-power signalling…"

Ted shook his head, firmly. "If there are survivors, we will have to hope they hold out until the end of the war," he said. "One shuttle flight was dangerously revealing."

The Marine looked as though he wanted to argue, but didn't. Instead, he saluted and left the compartment. Ted watched him go, then turned back to the display. One tramline had been explored, the other…God alone knew where it went. No, that wasn't entirely accurate. They knew which *star* held the other end of the tramline; they just didn't know what might be orbiting that star. An alien homeworld…or merely a staging base?

"One day," Ted said, out loud. "And then we will know."

CHAPTER
TWENTY EIGHT

"So," Rose said. "What do you think of our chances?"

Kurt considered it. She'd come to his office, they'd fucked, they'd showered…and every instinct told him to get her out of his office before someone caught them together. Every time he was called to a meeting, he wondered if the senior officers knew. But he knew Rose and he needed to talk…and besides, he didn't *want* to chase her out. They *were* supposed to be working together, after all.

"I wish I knew," he said. Every war the Royal Navy had simulated had involved purely human opponents, with both sides aware of the tramline networks reaching through their territories. Now…tramlines could be predicted, to a certain extent, but there was no way of knowing what might lie ahead of *Ark Royal* as she made her way through enemy territory. "Too little data to calculate."

Rose smiled. "You don't think this is a lucky ship?"

Kurt shrugged. They'd won their first engagement through surprise and superior firepower, the second when the enemy had broken off and the third…technically, they'd fled the battlefield, after giving the enemy a bloody nose. Luck had played a large role in their success, he had to agree, but he preferred careful planning. Planning tended to be more reliable, in the long run.

"I think we need to keep ahead of the bastards," he said. Whatever damage they'd done at New Russia, the aliens would still be in command of the territory – and priming themselves for a drive on Earth. Or maybe head around the edge of human space and attack one of the other settled worlds. There was no way to know what they might have in mind. "And I also think we have to concentrate on our planning."

Rose gave him a bewitching glance. It was funny how he could no longer think of her as anything other than beautiful. And she *was* beautiful. But dangerous, so dangerous...Molly was comforting, when Rose burned like a candle alight at both ends. And yet...how long had it been since he and Molly had made love, even before his recall to duty?

"Planning," she repeated. One hand reached for her tunic, threatening to pull it open to reveal her breasts. "Isn't there something else you would like to do?"

"I'm not a young man any longer," Kurt reminded her, embarrassed. "I need time to recharge my batteries before doing it again."

Rose smirked. "And there I was thinking that you were behind the stimulant shortage," she said. She went on at his questioning glance. "Someone – probably more than one person – has been talking the doctor into issuing stimulants. The doctor won't say who."

"Not me," Kurt said. There were warnings about using stimulants for sexual pleasure. In the long term, they could create dependency or reduce potency. But if someone believed that the entire ship was doomed, they might not care about the long-term effects. "I still need to recharge naturally."

He looked down at the flight rosters, although – in truth – they'd been over the same thing several times already. It provided an excuse to meet in private, yet it had long since worn out its usefulness. But the only alternative was to draw up new training simulations, which they would then have to fly out with their pilots...angrily, he scowled down at the list of names. Surely his life hadn't been so complicated before he'd started an illicit affair?

Rose leaned forward and placed her hand on his knee. "Thinking about your children?"

Kurt flushed. He *hadn't* been thinking about his children...but now she'd mentioned them, the guilt flooded back into his mind. Whatever happened between Molly and him was one thing, yet he would always be the father of Penny and Percy. His affair, his betrayal of their mother, would hurt them badly. He knew that for a fact. And yet he couldn't stop himself from touching Rose, now she'd broken the barrier between them.

"I miss them," he admitted, partly to cover his real thoughts. "And I may miss the rest of their lives."

The thought overwhelmed him. Penny would walk down the aisle... and he wouldn't be there to escort her. Percy would grow up, perhaps join the Royal Navy to be like the father he'd started to admire...and then marry himself, without his father to watch and advise him. And Molly... what would Molly do to make ends meet? Maybe she would marry again, even though her best years were past. Or maybe she would just work longer hours to keep the kids in their private school.

"You'll see them again, I'm sure," Rose said. She withdrew her hand and stood up, pacing around the cabin. "Tell me something. Where do you see *us* going?"

Kurt blanched. It was the question he had studiously refrained from even contemplating, as if refusing to think about it would make the question go away. But it hadn't and it wouldn't.

"I don't know," he admitted, finally.

Rose made him feel young again, he admitted, in the privacy of his own thoughts. He was old enough to be her father, just about; there was no denying that the thought of making love to her was a hell of a turn-on. And the danger, the looming threat of death or discovery, added a certain kind of spice to the whole affair. But afterwards, assuming they made it home, where would they be?

It wasn't fair on Rose, he knew, to tell her that he would leave Molly. Even if he wanted to leave his wife, he wasn't sure what he could say to the children – and he didn't want to walk out of their lives. It was bad enough that his current job could end his life in a split-second leaving them alone. He knew it would be worse if he walked away from their mother, leaving them even though he was still alive. Or would he wind up competing with Molly for their affection?

"Neither do I," Rose said, practically. She walked forward and sat down on his lap, wrapping her arms around him. "I don't expect to survive the next few weeks and neither should you."

Kurt blinked at her. The feel of her body pressing against his was hellishly distracting, but he didn't want to forget what she'd said. "You don't expect to survive?"

"We've lost fourteen pilots so far," Rose pointed out. There was an oddly dispassionate note to her voice. "I had someone in the analysis section run through the numbers for me. The odds of any of us surviving any given battle with the aliens are terrifyingly low. Sooner or later, our luck is going to run out and the aliens will kill us. Don't you know that to be true?"

Kurt nodded, wordlessly. The fewer starfighters *Ark Royal* could deploy, the greater the number of alien pilots that could be vectored onto each starfighter. And the aliens, damn them, didn't need to worry about watching their ammunition. Rose was right; sooner or later, a lucky shot would blow them into flaming debris, ending their lives before they even knew what had hit them. And the odds of the carrier making it back to Earth were very low.

"So here's my idea," Rose said. She shifted position until her breasts were pressing into his chin. "We enjoy ourselves now, between duty shifts. If we die, we die; if we live, you can go back to your family and I won't say a word. This isn't...this isn't a normal situation."

"I know," Kurt whispered.

It was a troubling problem. Would he have cheated on Molly – and he knew that was what he was doing – if he hadn't felt trapped by the aliens? Or would he have remained untouched by her blandishments? His hands reached up, almost of their own accord, to pull at her tunic, letting her breasts bounce free. He felt himself stiffen as her hand reached into his pants...

...And knew he was lost.

The Captain, according to Royal Naval regulations, was the sole source of authority on any given starship. There was, James had learnt at the Academy, plenty of case law to back up the assertion that the Captain had a wide range of authority to reward or punish his crew, even rewrite the specific words of orders as long as the intent remained in place. But, by the same token, involving the Captain in a disciplinary matter meant that it *would* be recorded in the ship's log. If the matter was not serious,

XOs preferred to handle it off the record and ensure that nothing was ever written down.

He sighed as he studied the three crewmen facing him, both trying not to look guilty and failing miserably. It wouldn't have been a problem, he knew, if they'd kept their wits about them, but they'd been stupid enough to let rumours spread out. Crewwoman Sally Fletcher had lost a bet with Senior Crewman Daniel Meyer and Shuttle Technician Abdul Richardson and, as a result of the terms, had had to perform a striptease in front of a dozen crewmen. Gambling was bad enough – it wasn't technically forbidden, even though there were limits – but the striptease was a definite no-no. Luckily, the Boatswain had caught wind of the plot before Sally found herself humiliated in front of the entire crew.

"It's at times like these," James announced, carefully not looking at each of them, "that I wish it was the lash tradition that we'd kept, rather than alcohol and sodomy."

All three of the crewmen flinched. The Captain's Mast might be official punishment, but there were limits. James had a far wider range of authority to issue punishments, provided he didn't do anything that was brought to the Captain's attention. Whipping the three of them through the ship was permitted, if someone took a careful look at regulations, but it was normally reserved for thieves or idiots who endangered their fellow officers.

"I confess I have great difficulty in understanding what you were thinking," James added, sweetly. "Please. What *were* you thinking?"

He looked from face to face, feeling his temper start to flare. "Let me guess," he added, when none of them seemed inclined to answer the question. "You reached the limits of what could be legally gambled, so you started searching for forfeits. And one of you two idiots" – he gazed at the two men – "had the bright idea of a striptease. Right?"

"Yes, sir," Richardson stammered.

James rolled his eyes. Gambling rings existed on almost every large starship, often serving as a vehicle for the younger and more naive crewmen to be separated from a third of their wages. Normally, the Boatswain would supervise to ensure that no one was drained of *all* their available wages – a third of naval wages were banked on Earth or Britannia, rather than onboard ship – but this particular ring had clearly failed to remain under supervision. He made a mental note to have a few sharp words with the Boatswain, then glared at the two men.

"Here is my judgement," he said, coldly. He scowled at the two men until they were shifting uncomfortably. "You will return all the money you won over the past two weeks, then report to the Boatswain for shit duties for the next week or so. *And*, while we are on this cruise, you will refrain from any further gambling until we return to port. Do you wish to dispute my judgement?"

He smiled, inwardly, at their expressions. They could, legally, ask the Captain to review the judgement. It *had* been known to happen, from time to time, but it was far more likely that the Captain would confirm the punishment and add a few refinements of his own. And it would end up in their permanent records, where it would be a black mark when they applied for promotion or mustang status.

"Out," he ordered. "Fletcher, stay behind."

He waited until the hatch had closed, then studied the younger crewwoman. She was a year or two younger than Midshipwoman Lopez; her file stated that she was the youngest child of a merchant family. James was surprised she'd fallen for such an obvious trick – non-money forfeits weren't covered by any rules – but this *was* her first cruise. And perhaps she was foolish enough to believe that the next round would allow her to make up her winnings.

James rolled his eyes as she twitched under his gaze. If the two men hadn't rigged the game, James would have eaten his uniform hat. She looked too sweet and innocent to deserve the chewing out she was going to get, but he pushed that aside and straightened up.

"Agreeing to that bet was stupid," he said, sharply. "What were you thinking, precisely?"

"I ran out of money," Sally said. She sounded on the verge of tears. "I…"

"So you agreed to a forfeit without checking the terms in advance?" James interrupted. "Or were you idiotic enough to believe you could *win*?"

He paused, long enough for her to pull herself together. "I know; idiotic gamblers *will* agree to idiotic forfeits. And I'm sure they would have pushed you into it if you tried to back out. But there are regulations against such matters, young lady, and *you* would have been left holding the bag. *You* could have been summarily charged with breaking those regulations and booted out of the navy.

"Which might not matter," he added, "if we don't make it home."

She flinched, again. "You will not recover whatever money you lost to them," James said. "Instead, it will go into the kitty – which should win you some plaudits from your comrades who might otherwise be disappointed. And, for the rest of this cruise, you will be barred from any further gambling, with *anyone*."

He paused. Chances were she no longer had the money to gamble with, whatever else happened. "I would suggest, in addition, that you never played for forfeits again," he added. "You are not experienced enough to tell the difference between something tolerable and something that will pose a threat to good order."

"Yes, sir," Sally said. "Thank you, sir."

James smiled. He *had* let her off lightly...but it was her first cruise. Maybe she'd learn a lesson, without needing to face more formal punishment.

"One other thing," he added. He glanced down at the duty roster, then looked back at her suddenly nervous face. "I'm assigning you to work under Deputy Boatswain Harrison. You will find her a good mentor, if you learn to listen."

He watched her go, then sighed. Seven hours to the jump into unexplored space, seven hours until they knew what was waiting on the other side...and he was busy dealing with disciplinary problems. But at least it was a distraction from worrying about the future. His lips quirked as he realised that was probably what the gamblers had had in mind, too.

But she *had* been idiotic, he knew. Naval life could be hard for a woman, particularly one who went out of her way to make it plain she *was* a woman. Poor Sally would have lost all the respect she'd earned if she'd gone through with the striptease, her status plunging instantly from fellow crewmember to whore. Even now, her status had probably been weakened. At least she'd shared in *some* of the punishment the two men had earned. It would save her from losing everything.

But enough of a punishment, he decided, ruefully. She didn't deserve additional punishment duties – shit duties, as they were called – let alone a public whipping. Hell, jokes aside, there had only ever been four since the Royal Navy had become a space-based service. It was far more common for someone to be dumped in the brig and then discharged as soon as the carrier returned to port. Maybe Sally could be transferred to another starship, one where her new reputation wouldn't follow her.

Shaking his head, he made a note in his private log of what had happened, then stood. The reporters had been badgering for a briefing and he couldn't put it off any longer. Maybe answering a few silly questions would help him relax.

And if they didn't, he told himself, he could always discuss the odds of them reaching home, once again. The reporters always found it alarming to hear the odds from a naval crewman.

———

"*Kiev* is in place, sir," Farley reported. Ahead of them, the tramline glimmered on the display, waiting. "They're reporting ready to jump."

Ted sucked in a breath. They'd repaired the damage, reloaded the mass drivers and reorganised the starfighter squadrons. But they weren't at tip-top condition, he knew, and they wouldn't be until they gained an additional handful of starfighter pilots, as well as some additional repairs.

"Order them to jump," he said, finally. He couldn't help a thrill of excitement, even though he knew it was dangerous. *This* was real exploration, the sort of work he'd hoped to do as a younger man. But instead he'd been assigned to *Ark Royal*...he shook his head, amused. It was funny how the world worked out, sometimes. "And then power up the Puller Drive."

Kiev vanished from the display. Long seconds passed before she popped back into existence, signalling urgently. There was no alien fleet waiting for them, Ted saw to his relief, but there was a source of radio signals orbiting the G2 star. An alien settlement? There shouldn't be anything human on the other side of the tramline.

He smiled to himself. No one had explored the tramline, according to the latest records. In hindsight, that had clearly been a disastrous mistake. Who knew what precautions could have been taken if the aliens had been discovered before the first encounter? But now…One way or another, they were definitely going where no man had gone before.

"Jump," he ordered, quietly.

CHAPTER
TWENTY NINE

"Disappointing, isn't it?"

Ted had to smile at Fitzwilliam's judgement. The first alien star system – the first star system humanity had ever discovered belonging to another intelligent race – was disappointing, in one sense. It didn't *look* any different from a human-occupied star system. In many ways, it reminded Ted of Vera Cruz, except the alien system was lucky enough to have a gas giant for later mining. But it was an alien world orbiting an alien star and that made all the difference.

He looked up at the display, watching as the passive sensors sucked in data from across the star system and channelled it down to the analyst section. A number of signal sources – strong signal sources – on the planet itself or in close orbit, a handful of smaller signal sources scattered across the star system and very little else. If it *was* a forward alien base, Ted decided, feeling an odd hint of disappointment himself, the aliens had been criminally lax about fortifying it. But another part of him was relieved for the very same reason. A fleet of alien battleships would not be a pleasant discovery, not now.

"Locate the other tramlines," he ordered. Tramlines were largely predicable, but there were times when reality didn't follow the laws laid down by human theorists. Ted had always been amused by how shocked the scientists sounded when they realised there was something in the universe they hadn't accounted for in their models, no matter how elegant they seemed. "Where do they go?"

There was a long pause as the passive sensors measured the gravimetric flickers around the local star. "Four tramlines," Farley said, finally. "One leading back the way we came; two heading further into unexplored space, one dogging back along the edge of human space."

Ted found himself seriously considering taking the tramlines that led further into alien territory, then quashed the impulse ruthlessly. "Launch probes towards the alien world," he ordered, once he was reasonably sure that they weren't about to be attacked by alien starships guarding the tramline. "And then take us towards" – he glanced at the display – "Tramline Two."

Fitzwilliam's voice echoed in his ear. "You don't mean to engage the planetary defences?"

"It depends on what kind of defences there are," Ted replied. "We will just have to wait and see."

The thought made him scowl. He couldn't blame Fitzwilliam for wondering; they had, on the face of it, a rare chance to attack an alien-settled world and rock them back on their heels. But the sheer *lack* of noticeable defences was worrying him. Had the aliens only discovered humanity when they'd stumbled across Vera Cruz and attacked at once? Where they facing the equivalent of a quick-reaction force? If that was true – and he doubted it – what would they face when the enemy actually *mobilised*?

Or would they make a deliberate decision not to fortify Alien-One? The thought was odd – in their place, he would certainly have insisted that the sole known point of contact between human and alien was heavily fortified – but perhaps it made a certain kind of sense. *We might survey the system before they were ready to meet us.*

He had a sudden mental image of humanity's territory reaching out further and further, spreading the levels of deployable military forces ever thinner as their responsibilities grew rapidly. Perhaps, sooner or later, their ability to respond to a crisis before it got out of hand would be completely lost. He shook his head, putting the thought aside for later contemplation. Now humanity knew it was no longer alone in the universe, it was unlikely that petty nationalism could be tolerated any longer.

But we have aliens to hate now, he thought, cynically. *There's no point in hating humans when we have aliens to hate.*

Hours passed slowly as the display continued to fill up with data. There was an asteroid belt in the system, several worlds that could have passed for Mars or Venus…and one Earth-like world, the source of the radio signals. Analysis indicated that the world rated at least 80% Earth-like; the atmosphere was breathable, the sea water was suitable for fish from Earth…from afar, it seemed the perfect colony. The drones kept creeping closer, boring their way through space on ballistic courses, sending data back via laser link to the carrier. There was no way – yet – to get pictures of the surface, but the alien orbital facilities were all too clear.

"It looks like a transhipment hub," Anderson said. He sounded a little disappointed too, perhaps by the sheer normality of the alien structure. It was a boxy mass that looked too like some of *Ark Royal's* contemporaries for comfort. But it was necessary. Humanity's giant colonist-carriers couldn't land on planetary surfaces; judging by the presence of the station, nor could their alien counterparts. "I don't even think its armed."

"We have to be careful," Fitzwilliam reminded him. "The aliens might have different ideas about arming their settlements against possible attack."

Ted couldn't disagree. Now, with alien attack a very real possibility, even the smallest colony worlds were bolting weapons to their orbital stations. Few of them had any real chance of standing off an alien attack, even one carried out by a single starship, but there was no way they would agree to leave themselves defenceless. Just before they'd left Earth for the second time, he'd heard that stocks in companies producing war material had skyrocketed. It almost made him wish he'd taken the time to invest some of his salary in such corporations. God knew he wasn't doing anything with it.

He shook his head, studying the display. "Is there anything else in orbit?"

"A handful of satellites, but nothing else," the analyst said, firmly. "Unless they have a way to cloak an entire battlestation from our view."

He paused, looking down at the live feed from the drones. "Sir," one of the drones just got into orbit," he said. "It found a camp on the surface. "I think it's a POW camp."

Ted leaned forward, alarmed. "Show me," he ordered. "Are you sure?"

He scowled as the images appeared on the display. The settlement was encircled by solid metal walls, guarded by aliens…and, inside, there were

CHRISTOPHER G. NUTTALL

humans. They wore nothing, but the clothes they were born in; listlessly, they wandered around the camp.

"Two hundred and forty-seven men, women and children," the analyst said, with heavy satisfaction. "Source unknown."

Fitzwilliam coughed. "Are there any other alien settlements on the planet?"

"Not as far as we can tell," the analyst said. He paused. "There is a handful of buildings outside the camp's walls, but I don't think they're large enough to be a full-scale settlement."

"We're missing something," Ted mused. The aliens had installed a transhipment hub; clearly, they'd intended to settle the world. Had they changed their minds when they'd discovered Vera Cruz or were the human observers missing something? "But what?"

Fitzwilliam spoke rapidly. "Sir," he said, "we cannot let this opportunity go to waste. This is a rare chance to recover a number of human prisoners from alien hands!"

"I know," Ted said, rather more tartly than he intended. "But this could easily be a trap."

He looked down at the display, contemplatively. Fitzwilliam was right; this *was* a rare chance to give the aliens a bloody nose, as well as removing human prisoners from their hands. But if it was a trap…he looked over at Major Parnell's image on the display, quirking his eyebrows. The Major nodded, accepting the challenge.

"Very well," Ted said. "We will act to recover the prisoners."

It took nearly thirty minutes to draw up a plan of attack. On the face of it, *destroying* the alien transhipment hub and the handful of satellites would be easy, but if the aliens had intended to make it hard for the humans to recover the POWs it would be very tricky. His imagination provided a dozen possibilities, all based on human history. There could be a nuke buried under the POW camp, the prisoners could all have been forcibly addicted to something only the aliens could produce…or they could simply have been brainwashed into servitude. Even if Ted and his crew did manage to get them all home, they might never be trusted again.

"Hostage rescue is always a pain," Parnell had said. The Marine had sounded as enthusiastic as ever, but there had been an undertone of worry in his voice that bothered Ted. "The hostages have to be treated with great suspicion, because they might have bonded with their captors."

It seemed absurd, Ted considered, for anyone to bond with the aliens. But after their images had been released, there had been humans extolling the virtues in their noble bodies...or something like that. Ted hadn't been paying close attention to the lunatic fringe. But, if someone felt completely cut off from Earth and the rest of the human community, could they be seduced by the aliens? It was a definite possibility.

"Take us into attack position," he ordered. The closer they sneaked to Alien-One, the greater the chance of detection. He'd been tempted to snipe at the alien transhipment hub from a distance, just like they'd done at New Russia, but there was too great a chance of a projectile missing its target and striking the planet instead. "Is the fleet ready?"

"Yes, sir," Farley said. He nodded towards one of the monitors, tracking the location and status of every ship in the flotilla. "The fleet is standing by."

"Good," Ted said. He smiled, inwardly. As tiny as the alien settlement was – although he couldn't escape the feeling they were missing something – it was still the first alien world to be attacked by human forces. *Ark Royal* and her crew would go down in the history books...absently, he wondered just who would be writing the histories of the war. Humans... or the aliens? "Launch the first spread of unpowered missiles."

He settled back in his chair as the flight of blue icons darted out from the icons representing *Ark Royal* and headed towards their target. Unpowered as they were, not even *Ark Royal* could track them, but as long as they kept their drives deactivated they would follow a strictly predicable ballistic course. Long minutes ticked away until the missiles finally entered attack range and went active, bringing up their drives and lancing towards the alien station. There was a brief flurry of activity as the aliens realised the danger, too late. The missiles slammed home, blasting the space station into flaming debris. Ted watched, emotionlessly, as the debris started to de-orbit and fall towards the planet below.

Too much firepower, he thought, ruefully. If they'd realised the alien point defence would have been so pitiful, he could have saved a handful of missiles. *But at least we killed it.*

"Target destroyed," Farley reported, with heavy satisfaction. "I say again, target destroyed."

"There's nothing large enough to pose a threat to the ecosystem," one of the analysts added. "The pieces of junk should all burn up in the planetary atmosphere."

Ted kept his thoughts to himself. It was quite possible that there had been human POWs on the station, humans who had been killed without ever knowing what had hit them. There had been no choice, he told himself; the station had to be destroyed as quickly as possible. But he would never know for sure if humans had died because of him. The thought would torment him for the rest of his life.

"Launch starfighters," he ordered. "I want orbital space swept *clean*."

———

Kurt put thoughts of Rose out of his mind as the starfighter lurched forward and crashed out into interplanetary space at a colossal speed. Ahead of him, Alien-One glowed in the inky darkness of space, surrounded by unblinking stars that seemed to gaze pitilessly at the tiny humans infesting their domain. He shivered, helplessly, as he looked back at them. Most humans, even starship crewmen, didn't really comprehend the true vastness of space. He and his fellow pilots, however, knew it all too well. They were utterly insignificant on such a scale.

Bracing himself, he took the shuttle down towards planetary orbit, wishing – again – that the designers had solved the problem of crafting a starfighter that functioned equally well in space as on the ground. There were humans down there, according to the announcement, humans who had been taken prisoner by the aliens. He wanted to get down to the surface and tear into the alien defenders, pulling the prisoners out before they died in alien hands. But his craft couldn't hope to survive a trip through the atmosphere…

An alien satellite loomed up ahead of him. The computers engaged it automatically, blowing it apart before it could do anything threatening. Tiny pieces of debris fell towards the planet's atmosphere as Kurt led the rest of the squadron forward, searching for other alien satellites. None of the satellites seemed anything other than civilian designs – not too different from anything human – but Kurt knew just how easy it was to hide a weapon in space. They didn't even dare risk trying to take one of the satellites intact.

"Space is clear, sir," he reported, finally.

Despite himself, Kurt was almost disappointed. If *he'd* taken prisoners from an alien race, he would have made damn sure they were held somewhere that was heavily defended. But the aliens, for whatever reasons of their own, clearly disagreed with his logic. Maybe they'd assumed that humanity wouldn't bother to try to recover POWs. Or maybe they just hadn't had the shipping to move them further into their territory.

"Very clear," Rose agreed. As always, hearing her voice while they were on duty provoked a multitude of contradictory responses in his mind. It had been much easier before they'd become lovers…now, he was in danger of obsessing over her. But, at the same time, he found it more than a little irritating. "Even the debris is falling rapidly."

Kurt nodded. Earth had always had nightmares about a settled asteroid or a massive space station falling out of orbit, even if it shattered into countless pieces first. Adding that much junk to the planet's ecosystem couldn't possibly be healthy. But the alien world wouldn't be badly affected by the relatively small amount of debris…and besides, it was an *alien* world, not a human colony. The aliens could take care of themselves.

"Return to CSP positions," he ordered. *Ark Royal* was holding position some distance from the planet, making it easier to run for the tramline if necessary. A handful of frigates, however, were moving into orbit, ready to provide fire support if the Marines needed it. "And keep your eyes peeled. These bastards have very good stealth, remember?"

————

"Space is clear, sir," Farley reported. "No sign of any ground-based defences."

Ted wasn't too surprised. Ground-based defences were expensive and unreliable…although, with their technology, the aliens could probably create something more capable than humanity had been able to produce. But Alien-One was clearly nothing more than a tiny settlement and a

POW camp, perhaps a clearinghouse for the aliens to use to sort through their prisoners and work out who they wanted to interrogate more carefully. Or perhaps they just wanted to put the POWs out of the way and forget about them.

He shook his head. The aliens had gone to too much effort to gather the POWs merely to leave them alone. Perhaps, once the POWs were recovered, they could shed light on how they'd been treated – and why. Or perhaps they'd be as ignorant as their fellow humans.

There was a bleep from the tactical console. "Wait," Farley said. "One large ground-based transmitted, several hundred miles from the POW camp. It's broadcasting out into space."

Ted didn't hesitate. "Kill it," he ordered. That far from the POW camp there would be no risk of hurting the prisoners. "Can you identify the intended destination?"

Farley shook his head. "The signal was beamed towards Tramline Four," he said. "But I don't know what – if anything – actually heard it."

They won't have heard it yet, Ted thought. Tramline Four – leading further into alien-controlled space - was five light minutes from the planet. But even though the transmission had been terminated, there was no stopping the first signal burst from reaching its destination. *There must be a ship there, lying doggo. They'll bring help from the next system.*

Farley looked up. "The transmitter is dead, sir," he said. On the display, a fireball was rising from where the frigate-launched KEW had struck the transmitter. "But I still don't know where it was aimed."

"Launch a pair of additional drones towards Tramline Four," Ted ordered. "If there are reinforcements within shouting distance, they'll have to come from there."

He tried to work it out in his head, then gave up as he realised there just wasn't enough data to make even educated guesses. What was on the other end of Tramline Four? If there was an alien fleet in the system, how long would it take them to power up and advanced to Alien-One? Long enough to get the POWs off the surface…or quickly enough to force Ted to abandon some of them on the ground.

"Vector two frigates towards the tramline," he ordered, after a moment. The frigates weren't stealthy, but their sensors were better than the drones. Besides, they could pop through the tramline themselves and see what was on the other side. "I want advance warning if something pops through. If nothing does by the time the frigates arrive, one of them is to jump into the tramline and investigate."

He turned back to the main display. "And order the Marines to proceed with all due dispatch," he added. "We may be running short of time."

CHAPTER
THIRTY

Charles suppressed the urge to whoop and cry hurrah as the shuttles plunged through the planetary atmosphere, lurching from side to side as if they expected the alien ground-based defences – if there *were* any defences – to open fire at any moment. This was what he'd signed up for, a daring combat drop right into the heart of enemy territory. Maybe the enemy weren't as heavily armed as he assumed they would be, when the human military actually hit an alien colony world, but it was still a combat drop. Drills just weren't the same.

"Ten seconds," he called, as the shuttle lurched violently. There was no incoming fire, thankfully, but he was sure it was just a matter of time until they hit a heavily-defended world. By then, the lessons from a reasonably placid combat drop would have to be learned and learned well. "Five seconds…"

He was first out of the shuttle, as it should be. The magnetic field tossed him through the hatch and sent him plunging down towards the world below. Beside him, combat drones came online, spoofing enemy sensors and giving them a multitude of targets to engage…if they'd had anything to use to engage the onrushing humans. Behind him, the remainder of the Marines streamed out of the shuttle. He spared a moment of sympathy for the damn reporter – no matter how hard he'd worked over the last few days, he was utterly unprepared for a combat drop – then turned his mind back to the landing. Below, the alien camp was rapidly coming into view.

The chute popped bare seconds before he would have hit the ground, yanking him to a slow fall that allowed him to land reasonably gently. It disintegrated a second later as Charles moved forward, weapons and sensors searching for targets. The combat datanet came online as the other Marines landed, most of them fanning out in a wide circle around the alien camp. A smaller group would take care of the alien buildings to the south, dealing with any defences as rapidly and brutally as necessary, but taking aliens alive if possible. Charles knew better than to think that taking prisoners would be easy, yet he knew the human race needed to learn to understand its foe.

Pushing the thought aside, he led the way towards the alien camp. The wall surrounding it was solid metal; despite seeing it from orbit, he'd expected to discover that it was actually a fence when they hit the ground. It seemed excessive, somehow. The alien guards swung around, then opened fire, confirming Charles's suspicion that the aliens had managed to construct plasma weapons that could be comfortably carried by a single soldier. Each of them, he recognised unwillingly, was capable of burning through a Marine-issue battlesuit…

"Return fire," he ordered. Shots rang out as the Marines engaged their targets. He saw an alien head disintegrate as an armour-piercing bullet, intended to punch through armour comparable to the armour the Marines themselves wore, slammed through its target and went onwards. "Take them all out."

Two Marines fell, alerts popping up in his HUD, as they rushed the camp, but the aliens suffered worse. Despite not being taken by surprise, they had had no time to prepare proper defences before the Marines came down and surrounded them. Charles couldn't help wondering if the aliens had seriously believed the human forces would never reach the camp or if the soldiers guarded it had been rated as expendable. But the aliens still fought, no matter how helpless their position, and died in place. Charles found himself caught between a kind of reluctant admiration and a cold, dispassionate disdain. The aliens could have withdrawn from the camp before the Marines landed and saved their lives.

The camp's gateway was another piece of solid metal. Charles muttered orders and the demolition team went to work, blowing the gateway right off its hinges. Inside, he saw a handful of metal buildings – they looked to have been designed by humans, rather than aliens – and a number of human prisoners, staring at the Marines as if they were creatures from another world. All of them were naked, even the women and children. It made sense, he knew; it was hard for a naked human to conceal a weapon. Hell, the aliens weren't likely to be interested in human bodies...

...But it still didn't make it any easier to bear.

"Most of them are clearly Mexican," Yang muttered. "But some of the others are not so recognisable."

He was right, Charles realised. Who would have thought that the reporter had actually come in useful? Pushing the thought aside, he activated his suit's speakers. It struck him, a moment later, that they might not actually speak English, before dismissing the thought as absurd. English was a common second language in space, as well as the official language for all deep space activities. Most of the POWs would definitely speak English.

"Attention," he said. The POWs still looked listless, despite the appearance of salvation. It bothered him more than he cared to admit. "We're the Royal Marines, from Earth. We're here to take you off this mudball, assuming you want to go."

The shuttles flew lower, then dropped down towards the cleared LZ. For once, the POWs showed some reaction – absolute terror. Charles blinked in surprise, wondering if they would have to knock the POWs out just to get them onto the shuttles, then relaxed as the shuttles touched down. As soon as the roar of their engines faded away, the POWs relaxed and stopped panicking.

"Women and children first," Charles ordered. Thankfully, the POWs didn't seem inclined to argue. "Get into the shuttles and strap yourselves down. Hurry!"

A team of Marines swept the camp as the naked women and children made their way towards the shuttles. The medic – the closest thing they had to a war crimes assessor – reported that the camp's water contained a combination of various drugs. One of them would make the POWs listless and biddable, another heightened their fears while dampening their other emotions. At least that explained why the POWs had been able to endure their nakedness, the medic concluded, but he had no idea what the long-term effects of such treatment would be.

"The drug has some similarities to a number of penal drugs," he said. "They may well have taken them from our supplies, perhaps from New Russia."

Charles shuddered. Before discovering a suitable world for housing dangerous criminals and lacking the political backing to execute them, the human race had experimented with various forms of drugs to control their behaviour. Some of them permanently dampened sexual ardour, others encouraged compliance and obedience. But none of the drugs had been completely effective, he recalled, or they turned out to have thoroughly unpleasant side effects. He found it hard to care about murderers or child molesters who'd been forced to take the drugs, but it was alarmingly easy to imagine them being used for less savoury purposes.

He turned to watch as the remaining women were shoed into the shuttle by the Marines, then looked back at the medic. "Can they be purged of the drugs?"

"I imagine they're in for a rough few weeks," he said, shortly. "Like all such drugs, they can be quite addictive if taken regularly. But after that they should be fine."

Charles had his doubts. Back during his first year of training, there had been a young recruit who had been a drug addict before trying to join the military. Somehow, he'd stayed clean long enough for routine drug screening to miss him, but eventually his body's demands for the drug had become overpowering. He'd fallen off the wagon and he'd fallen off hard.

"Make sure the doctors on the carrier know the situation," he ordered. "And you can detach yourself to assist them if necessary."

He strode through the rest of the camp, examining it quickly. It was actually nicer than some of the camps he'd seen on Earth, complete with hot and cold running water, surprisingly comfortable beds and regular food. A quick check revealed that the aliens were feeding their captives proper meals, rather than nutrient mush or something edible, but tasteless. Charles couldn't help frowning as he walked back out of the building, wondering at their odd behaviour. One moment they attacked mercilessly, the next they treated their captives with a curious mixture of kindness and ruthlessness.

The remaining POWs started to panic again as the shuttles took off, clawing for the sky. Some of the Marines attempted to calm them, but it was impossible until the shuttles had vanished into the wild blue yonder. Charles looked at the panic in their eyes and found himself wondering, despite the medic's words, if they would ever be normal again. The drugs had clearly influenced their behaviour…and not for the better.

His radio buzzed. "Sir," one of the Marines said, "I think you should take a look at this."

Charles located the Marine on the datanet, then walked back to one of the buildings in the centre of the camp. Corporal Glen was standing by a hatch, pointing to it with an armoured hand. Charles followed the pointing hand and frowned as he saw English letters written on the metal. *Robert A. Heinlein.* For a moment, he puzzled over it before recalling one of the endless briefings he'd had to attend before boarding *Ark Royal.* The *Heinlein* had been a colony ship, owned by a consortium of settlers who wanted to leave the rest of the human race far behind…and they'd done it too. They'd left human space before Vera Cruz had been settled and had never been seen again, until now.

"Interesting," he said. Had the settlers gone far enough to encounter the aliens? Had *that* been First Contact, not the attack on Vera Cruz? Had the settlers somehow provoked the war? "Take all the recordings you can for the analysts."

He stepped backwards, staring at the buildings. Now he knew about the *Heinlein,* it was clear that the POW barracks were little more than prefabricated human buildings from a previous era. The aliens, for whatever reason, had given humans human buildings. It was yet another oddity for the social scientists to puzzle over, he decided, making a mental note to see to it that some of the more reliable researchers received a full report. Some of the civilian ones made mistakes, misreading situations…and then refused to confess to their errors. And some of those errors had cost lives.

His radio buzzed, again. "Sir, we captured a handful of aliens," Captain Jackson reported. "I think you're going to want to see this."

"Understood," Charles said. He couldn't help a flicker of excitement. "I'm on my way."

———

James watched in horror as the first POWs stumbled out of the shuttles and onto the deck. They were naked – drawing the attention of most of the shuttlebay crewmen, he noticed – but they walked like zombies, rather than human beings. Even the children, young girls and boys, stumbled about as though they needed to be prodded in the right direction to keep them moving. The reporters, who had hoped to make history by conducting the first set of interviews with alien POWs, stared in horror.

He'd been worried that the POWs might pose a threat to the carrier. As XO, it was his job to worry about such possibilities. But right now, looking at their blank faces, he knew that they posed no threat. The real problem was keeping them alive long enough to get to a proper medical facility. *Ark Royal's* sickbay was huge – frigates and other smaller ships were meant to ship their casualties to the carrier – but it wasn't large enough to handle three hundred former POWs.

"Get them sedated," the doctor ordered, briskly.

"Move them to another room first," James ordered, silently grateful for the over-engineering *Ark Royal's* designers had indulged in. There was plenty of space for the POWs, once they were away from the shuttlebay. "The shuttles have to go out again."

His communicator bleeped. "You'll need to secure the brig," the Captain ordered. "They caught some aliens."

James nodded, grimly. Aliens…aliens might well pose a real threat.

He turned and directed the reporters to help the doctor and her staff urge the POWs out of the shuttlebay and into their new quarters. For once, they didn't argue.

———

The alien buildings were right next to the shore, Marcus saw, as he followed Major Parnell towards the odd-looking buildings. Human prefabricated structures were ugly blocks – designed that way to encourage the inhabitants to work towards building something more aesthetic for themselves – but there was something oddly attractive about the alien buildings. They glimmered an eerie green and gold, shimmering faintly in the sunlight. But it was the aliens themselves who really caught his attention.

He'd seen images of the bodies that had been recovered from the wreckage *Ark Royal* had left in her wake, but this was different. Up close, the aliens were a shimmering multitude of colours, some bright green, others orange or even yellow. Compared to them, the difference between white and black humans – or even his father's brown and his mother's yellow – looked imperceptible. He felt a chill running down his spine as he saw one of the aliens staring at him, his – or her – black orbs meeting his and refusing to look away. It was impossible to escape the feeling that he had been weighed in the balance and found wanting.

Somehow, he managed to pull his gaze away from the alien eyes and inspect the rest of their bodies. There was something oddly snake-like about their bodies, ululating slightly as if they couldn't stay completely still, despite the weapons pointed at them. They wore no clothes, as far as he could tell; their skins seemed faintly watery, as if they were used to swimming through the sea. Perhaps they were, he guessed, as he saw one of the aliens turn to look at the shore. Chances were they could swim far better than the Marines, no matter how intensely the Marines had trained.

"One of the shuttles has been diverted," a Marine called. "They'll take the aliens up into space."

"Good," Parnell said. He switched his suit's speakers on, then addressed the aliens. "Can you understand me?"

The aliens seemed to flinch backwards, but said nothing. It was impossible to tell if they were playing dumb or if they genuinely didn't understand. Their bodies were still quivering faintly; fear, Marcus wondered, or was he trying to interpret their actions in light of human body language? There was no way to understand the meaning of their motions.

"Maybe the POWs know how to speak to them," he said, out loud.

"I doubt it," Parnell replied. "The aliens would be fools to let the POWs learn their language."

Markus smiled. "I had a friend who had no gift for languages at all, but married a Malay girl," he said. "He insisted she talked to him in English. Maybe the aliens think the same way."

He felt his smile widen as the shuttle swept down from high overhead, eventually coming to rest on the sandy beach. Despite over three hundred years of effort, the human race had yet to develop a viable AI…and without one, automated language translators were fundamentally unreliable. And that was when *human* languages were taken into account. Who knew just how complex an *alien* language would be? And the POWs would have ample motives to learn how to speak to their captors. How else could they tell the aliens they were in pain?

But if they had been drugged, he asked himself silently, how would they know they were in pain?

The aliens started to produce hissing noises as soon as the Marines started to prod them towards the shuttle. Markus wondered if they were trying to talk to their captors, but no matter how hard he listened he couldn't make out any understandable words. He quickly checked to make sure that it was all being recorded – later, perhaps, he could get a translation – and then followed the protesting aliens as they marched towards the shuttle. One of them broke free and ran, with a curious waddling motion, towards the water. A Marine shouted after him, then shot the alien in the leg. The alien toppled over and lay still.

Markus swallowed hard as the alien was recovered by two Marines, then carried bodily into the shuttle. The remaining aliens didn't show any further reluctance to move; they inched into the shuttle, then sat on the deck. Markus watched the Marines secure them as best as they could, then sit back and wait for liftoff. Moments later, the shuttle shuddered and lurched into the air.

He heard one of the aliens let out a keening sound and winced, feeling an odd twinge of sympathy. The aliens had been living with the POWs, performing odd experiments on the POWs...and yet he couldn't help feeling a little sorry for the nine aliens. They were going to be delivered to a secure facility in the Sol System...or, perhaps, wind up killed by their own people if the aliens caught up with *Ark Royal*. It was easy to believe that they would never see their home again.

"He ran towards the water," Parnell mused. "There could be an entire alien settlement under the waves."

Markus stared at him. The orbital sensors hadn't detected any settlements...but they hadn't looked under the water. How could they?

"You think they stay in the water?"

"They're certainly built for it," Parnell said. "They remind me of that character from the TV show...the guy who was a merman or something. But thousands of them could be under the waves, hiding from us."

Markus shuddered. He hoped the Marine was wrong.

CHAPTER
THIRTY ONE

"There will be a review, of course."

Ted nodded, glumly. There were strict rules for handling POWs, rules that would logically be applied to their alien captives too. Humanity's treatment of POWs tended to range widely, but the war wasn't old enough for common decency to be forgotten – and besides, the aliens would be a source of intelligence in their own right. There was no need to mistreat them even if there wasn't a political lobby that would rise up in arms at the merest hint the aliens weren't being treated gently.

"Under the circumstances, I think we can agree that no action is required," he said. It was legal to use all necessary force to prevent prisoners from escaping – and while he was sure the Marines would face a great deal of second-guessing, the Admiralty would probably take their side. "And the other aliens? Are they healthy?"

The doctor sighed. She'd been irked at being called away from the rescued POWs in order to tend to the aliens, even though they were valuable prisoners. "I am no expert in the care and feeding of alien life forms," she said, "and nor is anyone else in the navy. We have no baseline for what is normal for their race and what isn't. There are steps we can take to ensure that their quarters are suitable for them, and we *think* we can provide them with proper foodstuffs, but there are too many unanswered questions for us to be completely sure."

She gazed down at her terminal. "I've used medical nanites to start building up a profile of a living alien," she added. "I'm reluctant to risk more invasive procedures until we have an excellent idea of how their bodies will respond. The injured alien has been placed in a stasis capsule until we can work out how best to proceed with treatment. For the moment, sir, there isn't much more we can do."

Fitzwilliam smiled. "Should we place them *all* in stasis?"

"If we had the capsules to spare, I'd recommend it," the doctor said. "As it is, I'm worried about the condition of several of the former POWs. I'd prefer to put them in stasis if their condition worsens."

Ted sighed. "What *is* their condition?"

"Drugged, mainly," the doctor said. "Varying levels of dosage. My subordinates and I have had a chance to inspect a handful of the POWs; there's very little actual damage, but there are signs that the aliens took blood and skin samples. I don't think they did anything more invasive themselves, at least to the surviving prisoners."

"Anyone they killed might have been forgotten," Ted commented. Drugged as they were, the prisoners might not have noticed if they'd lost friends or family to the aliens. "Or simply held at another compound."

"We will ask them when they recover enough to talk to us," the doctor assured him. "For the moment, however, we can only treat their withdrawal symptoms and pray none of them die."

"I have a question," Fitzwilliam said. "Couldn't we drug them ourselves?"

"Keep them on the drugs, you mean?" The doctor shook her head. "Quite apart from the violation of medical ethics, *Commander*, the human body isn't designed for long-term addiction to anything. Nor do we have the supplies to start easing them off the drugs. All we can do is let them slowly clear their own systems and clean up the mess."

"Understood," Ted said. "Dismissed, doctor."

He watched the doctor leave the compartment, then turned to Fitzwilliam. "Is there an alien city, after all?"

"It looks that way," Fitzwilliam confirmed. "There's nothing to be detected from orbit, but we flew a couple of drones over the ocean and picked up low-level emissions from below the waves. We don't have any suitable probes to drop into the water…"

"We could put one together," the Chief Engineer suggested. "It wouldn't take too long, if we recycle a number of spare parts."

"We can't stay in this system for much longer," Ted said. He considered it for a long moment, then shook his head. "We'll come back, one day, and uncover the aliens then."

"There is another possibility," Farley pointed out. "We could drop rocks on the alien city from orbit."

Ted was revolted at the idea, although he had the uneasy feeling that suggestions like that were going to become more and more common as the war raged on. The aliens had depopulated Vera Cruz and invaded New Russia. God alone knew what was happening on the surface...and, by now, they could easily have found other targets. There was no shortage of tramlines within two or three jumps from New Russia that would take them to more populated worlds.

"No," he said, firmly. "As long as we believe the aliens aren't committing mass slaughter, we will refrain from committing it ourselves."

"The Admiralty might disagree," Farley pointed out, mulishly.

Ted swallowed the urge to bite the young man's head off. Tired as they were, stressed as they were, that was pushing the limits for addressing one's commanding officer.

"Yes, they might," he said. He kept his voice very cold. "But we have received no specific orders to bombard alien civilian settlements and we will not act without them."

And such an order would be illegal, he knew. Killing enemy soldiers was one thing, butchering civilians was quite another. If he gave such an order, his crew would be quite within their rights to refuse to carry it out. And if they *did* carry it out, the Admiralty would charge them as being accomplices to genocide. The entire crew might go on trial...

Would it ever be legal? The thought was terrifying. Even the most heavily-militarised human society hadn't managed to turn *everyone* into a warrior. But what if the aliens had actually *succeeded* in producing a completely militarised society? Would there come a time when genocide was the only way to end the war? He shuddered, remembering the debates and moral quandaries they'd been forced to study at the Academy. The Bug Scenario, they'd called it, a situation where humanity waged a war with a completely alien race, one bent on exterminating humanity. Should the bugs be exterminated to save mankind?

Angrily, he changed the subject. "Do we know where the prisoners came from?"

"Most of them are clearly Latin American in origin," Fitzwilliam said. "We assume they came from Vera Cruz, although in that case several hundred more remain unaccounted for. The remainder...we don't know yet. None of the DNA samples we drew matched with any of our records."

Ted wasn't surprised. The Mexican Government hadn't been in the habit of sharing its files with anyone, least of all the major interstellar powers. They would have to ask the Mexicans once they got back to Earth, maybe sharing the other DNA codes with everyone else and seeing who got a match. Perhaps the aliens had jumped more than one colony mission before the attack on Vera Cruz.

"See to their care and feeding," he ordered. He looked over at Parnell. "And the alien prisoners?"

"I have a squad of Marines stationed in position to provide security for the aliens," Parnell reported. Left unspoken was the very real possibility that the aliens could be threatened by *Ark Royal's* crew. "As far as we can tell, the aliens themselves don't pose a threat, but we're taking every precaution regardless."

"Good," Ted said, silently blessing his ship's paranoid designers. The quarantine ward was completely self-contained, to the point where the prisoners and their monitors could be completely isolated from the rest of the ship. If they had any viruses that could spread to humanity, they wouldn't get very far. "Make sure the guards are rotated regularly. I don't want to take any chances."

"Lots of curious crewmen," Parnell added. "We might want to place recordings of the aliens on the datanet."

Ted hesitated, then shook his head. He could understand the crew being curious about their alien captives, but he had no way of knowing how the aliens or their superiors would react to such treatment. Humans wouldn't be happy when they found out about the nude prison camp, even if cold logic suggested the aliens hadn't meant any harm.

"No," he said. He looked around the compartment. "Have we pulled everything useful from the penal camp and the alien base?"

"We pulled a few samples of alien technology from their base," Parnell said.

"Aye," Anderson growled. "I'm looking forward to studying it, I am."

"As soon as we're on our way," Ted assured him. "And the camp itself?"

"There's nothing apart from the prefabricated buildings," Parnell said. "We searched thoroughly and found nothing else from the *Heinlein*. I was hoping for a flight recorder, but…"

He shrugged. "I suspect the full story of their colony mission won't be known until we actually manage to talk to the aliens," he admitted. "Overall, if the prisoners hadn't been drugged, they would have been bored out of their minds."

Ted nodded. Even when he'd been commander of a starship permanently stuck in the reserves, he'd had something to do. *Ark Royal* had had no shortage of repair or modification jobs…and when those palled, he'd had access to a vast entertainment library and the ship's own production of rotgut. But staying in a prison camp for weeks, perhaps months, with nothing to do would have driven him out of his mind.

"Unless anyone sees a strong reason to remain in this system," he said, "we will proceed to Tramline Two within the hour. That should take us back on a course towards human space."

There was no disagreement. Everyone knew that the aliens had signalled for help – and no one knew how long it would take for help to arrive. If there *was* a large alien colony under the waves, help might well come sooner than later. Ted couldn't imagine the Royal Navy abandoning Britannia as long as there was a hope of saving it, or even Nova Scotia. No, the aliens would be on their way. The only question was how long they had before the shit hit the fan.

"Good," Ted said. He rose to his feet. "Dismissed."

———

"It must have been horrifically dangerous down there," Barbie said.

"It was," Markus said, dramatically. "And the worst of it was jumping out of the shuttle in a combat suit."

The Marines had gone out of their way to tell him how horrific the whole experience was – and, if anything, they'd understated. Maybe there were people who skydived for fun, but Markus had already decided he wasn't one of them. He'd taken one look at the ground coming closer, his sense of perspective so badly screwed up that he'd been unsure if he was falling or rising, then closed his eyes tightly. The whole experience had left him trembling in his suit, permanently hovering on the verge of throwing up until he'd finally hit the ground.

But there hadn't been any real danger, he knew, once they'd actually reached the ground. The aliens hadn't tried to prevent them from landing or even reinforce the guards on the penal camp. It was almost as if they *wanted* the POWs to be rescued. But why?

He thought back through the recordings he'd taken – or borrowed from the Marines. Was the whole world a subtle trap? Or had the aliens simply decided not to risk more than a token attempt to defend the camp with *Ark Royal* hovering high overhead, ready to pour fire down onto alien defensive stations? But if it was a trap, the aliens would have had to know that *Ark Royal* had survived Russia…

The XO entered the briefing room, looking businesslike. "Mister Yang, I need to speak with you," he said, bluntly. "Come with me."

Markus smiled as he followed the XO out of the compartment, feeling several reporters staring at his retreating back. No matter how they pretended, they knew that they weren't really capable of understanding what was going on. No, the only way to do that was to have friends and allies – sources, rather – among the military crew. Markus's status within the group, already high because he had been allowed to embed with the Marines, would rise even higher if they thought he had the XO's ear.

"I understand that you took recordings from the prison camp," the XO said. It wasn't a question. "We would appreciate it if you kept them to yourself for the moment."

"As you wish," Markus said, quickly. There was no point in arguing. Besides, they weren't trying to confiscate his recordings. "Do you think the aliens *wanted* us here?"

"It's a possibility," the XO conceded. "If they believed we survived New Russia, there aren't many other places we could go. But why?"

"The POWs," Markus suggested. "They could have been conditioned…"

"We thought of that," the XO said. Markus let out a sigh of relief. "For the moment, they will remain confined."

He smiled, rather dryly. "Do you have any other questions?"

"Just one," Markus said. "Where are we going next?"

The XO hesitated, clearly weighing the question in the balance, then shrugged. "There are a handful of systems with tramlines that lead back to human space," he said. "We'll pick our way through them, trying to avoid contact with the aliens – if possible."

Markus frowned. "We're not heading further into alien space?"

"Not yet," the XO said. "We need to report in to Earth and…"

He broke off as the alert howled, bringing the ship to battlestations. "I need to go to the CIC," he said. "You get back to your compartment. Now."

"Yes, sir," Markus said.

———

"Apparently," Gladys said, "they were all naked. The aliens and prisoners alike, I mean."

Kurt rolled his eyes. Gladys was older than Rose, younger than him… and queen of the chatterboxes. When she wasn't flying her starfighter or resting, she was chatting to everyone from junior crewmen to Royal Marines. It made her very well informed of what was actually going on, although she heard too many rumours for them *all* to be true. Kurt rather doubted that anyone would have the nerve to organise a striptease onboard ship with the XO on the prowl.

"Maybe they were molested," one of the older male pilots grunted. "Wasn't there a film about Mars needing women?"

"That was about the shortage of women on the first colony," Rose reminded him. "There was an accident and twenty-seven colonists were killed, twenty-three of them women. It had Jeremy Underline in his first starring role. And Nasty Mildew."

Kurt smiled, despite the tension of being so close to Rose and yet pretending that everything was normal. Jeremy Underline was a heart-throb movie star; Penny had spent a year with her room utterly plastered in pictures of the handsome actor. It was odd to realise that Rose would have fancied him too…but then, she was only five years older than Penny. Nasty Mildew was worth watching, he recalled, yet the general theory at the time had been that she didn't really exist in reality. The unions might have objected to VR actors – they took work from real actors, they felt – but surely no living human could have boobs that big and still walk upright.

"There was a great nude scene," the male pilot said. "I remember it well…"

"I'm sure you did," Kurt said. He recalled, now, Molly throwing a fit at the filth Penny had been watching. Penny had been thirteen at the time, too young to watch anything even remotely sexual – and there had been nothing *remote* about Nasty Mildew. "But I don't think that was what the aliens had in mind."

"They'd have to work hard to find the wretched actor," the male pilot said. "I always knew she was a fake."

"You'd think a VR composite character could actually *act*," Rose said.

"I don't think anyone cared about her *acting*," Kurt said. "Coming to think of it, Underline couldn't act his way out of a paper bag either. Maybe he was a composite too."

Gladys cleared her throat, noisily. "Maybe the aliens just don't wear clothes and don't understand why *we* wear them," she suggested. "There are colonies where people walk around in the buff."

"Best shore leave destination ever," the male pilot exulted.

"Most people who go to nudist camps really shouldn't," Rose commented. She smiled at Kurt, a secret smile that was just a fraction too bright. "But didn't the alien bodies we recovered after the first battle have clothes?"

"Probably protective gear," Gladys suggested. She didn't seem to have noticed Rose's smile, but Kurt knew she rarely missed anything. "The aliens might well need protection, even if they don't wear clothes normally. Can you imagine trying to fly a starfighter in the nude?"

Kurt had to smile. "No," he said, finally. The very thought was absurd, outside appallingly bad pornographic movies. He'd be lucky if he didn't accidentally castrate himself with the flight stick. "And nor should you."

The alert sounded before he could say anything else. "To your fighters," he snapped, thankful to be away from the embarrassing discussion. The enemy had to have finally returned to the system, loaded for bear. "Hurry!"

Rose grinned at him as she ran out of the room. Kurt flushed, then followed her until they reached the fork in the corridor that led to the launch tubes. Nodding at her retreating back, he ran down his own corridor and scrambled into his starfighter. Moments later, he was ready to launch.

———

"Twelve enemy capital ships just jumped into the system through Tramline Four," Farley reported. "*Janus* sent us a full download before she was overwhelmed. Two carriers, one battlecruiser and nine frigates. Approaching on intercept vector."

Ted hesitated, then made up his mind. "Set course for Tramline Two," he ordered, coldly. "Maximum acceleration."

CHAPTER
THIRTY TWO

"I think we waited too long, sir," Fitzwilliam said.

Ted nodded, wordlessly. Both of the detached frigates had been destroyed, one of them at the other end of Tramline Four. But the drones were still intact and reporting back to *Ark Royal*. The alien ships were driving right towards them, not even bothering to leave a picket on the tramline. They were definitely out for blood.

"There must be something important on the other end of that tramline," Farley suggested. "If they managed to scramble a defensive force so quickly..."

"Immaterial at the moment," Ted said. If – when – they made it home, they could muster a large force to attack the alien system. "Run me the attack vectors, please."

He watched, grimly, as the display filled with projected courses and attack vectors. The alien craft definitely had a faster rate of acceleration than anything human, which meant they would overrun the flotilla halfway to Tramline Two. Ted briefly considered trying to slip back into silent running, but there were too many alien craft to make it a viable tactic. At best, they would remain undiscovered for a few hours...and at worst, the aliens would manage to get close to their hull before being detected themselves.

"Recall all starfighters," Ted ordered. It would be several hours before the alien craft entered engagement range. Until then, there was no point in running his pilots ragged. "And then concentrate on getting us towards Tramline Two."

"Aye, sir," Lightbridge said.

He didn't ask the question Ted saw on his face. What would they do if Tramline Two proved to have no link to human territory? The tramlines should lead back in the direction of human space, but what if their projections were wrong? Ted knew the answer, even if he was reluctant to say it out loud. They would have to keep going and hope they found a way to escape. If, of course, they even made it to Tramline Two.

The drones were sending back clear visuals of the alien starships now. Ted found himself grimacing as he mentally calculated the number of starfighters the alien carriers could launch, then studying the power curves of the alien battlecruiser. Despite its size, it was faster than any human frigate…and presumably armed to the teeth. Humanity hadn't bothered to build large military starships, apart from carriers, but the alien point defence gave them the ability to make the ships workable. He wondered, absently, just how badly the aliens had scaled up their plasma cannons before mounting them on the battlecruiser.

He smiled, remembering the handful of alien weapons that had been scooped up by the Marines as they retreated from Alien-One. Perhaps the engineering crew would be able to deduce their operating principles, which would allow the alien weapons to be duplicated. Or perhaps they would expose a weakness which made the aliens vulnerable…if EMP could be used to disrupt ship-mounted weapons, what could it do to handheld pistols and rifles?

Humanity had experimented with EMP weapons – and EMP protections – for over two centuries. The weapons had been quite successful in tests, but so had the protections worked into military technology. *Ark Royal's* sensor network wouldn't be badly dented if an EMP warhead went off too close to the hull, let alone her weapons and drives. But the aliens…

They mount their plasma weapons on their hulls, he thought. *They cannot protect them without rendering the weapons completely useless.*

Shaking his head, he settled back to watch as the alien ships drew closer.

"I'm picking up a stream of signals from the planet," Annie reported. The communications officer looked surprised. "They're beamed towards the alien ships, but our drones are picking them up."

"Probably reporting in," Fitzwilliam said. "And telling them that we took prisoners."

Ted tended to agree…which raised the question of precisely what the alien ships would do, now they knew that *Ark Royal* carried nine aliens as well as the liberated POWs. Would they give chase anyway…or would they pull back, refusing to kill their own kind? Ted had studied such moral dilemmas at the Academy and had been left with the feeling that they depended on circumstances. Would it be wise to fire on a starship carrying prisoners if that starship was also carrying information that could not be allowed to reach enemy territory?

He leaned forward. "Can you decipher it?"

"No, sir, not with the technology we have," Annie said. "My computers are still analysing the signal, but we don't have an understanding of the alien language, let alone whatever encryption programs they might be using."

Ted sighed. Once, years ago, he'd taken part in an exercise where one side had been forced to send messages in the clear. Most such exercises had the leaders devising codes to pass messages without being understood by anyone who might want to listen in, but this particular leader had taken advantage of having a handful of Gaelic speakers in his company by using them as code-talkers. His opponents had claimed he was cheating, afterwards, yet the umpires had ruled in his favour. If someone wasn't making the best use of his personnel, they'd pointed out, he was failing.

But it was unlikely that combat decryption would ever be a viable tactic in its own right, he knew, even without adding the complexities of an alien language and alien encryption programs. It just took too long to decrypt even a short message, by which time the window of opportunity for using the message might have already closed…

"The alien ships sent a short reply," Annie said. "Nothing else."

Somehow, Ted wasn't surprised when the aliens just kept coming.

———

"Enemy carriers are launching starfighters," Farley reported, four hours later. "Alien frigates are spreading out, but otherwise keeping their distance."

At least we taught them respect, Ted thought. It was still another hour to Tramline Two, he calculated, by which time the aliens might well have overwhelmed them completely. If nothing else, he privately resolved, the aliens were going to know they'd been kissed. Hell, trading two of their modern carriers for *Ark Royal* would cost them dearly.

"Launch starfighters," he ordered. "And then prepare to engage with mass drivers and unpowered missiles."

The aliens would know their tricks by now, he knew. But they'd still have to be careful. One hit from a mass driver would shatter their carriers .., maybe even their battlecruiser. It might just allow him time to get his ship to the tramline…

"First enemy attack force inbound," Farley added. "Targets; our frigates."

Ted nodded, unsurprised. Strip the carrier of her escorts first, then close in and wipe her weapons and sensors off her hull. It made sense, he knew, which didn't make it any less irritating. The alien weapons, combined with their speed and agility, would ensure that that the following hour was going to be very unpleasant. He wished, suddenly, that he'd spent more time talking with the other commanders, rather than just issuing orders through his subordinates. But he had never commanded a multinational force before…

Hell, he thought. *There has never been a multinational space force until the aliens arrived.*

"Keep one squadron of starfighters to cover our hull, then direct the remaining craft to cover the frigates," he ordered. "And then target the mass drivers on the alien carriers and open fire."

On the display, the cloud of alien starfighters split up into several smaller formations as they entered engagement range, screeching down on the human frigates like a pack of wolves on helpless sheep. Ted noted, absently, that they were clearly taking precautions against nukes or EMP-weapons, although there were limits to how much space the alien pilots could put between themselves and their fellows. The frigates opened fire, picking off a handful of alien fighters as they closed in, then shuddered under the weight of alien plasma fire.

Ted silently thanked God for the armoured warships. Old they might be, primitive and slow they might be, but they were tough enough to stand up to the aliens. But damage was mounting rapidly on their hulls as their weapons and sensors were stripped away. One frigate stumbled out of formation as her drive failed, another vanished in a ball of fire when a lucky alien shot slipped through a gash in the hull and triggered an explosion. Ted noted lifepods launching from the stricken ship, knowing that they were futile. Unless the aliens saw fit to recover the human survivors, they were going to die in the vastness of interstellar space.

Poor bastards, he thought. He could launch shuttles to recover them – and there would definitely be volunteers to mount SAR missions – but the aliens would simply fire on the shuttles, assuming them to be warships. There were protocols among human powers for recovering stranded personnel, yet the aliens had probably never even *heard* of them. Besides, why would they allow humanity to recover personnel who could be turned around and sent right back to the war?

"*Franco* is taking heavy damage," Farley reported. "Her drives are being targeted specifically."

Ted winced as he peered down at the display. The alien starfighters had converged to the rear of the frigate and were pouring fire into her, shattering her armour piece by piece. There was no escape, he saw; even as his starfighters raced desperately towards the frigate the aliens finally succeeded. A series of explosions blew the frigate into a ball of radioactive plasma. Her tormentors slipped away and vanished into the distance, then turned and zoomed back towards another frigate. The human starfighters moved to block them.

"Beta Squadron needs to reload," Fitzwilliam said. "Alpha Squadron is running dry too."

"Call them back," Ted ordered.

Gritting his teeth, he mentally cursed the aliens for having such effective weapons – and for not needing to reload in the middle of an engagement. If *Ark Royal* had been a modern carrier, recalling her fighters to reload would have been disastrous. Even with her heavy armour and heavier weapons, it still wasn't particularly safe for *Ark Royal* to have a quarter of her remaining starfighters out of the battle. But there was no alternative…

"Hit," Farley exulted, suddenly. "We *got* one of the bastards!"

Ted felt a desperate flash of hope as he saw one of the alien carriers staggering out of formation, having taken a bomb-pumped laser to her main hull. He found himself torn in two as the aliens struggled to save their ship, torn between praying for them to succeed and praying for them to fail. There was a brotherhood between human spacers, no matter what interstellar power they served, but did that brotherhood include the aliens? For all he knew, they didn't even have the *concept* of brotherhood. But he couldn't help feeling torn in two...

The display blinked, then replaced the icon representing the alien carrier with an expanding sphere marking a cloud of debris. "Target destroyed," Farley reported. "I say again, target destroyed."

"Good," Ted said. The aliens had to *feel* the loss of a carrier...although God knew they'd killed almost ten alien carriers since they'd gone to war. But would it be enough to force them to take a step backwards and let *Ark Royal* escape? "Target the other carrier and continue firing."

On the display, the alien craft converged, then flashed back towards *Ark Royal* with murderous intent.

———

Kurt was finding it hard to keep track of everything that was going on in the combat zone, despite his best efforts. His carefully-planned formations had fallen apart as soon as the battle had begun, forcing pilots to fly with whatever wingmen they could find. The aliens seemed to have definitely learnt from experience, filling space with thousands upon thousands of plasma bolts that threatened to wipe the human starfighters from existence. At least one of his pilots, he'd noted savagely, had died because he'd flown right *into* the path of one of the plasma bolts, his craft exploding before he'd even recognised his mistake.

He took a shot at an alien fighter, then gave chase...but the alien pilot rapidly outpaced him, then flipped around and came darting back. Kurt braced himself, allowed the computers to take the shot as soon as it became possible, then yanked his starfighter to one side. Warning lights blinked up as plasma blasts flashed past his position, but none of them managed to score a hit. The alien pilot wasn't so lucky. A direct hit smashed his starfighter to atoms.

"Good shot, boss," Gladys called. "A little help over here, perhaps?"

Kurt nodded, barking orders as he flipped his starfighter around and moved to her assistance. The aliens were taking ruthless advantage of their numerical superiority, ganging up on the human pilots and forcing them to scatter. Kurt drove at one alien craft and had the satisfaction of seeing its pilot jumping out of the way, then broke through to cover Gladys as she turned to make the run back to the carrier.

Clever bastards, he thought, sourly. The aliens knew the human pilots needed to reload, so they were trying to make it impossible for them to return to the carrier. He ordered Beta Squadron to cover the incoming fighters, but he was rapidly running out of pilots with loaded weapons. The entire wing was running low on ammunition.

"Alpha and Gamma, prepare to return," he ordered. Both squadrons were low, but most of the pilots still had some ammunition left. "Let them come close before you open fire."

He felt a moment of unwilling admiration for the alien pilots as they streaked to block their path back to the human carrier. They'd already picked off the point defence weapons covering the landing deck, allowing themselves to lurk there and pick off human starfighters trying to land. It was clever, he admitted, although they weren't trying to fire *into* the carrier. The armour would prevent a series of explosions that would destroy the ship, but they could easily render the landing bay effectively useless. Or were they more interested in picking off the starfighters?

Kindred, he thought. Successful starfighter pilots were neither the wild untamed dogs the movies made them out to be or slavishly obedient servants of the military. It was strange to realise that they might have something in common with the alien pilots...

"Fire," he ordered.

Caught by surprise, five alien starfighters were picked off before they even realised that their intended prey was far from toothless. The remainder scattered, just long enough to allow the human pilots to land and rush through the reloading cycle. Kurt slumped in his seat as the ground crew went to work, feeling utterly exhausted. They were in deep trouble and it was far from over. He'd have to go back out within moments...

He looked over at Rose's starfighter, then cursed himself angrily. Whatever else happened, he wanted her to survive...and that was the kind of emotion he could not allow.

Moments later, the starfighter lurched as it was shoved back into the battle.

———

"The starfighters are down to three squadrons worth of starfighters," Farley said, quietly.

Ted nodded. Only three frigates remained intact and largely undamaged, allowing the aliens to concentrate their efforts on *Ark Royal* herself. The repairs they'd carried out had made it harder for the alien pilots to get into range, but not impossible. Ted had deduced that the aliens had no tradition of actually repairing their ships outside a shipyard, as the alien pilots seemed to have assumed that weapons damaged or destroyed at New Russia hadn't been replaced. And they were still thirty minutes from Tramline Two.

"Understood," he said. They needed time to recuperate, then reorganise their squadrons. The CAG had done an excellent job, but the pilots needed more guidance than could be provided in the middle of a battle. "And our mass drivers?"

"Down to one-third projectiles," Farley said. "We haven't scored a single hit."

"I know," Ted said. "But keep firing."

He scowled. The aliens were aware of the danger now and were taking precautions, even if it meant withholding some of their starfighters from the swarms tearing the human fleet apart. They'd come close to scoring a hit on the other carrier, but there was no such thing as proximity damage where mass drivers and inert projectiles were concerned. They either scored a hit or they didn't. There was no middle ground. But, he told himself, if they kept spitting projectiles towards the carrier, the aliens would be forced to keep some of their starfighters back to cover their ship...

The only consolation, he told himself, *is that we wiped out six of their frigates with nukes.*

Farley swore, suddenly. "Sir, the *Rubicon*..."

Ted blinked, then stared at the display. The Italian frigate was lurching out of formation, her drives spluttering madly...but she didn't seem to be damaged. Beside her, the French and German frigates followed, altering course until they were plunging back towards the onrushing alien ships. Ted stared, not understanding – at first – what he was seeing. And then the frigates opened fire. Their weapons seemed puny compared to the alien energy cannons...

"They'll be in range of the plasma gun," Fitzwilliam said, in shocked disbelief. One of the alien frigates glowed, then vanished from the display. The German frigate followed moments later, blown apart by a direct hit from the battlecruiser. "Call them back!"

Ted shook his head. The French and Italian crewmen were committed now, he knew. There was no way they could reverse course again and escape before it was too late. He watched, torn between horror and respect, as the Italian frigate and the remaining alien frigate killed each other...and the French frigate rammed the alien carrier directly. Both starships vanished in a colossal explosion.

CHAPTER
THIRTY THREE

"Dear God," Farley said, very quietly.

Ted was stunned. It was rare, very rare, for one starship to try to deliberately ram another – and to succeed in ramming her target. No matter what civilians might say, it was about as likely to happen as crashing into an asteroid while flying through an asteroid belt without bothering to keep a careful eye on the sensors. But the frigates had sacrificed themselves to give the carrier – and the POWs – time to escape.

The aliens seemed equally stunned. Their starfighters flipped backwards, away from *Ark Royal*, even though they had nowhere to go. Could the one remaining alien craft, the giant battlecruiser, take them onboard? Or could they return to the planet and land under their own power? Intelligence's best guess was that the alien starfighters were no more capable of landing on a planet than humanity's starfighters, but what if they were wrong? Ted shook his head, dismissing the thought. As long as the starfighters stayed away from his ship, it didn't matter what happened to them.

"The ship-mounted plasma cannon must have a recharge period," Anderson muttered, through the intercom. "That would make sense, I think; they'd need to refill the containment chamber between shots…"

Ted couldn't disagree. If the aliens had been capable of firing multiple shots without pause, all three frigates would have been destroyed as soon as they entered firing range. Instead, they'd taken out a carrier and damaged the alien chances of catching their target.

"Recall our starfighters, then keep us heading towards Tramline Two," he ordered. "Target the battlecruiser with the mass driver, then open fire if you believe you have a reasonable chance of scoring a hit."

"Understood," Farley said, although he sounded doubtful. The alien battlecruiser was surrounded by a swarm of starfighters, buzzing around like angry bees. It was unlikely that a projectile would get within kilometres of its target without being engaged and deflected or destroyed by the starfighters. Or an unpowered missile, for that matter. "I'll watch for a suitable opportunity."

Ted kept one eye on the alien ships as his starfighters reloaded, then repositioned themselves in the launch bay. His pilots needed a chance to rest and recuperate, but they were unlikely to get it; silently, he made a mental note to insist on training up new starfighter pilots if the war threatened to go on for much longer. There was no reason why a carrier the size of *Ark Royal* couldn't carry more than one starfighter pilot per starfighter, allowing the starfighters to be turned around and pushed back into combat quicker than before.

The aliens kept their distance as the giant carrier moved rapidly towards Tramline Two. Ted couldn't help wondering if they'd learned caution...or if they were merely waiting for reinforcements. His imagination provided too many possibilities, including the very real danger of running into an alien ambush as soon as they jumped through the tramline. But if there *was* an ambush waiting for them, the optimistic side of his mind pointed out, why had the aliens sought to bring them to combat already? They could just have herded *Ark Royal* and her flotilla towards Tramline Two without coming close enough to engage the carrier.

No way to know, he reminded himself.

He keyed his console, instead. "James, make sure that everyone has a bite to eat," he ordered. "I want them as alert as possible when we jump through the tramline."

"Understood," his XO said. "I'll see to it at once."

Ted wondered, in a moment of mischievous amusement, just how badly the reporters were taking the running battle. Had they learned to read the display well enough to realise that all of the frigates were now gone? Or had they concluded that *Ark Royal* had actually won the battle outright, rather than scoring a victory on points? He considered, briefly, calling their compartment and asking them, before dismissing the thought as unworthy of him. There was no point in wasting time...

Midshipwoman Lopez appeared with a tray of food packets, which she passed around the bridge. Ted took his gratefully, silently impressed that the young woman was bearing up well under the stress of combat – and dealing with reporters. He made a mental note to ensure she was promoted when they returned to Earth, perhaps with a transfer to a more modern starship if it was what she wanted. Or maybe she'd prefer to stay on *Ark Royal*. Unless the human race made a definite breakthrough in point defence – and light armour – the modern carriers were little more than death traps.

"Thank you," he said. The packaged food had no taste, as far as he or anyone else had been able to determine, but it did help him to become more alert. He ate the two ration bars – they had the consistency of fudge, although not the taste – and then passed her the empty package. "How are the reporters coping?"

Midshipwoman Lopez smiled. "They're coping about as well as can be expected," she said. "I don't think they understand the situation."

Ted smiled. It was a very diplomatic answer. "Good," he said. "Keep an eye on them, once you have finished with the food."

He turned back to the display as Tramline Two loomed up in front of them. The aliens might well have left a stealthed picket somewhere along the tramline, watching the human ships as they fought their desperate battle for survival. They'd clearly had a ship at Tramline Four, so why not one at Tramline Two. And they'd have a very good idea of where – precisely – the human ships would jump into the system. There was no time to do anything to make their jumping coordinates more random. If the aliens had an ambush waiting for them, it would be impossible to avoid. They'd just have to hope they could fight their way through it.

"All starfighters are ready to launch," Fitzwilliam reported. "The pilots are standing by."

Ted scowled. The pilots had waited for hours, then fought savagely... and all the best studies agreed that starfighter pilots should have hours of rest between bouts of combat. But the scientists who had carried out the studies weren't on the carrier. He had no choice, apart from sending his exhausted pilots back into the fight. Assuming, of course, the aliens were lurking in ambush.

"Jump," he ordered.

He braced himself as the display went dark, then flickered back to life as they materialised within the new star system. The aliens could be waiting...but nothing materialised, apart from a single icon that was drifting five hundred thousand kilometres from their position. It looked like a monitoring satellite, Ted decided, which was confirmed when the satellite started to send a stream of data into the inner system. Ted ordered its immediate destruction – a single blast from a railgun would suffice – then turned his attention to the sensor reports. There was one source of signals within the inner system...and only one other tramline.

"It isn't jumping back towards human space," Annie reported.

Ted shrugged, briefly considering their options. He could launch an ambush himself, when – if – the alien ship came through the tramline, but it would be too risky. God alone knew what was lurking within the alien system, yet if they'd left Alien-One largely undeveloped to avoid alerting human survey ships, there was no guarantee that they'd done the same for Alien-Two. At some point, he knew, they would have to fortify their worlds to prevent the humans from accidentally stumbling over their settlements and then escaping to alert the human race.

"Take us towards it anyway, best possible speed," he ordered. Turning, he looked over at Farley. "Launch two of our remaining drones towards the alien world. I want to know what – if anything – is there, waiting for us."

There was a chime from his console. "I'd like to withdraw half of the pilots for a rest in the sleep machine," Fitzwilliam said. "They need it, desperately."

Ted cursed under his breath. They were still too close to the tramline for him to be sanguine about stripping half of the starfighters from the launch roster. But, at the same time, he knew his pilots were exhausted.

"Hold for ten minutes," he said, studying the tramline as it fell behind them. "I want to see what the aliens do."

"Understood," Fitzwilliam said.

He didn't say anything else, for which Ted was grateful. Maybe he *had* wanted to steal command for himself, once upon a time. Ted couldn't really blame him for wanting to promote himself by any means possible. But he was smart enough to know that they couldn't afford internal bickering, not now. The minutes ticked away with no sign of the alien battlecruiser.

"Launch another drone," Ted ordered. The further they moved from the tramline, the harder it would be to pick up a transit signature when the alien ship finally made its appearance. "I want to know when it arrives."

"Yes, sir," Farley said. He hesitated, noticeably. "We only have three drones left."

Ted sighed. "Launch it anyway," he ordered. The beancounters would make a terrible fuss, but without that information they might well be caught by surprise when the battlecruiser made its return appearance. He keyed his console. "James, send half the pilots for their rest now."

"Aye, sir," the XO said. "And you should get some rest too, sir."

Ted rubbed his eyes. The XO was right, he knew. But he was unwilling to leave the bridge until the battle was over.

"You get some rest," he ordered, instead. "I need to stay here."

Oddly, Fitzwilliam didn't argue.

Ted leaned back in his chair and watched the reports from the drones plunging into the inner system. The second tramline was on the other side of the source of alien signals, a Mars-like world that seemed to have nothing going for it apart from a surprisingly large number of small moons orbiting it. Ted found himself wondering if the aliens had actually captured hundreds of asteroids and steered them into planetary orbit, producing a vast network of habitats and industrial nodes. But the world seemed surprisingly undefended for an industrial complex…and besides, it was far too close to the front lines.

But the Russians wanted to turn New Russia into a centre of industry, he thought. *They didn't know that the aliens might come on the offensive at any moment.*

He puzzled over the issue as the data continued to flood into the computers. The analyst section identified a handful of small mining complexes, all disappointingly comparable to human systems. It seemed the aliens didn't bother to waste ultra-advanced technology on mining camps, any more than the human industrial complexes. Most of the technology used to mine the asteroids and the lunar surface predated the general advance into space itself.

"Curious," he muttered, out loud. "All that industry and hardly any defences."

"We might not be able to *see* the defences, sir," Farley pointed out. "We're operating at quite some distance from the planet."

Ted smiled, calculating the vectors. If the alien battlecruiser didn't make its appearance, he would be tempted – very tempted – to pause long enough to lay waste to the system. The outcome of modern wars were largely determined by the production war, with one side out-producing its rival and crushing its enemies under the sheer weight of its produce. But the aliens knew where humanity's industrial centres were located, allowing them to target their attacks on facilities that had taken years to produce, while the human race had no idea where to hit their enemy's industrial base. A few deep-strike raids, Ted realised, and the human race would lose many of its industrial complexes. And the war itself would be lost with them.

"Continue on our present course," he ordered, finally. Where *was* the damn battlecruiser? Surely the aliens would want to keep tabs on *Ark Royal*, rather than let her wander through alien-controlled space without supervision. "Alert me when we make our closest approach to the planet."

He glanced at the timer. Nine hours to go. Fitzwilliam was right. He did need to sleep.

Once he's had his shot in the sleep machines, I'll take mine, Ted thought. He disliked the sleep machines – they just didn't feel right – but there was no alternative. *And then I might feel more alert.*

———

"They reacted rather oddly, sir," the Marine reported. "As soon as we jumped, they started keening."

Charles frowned, studying the alien prisoners through the surveillance sensors. The aliens hadn't shown much reaction to the quarantine compartment or the human observers, but that could be nothing more than lessons from an alien version of the dreaded Conduct After Capture course. What would the aliens, who had presumably known about humanity long enough to devise protocols for any of their race who happened to be taken prisoner, have told them to do? Humans were supposed to restrict themselves to name, rank and serial number…although if the captors felt like conducting a more rigorous interrogation, it was unlikely that any of the prisoners could have held anything back.

Not that it matters, he thought, wryly. *They can't speak English and we can't speak their language. We might have captured the King of all the Aliens and we'd never know it.*

"Interesting," he said. The human observers had retreated hastily, complaining about their ears hurting. "Have they done anything else?"

"No, but they must have sensed the jump," the Marine said. "They know there's no hope of recovery now."

Charles sighed. No one had seriously considered having to deal with prisoners from an alien race, not until Vera Cruz…and, as far as he knew, no real protocols had been developed to handle the situation. The planned First Contact bore no resemblance to what had actually happened. Between them, the doctors and the Marines were making it up as they went along.

"It would give them a reason to talk to us," Charles said. "But if they can't…"

He shook his head. These days, human prisoners were either treated under the laws of war or rated as terrorists, depending on when and where they were captured. The Third World War had left massive scars on the human psyche, sweeping away much of the idealism that had marked the previous century. POWs could expect to be held until the end of the war – unless someone arranged a prisoner exchange – or to be interrogated and then shot. Aliens, on the other hand…even if they'd merely captured the alien version of junior crewmen, they still needed to be treated carefully.

"I'll discuss it with the Captain," he said. "Have they managed to master their cell?"

The Marine smiled. "They didn't have any problems with the knobs," he said. "Turns out they like the cell warm, but moist. Feels like Kuala Lumpur in there, sir. I think they would put it even higher if they could."

"We'll have to build them a better cell, when we get them home," Charles said. He looked up as Doctor Hastings stepped into the observation sector. "Doctor."

"Major," the doctor responded.

Charles looked at her, thoughtfully. She looked as tired as everyone else felt, but there was a curious excitement pushing her onwards. "What have you discovered?"

"I've been trying to work out a baseline for this race," the doctor said. She smiled as she pushed past him to look at the aliens. "Of our nine captives, I believe that four of them are actually female."

"Oh," Charles said. He looked back at the aliens, puzzled. As far as he could tell, there were no physical differences beyond skin colour. There were no breasts or penises. "How do you tell the difference?"

"There are none, on the surface," the doctor said. "But internally there are some quite significant differences. That one there" – she pointed to a green-skinned alien who looked identical to the others – "is female, with an organ that seems to produce eggs for expulsion into the water. Males" – she nodded to another alien – "produce sperm, which is also expelled into the water."

"Tadpoles," Charles said, in sudden understanding.

"Indeed," the doctor said, giving him a smile that made her tired face look strikingly pretty. "My best guess, Major, is that they reproduce by ejaculating into warm water, rather than direct sexual contact. It's quite likely that they don't have any real concept of physical love as we understand the term, or bastardry for that matter. Their society might well be very different from ours."

Charles had a sudden vision of the aliens leaving sperm and eggs everywhere they went, hoping that they would match up and produce children. Once conceived, what would happen to the child? Instead of one parent...who would take the children in? Their society must have people trained to serve as mothers and fathers, even if they weren't biologically related to the child's parents. Hell, the child's parents might never even have met!

"There are no other major differences between the sexes," the doctor added. "I think that they won't have invented any form of sexual discrimination, not when females are fully as strong as males."

"But they miss out on a lot," Charles mused. "No sex."

"It would seem perfectly normal to them," the doctor pointed out, tartly. "And besides, do you know how much time is wasting having and rearing children?"

Charles shrugged. "It used to be that the best years of a woman's life were the ones where she was expected to have children and bear the burden of raising them," the doctor explained. "By the time the children were old enough to flee the nest, their mother couldn't really do anything else. It was only since the development of technology that the women could go back to work – and now, with life-extension treatments, the women have more years to play with. How many female geniuses were lost to the ages because of the demands of childbirth?"

The alarms howled before Charles could reply. He glanced at his terminal, then swore.

"They're back," he said.

CHAPTER
THIRTY FOUR

Ted jerked back to full awareness as the alarms sounded.

Shit, he swore, inwardly. He'd committed the cardinal sin of almost falling asleep on the bridge. A young midshipman who dozed off while on watch would be lucky if he wasn't demoted all the way back to cadet by his outraged CO. Ted forced himself to put the thought aside, then stared at the display. A single red icon was emerging from the tramline they'd taken to reach Alien-Two.

"The battlecruiser, sir," Farley said. If he'd noted Ted's near-collapse, he said nothing. "They must have assumed that we were planning an ambush."

Ted nodded, silently giving thanks for the alien commander's paranoia. He'd taken the time to enter the tramline at a different point, thwarting any planned ambush…but, incidentally, giving *Ark Royal* some time to put distance between the two ships. He watched, coldly, as the alien ship started after them, without waiting for any sensor reports. It took his tired mind a long moment to realise that the aliens already knew their destination. There was literally nowhere else the human ship could go.

"They're keeping their distance too," Farley added. "They could overrun us well before we reached the tramline, if they pleased."

"True," Ted agreed.

He ran his hand though his hair, considering the possibilities. Maybe the aliens weren't as confident of their predictions as they acted. Or maybe they thought the human ship was powerful enough to best the battlecruiser, even though her starfighter squadrons had been shot to ribbons. Or maybe they were still herding her towards a final ambush. He silently cursed the alien FTL drive under his breath. With a bit of luck, the aliens could muster an ambush while *Ark Royal* followed a predictable path.

"Continue on course towards the tramline," he ordered. There was no point in trying to hide, not now. The aliens knew roughly where they were. "And draw up a strike pattern for targeting the alien facilities in orbit around the planet."

It was risky, he knew; if the aliens had a major colony on the surface there was a very definite possibility that one of the human projectiles would strike the planet's surface and carry out an atrocity. But there was no time to target their weapons more precisely – and he had no intention of wasting irreplaceable missiles on targets that couldn't shoot back. He simply didn't have enough to spare.

"They didn't bring any starfighters," Fitzwilliam said. He sounded disgustingly alert after half an hour in the sleep machine. He'd pay for that later, but for the moment he could carry out his duties without tiredness blunting his edge. "What happened to them?"

Ted shrugged. Maybe the alien pilots had made it back to Alien-One, maybe they'd been picked up by the battlecruiser...or maybe they'd expired in the merciless reaches of outer space. There was no way to know.

"Take command," he ordered, surrendering to the inevitable. "I'm going to take some rest in the sleep machine. Alert me if the aliens start to run us down."

———

Kurt cracked open the lid and sat up, feeling his head spinning slightly. It wasn't quite a headache, but it was bad enough to blunt him. His chronometer stated that he'd been in the sleep machine for barely an hour, nowhere near enough to replenish his reserves. But there was no more time to rest, not now. A quick look at the status display showed the alien battlecruiser, tracking *Ark Royal* with murderous intent.

He sighed as the other sleep machines opened, revealing two-thirds of his remaining pilots. The remainder, waiting in the launch tubes, were even more tired than the rest of them. Kurt forced his head to start working, thinking hard. The squadrons needed to be reorganised – Delta Squadron was effectively out of service, having one surviving pilot – but he was too tired to do it properly.

"Dave, Gus, Gladys and Mike, take the ready starfighters," he ordered. "You're now classed as Beta Squadron. Everyone else in this compartment is part of Alpha Squadron."

Rose looked irked – he'd effectively demoted her – but she looked too tired to argue in front of the others. If they made it home, Rose would probably be given a whole new starfighter squadron on a different starship, one where her experience could be passed on to starfighter pilots who had never even *seen* an enemy starfighter. Kurt allowed himself a moment of relief, then pushed it aside ruthlessly. Their relationship, their *secret* relationship, meant nothing. All that mattered was staying alive long enough to give the aliens one final bloody nose before they were overwhelmed.

"Alpha, go get a shower," he added, after taking another look at the display and calculating the vectors in his head. The aliens, unless they sped up, would need at least two hours to overrun the carrier. By his assessment, the aliens were keeping tabs on their location rather than attempting to actually *stop Ark Royal.* "You all stink like…" – his imagination failed him – "a very stinky thing."

"Same to you, sir," Oxford said. "You shouldn't have worn your socks in the sleeping machine."

It was a measure of how tried he was, Kurt decided, that he found himself giggling helplessly for several seconds. "Shower," he snapped, when he could finally talk again. "Now."

He watched them go, then looked over at Rose. "I understand," she said. She leaned forward and kissed his lips hard, then strode past him into the shower. Kurt glared at her back, then forced his body back under control. She called back to him as her clothes hit the deck. "Come on, sir. The water's fine."

Kurt gritted his teeth, realising that he'd lost his detachment once and for all. Somehow, he managed to keep his eyes off her, covering himself by scrubbing thoroughly at his feet and legs as the water ran down his body.

As soon as he felt clean, he stepped back out of the shower, towelled himself down and checked the display. The alien battlecruiser hadn't moved any closer. Indeed, it seemed to have decided to match the carrier's speed even though it could have easily moved a great deal faster.

It's precisely what we want them to do, Kurt thought, as he pulled on a clean flight suit. *They're being very obliging. And that's what bothers us.*

"Stay here," he ordered, as the other pilots scrambled out of the shower, water running off their bodies. "If the alert sounds, go to your fighters at once."

The hatch opened as he reached it, revealing Gamma Squadron's pilots. They looked even more haggard than the other pilots, unsurprisingly. And they stank too, just like the others before they'd showered. None of them really cared to remain in the cockpits for so long.

"Have your showers, then get a nap," Kurt ordered. "And then join the remaining pilots here."

He walked down to his office, closed the door firmly and brought up the squadron rosters. It seemed absurd to be doing the paperwork now, when the aliens were tracking them, but it helped keep his mind off other things. He could record a message for Molly and the children, yet it was unlikely they would ever hear it. Or he could call Rose...

Angrily, he shook his head. The aliens were in hot pursuit. They couldn't afford to be caught with their pants down, not now.

———

Ted didn't feel much better after several hours in the sleep machine – Fitzwilliam had evidently decided to let him sleep longer than he'd planned - but one glance at the display was enough to reassure him that the alien battlecruiser was still keeping its distance from the carrier. Unfortunately, it had also launched a spread of drones of its own, ensuring that *Ark Royal* couldn't hide without being detected.

"We have a lock on several targets in orbit around the alien world," Farley informed him, when he stepped back onto the bridge. A shave and a shower had made him feel much better about himself. "I don't think there is a major risk to the planet itself."

Ted nodded, studying the reports from the drones. There were dozens of large structures in orbit, most of them clearly industrial nodes. But there were relatively few defences, as far as he could see. Was it possible, he asked himself, that some of the nodes were actually *drones* or ECM beacons? If human technology could fool the aliens long enough to let *Ark Royal* launch an ambush, why couldn't the aliens do the same?

"It's impossible to be certain at this distance," Farley admitted, when Ted asked. ""But they would have had to set up the trap well before we arrived in the system."

"True," Ted agreed. "Are you ready to open fire?"

"The mass drivers are armed and ready," Farley said. "We can fire on your command."

Ted nodded. Given the distance between themselves and the planet, they would be past the perfect firing location before they knew if they'd hit their targets or not. But it didn't matter, he told himself. If they missed, or if the alien point defence was sufficient to stop the projectiles, he had no intention of wasting any more. Besides, the aliens were unlikely to give them time to stop and reload from the local asteroid belt.

"Fire," he ordered.

Long hours ticked away as the silent projectiles rocketed towards their targets. Ted watched, keeping one eye on the alien battlecruiser, until the first reports started to come back into the display. Four facilities had been hit and destroyed, seven had turned out to have a surprisingly heavy concentration of point defence weapons and two more were missed outright. Under the circumstances, Ted decided, it was the best they could reasonably hope for.

The alien battlecruiser showed no reaction, no inclination to accelerate and enter engagement range. Indeed, the distance it was keeping was safe by several orders of magnitude. Ted puzzled over it, wondering just what the aliens would think of a CO who didn't try to save the facilities. A naval officer would understand that there was nothing the battlecruiser could have done, but his civilian superiors would have complained loudly at the absence of any actual *attempt* to save the planet. *They* wouldn't understand the realities of naval combat...he wondered, with a sudden flicker of envy, if the alien government was composed of naval officers.

God knew there was a human colony that believed that military service was the only way to gain the vote.

He turned back to look at the tramline, stretching out ahead of them. At this rate, the aliens would let them leave the system without interference...and he couldn't help, but wonder if that was what the aliens *wanted* the human ship to do. It was easy enough to project the destination of the tramline, yet there was no way of knowing what might be waiting for them at the other end. And, with a stealthed picket ship, the aliens would have plenty of time to note *Ark Royal's* course and set an ambush.

"Prepare two more drones," he ordered, looking over at Farley. "I want to cause as much confusion as possible as we come out of the tramline."

It might be wasted effort, he knew. Given enough time, the aliens could have seeded space with beacons and detectors. But he had to try.

Shaking his head, he picked up the latest report from the doctors and started to read. The aliens were very alien, unsurprisingly. But there didn't seem to be any threat of disease, thankfully. God alone knew what would happen if the Admiralty believed *Ark Royal* to be compromised. They'd probably insist on flying the carrier right into the nearest star.

But there was one thing the report couldn't answer. How, precisely, did the alien thought processes differ from human ones?

And just what were they planning for *Ark Royal*?

"Angle us towards the tramline," he added, watching the timer closely. Soon enough, the aliens wouldn't be able to intercept them before they made the jump. There would be an opportunity, Ted calculated, to make an escape into silent running before the battlecruiser caught up...assuming that there was no waiting ambush. If there was...they'd just have to fight and pray. "Give me a countdown as soon as we reach the two-minute mark."

"Why don't we just go faster?"

James concealed his tired amusement at Barbie's question. *Ark Royal* wasn't *trying* to crawl through space, not with her drives straining desperately to push them faster and faster towards the tramline. But, compared to a modern human carrier – or the alien battlecruiser – she was a wallowing hippo. The only thing preventing the alien ship from closing to engagement range was her commander's reluctance to close the distance between them and the carrier.

"Because we don't have the drives to go faster," he said. "It was a terrible oversight on the part of the designers."

The thought made him scowl. He'd read all the debates in the various naval forums, after *Ark Royal* had been commissioned into the Royal Navy, in what little spare time he'd had since becoming fascinated with the ship. Some designers had argued that the carrier was simply too heavily armoured for her own good, that she would hold back the fleet if the Royal Navy ever went on the offensive. And she was cripplingly expensive. Even the American and Russian carriers that had come into service at the same time were lighter.

But now...now *Ark Royal* had a survival rate the modern carriers could only envy. New Russia had proven that; twelve modern human carriers, all wiped out with ease. Even now the alien weapons were a known quality, the modern carriers would still be in trouble. The last he'd heard, the designers were planning to add extra armour, hoping it would give the ships a fighting chance.

I guess the designers got the last laugh, after all, he thought. *But will they ever know what happened to us?*

"Heads should roll," Barbie said, with great certainty. "When we get home, we will make sure everyone knows just how badly the designers performed."

"Don't tell them that," James said, quickly. "They did better than the more modern designers."

His communicator buzzed. "We cross the tramline in ten minutes," the Captain said. "Report to the CIC."

"Understood," James said. "I'm on my way."

Barbie caught his hand before he could leave the compartment. "Commander," she said, "once we cross the tramline we'll be safe, right?"

James hesitated. The truth was that the alien battlecruiser would have no difficulty in crossing the tramline after them, although it might take the time to ensure that the humans couldn't lay an ambush. He'd thought about advising the Captain to do that, but it would be chancy. Too chancy, perhaps.

"We'll be out of this system," he said. He didn't have the heart to tell her that they might fly straight into an ambush. "I don't know what will happen afterwards."

Shaking his head, he turned and walked out of the hatch.

———

"No sign of any picket ships," Farley reported. "The tramline seems to be empty."

Ted nodded, although he knew it meant nothing. The aliens could be hiding under stealth or simply running silent. It wouldn't be hard to use passive sensors to track the carrier's progress, not now they were close to the tramline. And the battlecruiser was still keeping its distance.

"Sound the alert," he ordered, quietly. The alarm howled through the ship, bringing the crew to battlestations. Ted watched as the ship's weapons came online, followed rapidly by the starfighter pilots checking in. Tired as they were, they were still ready to fight to defend their carrier. "Reports?"

"All decks report ready, sir," Farley reported.

Ted took a breath. "Jump," he ordered. "Now!"

Space twisted around them, the display fading into darkness before lighting up again. Ahead of them, there was a dull red star, surrounded by hundreds of asteroids.

"No contacts," Farley said. "No alien contacts detected at all."

Ted stared at the display, wonderingly. Had the aliens merely sought to keep an eye on them rather than placing an ambush ahead of their course?

An alarm sounded from the helm console. "Captain," Lightbridge said. "There are no other tramlines here."

Ted swore in sudden understanding. The aliens hadn't engaged because they'd known *Ark Royal* was heading towards a dead end. She'd been heading in precisely the direction the aliens wanted her to go. Hell, the bastards could use the battlecruiser to keep the carrier penned in while they summoned additional reinforcements. He thought, desperately, as the carrier moved away from the tramline, but nothing came to mind. They were trapped.

"Silent running," he ordered. Unless the aliens had surveyed the system very carefully, *Ark Royal* could pose as just another asteroid. One battlecruiser couldn't hope to identify them among the other pieces of space junk. "Leave one powered-down drone by the tramline, but hold the others. We need to hide."

"Yes, sir," Farley said.

Ted scowled down at the display. A thin translucent line – an alien tramline – winked into existence, mocking him. *They* couldn't use it to escape, even though it seemed to head back into human space. There was no way they could build an improved Puller Drive in time to make it out. Moments later, the alien battlecruiser popped into existence. Ted watched, holding his breath, then sighed in relief as he realised the aliens had lost them. But that wouldn't last indefinitely.

The conclusion was inescapable. They were trapped.

"You have the bridge," he growled. Bitter helplessness warred in his mind. They were trapped – and it was his fault. If he'd taken the risk of jumping back towards New Russia instead...he shook his head, angrily. Now, he would have all the time in the world to second-guess himself. "Keep us drifting here."

With that, he strode through the hatch and headed down towards his cabin.

CHAPTER
THIRTY FIVE

James studied the display, feeling cold ice congealing around his heart.

The realities of the tramline network were well-understood, he knew. Without a tramline, travel from star to star was impossible. God knew that at least one sublight colony venture had deliberately aimed for a star that was believed to have no tramlines, putting six light years between them and the closest human world. But every other star system reached by humanity had at least one tramline. Here, through, they had come to the end of the line.

He sucked in a breath as the alien battlecruiser made her appearance, sitting on top of the tramline and showing no sign of budging. Once again, thankfully, the aliens had prepared for an ambush that hadn't been prepared, giving the human ship time to hide. *Ark Royal* would remain undetected as long as she remained still, he knew, particularly since the aliens didn't seem to be actually *looking* for her. But they wouldn't be able to re-enter the tramline at a different point without altering course radically enough to risk detection…and even if they did, they'd only jump back to Alien-Two. No, they were trapped…and the aliens would be gathering the force to destroy them.

A note blinked up on his display. Someone – Midshipwomen Lopez – was asking for a private conversation. *That* was rare, particularly in the middle of a battle. Alarmed, unsure of *why* he was alarmed, James reached for his earpiece and voder, pressing one into his ear and the other against his throat. It had been years since he had used either of the pieces of equipment, but his body remembered how to use them.

"Sir, it's the Captain," the young woman said. James frowned in puzzlement, then recalled that he'd asked her to keep a subtle eye on her commander. "He just left the bridge."

James felt his brow furrow in alarm. He'd known Captains who were tyrants and Captains who were too soft, but he'd never known a Captain who had abandoned his bridge when his starship was in deadly danger. Whatever else could be said about Captain Smith, he'd definitely had the same worth ethic. It had been hard enough to convince the Captain to take a nap when the alien battlecruiser had been maintaining her distance. But why would he leave the bridge now?

"I see," he subvocalised. He didn't dare speak out loud. God alone knew what the CIC's officers would think if they heard him. "Who's in command now?"

Midshipwomen Lopez spluttered. "You, I think," she said. "But he passed bridge command over to Commander Farley..."

James felt a shiver run down his spine. Something was *definitely* wrong. Traditionally, the officer on the bridge held command, even if he was outranked by someone elsewhere on the ship. Captain Smith should have called James himself to the bridge or at least informed him that someone else would be holding formal command, if James couldn't leave the CIC...

"Inform Commander Farley that he is still in command, but he is to alert me if the situation changes," James said, pulling up the personnel display. *Ark Royal* automatically tracked and logged the locations of everyone on the ship, including the aliens and their former captives, snug in their secure quarters. The Captain wasn't in his office, but his cabin. "I will deal with the situation."

"But..."

"I will deal with the situation," James repeated. The young woman had done enough – more than enough. No matter what had happened, her career wouldn't survive if the Admiralty found out what she'd done. "Remain on the bridge."

He passed CIC command over to his second, took one final look at the tactical display – the alien ship was *still* holding position, mocking them – and hurried out of the CIC.

———

Ted entered his cabin, closed and locked the hatch behind him and sat down on the sofa, feeling absolute despair working its way through his mind. He'd failed; he'd failed everyone from the First Space Lord to the lowliest crewman on his ship. The aliens had them trapped now, holding in place and waiting for the force they needed to smash *Ark Royal* like a bug. Ted had no illusions. The aliens *knew* his ship now; they knew what they needed to destroy her. When they came, it would be the final battle.

He cursed his own stubbornness as he stared down at the deck. If he'd been thinking, he would have gracefully accepted the First Space Lord's attempt to remove him from starship command. God knew there were few officers who had served on armoured carriers, let alone spent so long improvising improvements to the original design. Ted could have worked in the planning office, assisting the designers to prepare updated designs for carriers and battleships that would have combined modern technology and older systems to create powerful warships. Or he could have found a place in the Admiralty, doing paperwork to allow other – more capable – officers to take command.

But no, he'd had to keep his starship. He'd had to keep command.

He pulled himself to his feet and stumbled over towards the safe in the bulkhead, pressing his hand against the sensor so it could read the implant buried within his palm. It clicked open, revealing ten bottles of expensive alcohol. He'd considered disposing of them when he'd realised that *Ark Royal* was going back into active service, but he hadn't been able to convince himself to take the plunge. Maybe he would have served them at a dinner for his fellow commanders – he damned himself, silently, for not speaking more with them – if they hadn't all died because of his mistakes. *Ark Royal* had only escaped because the European frigates had sacrificed themselves...

Their sacrifice was in vain, he told himself, as he picked up a bottle at random. Fancy wine, he noted, from the Picard Vineyards on Mars. Who would have thought that humanity's first and last full-scale experiment with terraforming would have produced a modified grape that could be made into an elegant wine? Not that Ted really cared about the details, he had to admit, or the pretensions harboured by wine snobs. All he really cared about was the alcoholic content, the ability to blot out his mind and escape the pain. He would have called the Chief Engineer and ordered rotgut if Anderson hadn't been so busy.

Ted poured himself a glass, then took a long swig. The wine tasted fruity on his tongue, leaving a pleasant trail of fire as it ran down his throat and into his stomach. It had been months since he'd touched a drop, he realised, as he felt his head start to spin. There was no longer any need to drink heavily in order to achieve drunkenness. His fingers twitched, dropping the glass on the deck. Cursing, Ted picked up the bottle and put it to his lips.

He felt a flicker of guilt as he felt the cold glass touching his bare flesh. The crew needed him, he knew, yet he was useless. They would be better off with Commander Fitzwilliam or even an untrained newcomer from the Academy, not a drunkard like himself. Fitzwilliam had proved himself, in the end, to be more than just a well-born little bastard who had thought his connections would prove sufficient to take command of a starship. He'd make the Royal Navy proud.

Or he would, Ted considered, if he ever made it home.

Bracing himself, he took another long swig.

The buzzer sounded, but he ignored it. Let someone else worry for once.

———

The Captain's quarters were inviolate, James knew, as he came to a halt outside the hatch. A press of the buzzer brought no response. He hesitated, unsure of what to do. Technically, he could relieve the Captain of command...but he was surprised to discover that he didn't want to assert his authority. It would destroy his career, no matter how many friends and family he had in the Admiralty, yet that wasn't what was bothering him. He'd come to respect Captain Smith too much to want to destroy his career too.

He hesitated, then reached into his pocket and produced a standard multitool. One of the less standard classes at the Academy had shown the cadets how to bypass certain systems, acknowledging that sometimes the non-standard approach was necessary. James flipped open the panel beside the hatch, found the locking system and carefully removed it from operation. The hatch clicked as it unlocked itself, but didn't open. James cursed his decision to come alone as he pushed the door open, then squeezed through the gap into the Captain's cabin. Inside, the Captain was sitting on the sofa, halfway to drunkenness.

James swore out loud as he saw the bottle in the Captain's hand, torn between being impressed and being horrified. He'd never heard of anyone drunk on wine from Mars before, but that was because it was hideously expensive, even by aristocratic standards. James had tasted a small glass of it once, years ago, and had been left with the impression that it was grossly overrated. He certainly hadn't drunk enough of it to affect his feelings. Putting the memories aside, he walked over to the Captain, pulled the bottle out of his hand and placed it on the side table. The Captain looked up at him, blearily.

His mouth opened, but his lips worked incoherently for a few minutes before he managed to produce a few words. "Piss off."

"No," James said.

"Piss off," the Captain repeated. His voice sounded stronger this time, suggesting he wasn't as drunk as he looked. "That's an order, mister."

James hesitated, staring down at the wreck his commanding officer had become. The part of him that was ambitious knew that he could go to the bridge and claim command – and no one would be able to dispute it. Even if they did, what could they do? Back home, if they made it home, even the most rule-bound Admiral wouldn't object to James relieving his commanding officer for drunkenness in the face of the enemy. The Captain could be beached; hell, James knew that Uncle Winchester would be able to find a place for him. It wouldn't be the end of his life…

But he didn't *want* to throw the Captain to the wolves. Captain Smith had done well, first in building up a crew and then in leading it into battle against the aliens. He was, by any standard, the most effective naval officer the war had yet produced. Six months ago, he had merely been a drunkard James had aimed to remove from his post. Now…now he was a friend. They'd learned to work together as partners.

He *owed* the Captain.

Duty warred with loyalty in his head. Duty demanded that he relieve the Captain of command at once, the sooner the better. Loyalty demanded that he assist the Captain in overcoming his demons so he could resume command of his ship. James hesitated, then stood up and walked into the washroom. Inside, he turned the shower on, lowered the water's temperature until it was just above freezing, then walked back to where the Captain was sprawling on the sofa. Before the older man could muster an objection, James pulled him to his feet, half-dragged him into the shower and shoved his head under the water.

The Captain spluttered with anger, producing a string of swearwords so vile that James could only listen, impressed. He'd only ever heard one other person swear like that, an old family friend who'd served in the Royal Navy for years before leaving under a cloud. In hindsight, James realised that his family's friend had had problems with drinking too. Pushing the thought aside, he helped the Captain out of the shower and reached for a towel. The Captain snatched it from his hands and started to dry himself.

James hesitated, then stepped back into the main cabin and found the collection of alcohol. It was oddly impressive, given that the Captain wouldn't have drawn *that* large a salary while he remained in the Royal Navy. Even his knighthood had come with his promotion to Commodore, rather than being awarded for heroism. Absently, he wondered why the Captain hadn't been granted further honours after the first encounter with the aliens, then dismissed the thought. While the Captain dried himself, he scooped up the bottles, dumped them into a bag and placed them outside the cabin. They could be concealed in his cabin until *Ark Royal* returned to Earth.

And what, a nasty voice at the back of his mind asked, *will you do when the Captain orders you to return them?*

He had no answer.

———

Ted rubbed his wet uniform with the towel, then gave it up as a bad job and removed his jacket and shirt completely. The XO had shoved him into the shower fully clothed…absently, Ted found himself wondering just what regulation had been broken by wetting the Captain's uniform. Wasn't there something about not tampering with the Captain's dignity?

He shook his head, sourly. The water had done an effective job of sobering him up, leaving him grimly aware of just how badly he'd played the fool. If he had realised that the alcohol he'd consumed before the call to war had worked its way out of his system, he might have realised that he couldn't drink freely any longer. And to think he was meant to be in command! What a fool he'd been, he told himself. How could he really blame the XO for considering relieving him of command?

Maybe he should relieve himself, part of his mind suggested. But regulations, which declined to offer many acceptable reasons for relieving a commanding officer, flatly forbade the commanding officer from surrendering command while underway. He could put the XO or another officer on the bridge, in position to act rapidly if necessary, but he could never give them the full weight of his authority. No matter what he did, he – Captain Sir Theodore Smith – was the commanding officer, master under God. He could not shirk that responsibility for a second time.

He walked back into the main room and scooped up a dressing gown, pulling it on to cover his bare chest. The XO was seated in one of the chairs, a cup of steaming coffee in front of him. Another was positioned on Ted's desk, waiting for him. Ted wasn't fond of coffee – he strongly preferred tea – but he had to admit that it would be good for him. Sitting down, he wondered who'd made it – and what they knew about his situation.

"I made it," Fitzwilliam said, answering the unspoken question. "No one else has come here…ah, I think I broke your door."

Ted smiled at the sudden uncertainty in his XO's voice, then glanced over at the hatch. It was pinned open, barely wide enough to allow someone as skinny as Fitzwilliam to slip through the gap. He shook his head in droll amusement; apart from himself, only Midshipwoman Lopez had access to his cabin. It had never occurred to him that the XO would need to enter too without breaking the locks. He'd acquired too many bad habits when his ship had been drifting at anchor, with no hope of ever returning to active service.

"Yes, you did," he said. He couldn't help a sudden laugh. Under the circumstances, a broken door was the least of their worries. "A court-martial offense if I ever saw one."

He hesitated, looking at the younger man's uncertain face. "I'm sorry," he said, quietly. He found himself struggling for words, then realised he was trying to excuse the inexcusable. It would be better to take his punishment like a man, except there was no one who could punish him. "Thank you."

Commander Fitzwilliam seemed to understand, thankfully. Ted cursed himself under his breath, wondering just how much of the younger man's respect he'd lost when he'd tried to crawl back into a bottle. There was no point in deluding himself, he told himself savagely. He'd probably lost *all* of it. The belief that he'd led his crew into a trap didn't excuse abandoning them now...

He took a sip of his coffee, weighing up the options. Getting back through the tramline would mean confronting the alien battlecruiser... and it would be a very close-run thing. He didn't have the starfighter numbers to take her down without closing to engagement range, which would expose his carrier's hull to her plasma cannons. One shot, assuming the analysts were right, would be enough to melt the carrier's armour and ravage her innards. The second would blow them apart...

No, he thought. *We cannot allow them to close to point-blank range.*

Mass driver projectiles would work, he knew, if they succeeded in scoring a hit. Maybe they could snipe at the battlecruiser. But the alien battlecruiser was watching for incoming projectiles, he was sure. They might just give away their position for nothing. And, even if they did manage to sneak around the battlecruiser and enter the tramline, they'd still have to crawl past Alien-Two, then Alien-One. They would encounter the alien reinforcements on their way.

And there was no hope of modifying their Puller Drive to work like an alien drive…

A thought occurred to him. For a moment, he dismissed it as the last vestiges of the alcohol, then he started to take it seriously. It was insane, but it might just be workable. And besides, they were trapped. Thinking inside the box would only lead to a suicidal direct confrontation with the alien ship. But thinking outside it…

He swallowed the rest of his coffee, then jumped to his feet. "Come on," he said. The XO stood up, looking confused. "We have an operation to plan."

CHAPTER
THIRTY SIX

James followed the Captain, not to the bridge but down to the engineering compartment. It was heartening to see the confident looks many of the crew had as their commander passed, even though James knew just how close the Captain had come to betraying their trust. Maybe he should have chewed the Captain out more, James told himself, even if it cost him his career. But at least the Captain had an idea...

They stepped into Main Engineering, then straight into one of the side compartments. Anderson was sitting on a stool in front of a table, slowly dismantling one of the alien plasma guns. James wondered, angrily, why the Chief Engineer wasn't working on the drives or replacing destroyed weapons, then realised that those tasks could be passed to subordinates while unlocking the mysteries of alien tech was something for an older man.

"Interesting piece of technology," Anderson said, as the hatch closed behind them. "Do you realise that an EMP-bomb wouldn't just disarm the aliens, it would cause their weapons to blow up in their faces?"

James smiled at the mental image. "Seems like an odd choice of weapons, then."

"Not too odd, unfortunately," Anderson said. "The Yanks issued a laser rifle for their troops a couple of decades ago. It turned out that the power packs couldn't hold a charge for longer than a few days, while localised interference and jammers could interfere with the weapon's subsystems. Nor could they really be repaired in the field. Luckily, they didn't have to take them into combat before the weapons were withdrawn from service."

He shrugged. "In this case, the weapons are devastating while they work," he added. "Their plasma pulses can and do burn through our best personal armour. They could probably shoot through anything short of starship or tank armour. I wouldn't care to take a tank up against an infantry platoon armed with these weapons. But I suspect they have a very real danger of overheating if fired for more than a few minutes."

"Good," the Captain said. "What progress have you made with the rest of the recovered alien technology?"

"Most of it isn't that different from ours," Anderson said. "I've got one of our supercomputers trying to hack the recovered alien computer, but all its producing is gibberish. We will need to ship it to a proper geek on Earth, sir, although in all honesty I think the aliens corrupted the files before we captured the system."

James nodded. Standard human precautions called for wiping the files, then destroying the computers physically to render the date hopelessly beyond recovery. There was no reason to assume the aliens couldn't or wouldn't do the same themselves. Indeed, he was mildly surprised that the Marines had managed to take the computer at all. Had the aliens been careless...or had the Marines captured alien civilians rather than military personnel?

The Captain sat down and rested his elbows on the table. "If we took the alien ship," he said, "could you operate it?"

James and Anderson both stared at him. The Captain met their gaze evenly. James wondered, absurdly, if the Captain had drunk far too much...and then wondered if he should relieve him of command at once. No one had managed to board and capture a military starship in all of humanity's exploration of space. But then, no one had really tried.

"...Maybe," Anderson said. "If they had the time to purge and destroy the computer systems, it would probably become impossible."

James hesitated, then looked at the engineer. "Could someone operate *Ark Royal* without the computers?"

Anderson smiled. "They'd have to run their own control systems through the drives," he said, "but it might be possible. Our security protocols purge the local control networks too, sir. We didn't want to take the risk of the datanet collapsing at an inappropriate moment."

"I see," James said. Unlike more modern carriers, *Ark Royal's* data-net was largely decentralised. Normally, it would prevent battle damage to one section taking down the entire system, but it might also regard a self-destruct command as a network failure and ignore it, particularly if the system was already damaged. It was why there were backup systems worked into the fusion cores as well as the main computer nodes. "Captain, do you seriously intend to capture the alien ship?"

The Captain smiled. "If we get past them, we go back to Alien-Two," he reminded him, dryly. "But if we take the alien tramline..."

James swallowed. It sounded like a recipe for disaster. But the more he thought about it, the more he realised the Captain was right. They were trapped. Why not place a bet on one last throw of the dice?

"We know nothing about the interior of the alien ship," Anderson warned. "The Marines have never gone into an alien ship."

"No," the Captain agreed. "No one ever has. But we have to try."

"If nothing else," James said slowly, "we can take out the alien ship and sneak back into Alien-Two. We might just avoid detection without that bastard chasing us."

"We'd still have to crawl all the way to New Russia," the Captain said. He shrugged. "But it's workable as a backup plan."

James sighed. "Then the sooner the better," he said. "Before more alien ships arrive."

The Captain nodded. "Call Major Parnell and the CAG," he ordered. "And don't say a word to the reporters. They don't need to know the truth."

"Understood," James said. "I won't say a word."

He wondered, absently, just how many of the reporters knew that they were trapped. Yang probably understood the implications of only one tramline leaving the system – and the alien battlecruiser blocking their retreat – but how many of the others had guessed the truth? Perhaps, by now, they were so used to coming to the brink of disaster that they didn't really have the capacity to feel alarm any longer.

"Sir," he said, "whatever happens, we know the aliens have been hurt."

The Captain smiled. *Ark Royal* had inflicted colossal damage on the aliens, even though no one knew just how badly they'd weakened the alien navy. And the aliens had had to devote a vast amount of firepower to hunting the carrier down, buying time for Earth to organise her defences. *Ark Royal* might be lost, but she might have ensured that humanity won the war.

If we have time to build more armoured carriers and a few new battle-ships, he thought. *But will the Admiralty have enough time?*

"Yes," the Captain said. The smile he gave James was the smile of a true predator. "We know we hurt the bastards."

————

There had been no discussion when Rose came to his office, Kurt recalled, through a post-orgasmic haze. She'd pushed him to the deck and strad-dled him, her hands hastily unsnapping his uniform trousers and pushing them down to his knees. Moments later, she'd impaled herself on Kurt and ridden him savagely, panting out loud as she moved up and down on his cock. He came so quickly that, for a long moment, he thought he'd left her unsatisfied. But it was clear from the mewling noises she made that she'd come too.

"I'm sorry," she said, afterwards. She lay on top of him, still clutching his penis within her. "I just wanted to…"

She shook her head. "I think Gladys and Tom went to find a private place of their own too," she added. "How naughty of them."

"Hypocrite," Kurt said, without heat. Just what sort of reputation was *Ark Royal* going to have when she returned home? The media, if they ever caught wind of it, would turn her into a regular pleasure cruise. "What are you and I doing?"

Rose coloured, then straightened up. His limp cock fell out of her as she rolled off him and onto the deck. Kurt sighed, pushed his trousers all the way off and then stood up to go to the washroom. Whatever hap-pened, he knew they had no time to just relax and enjoy the aftermath. The aliens might attack at any moment.

She followed him into the shower, carefully removing her own clothes. Kurt hesitated, then allowed her to climb into the small cubicle with him. She washed his back, her breasts pressing into his body, then turned so he could do the same to her. Kurt was struck by the sheer perfection of her young body, almost completely unscarred by age or experience, and felt a pang of guilt. He was cheating on his wife with a girl almost young enough to be his daughter. The guilt grew stronger as he washed her, then stepped out of the shower and reached for a towel. What was he doing?

"Do you think," Rose said, "that the other CAGs have fun with their pilots?"

Kurt flushed, angrily. "I think they have the shower because they're not meant to fly or sleep with the pilots," he retorted. Ideally, the CAG wasn't meant to identify with any of the squadrons under his command. The Royal Navy worked hard to encourage a certain rivalry between squadrons, but the CAG was meant to be above it. "And because they're important people."

"Don't get too big-headed," Rose warned him. "You'll never be able to leave your office."

"How true," Kurt mused. He turned to look at her, then looked away, embarrassed, as she slid her panties back over her knees. Those weren't regulation panties, he noted…but who was going to know? It wasn't as if even the most stringent inspection included ordering pilots to lower their trousers long enough for their underwear to be checked. The very thought was absurd. "And I wouldn't be able to fit in the cockpit either."

He looked over at his terminal, feeling another pang of guilt. Part of his duty as a CAG was to analyse the alien starfighter tactics and propose countermeasures. He hadn't been doing it, first because he'd been too busy being a Squadron Leader as well as CAG, then because he'd reasoned they were trapped and about to die when the aliens caught them. There was no point in doing paperwork when no one would ever read it, even the XO. But if he returned home, he could look forward to a year or two on the beach, helping the tutors at the Academy to prepare new starfighter pilot trainees for combat.

I could see Molly and the kids every day, he thought. He might not have to take up a teaching post – and, if he did, his family could come with them to the moon. *And then…*

The communicator bleeped, pulling him out of his thoughts. "CAG, report to the briefing compartment," the XO ordered. "I say again, report to the briefing compartment."

"Good luck," Rose said.

She straightened up her jacket, glanced down at herself to make sure she looked decent, then strode out of the office without a backwards glance. Kurt glared after her, then hastily finished pulling on his uniform and stepped out of the hatch. One way or another, he was sure, their affair couldn't continue for much longer. Sooner or later, someone was bound to notice and then...

He shook his head, tiredly. If they didn't make it home, it didn't matter. And it certainly didn't *look* like they were going to make it home. But if they did...

Idiot, he told himself, as he made his way to the briefing room. *Concentrate on the here and now. The future can take care of itself.*

———

Charles hadn't expected the summons to the briefing compartment – or, when he entered, to discover that only the XO and the CAG had also been invited. Technically, the Marine contingent reported directly to the Captain; he'd been on ships where the Marine CO had refused to even talk formally to the XO. But with no task for the Marines apart from monitoring the captives – and the humans they'd liberated from the aliens – he hadn't expected to do anything other than keep his Marines busy.

"We have a plan," the Captain explained. He outlined the plan, piece by piece. "We have to take that ship or destroy it without risking ourselves."

He had the grace to look embarrassed, Charles noted. Traditionally, the commander of any Royal Navy squadron would ride into danger alongside his subordinates, even if he was often on the most heavily armoured ship in the navy. But the Captain couldn't abandon his ship and join the Marines as they boarded the alien ship, even if he'd been trained for the job. The Marines would be going into action alone...and if the first part of the operation failed, they were all dead. They'd detonate a nuke inside the alien hull to make sure of it.

But he couldn't help feeling a thrill at the mere *concept* of the operation. The Royal Marines had a long and illustrious history of death-defying stunts, but no one had ever tried to board an alien starship before. One way or another, they would go down in history.

If the carrier makes it home, he thought.

"I understand," he said, finally. His subordinates would love it, if only for the bragging rights when they finally made it home. The SAS, SBS or SRS claimed most of the bragging rights in Britain, while operations with Western Alliance partners exposed the Royal Marines to bragging from American or European operatives. But none of *them* had ever boarded an alien ship. "We won't let you down."

He pushed the exultation aside and began to think, mentally outlining the operational plan for the deployment. There were too many unknowns for him to be entirely comfortable, even though he relished the challenge. They knew nothing about the interior of the alien starship or how the aliens would respond to a boarding party. The Royal Navy's protocols called for the compromised compartments to be sealed off, then counterattacks mounted by the Marines and armed crewmen. But no one had ever tried to handle a counterattack outside drills few took very seriously. Did the *aliens* take their drills seriously?

"They're sweeping space for threats," he said, after a moment. "How do you intend to get the shuttles though their defences?"

"By giving them a threat," the Captain said, grimly. "*Ark Royal* will reveal herself here" – he tapped a point on the display – "and launch starfighters on attack vector. I believe they will focus all of their sensors on us so they can detect incoming projectiles. But we don't dare move towards them *too* aggressively."

Charles understood. If the alien craft wanted to break contact, it could...and the humans would be unable to escape their shadow. They could start running back up the chain towards Vera Cruz, only to run into the alien reinforcements on the way. But the aliens wouldn't think their ship could be attacked, would they?

He shook his head. Sometimes, no matter what the bureaucrats thought, you just had to gamble.

"I shall prepare my men," he said. They'd relish the challenge, he knew, despite the danger of being blown up by the aliens if they scuttled their ship. Or by the human nuke, if the operation failed spectacularly. "When do you wish us to depart?"

"As soon as possible," the Captain said. "You'll have to sneak towards the target, then move in from behind."

"I understand," Charles said. In one respect, it was just like boarding a rogue asteroid settlement. Marines in a shuttle were hideously vulnerable, Marines inside the asteroid – or the enemy ship – could fight to secure and expand their bridgehead. "We won't let you down."

"Good luck," the CAG said, quietly.

Charles gave the older man an odd look. Marines might bitch and moan about starfighter pilots having a comfortable seat while they fought – and all the women when they went on leave – but Charles knew the average life expectancy of a starfighter pilot facing the aliens. Even Marines might last longer…when the time came to finally hit a defended alien world.

"Thank you," he said.

———

Ted waited until the other men had left the compartment, then sagged back in his chair, feeling an odd tiredness fall over him. He knew, despite his show of confidence, just how many things could go wrong with the operation…and just how easily it could cost them everything. Every time he thought about it, he wondered if he'd trusted too much in the alcohol. Surely, if he hadn't touched the bottle, he would have thought of something better…

But he hadn't, he knew, and nor had anyone else. He was hardly the type of commanding officer to reject an idea, purely because it wasn't his. The Royal Navy discouraged the Darth Vader style of command, believing it to be dangerously inefficient. But Ted could understand why commanding officers worried about accepting outside ideas. Theirs was the authority – and the responsibility. The person who had proposed the idea wouldn't be blamed if it failed.

But this is my idea, he told himself. *I will be blamed if it fails.*

He wanted a drink. God, how he wanted a drink. But he knew he didn't dare touch a drop, not now. Instead, he pulled himself to his feet, took a moment to compose himself and then strode through the hatch and onto the bridge. It was time to brief the bridge crew on the planned operation.

"We've come a long way," he concluded. "Everyone believed that *Ark Royal* would head to the scrapheap, one day. Instead, we have devastated the alien fleets and scored victories that have knocked them back on their heels. Whatever happens today, they will know that we will never surrender, never give in."

He looked down at the console. The Marines were reporting in, ready to go. They'd be on their way within minutes, then Ted would have to wait for them to reach the first waypoint before he could launch his starfighters. But then...

There was no longer any time to fret, he told himself, firmly.

"Launch the Marines," he ordered.

CHAPTER
THIRTY SEVEN

There was no need for silence in the shuttlecraft. Sound didn't travel in space; there was no way the aliens could hear a spoken word. But the Marines said nothing as the pilot guided them though space towards the first waypoint, each one of them locked in his own thoughts and feelings. They'd all made wills before they'd departed Earth, Charles knew, but it was unlikely their final messages would ever get back to their families. Unless, of course, they did manage to escape the alien trap.

He accessed the live feed from the shuttle's passive sensors and nodded to himself. The aliens still weren't moving, but they were sweeping space with their active sensors. Marine shuttles were stealthy, yet Charles knew better than to assume they were stealthy enough to creep through an active sensor sweep. They needed one of the alien stealth systems, he told himself, and wondered if the boffins on Earth had unlocked their secrets since *Ark Royal* had set out on deployment. If not…the answers to their questions about the system might be dead ahead of them, waiting to be taken.

A faint quiver ran through the shuttle as it slowed to a halt, relative to the alien battlecruiser. Behind them, the other shuttles held their position and waited, linked to the command ship through pinpoint laser beams. Charles sucked in his breath and studied the alien craft through the passive sensors, recalling what little had been gleaned from sensor sweeps during the Battle of Alien-One. The ship was half the size of *Ark Royal*, its gleaming hull seemingly untouched by weapons and sensor blisters. But, given the alien capabilities, that meant nothing.

She was more elegant than a human ship, he had to admit. Unlike the boxy *Ark Royal* or the newer carriers, the alien craft was a black triangle, hovering against the darkness of interplanetary space. Twin engine nodes glowed at the rear of the ship – their in-system drives were definitely a step or two above humanity's technology – while the faint bulge of a Puller Drive was easily detectable. The aliens, it seemed, were ready to nip back through the tramline if the shit hit the fan.

The only rupture in her otherwise seamless hull, he noted, came at the very prow of the ship. It looked like her hull should taper down to a fine point, but instead there was a large aperture big enough to take the shuttlecraft or a couple of starfighters. He wondered, vaguely, if the aliens had actually outfitted the battlecruiser with a starfighter launch tube – there had been early human designs that had been nothing more than engines wrapped around a starfighter launching system – but it was grossly inefficient. Besides, the passive sensors were picking up faint traces of radiation from the opening.

That must be their plasma cannon, he thought, as he eyed the alien ship. It was a curious design, all the more so after witnessing what EMP pulses did to plasma containment systems. *I wonder what they would do if the ship was attacked by a nuke...*

He pushed the thought out of his mind as the shuttle sent back an automated acknowledgement to *Ark Royal*. The Marines were in position. All they could do now, he told himself, was wait.

And hope that the aliens took the bait.

———

"The Marines are in position, sir."

Ted nodded. The aliens hadn't reacted at all to the shuttles, which was a colossal relief. It was impossible to forget that their technology was often more advanced than humanity's...and equally impossible to gauge the ways it might be more advanced without actually seeing it in operation. He'd been dreading a sensor field or some other trick that would allow the aliens to track the shuttles, but nothing had shown itself. Or were the aliens merely holding their fire for their own inscrutable reasons?

He pushed his doubts aside, then looked over at Farley. "Bring us to full alert," he ordered, refusing to allow any of his trepidations to show on his face. "And then launch starfighters."

The aliens would notice, of course, the moment *Ark Royal's* active sensors came online. There was no way they could hide, which should puzzle the aliens…perhaps they'd jump back into the previous system, leaving him with a terrible dilemma. Or maybe they would see it as one last desperate attempt to escape the tightening noose.

"Starfighters away," Farley reported. "The aliens are powering up their drives."

"Lock full active sensors on them," Ted ordered. At such a distance, targeting data would be imprecise, to say the least. But it would keep the aliens firmly aware of their location – and not, he devoutly hoped, looking anywhere else. "And prepare to engage with the mass driver."

———

Gladys and Tom were fucking, Kurt had noted, as soon as he'd returned to the pilot ready room. They were trying to hide it, but his experienced eyes had picked out the signs. Thankfully, they were in different squadrons or he would have been forced to say something to them at once, which could have turned unpleasant if they'd found out about Rose and himself. The resulting shouting match, he was sure, would have ended with them all standing in front of the Captain, trying to excuse the inexcusable.

He braced himself as the starfighter rocketed out of the launch tube, followed by the remaining twenty-one pilots under his command. Barely two squadrons, he noted, composed of survivors from six separate units. His idea for expanding Starfighter Command, he decided, would have to be implemented as soon as they got home. The Royal Navy couldn't afford these loss rates – there was a shortage of trained personnel – and nor could any of the other human powers.

We might have to do more than just train more starfighter pilots, he thought. No one had ever foreseen a joint campaign against an alien enemy…at least as far as he knew. Soon, they might have to take Russian or Chinese pilots onboard *Ark Royal* or assign British pilots to fly off their carriers. *We will have to unify everything.*

Ark Royal had plenty of non-British components packed into her hull, but *Ark Royal* was unique. It would be harder to add Russian components to a modern British carrier, even American or European components required careful modification before they could be used without causing problems down the line. That would have to change, he knew; the next generation of human warships would have to be completely compatible, even among human states that were historical enemies. He wondered, absently, if their mission – if it succeeded – would give Britain the diplomatic clout to insist on standardising everything… or if the Admiralty would attempt to keep the alien starship to itself. There was precedent for both, he knew, and no way to know how the politicians would jump.

He pushed his meditations aside as the alien battlecruiser started to turn, angling its prow towards the oncoming starfighters. Kurt puzzled over the movement for a long moment, then realised that the aliens were revealing as little of themselves as possible to *Ark Royal's* mass drivers. They seemed less concerned about the starfighters, he decided, which wasn't too surprising. Unlike a human ship, their point defence could fire randomly, sweeping through space in the hopes of scoring a lucky hit. The closer the starfighters came, the greater the chance of the aliens hitting their target.

"*Ark Royal* is engaging now," a voice said, though the datanet. "Missiles inbound; I say again, missiles inbound."

Kurt nodded. They were placing everything on one last throw of the dice. Every missile, every remaining projectile – although those could be replaced, given time – and every starfighter. He wondered, again, just how much the aliens actually *knew*. Did they realise that their target was about to expend the last of its weapons?

They configured their weapons for our modern ships, he thought. It made sense, he decided; the aliens had taken the measure of their opponents, then attacked with savage force. Earth would have fallen as easily as New Russia, he suspected, if *Ark Royal* hadn't intercepted the alien task force. And now the aliens were taking stock, presumably building up their own weapons to confront a new and unexpected threat. He smirked at the thought. *Didn't expect the Old Lady, did they?*

"Picking up power surges around the alien prow," Rose reported. She paused, then spoke in a dramatic tone of voice. "If I don't come back, get in touch with my mother and tell her I was alive all this time, I just couldn't be bothered to call the old bat."

"It was a mistake to let you pick the entertainment for the ready room," Kurt said. He grinned, imagining her outraged expression. "On my command, break and attack; I say again, break and attack!"

———

"The alien energy signature is growing stronger," Farley reported. "The analysts are unsure what we're facing."

Ted nodded, studying the display as if the answers would magically appear. It didn't *look* like anything they recognised, not a point defence system or a FTL drive. Or a normal space drive, for that matter. There was a sudden energy spike...

Ark Royal rocked, violently. Ted was nearly pitched out of his chair as the compensators struggled to handle the unexpected assault. Alarms sounded; the display glowed red, sounding the alert. Ted gripped hold of his chair and held on for dear life as the network attempted to identify the damage.

"Direct hit to our starboard launch tube," Farley reported. He sounded badly shaken. "Our armour took most of the blow, but there's some internal damage."

He paused. "Something damaged our external sensors too," he added. "We're down thirty percent of capacity."

Ted swore. He'd thought they were out of alien weapons range. Clearly, the aliens had had other ideas. But why hadn't they used the system earlier?

"Rotate us," he ordered, quickly. Damage control teams were already on their way, he was pleased to note, although they were somewhat undermanned with the absence of the Marines. If worst came to worst, they could withdraw the crew to the main hull and then separate the launch tube from the remainder of the starship. "Present our strongest armour to them, then launch decoy drones."

"Aye, sir," Farley said.

Ted looked back the alien ship, clearly preparing to take another shot. *Ark Royal* was tough, but tough enough to take several more blows like that? Somehow, he doubted it.

"Launch sensor drones too," he added. His display pinged as the analysts finally came up with a theory about the alien weapon. They'd supercharged a plasma cannon, then used it to take shots at *Ark Royal*. Their best guess, he saw at the bottom, was that the weapon couldn't be fired very rapidly or the aliens would burn out their own systems. "And hold us here."

He wanted to pull back, to escape the alien weapon. But he needed to keep their attention focused firmly on the carrier, not on anything else.

"Continue firing," he ordered. It would be the height of irony, he decided, if they actually scored a *hit* with the mass drivers. The alien battlecruiser didn't look tough enough to survive a direct hit. "Don't give them a moment to think."

———

"They're advancing towards us," Rose reported. "Alien point defence is coming online."

Kurt nodded, then threw his craft into a series of evasive patterns that no computer could hope to match, let alone predict. It was just in time. Apparently heartened by scoring a hit on *Ark Royal*, the alien battlecruiser was gliding forward, intent on getting into range for another shot. According to a stream of data at the bottom of his screen, the alien weapon lost its effectiveness at long range. A shot at close range might blow the carrier apart like an eggshell.

"Noted," he said. The rate of alien fire was increasing, picking off missiles and inert projectiles with surprising accuracy. "We need to keep them busy."

Bracing himself, he altered course and zoomed towards the alien craft in a straight line for as long as he dared, around five seconds. His spine prickled as he altered course sharply, just as a spray of plasma fire lanced through where he'd been. Moments later, a warhead detonated close to the alien craft, blasting an EMP straight towards her hull. The rate of plasma fire slacked rapidly, but didn't come to an end. Their targeting, on the other hand, seemed to go entirely to hell.

"They didn't lose the big gun," Gladys exclaimed. "It's still charging up."

"Then we'll deal with it," Kurt said. He yanked his starfighter back, then powered down towards the alien hull. Most of the plasma cannon was embedded into the alien ship, but enough of the containment system was exposed to make it an easy target. "Fire at will."

The alien cannon buckled under the spray of pellets from his railgun. Kurt watched a sudden surge of energy spike, then fade back into nothingness. He thought, for a brief chilling moment, that they'd actually succeeded in starting a chain reaction that would take out the entire ship. Normally, that would have let them paint an alien silhouette on their starfighters, but now it would be a disaster. Thankfully, the aliens merely altered course as they powered down their weapons.

"They're rebuilding their sensors," Tom reported. "I..."

His voice disappeared with a sudden, terrible finality. Kurt risked a glance at the datanet and saw that Tom had been hit, blotted out of existence in a split second. He heard Gladys gasp in shock, then bring herself back under control. She wanted revenge, but at least she could hold it back enough to keep flying in unison with the remaining pilots.

This, a voice said at the back of his head, *is why starfighter pilots should not develop relationships with one another.*

"Damn it," he muttered. Out loud, he barked orders. "Regroup and attack; I say again, regroup and attack."

———

"The launch tube is going to need a complete refurbishment," Anderson reported. "I've given orders to evacuate the section, sir; there's no point in leaving anyone there."

"Understood," Ted said, absently. On the display, the alien ship was slowly turning back towards the tramline. They couldn't be allowed to run, but he didn't have any way to stop them without destroying the systems he needed to capture. "Keep me informed."

He closed the channel, then looked over at the display. The Marines were drawing closer to their target. Close enough to board...and to be detected.

———

Charles braced himself as the alien craft came closer, its hull shining faintly with scars from the EMP strike. They must have suffered local power overloads and explosions, he guessed, which had damaged the superconductor hull. It was funny, he thought, just how a strength could so easily become a weakness, under the right circumstances. But there was no longer any time to think...

An alarm sounded. "They have us," the pilot snapped. "Launching flares, now!"

Charles braced himself as the shuttle jerked, then accelerated towards the alien hull. The aliens might have mistaken them for missiles, or they might have realised what the humans actually had in mind, but it was too late. Between the shuttle's erratic courses and the disruptive flares – actually, tiny drones intended to create false sensor readings – the aliens would have real difficulty tracking them properly.

A red icon flared on the display briefly, then faded. Charles felt a wrench as Shuttle Three vanished from the display, picked off by the alien blast. Fifteen Marines vaporised in a split second, he told himself, then pushed the grief and rage out of his mind. There was no time to mourn the dead now. Afterwards, if they survived, they would hold a proper funeral for the lost men.

The alien hull loomed up in front of them, then glowed white as the shuttle's drives flared, burning through the alien metal. Charles allowed himself a tight smile, imagining the carnage inside the alien ship. *Ark Royal's* armour would have melted under a fusion light, he knew; the alien hull, whatever it was, didn't seem to be anything like as resistant. The Marines braced themselves, ran one final check on their armour, and then scrambled to their feet as the shuttle came to rest. Outside, the alien ship was waiting...

And how much, he asked himself suddenly, *will the ship be worth in prize money?*

"Deploy probes," he ordered. It had been a long time since he'd plunged into the unknown – even terrorist or insurgent bases were scoped out carefully before the Marines moved in - but he was looking forward to the challenge. "And then follow me."

———

"Four of the shuttles made it, sir," Farley reported.

Ted grimaced. Two shuttles were gone, then; one lost to point defence, one lost to unknown causes. They'd have to replay the sensor records piece by piece to find out what had actually happened, he knew, which would take hours. He wouldn't know until after the battle.

"Good," he said. He looked over at the helmsman. "Pull us back."

"Aye, sir," Lightbridge said. *Ark Royal* felt uncomfortably sluggish as she moved, slowly, away from the alien craft. On the display, the starfighters pulled back too. There was nothing further they could do to help the Marines. "Two minutes to minimum safe range."

If they're right about the weapon's range, Ted thought.

He looked down at the final damage reports, then resigned himself to waiting – again. They thought they'd taken out the alien cannon, but if they were wrong…the bastards wouldn't get another shot at his ship. But they were almost defenceless now…quite apart from the damage to the sensor network, their missiles were completely expended.

Pushing his thoughts aside, he forced himself to watch…

…And wait.

CHAPTER
THIRTY EIGHT

Charles hadn't been sure what to expect when they plunged into the alien ship. There had been no way to train for the mission, nor had they had any data to use in training simulations, not when the ships they'd examined after the first battle had been shattered by *Ark Royal*. All they could do was improvise – and pray that the aliens didn't manage to blow the ship before they were wiped out or captured.

Tiny nanoprobes raced ahead of the Marines, rapidly sending back data to the shared combat datanet. Charles expected to see hunter-killer probes deployed in response – it was the standard human procedure – but none of the nanoprobes vanished from the display. Instead, they rapidly started to map out the interior of the ship, updating the HUD with notes on alien positions and internal environment. The atmosphere was breathable, they noted, but hot and moist enough to make most humans sweaty and uncomfortable. Charles noted it in passing – the Marines wore battle-suits, allowing them to ignore the local environment – as they slipped through a gash in the hull. A scene from hell greeted them.

Atmosphere – the water droplets already freezing to ice – streamed past the Marines as they entered the alien ship. The fusion flame had melted metal into molten streams of liquid, which were cooling rapidly now the flame was gone. Even so, the interior of the alien ship looked like a melted honeycomb, with decks destroyed or warped into something unusable by human or alien. The gravity field caught them as they pressed onwards, the stream of atmosphere coming to an end. Their safety precautions must have finally taken effect, Charles noted inwardly. The aliens designers, like humanity's designers, clearly believed in devising hulls so compromised sections could be sealed off at a moment's notice.

They saw their first alien body as they made their way down towards the closest airlock the nanoprobes could identify. Charles was no stranger to horror – nothing the aliens had done matched the horrors humans had inflicted on other humans – but he couldn't help feeling uncomfortable at the sight of an alien torso permanently separated from the lower half of its body. A human would probably have been killed instantly through shock, Charles knew, but would an alien be just as fragile? There was no way to know.

Two Marines attached an atmospheric bubble to the airlock, then went to work with cutting torches. If anything, the alien hull was *less* resistant than *Ark Royal's* armour – although, to be fair, it *was* an internal airlock. Charles watched the airlock come loose, then motioned for the first Marines to step into the interior of the ship. A swarm of nanoprobes shot past them, racing deeper and deeper into the alien ship. His HUD constantly updated as they mapped out the alien interior.

Inside, the atmosphere was misty. Visibility was poor, something that puzzled him. Surely the aliens would have wanted to see clearly onboard a starship? But he recalled the sheer size of their eyes – and the speculation that they normally lived in water – and guessed that the aliens probably had far better eyesight than humans. Besides, their helmet sensors could peer through the muck, although the IR sensors kept sounding false alarms. The environment was hot enough to confuse them.

He took a glance at the updating map, then issued orders. One team would advance towards where they thought the alien bridge was, another would head down to engineering. The remaining Marines would expand through the ship, capturing or killing any aliens they encountered. Charles had given serious thought to declining to take prisoners at all, but he'd eventually dismissed that thought. No matter the dangers, he wasn't about to start committing atrocities against an alien race. Particularly, as he'd pointed out to his subordinates, one that might still win the war.

The interior of the alien ship looked faintly distorted, oddly disconcerting to the eye. Some of the passageways seemed normal, as if they could easily have been found on a human ship, others were oddly proportioned. It took him a long moment to realise that the aliens didn't seem to have designed their interior to resemble something on the ground, with a definite floor and ceiling. Indeed, were it not for the gravity field holding them down, he would have thought the aliens didn't bother to maintain an artificial gravity field at all. He puzzled over it for a long moment, then realised that the aliens were born in water. They would have an instinctive understanding of zero-gravity environments that only asteroid-born humans would be able to match.

"Curious wall decorations," Sergeant Patterson noted. He sounded faintly jumpy, clearly worried about what might spring up ahead of them. "Do you think they can see at all?"

Charles followed his gaze. The aliens had decorated their passageways with artworks, but there was no recognisable pattern at all. It looked as though a child had taken a paint box and splashed its contents randomly over the bulkheads. Charles suspected his five-year-old nephew could have done a better job, then he touched the bulkhead and realised that the texture changed from colour to colour. Could the aliens be colour-blind? It might explain their choice of artwork...and, for that matter, the apparent shifts in their own skin colours.

Or maybe they just have a different set of aesthetics, he told himself. *If humans can't agree on what makes a good painting and what doesn't, why should they?*

The explosion caught them by surprise, despite the drones. An entire bulkhead blasted out at them, forcing the Marines to duck and dive for cover, despite their armour. Behind it, a squad of aliens lunged forward, firing plasma bolts towards the human intruders. The Marines returned fire, blasting the aliens to the ground. Their tactics made no sense, Charles noted absently, part of his mind analysing the brief engagement. Or perhaps they did make sense, he realised, as the second group of aliens appeared. *This* group seemed far more professional, sniping at the humans from cover rather than merely charging at the intruders and being gunned down.

There was no time to pick out an alternate path through the rabbit warren. Instead, Charles barked orders, commanding his men to launch grenades into the alien position. The deck shook violently as the grenades detonated, followed rapidly by a sudden reduction in enemy fire. A small group of Marines ran forward, crouching low, and finished off the remaining aliens before they could escape or recover from the blasts. But a second set of aliens had taken up position behind the first...

Charles sighed, resigning himself to heavy fighting. The HUD kept updating rapidly, showing more and more concentrations of alien crewmen. It was impossible to tell which of them were trained soldiers – alien Marines, he guessed – and which ones were merely crewmen who barely knew which end of a weapon to point at the enemy. The Royal Navy was often careless about ensuring that its starship crewmen kept up with their personal weapons; he couldn't help feeling a flicker of amusement at the thought of the aliens having the same problem. Making a mental note to suggest to the Captain that weapons practice should be made mandatory – the aliens might be the next ones to board a crippled starship – he barked orders, leading his Marines further and further into the alien ship.

His HUD bleeped as it signalled an alert. Charles puzzled over the sudden detection of poison gas, then realised that one of their shots – or an alien plasma burst – had burned into a coolant conduit. The Marines ignored it, even though the aliens retreated hastily. Most of them had no armour. Charles briefly rethought his decision not to blow the ship's integrity and release its atmosphere, allowing the aliens to suffocate, then reminded himself that all the arguments against it were still valid. But the aliens weren't even *trying* to surrender...

Get real, he told himself, as he snapped off a burst at an alien soldier. The alien tactics seemed haphazard, even random...but with their weapons, they made a great deal of sense. They didn't have to worry about reloading their weapons, so why not spray at random like a primitive machine gun? The worst that could happen was that they forced the advancing enemy to keep their heads down. *We don't even know how to ask them to surrender.*

The thought nagged at him as he saw his target fall to the deck and lie still. If they'd been facing humans, they would have been shouting demands for surrender in every language they thought their opponents faced. Not that it would have been enough, for some humans; insurgents and terrorists knew what to expect if they fell into military hands. They rarely surrendered – and, unless there were hostages or human shields, they were rarely given a chance to fight back. But the aliens...how could they tell them to put their hands up when they couldn't speak to them?

We have to fix this problem, he thought. Another series of explosions shook the deck as the Marines blasted their way through an alien strongpoint. It looked as though the aliens were organising their defence on the fly, which was fortunate. Given time, they could have stalled the Marines long enough to blow the ship. *Somehow, we have to get them to surrender.*

"I've found a tube, sir," one of the Marines called. "That's how they're evading us."

"Snaky little bastards," another Marine observed. "*We* couldn't fit in that tube."

"Not unless we start recruiting children," Charles agreed, as he saw the alien tube. It looked like a Jefferies Tube from a human starship, but it was alarmingly thin, too thin for the Marines to use even without armour. The tubes on *Ark Royal* were wide enough for human adults to use; the alien tubes were simply too thin. But, given their biology, it probably wouldn't be a problem for the aliens. "Send drones up it, then seal the hatch and hope they can't break out again."

He scowled. It was easy enough to imagine the aliens using the tubes to sneak past human strongpoints and take them in the rear. Hell, humans planned to do the same thing if their ships were boarded. But these tubes couldn't be sealed so easily, nor could the aliens be flushed out. They'd have to start cutting through the bulkheads just to get at the aliens hiding within the tubes, doing untold damage to the alien command and control system. Normally, that wouldn't have been a problem. But now, when they needed the alien ship largely intact...

"Keep moving," he ordered. Somehow, they had to take the fight out of the aliens, but how? "Don't give them a moment to relax."

Charles let the NCOs lead the advance while he fell back, thinking hard. What did they actually *know* about the aliens? They seemed to breathe the same atmosphere as humans, but they liked it hot and moist...indeed, when the alien captives had been shown how to alter the temperature in their cell, they'd cranked it up as far as it would go. Could they cool down the ship, making the aliens sluggish? But how could they do that without cracking open the hull and releasing the atmosphere? What about gas…?

But they had no idea what gases designed to stun or kill humans would do to the aliens.

His HUD bleeped again as the final outline of the alien ship lay in front of him. The analysts were adding their notes to the combat datanet, pointing out how similar – in many ways – the alien ship was to human starships. Charles dismissed their work angrily, cursing the distraction under his breath, then issued orders to his Marines. The alien engineering compartment lay dead ahead of them.

"They're fighting like mad bastards to hold the bridge, sir," Captain Jackson called. "We may need to use grenades."

Charles winced. A human bridge had all of its vital components armoured under the deck, allowing attackers to lay waste to the command consoles without doing any real damage. But what if that wasn't true for the alien ship? They could smash up the bridge, only to discover that they'd accidentally crippled the whole ship. And yet…the longer they waited, the greater the chance the aliens would succeed in blowing up the ship. Right now, Charles knew that *he* would be preparing the self-destruct. Their position was hopeless. All that remained was to take as many of the humans with them as they could.

"Do it," he ordered. He hesitated, then added an additional order. "Use gas first, see what it does. Then use HE if there's no other alternative."

"Understood, sir," Jackson said.

Charles tore his attention back to the main engineering compartment, just as the main door crashed inward, revealing a compartment that was strikingly different from its human counterpart. The modular design he had expected was non-existent; instead, all of the alien subsystems appeared to be linked together into a single unprotected mass. It made no sense to him; half of the systems appeared to be exposed to any stray shot or power surge. Or were the aliens in the middle of trying to blow up the ship when the Marines burst in?

"The gas seemed to make them convulse," Jackson reported, as the Marines slowly advanced into the engineering compartment. The aliens seemed to have vanished completely, abandoning the section. "They weren't in any fit state for a fight. We've taken them prisoner."

The bridge crew, Charles told himself. "Keep a sharp eye on them," he ordered, remembering how bendy and flexible alien bodies could be. Standard zip-ties might not be enough to keep them helpless, not if they could flex their way out of the tie. "Actually, secure them thoroughly. We don't know how easily they can escape."

"Yes, sir," Jackson said.

The Marines prowled through the deserted compartment, looking for the aliens. There was so much interference in the section that the nano-probes, otherwise very useful at tracking alien movements, were largely useless. Charles heard bursts of interference over the datanet, wondering absently just what the aliens used to operate their starships. Nothing human produced such effects, of that he was sure. Or would human fusion cores produce interference, if they were unshielded? The prospect of fighting in a radiation-filled zone was chilling. But the battlesuits weren't reading any dangerous radiation in the vicinity.

"It's like they abandoned the entire section," Corporal Pollock said.

Charles rather doubted it. There were four compartments on a human starship that had to be held at any cost; the bridge, main engineering, the armoury and life support. Losing control of one of them could mean losing control of the ship. The contingency plans the Marines had practiced for *Ark Royal* included stationing a whole platoon of armoured Marines in all four locations, ready to repel attack or buy time for the ship to be destroyed. But the aliens seemed to have retreated instead...

The mists grew heavier as they advanced, making it harder and harder to see. Charles sensed the tension among his Marines, understanding and cursing it at the same time. What they couldn't see *could* hurt them – and the tension would make them fire off a shot at nothing, sooner or later. And then he saw very definite movement, something twitching...

"Keep back," he ordered. Something was barely visible in the gloom. "Sergeant..."

The Sergeant advanced forward, weapon at the ready. Charles silently cursed the rules that forced him to stay back, then almost jumped as the Sergeant swore out loud. "Sir," he said, "they're dying."

Charles threw caution to the winds and ran forward. There was a heap of alien bodies, twitching unpleasantly, lying at the far end of the compartment. Several of them were already dead – even when sleeping, according to the doctors, they moved constantly – and others were definitely dying. Their skins, normally bright vivid colours, were shading down towards the murky grey he remembered from the first body. But what did it mean?

"They thought they were going to be captured," the Sergeant speculated. "Instead, they chose to die"

Charles nodded, then listened as reports started to come in from the rest of the ship. Some aliens had been captured, but others had killed themselves, either through poison or simply shooting themselves in the head. Were they that fearful, Charles asked himself, of being taken prisoner? For all he knew, the aliens had a long tradition of murdering prisoners...although the treatment of their human captives seemed to suggest otherwise. But they'd also drugged the humans mercilessly...

He shook his head. That too was something that might be answered when human analysts went prowling through the alien ship, trying to recover computer files. There was a great deal of information in any standard teaching program on humanity, from biology to psychology. The aliens had probably cracked the systems they'd taken from Vera Cruz by now, if they hadn't recovered any from the *Heinlein*. But then, the aliens wouldn't really have had to work hard. Civilian teaching machines weren't designed to make it *hard* to learn.

"We need to find a way of talking to them," he said, as the prisoners were hauled back towards where the shuttles were docked. It would take some ingenuity to link up the shuttle's airlock to the alien ship, but they didn't have any spacesuits suitable for the alien captives. "Some way to tell them that they won't be killed on sight."

He fought down the urge to rub his forehead. There was no way to touch his skin through the suit. "And contact *Ark Royal*," he added. "Tell them...tell them that the ship is ours."

And hope that the engineering crew can make use of it, he added, silently. *Because alien reinforcements are already on their way.*

CHAPTER
THIRTY NINE

It had taken a considerable amount of polite arguing before Ted had been able to convince Commander Fitzwilliam that he should be allowed to board the alien craft. Captains were not supposed to risk themselves, Fitzwilliam had pointed out, reminding Ted that most television or data-net programs were grossly unrealistic. Ted had countered by reminding his XO that the alien ship had been rendered safe and he was damned if he wasn't going to take a look at it, just once. He certainly had never expected to be able to visit an alien ship before the war started – or even after it, for that matter.

Oddly, the alien craft was slightly disappointing. Once he'd come to terms with the moist atmosphere – the doctors insisted on everyone using breathmasks until they were sure there was nothing harmful in the alien atmosphere – he'd realised that there wasn't anything too different from human technology at all. Part of his mind realised that wasn't actually a bad thing – something based on completely different principles would require *years* to unravel, if it could be unravelled at all – but he couldn't help feeling as if some of the wonder of the universe had faded away.

He couldn't help envying the aliens for the sheer amount of *joy* they'd worked into their creation. Human starships were boxy, built more for utility than elegance; the only truly elegant human ships were the handful of luxury liners that plied the tramlines between Earth and the various wonders of the human sphere. *They'd* been built by shipping corporations willing to expend the money to design ships that *looked* spectacular, despite the inefficiencies. The aliens, it seemed, cared less for cost and more for elegance.

Or maybe there's something in them that wants to beautify their ships, he thought. There were human movements that wanted to produce ships identical to science-fantasy ships from the previous two centuries. Most of *them* were utterly unworkable, at least as military starships, but civilian models could work if someone put up the cash. *Wouldn't we, if we could get it to work?*

"We've moved the prisoners to *Ark Royal*," Major Parnell said, when Ted finally reached the alien engineering compartment. "None of them talked to us, so we put them in with the others, in hopes they would speak."

Ted nodded. The more samples of alien words they recorded, the quicker it would be to decipher the alien tongue. "And the self-destruct?"

"We accidentally disabled it, according to the engineers," Parnell admitted. "We got lucky, sir."

"I know," Ted said. He looked over at Anderson, who seemed to have merged a chunk of human technology into an alien control system. "What can you tell me?"

"Good news and bad," Anderson grunted. The engineer pulled himself away from the merged system with obvious reluctance. "I think I've figured out how they extend the range of their FTL drive; they actually create a stream of gravity pulses that boost the potential tramline into reality long enough for them to use it. It's actually much more flexible than we realised, sir. We may discover that there are more than two tramlines in this system."

Ted blinked in surprise. "How do you figure that?"

He held up a hand. "Spare me the technobabble," he said, quickly. "Just plain English, please."

"There's a difference between potential tramlines and real ones," Anderson said. "Our assumption was that it was impossible to actually do more than ride the tramlines we knew to be real. But this left us with the mystery of why some tramlines exist and others do not – or at least *seem* not to exist. It's possible that space is threaded with potential tramlines the aliens might be able to activate at will."

"I see," Ted said. There were five known tramlines leading from the Sol System to various destinations, nine counting the projected *alien* tramlines. But what if there were more? The aliens might be able to leapfrog across far more of humanity's territory than the Admiralty had realised. "Can we duplicate the system?"

"There shouldn't be any problems with producing a duplicate," Anderson said. "I'd prefer not to start dissecting the system until we got back to Earth, though. The alien command and control unit is quite complex and I don't want to risk annoying it."

"Which leads back to the important question," Ted said. "Can we use the drive to get back home?"

"Easily," Anderson said. He grinned, suddenly. "We'd just have to secure *Ark Royal's* hull to the alien ship."

Ted blanched. Securing one capital ship to another was dangerous, even when both ships belonged to the Royal Navy. If something went wrong on the alien ship and she exploded – he found himself wishing that he knew the ship's *name* – *Ark Royal* would be caught in the blast. Even *her* armour probably wouldn't provide protection against such a close encounter.

"Do it," he ordered. If nothing else, the reporters would get one hell of a story. And besides, if they got home, the entire crew would be eligible for the prize money. "But I suggest you hurry."

————

James couldn't help feeling nervous as the engineering crew carefully linked the two starships together, ensuring that parting contact was impossible. He couldn't help the feeling that it would be impossible with or without the cords; *Ark Royal* moved like a wallowing pig and the alien starship, as yet unnamed, was little better. The engineers might be fascinated by the chance to study so much alien technology, but James had to concentrate on the dangers. And it was perhaps the riskiest manoeuvre the Royal Navy had ever carried out, at least in the face of the enemy.

"We're linked, sir," Anderson reported, finally. "We've attached a tube so crewmen can move between the two ships, as well as supervising the alien drive."

"Understood," James said. The reporters had been begging for a chance to board the alien craft as soon as they'd realised what had been accomplished. He sighed; sooner or later, he would have to surrender to their request, even though it was quite likely that all of the details would be thoroughly classified. The Royal Navy wouldn't want to give up any intelligence on the alien ships without a fight – or at least getting something of equal value in return. "When can we jump?"

"I'd prefer to spend more time monitoring the alien power curves," Anderson said, "but we should be able to jump as soon as we reach the tramline."

James smiled, ruefully. The longest jump ever recorded – at least before the aliens arrived – was ten light years – and that had only been possible because both stars were massive enough to create a longer than normal tramline running between them. Now, *Ark Royal* was going to set a record, at least until human researchers started messing around with the potentials of the alien drive system. Genuine original science would be done, Anderson had claimed, during one of his brief naps. Humanity would learn a great deal from the alien ship.

"Good," he said. Manoeuvring interlinked ships through interplanetary space would be tricky, but doable. "We will leave as soon as the Captain gives the command."

———

Ted felt his heartbeat pounding faster and faster as the conjoined ships entered the phantom tramline. Human technology could barely detect its existence, let alone traverse it to an unknown destination. But the alien systems seemed to have no difficulty recognising that it was there. He hesitated as the two ships came to a halt – the whole jump was dangerous enough without trying to do it at speed – then gave the order. The universe seemed to darken...

For a terrified moment, he was sure he'd killed them all. The moment of darkness stretched on and on, then cleared with astonishing speed. He felt his ship lurch, as if it had rammed something, then quieten down. The display was already starting to fill up with data.

"We made it, sir," Lightbridge said. "All systems report nominal."

Ted sat back in his chair, feeling sweat running down his back. Fourteen light years. They'd jumped fourteen light years, effectively instantaneously. And the aliens did it all the time. The implications hadn't changed from the conclusions in the half-panicky reports he'd been sent the Admiralty, but they hadn't quite seemed *real*. Now...now he comprehended, finally, that the territory the aliens controlled might be much greater than the human sphere.

"We have several reports of crewmen fainting," Commander Fitzwilliam said. There was an odd note of amusement in his voice, which seemed out of place until he continued. "All, but two of the reporters also fainted."

Ted nodded, then looked down at his console as the reports flowed in from all over the ship – both ships. Spacers were used to normal jumps, but this one had been unusually violent, although no one was quite sure why. Perhaps it explained, he decided, why the aliens were so lax about chasing the human ships through the tramlines. Their drives reacted poorly when asked to jump at speed.

"Check the aliens," he ordered. Was it possible that they were stunned...or dead? "How did they handle the jump?"

"They seem fine, sir," Major Parnell reported, two minutes later. "But clearly a little agitated."

Ted nodded. Clearly, the aliens had sensed the jump...but they hadn't suffered any real ill effects. Were they experienced spacers, then, or were the aliens actually *less* inclined to be harmed by the jump?

"Understood," he said, finally. "Keep an eye on them."

He keyed his console, linking directly to Anderson. The Chief Engineer and a third of his staff had taken up permanent residence on the alien ship, despite the doctor's warnings that they *still* couldn't guarantee that the environment was safe. Anderson sounded tired, but very happy when he answered the call.

"The jump functioned as advertised," he said. "If we lose the alien Puller Drive next time, sir, we will probably still be able to devise our own version."

"Glad to hear it," Ted said. He looked at the new star system on the display, his eyes tracking the four tramlines leading out of it and back towards human space. Two of them were useless without the alien drive. "Can we jump again?"

"I think so," Anderson said. "We only need three more jumps to get us back to Earth."

Ted shook his head in disbelief. Three more jumps...when it had taken nine to reach New Russia from Earth. They'd be jumping through the scene of their first successful engagement, he saw, as the helmsman plotted out the series of jumps. Three more jumps...

"The sooner we duplicate this system, the better," he said, flatly. "We need it for ourselves."

———

"I never expected to survive," Rose said.

Kurt nodded. She'd come to his office...but instead of making love to him at once she'd sat down, twisting her hands in her lap. Oddly, he found himself torn between relief and disappointment. He might have cheated on his wife, but he wasn't going to deny that the sex had been great. But really...what kind of future could Rose and he have, even if he left Molly for her? He was old enough – almost – to be her father. He'd be old and gray long before her.

"Nor did I," he said. He swallowed. It was time to act the mature adult. "Rose...what do you actually *want* from me?"

"I don't know," Rose confessed. "I want you and I don't want you and I don't want to hurt your children and yet I don't care if they get hurt..."

It took Kurt a moment to untangle her words and understand just how conflicted she was. "I understand why you came to me," he said, carefully. "I wasn't only experienced" – Rose gave him a look that told him precisely where he could shove his experience – "but I was also safe."

"Most starfighter pilots are selfish," Rose said. "You weren't selfish."

Kurt almost pointed out that Rose had been having an affair with one, which had resulted in her assignment to *Ark Royal*, but stopped himself just in time. It would have been thoughtlessly cruel to say something like that to anyone, particularly someone who had lost the lover in question soon afterwards. Survivor's Guilt had probably played a big role in Rose's decision to find someone else as quickly as possible.

And you are not blameless, he told himself, shortly. *You didn't say no when she took off her top, did you?*

Rose had been more than a little selfish herself, he acknowledged, but he hadn't been much better. No, he corrected himself ruthlessly, he hadn't been better at all. He'd made love to her despite having a family back on Earth, a family that would be torn apart by his betrayal...and it *was* a betrayal. Perhaps he could have sat down with Molly and talked their way through their problems, sharing blame as well as responsibility to find a resolution. Who knew – maybe they'd separate, but stay close for the sake of the kids.

And that might be tricky, he thought. *Because you certainly didn't consult with Molly before finding someone else...*

"I was," Kurt said. Rose gave him an uncomprehending look. She was young and far too used to the immature idiocy of starfighter pilots who knew they could die at any second. It would be years before she gained the perspective that would show her that love wasn't just about sharing a bed, but sharing an entire life. "I could have told you to fuck off."

A faint smile ghosted over Rose's cheeks. "No man has ever said that to me," she said, deadpan. Someone her age would have missed the pain hidden under the boasting. "And I'd bet that none ever will."

"Probably not," Kurt said. He cursed himself mentally, then looked up at her, trying not to imagine her body under her flight suit. It would be so easy, he knew, to pull her to him...and he was certain she wouldn't object. His cock twitched at the thought. But it would send the wrong message. "Rose..."

He leaned forward. "What we did, when we thought we would both die, was wrong."

"I didn't notice you objecting," Rose pointed out, snidely.

"I didn't," Kurt said. "And if I'd known we would return to Earth, I would have objected strongly. But I didn't know."

He pressed on, remorselessly. "I have a wife and children as well as a career," he added. "You have a career, a career that has already been dented by one affair. And…I don't know how you feel about me, but I am not a good choice for you over the long term."

Rose looked down at the deck. "Are you going to report me? Report *us*?"

Kurt shook his head, not trusting himself to speak. The report would destroy both of their careers, even if they *were* heroes – and rich heroes at that, if the prize money came through as expected. They would probably be permanently beached or dishonourably discharged. And, in his case, it would probably cost him his marriage too.

"No," he said, when he could finally form words. "But I am not going to make love to you anymore."

He'd expected anger, he'd expected a shouting match…but she responded with a calm sadness that worried him. As CAG, it was his duty to counsel any of pilots who required counselling—he might have lacked training, but at least he wasn't an idiot psychologist – yet his relationship with her was hopelessly compromised. He couldn't play her father or a senior officer when they'd had sex countless times. And who could Rose talk to who wouldn't betray her confidences?

"I understand," she said, quietly.

She stood, gave him a brief and formal hug, then turned and marched out of his quarters as if she were passing out on parade. Kurt watched her go, torn between calling her back and letting her go – and, perhaps, asking the doctor to speak to her. The doctor would keep secrets unless they threatened the integrity of the crew.

Idiot, he told himself as the hatch hissed closed. *What do you think your secret has done?*

———

"Jump completed, sir."

Ted smiled as the familiar shape of the Sol System appeared on the display. He'd taken the precaution of insisting they came out of the tramline some distance from Earth, just in case Earth's defenders were in a shoot first and ask questions later mode, but it seemed as though his precautions had been unnecessary. The closest human starship was over a light minute away.

"Send our IFF," he ordered. The defenders, seeing them come out of a phantom tramline, would be more than a little suspicious. It would take time to reassure them. "And hold position here until they reply."

It was nearly thirty minutes before a giant modern carrier, surrounded by a dozen frigates, approached *Ark Royal*. Ted smiled as her IFF – USS *Enterprise* – popped up on the display. Like most American carriers, she was overpowered and over-engineered…and, like all of the other modern carriers, hopelessly vulnerable if faced with alien starfighters. Ted felt his smile grow wider as electronic handshakes were exchanged, confirming that neither ship was under alien control. Whatever he was offered, he was damned if he was exchanging *Ark Royal* for any modern starship.

"They're asking what the hell we've attached to our hull," Annie said, finally.

Ted smirked. "Tell them it's several billion pounds worth of prize money," he said. He wished, suddenly, that he'd thought to fly the skull and crossbones. Too late now. "And ask them for an escort back to Earth."

He sat back as the giant carrier turned back towards Earth, her starfighters flying past *Ark Royal* in welcome. They'd made it.

They were home.

CHAPTER
FORTY

"You will not, I suspect, be pleased to learn that the media is besieging the Admiralty Building in London," the First Space Lord said. "Word of your exploits – and the capture of an alien ship – has leaked out and the world has gone crazy."

Ted nodded, keeping his mouth firmly closed. He would have bet good money, after meeting the PR staff assigned to the reporters, that the Admiralty had deliberately allowed the news to leak. The human race needed good news and *Ark Royal's* successful cruise through alien territory was the best they'd had in quite some time. He had no doubt that the Admiralty would successfully minimise the simple fact that they'd come within bare millimetres of absolute disaster.

"The major interstellar powers have also contributed to a prize money fund," the First Space Lord continued. "I dare say your crew will be happy."

Ted nodded, feeling an unfamiliar twinge of gratitude for British diplomacy. Ten percent of the prize money went to him, ten percent went to the Marines and the remainder was shared out evenly among the crew. With contributions flowing in from all over the human sphere, even the lowliest crewman could look forward to becoming an instant millionaire. Taxes might have been raised to help fund the war effort – prize money wasn't tax-free, unfortunately – but they would still be quite wealthy. Not a bad outcome, he knew, for a crew that had been scraped together from officers and men the Admiralty couldn't be bothered to discharge.

"Yes, sir," he said. "And the former prisoners?"

"Most of them came from Vera Cruz, as you summarised," the First Space Lord said. "The remainder came from the handful of smaller colonies the aliens hit and destroyed. Their families have been informed, but they'll be remaining in custody for the moment."

Ted couldn't disagree, even though he knew it was cold. The former alien POWs would require time to decompress, time to recover from their ordeal…and most of them had yet to purge the alien drugs from their systems. On Earth, they would receive proper medical care and, when they were ready to talk, sympathetic ears. Being held captive was bad enough, Ted knew, even when the captors weren't alien monsters.

Or maybe humans would have been worse, Ted thought. *Apart from the drugs, the human captives were unhurt.*

He sighed. The alien POWs had been moved to a secure facility on the moon, where a mixture of military and civilian researchers would attempt to unlock the secrets of their language – and their biology. If they could talk to the aliens, they might figure out the truth behind this senseless war…and determine if there was a way it could be ended without one side being completely crushed. But Ted wasn't hopeful. None of the doctor's work on the aliens had managed to crack even part of their language.

"I will confess," the First Space Lord said, "that I had my doubts about you."

Ted kept his face expressionless, somehow. Had Fitzwilliam told the Admiralty about Ted's near collapse back into drunkenness? Or had the First Space Lord merely had his doubts from the start, despite recognising that Ted was uniquely qualified to command *Ark Royal*? It seemed quite likely.

"You were a drunk, put bluntly," the First Space Lord continued. "I fretted, even when it seemed that *Ark Royal* would be nothing more than an escort carrier or a backstop, before we learned the truth about the alien weapons. And when you had to take the ship into battle…"

He shook his head. "You have proved yourself," he admitted. "When the chips were down, you made the Royal Navy proud."

"Thank you, sir," Ted said. He knew it wasn't entirely true. If Fitzwilliam hadn't caught him before he could drink himself into a stupor, the entire cruise would have ended very differently. "I did my best."

"You did," the First Space Lord agreed. He nodded over towards the display. "But the war isn't over."

Ted followed his gaze. Two more star systems had joined New Russia in red, occupied by the aliens, while another three had been probed by alien forces. The aliens might not have dared go straight for Earth, but they'd weakened humanity still further. It was impossible to escape the feeling that the war was very far from over.

"It will take us at least a year to produce the new battleships and armoured carriers," the First Space Lord said. "We're trying to rearm a number of older ships that were converted into colonist-carriers or heavy bulk freighters, but that's an uphill chore too. The aliens may still hold the whip hand."

"So we go back on the offensive," Ted said.

"Soon," the First Space Lord said. He looked down at his desk for a long moment, then up at Ted. "When the time comes, it had been agreed" – he paused, significantly – "that you will command the offensive."

Ted wondered, absently, just how many deals had been cut to make that possible so quickly. Few of the interstellar powers liked the thought of having their starships serve under another power's command, no matter how closely allied they were. And Ted's previous command had been shot to pieces, with *Ark Royal* the only survivor. He was surprised that any other power had been willing to agree to let him take command.

"We're short on heroes," the First Space Lord said, when he asked. "Blame the reporters, if you like."

Ted rolled his eyes, inwardly. He'd only caught a couple of newscasts between debriefing sessions, but most of them bore little relationship to reality. One of the reporters – who hadn't even been on *Ark Royal* – insisted that Ted had led the boarding party in person. But if he had, the Royal Navy would have congratulated him and then removed him from command.

"Thank you, sir," he said, finally.

"Don't thank me," the First Space Lord said. "Your life is about to become a great deal more complicated."

"As long as I keep *Ark Royal* as a flagship, I don't mind," Ted said.

The First Space Lord smiled. "Congratulations, *Admiral* Smith," he said.

———

James couldn't help, but be mildly bothered by the summons to Nelson Base. Between debriefings and supervising the repairs to *Ark Royal*, he simply didn't have the time to spare. But the summons had left no room for objections, so he'd boarded the shuttle and made his way to the giant space station. Inside, it was no surprise when he was escorted to a private briefing room.

"My official weblog states that I am in a meeting with a design team leader," the First Space Lord said, as soon as the hatch had hissed closed and locked itself. "We don't have much time."

"Yes, sir," James said.

"Admiral Smith," the First Space Lord said, taking a seat. "Is he suited for independent command?"

"Yes," James said, without hesitation.

The First Space Lord looked up. "Are you sure?"

James kept his expression as blank as possible, even though the First Space Lord was probably used to reading people more inclined to deception than James.

"Yes, sir," he said, finally. The Captain had come alarmingly close to a relapse, but disaster had been averted…and he'd managed to get his ship and crew home. And he'd captured an alien starship in the process. "Permission to speak freely, sir?"

The First Space Lord nodded, impatiently.

"Captain Smith is responsible for the destruction of a number of alien carriers, along with smaller ships, the recovery of over two hundred former captives, the capture of thirty-two alien POWs and, last but not least, the capture of an intact alien starship," James said. "By any standards, *Ark Royal's* cruise through enemy-held territory was the most successful naval operation since Trafalgar. We successfully gave the enemy a bloody nose."

He paused. "We might not have succeeded in liberating New Russia," he added, "but that wasn't part of our mission orders."

The First Space Lord sighed. "Blame the media," he said. "They expect perfection – or nothing."

James nodded, silently grateful that the reporters were off the ship and tormenting someone else. They'd certainly helped promote the Captain – but they'd also raised the uncomfortable question of why New Russia hadn't been liberated. At least the Russian government had been smart enough to understand that the planet couldn't have been liberated, at least not without an unacceptable level of risk. *They* weren't fuelling the flames.

The First Space Lord looked up at him. "I believe that Captain – sorry, *Admiral* – Smith has proved himself," he added. "But I will still require you to keep an eye on him."

"Sir," James said, carefully, "can I ask why?"

"Two reasons," the First Space Lord said. "First, he will be placed in command of a multinational fleet…and he was not the most capable officer at building connections to the foreign starships. This time, the other commanders will not be from minor powers."

James nodded in reluctant understanding.

"Second, because fame and fortune may well go to his head," the First Space Lord added. "As his Flag Captain, you will be in position to advise him – and to report any problems before they become public."

"I don't like it, sir," James said, twisting uncomfortably. "With all due respect, sir, you're asking me to act like a spy."

"You *have* been acting like a spy," the First Space Lord pointed out, coldly.

"Yes, sir," James said. "And I didn't like it."

"You don't have a choice," the First Space Lord told him. "The war isn't over – and the deciding moment may come to rest on Admiral Smith. When it does, I want you to ensure that he's ready to handle it."

James hesitated, but knew there was no real choice.

"Yes, sir," he said.

———

Kurt couldn't help a thrill of excitement as the taxi made its way back to his home, even though he was nervous about seeing his wife once again. He'd rung ahead and asked the children to stay home from school, despite the probable anger of their teachers. He just couldn't wait to see them again.

The house was dark and cold when he opened the door, until he stepped into the kitchen. Inside, Molly, Penny and Percy greeted him, the two teenagers throwing their arms around him and hugging him tightly. Molly – and a young girl he assumed was the home help – seemed a little more standoffish, but he hugged her anyway. A pang of guilt, as sharp as a knife, echoed through him as he remembered everything he'd done with Rose.

"Welcome home, dad," Penny said. She pushed him towards a chair, then produced a sheet of paper. "I did very well on my exams."

"Well done," Kurt said, grinning like a madman. His kids were fine, his wife…well, she wasn't entirely fine, but at least she wasn't shouting and throwing things at him. "And you, Percy?"

"I'm going to apply to the Academy next year," Percy said. "I can go, with your permission…"

Kurt swallowed. "Later, son," he said. He knew it wouldn't be easy to convince Molly to agree – and he wasn't going to write any permission slip without her consent. "Later."

The home help stuck out a diffident hand. "I'm Gayle," she said. She was tall and muscular, reminding him of a handful of female servicewomen he knew. "I've been looking after your kids for the last two months."

Kurt frowned. Hadn't there been another girl?

"She's practically been living here," Penny said, crossly. "I can't get away from her."

"Good," Kurt said, unsympathetically. He ignored the whining about how Gayle put a crimp in Penny's social life. Constant supervision was probably good for her, even if she wasn't going out and having fun with her friends. "You have to get high marks in your exams or your social life will take a disastrous fall."

Penny looked sulky, but cheered up when Molly brought out the cake.

Afterwards, when the teenagers were in bed, he spoke to Molly. "What happened to their schooling?"

"The school said that it wasn't going to expel children from military families," Molly said. "But I don't know how we're going to keep them there."

She shook her head. "Penny acted quite badly for months," she explained. "I had to practically thrash her bottom red to stop her driving the teachers mad – and that was with supervision. I don't know what I would have done if she'd been expelled. As it is, we don't even have the money to keep them there past the end of the year."

Kurt smiled. "Prize money," he said, and produced the cheque from his pocket. "We can keep them there for a few years, if necessary."

Molly stared at the cheque, then shook her head in disbelief. "Where are you going now?"

"Luna Academy for several months," Kurt said. *Ark Royal's* fighter wings would have to be rebuilt from the ground up, so the Admiralty had decided his experience would be better used in teaching new trainees how to fight the aliens. He couldn't fault them – and besides, getting leave to visit Earth would be much simpler from the moon. "It's not as…sexy a job as CAG, but it will keep me nearby for a few months."

"That's good," Molly said, reluctantly. She took the cheque and folded it into her pocket. "I…"

"I missed you too," Kurt said. It was true, in a way. "And thank you for waiting."

He picked his wife up and carried her into the bedroom. It had been a long time, far longer than just his deployment to *Ark Royal*, yet there was something…odd about their lovemaking. Afterwards, he lay on his bed, looking up at the ceiling. What was different now? His experience with Rose…or realising that, perhaps, Molly didn't really miss him when he was gone.

His terminal bleeped. When he picked it up, he saw a message from Rose. She'd been assigned to Luna Academy too.

Kurt cursed under his breath, torn between delight and bitter guilt. It made sense to send Rose there; her experience, after all, wasn't too different from his. And she could relate to the younger pilots better than himself. But he also knew that he would be tempted, horribly tempted, to get back into bed with her. Maybe he could bring Molly and the kids to the moon with him…

…And Gayle had practically been living with the family.

He looked over at Molly's sleeping form, wonderingly. Had she been desperate enough to pay Gayle to stay when she was in the house…or had she been elsewhere? And, if so, where? Had she been having an affair

? Had she been having an affair *too*? But why didn't the prospect bother him? Had he fallen out of love with his wife and never really noticed?

Kurt sighed and tried to sleep, putting the mystery aside for a later day. But sleep was a long time in coming.

———

"Congratulations, Admiral," Commander – no, *Captain* – Fitzwilliam said.

"Thank you," Ted said. "And congratulations to you too."

They stood together, looking down through the observation blister at *Ark Royal's* dented launch tube. The shipyard workers were already at it, removing the damaged components and rapidly replacing them with devices built from scratch. Given a week, Ted had been promised, the carrier would be as good as new. He hoped, devoutly, that they were right.

"We did well, sir," Fitzwilliam said, finally. "I received a v-mail from Major Parnell. He and his men are being feted all over Hereford."

"I know," Ted agreed. Hereford was the home of the SAS, still the best special forces unit in the whole damn human sphere. For the Royal Marines to be feted so openly meant that they'd done something truly extraordinary. But then, who else had captured an alien ship? "He'll be back soon."

He smiled at the thought. The Admiralty had handed out promotions all round, although most of the senior crew had refused to leave the carrier. Given their fame, the Admiralty hadn't bothered to argue. Besides, who else was more experienced with the ancient carrier?

His smile grew wider. The aliens probably knew *Ark Royal* now, knew her and feared her. For a ship that had come alarmingly close to being scrapped, it was no small achievement.

And for a drunkard, the medals on his chest – from every spacefaring human power and some of the ones that remained trapped on Earth - were no small achievement either.

"Yes," he said, finally. "We did very well."

The End

The Story Continues In

THE NELSON TOUCH

Available Now!

Also Available:

THE SHARK BOATS
by Leo Champion

Built for speed and agility, Motor Torpedo Boats have armor made from thin plywood - and weapons that can smash a battleship. Powered by engines that can drive them into harm's way at 70 miles an hour, they bristle with machine-guns, cannon, torpedoes and rockets…and the men who command them are no less dangerous.

Jack Reiner had made his way from the orphanage to a stock-exchange desk, and joined the Reserves to protect a society where that was possible. When the citizen soldiers he'd known for a decade are massacred in the water with their hands raised…then an ideological war has just become very personal.

Hector Chavez had made himself an orphan when he reported his parents for illegal trading. An idealistic servant of the People, he's long ago sacrificed his personal conscience to the greater good, for President Ramirez' dream of peace and equality under one rule. Killing capitalists is his duty - but killing Reiner might just be a pleasure.

There'll be blood in the water when they meet.

"There are no weaknesses anywhere in this book.…The characters are brilliantly drawn and the plot is a tightly threaded mixture of adventure, political intrigue, and understated romance…I thoroughly recommend it."
-Kate Paulk, author of *Impaler*

CHAPTER SEVENTEEN

Engines. Loud engines, coming in from where they shouldn't be.

Reiner was agitated enough that *anything* would have made him jump. There was absolutely no reason for any USC MTBs to be moving fast at this time of night. Not even *his* ones.

It's impossible for anyone to get through this storm.

Not the case. Calina had told him that he'd made it through the open sea in worse storms than this on smuggling runs. Storms were the best time to make landings because most Nick patrols weren't active and the ones that were active, couldn't see shit. All of Goldstein's pilots were that good – that was why Goldstein had chosen them.

"Give us a flare," he snarled. "Let's see who the fuck that is."

Almost immediately, someone on the *Isabella* blasted a white flare into the sky. They must have already had the gun in hand.

Dark shapes silhouetted about two miles away.

Coming in fast.

"More flares, *now*! Battle stations! Hit searchlights!"

Reiner tensed as more flares went up. Calina revved the engines and whirled the *Isabella* around to face the oncoming shapes. Grey and Schaffer were moving, too.

He leaned over and hit the general frequency.

For a moment, he hesitated. *What if it's just some of our boys coming in? What if they're reinforcements?*

Then a blazing white flare shot up from either the *Ragnar* or the *Krantz*, at a forty-five degree angle so that it hung in the air above, for a moment, the leading shape.

Red dots glinted brightly in the flickering light.

It's not just the enemy.

It's Chavez.

"Red alert!" he snarled into the radio. "All USC units, this is Reiner on Ten, we have a *Red Alert!* Red red red!"

From the enemy shark boats came their own flares. Red ones, which left flickering trails and burst above the moored USC ships. Highlighting the *New Michigan City* and the *Robb*, and the two cruisers.

Reiner's teeth bared in a vicious snarl.

I get to have another crack at Chavez. And he's come to me.

"This one's for deKuyper, you piece of shit," he snarled as the *Isabella* roared towards the PNA boats.

Not personally needing radio communication beyond his squadron, Chavez had tuned his second radio to what Morales had said was the Southerners' general frequency.

As his boats sped in towards the now-visible *New Michigan City* and the *Robb*, he was rewarded with words he recognized:

Reiner. And *Ten*, the squadron Castro's murderer commanded.

Orders are not to engage. Fire our torpedoes and get out.

Yeah, well. The bastard might just turn out to be a target of opportunity.

One mile to the freighter. The three USC MTBs – Reiner's? – were coming in on a head-on intercept course. Their machine-guns began to blaze. One of their bow cannon fired, kicking up a waterspout not far from the *Carmen Quatro*.

The heavy machine-guns of Squadron Seven in turn began to blaze.

"Torpedoes ready!" Chavez shouted unnecessarily through the clattering din. His men were well-trained, and they'd been thoroughly briefed on this mission.

Searchlights began to light up on the Southern ships. One of their dormant MTBs began to move. In the flare-light, Chavez could see there were easily a dozen of them. More than a dozen.

"Red Alert!" came a voice over the enemy-tuned radio. "Bragg to all units, battle stations *now*! Repeat, battle stations!"

So the bastards were waking up. Too bad. It'd be minutes before they could get into action.

"I'm not ramming him," Calina snarled in response to Reiner's harsh order.

"You know this guy?" Turner asked. He was the calmest man on the boat right now.

"Long story," Reiner snapped.

A hundred yards, as the *Isabella* and what Reiner supposed was the *Rubina* raced towards each other. The *Rubina* was clearly on a torpedo run and just as clearly her target was the *New Michigan City*.

"Tex, *do it!*" Reiner yelled.

Without turning from his gun, Tex waved his hand in a calm-down gesture.

Fifty yards, forty. Pulli's machine-guns lashed wildly at the straight-moving *Rubina*. In his peripheral vision Reiner could see the *Krantz* and the *Ragnar* on either side of him, on similar intercept courses.

Tex fired.

The *Rubina*'s pilot swerved, *hard*, at that precise moment. Somehow not overturning his boat – a similar fishtail maneuver in the other direction righted her a second later.

Calina slowed the *Isabella* into the beginning of a sharp one-eighty. *God damn it*, Reiner thought, as they turned. *Kaye and deKuyper are aboard that tender! And a dozen other of my wounded men!*

They *had* to take Chavez out.

Now.

On a straight path. The only active Southern boats had passed them by – they'd need easily half a minute to turn.

Eight hundred yards to the tender. One of Chavez's torpedomen looked at the cockpit. Chavez shook his head, once.

You brilliant son of a bitch Albertino, he thought. He'd been *convinced* Reiner's near-point-blank shell would get them.

"Salina, kill the tanker," Chavez snarled into the radio. "Menendez, hit the tender."

Unnecessarily. Both captains already knew their assignments.

Searchlights were coming on all around the moored USC ships. A dozen flares already illuminated the night sky, silhouetting the unprepared fleet. Now, several dozen beams – from the sides of cruisers and destroyers, from the cockpits of MTBs, from the superstructure and sides of the *Robb* and the *New Michigan City* – began to probe the dark sea.

"*Faster!*" Reiner screamed to Calina. The *Isabella's* RPM needle was at the far right of its range, *beyond* the red area. They were pushing fifty knots, and still three or four hundred yards behind the *Rubina*. She was on the outside edge of torpedo range and moving in an obvious straight line that meant she was preparing to launch them.

Tex slammed another shell into the breech and fired.

Boom.

Explosion aboard one of the PNA boats. A red fireball spiralled up into the sky, followed by a sparkler display as belts of machine-gun ammunition started to detonate. The boat lay dead in the water.

Is that Chavez?

They rocketed past the stricken PNA boat a moment later, Pulli raking her with machine-gun fire just to make sure.

Didn't matter if it was or wasn't. Another shark boat was still on its way in.

"Mayday!" cried Senior Lieutenant Menendez on the *Carmen Quatro*. "We're hit and can't move! Mayday!"

"We'll try to come back for you," Chavez snapped into the radio. Six hundred yards to the enemy tender. Five hundred and fifty. Four hundred.

The torpedomen were looking at him expectantly. The tender was beginning to slip her moorings and move.

Albertino was keeping them on course, on a top-speed kamikaze run at the big tender. He'd turn when the torpedoes were fired and not before.

Chavez looked at the torpedomen and nodded.

The *Rubina's* torpedoes slid off their racks.

"She's turning!" someone on the *Isabella* shouted.

Oh no, thought Reiner. He knew what that meant.

Calina was turning to intercept the *Rubina's* escape path. Tex almost certainly had a shell in, but he was holding his fire until he had a better shot.

Explosion. Another one followed almost simultaneously. A gout of blazing fire erupted from the engine compartment of the *New Michigan City*.

A second later, from where the *Robb* had been, came a fireball. A massive fireball, a murderous wave of heat that blasted across Reiner's arms, face and chest like a flamethrower.

For a moment Reiner was blinded.

Graaf said the Robb *was down to dregs and fumes*, he thought. *Nothing more combustible than fumes.*

Except that there were a few hundred wounded men aboard the tanker, too.

Had been.

My God, Chavez.

"I don't care how far he runs," Reiner snarled. "We're going to catch that son of a bitch. And we're going to *kill* him."

"I hear you," Calina mouthed back.

"No chance we can save Menendez," Albertino snapped. "Those dormant ones – waking up now – we can't afford to stop."

The tender was burning, *hard*, and beginning to sink fast. Where the tanker had been, there was nothing but smoke and patches of burning gasoline. And yes, some of the other MTBs were waking up.

"We're heading *south*?" Chavez demanded. Looking around. South was down Lower Sudham Strait, the narrow channel between East and West Upham.

"Only route open," Albertino snapped.

Chavez nodded. Well, they had enough fuel to make it around the Uphams. The pilot was right. Going back past the fort, and through the remaining USC fleet in the Gap, wasn't an option.

The pilot, while intent on steering the *Rubina* on an attack run through the choppy waters of a still-subsiding storm, had somehow sized the tactical situation up before Chavez, whose responsibility such things really were.

I've got a couple of other books I'm going to make you read, Albertino.

Damn, you could be such an asset to the Revolution if only we could bring your heart around.

"Where's he going?" Turner asked. Braced against the side of the cockpit, he was scribbling notes on one of his pads.

"South. Only course open to him," said Reiner. "Son of a bitch is probably planning to beach his boats in friendly territory and make a run for it."

"You going to chase him on land behind PNA lines, if he does?" Turner asked.

Reiner gave a curt nod.

Not far away, another explosion bloomed on the rapidly-sinking *New Michigan City.*

"I'll chase him to hell if I've got to. That man killed three hundred wounded men on the Robb and probably deKuyper and Kaye and the others as well."

And D Company. While they surrendered helpless in the water off Rienfuegos.

No, Chavez, today's the day you die.

"They're chasing us," Munoz observed, coming up onto the bridge. "Think we should beach?"

"I'm not letting that bastard Reiner burn the *Rubina,*" said Chavez as they whipped past dark coast.

Map said there's uncharted reefs all over the Lower Sudham. And in this darkness we can barely make out the coastline proper.

Charts say the Lower Sudham is barely a mile wide in places. And that doesn't count the reefs.

Albertino had either memorized the charts in detail – and had a sixth sense for the reefs that *weren't* charted – or he didn't give a damn. He drove the *Rubina* hell-for-leather south.

A brief glance behind showed the *Charlina* following. And lashing searchlights from the pursuing USC boats. From their positions, they weren't far off. Not much more than a mile.

And closing.

"This is all barely charted," Calina snapped. "And they removed the buoys when the war started."

"You know these waters," Reiner said.

"Not *these* waters. Nothing worth shit in the Uphams. We'd go round the east side."

Almost in corroboration to Calina's words came a horrible sound: *Screeeeiiiiiiiiiiiiittttt*, like diesel-powered nails ripping across an accelerated blackboard.

Reiner braced himself. But no vibrations on the *Isabella*.

"Mayday!" came Grey's voice. "We're torn open and sinking fast! Mayday Mayday Mayday!"

The shore on this side of West Upham – on *both* sides of the Lower Sudham at this point – was firmly controlled by the PNA. Fort Bailey was a semi-besieged outpost that the PNA simply hadn't bothered to prioritize.

They *had* to catch Chavez before he beached the *Rubina* and ran for it. Or before he powered down out of the Lower Sudham and into open water.

We'll hit him with bombers. South side of both islands are still ours and we've got airbases. They can fly out of Angle.

I want him personally.

"Schaffer, *don't* rescue him," Reiner snarled into the radio. "Someone else can – Steele's boats or Brickley's or whoever's behind us. We're going to *kill* the bastard this time."

"That bastard murdered the XO," Schaffer replied. "I'm on him."

"You want to take it easy, Albertino? There's reefs *all around*," said Chavez.

"Looks like only two of 'em left," said the pilot.

"We could turn and fight," Chavez muttered, as the idea entered his mind. It was appealing.

"There's only two of them *right now*," said Munoz. "There's two dozen more ten minutes behind them. I know you and this guy have a history, Lieutenant-Commander, but I am *not* going to let you sacrifice the mission for that."

Mission?

Their original orders. To show the USC bastards in Angle that they weren't safe even there. Right.

Besides, these waters were too narrow for easy maneuver. Reefs everywhere. Their only option was to do what Albertino was already doing.

Stay as close as possible to the center of the channel, hope for the best, and run like hell.

Tex's cannon boomed. The fleeing *Rubina* had been holding them at about a mile for close to quarter of an hour.

No explosion to speak of. They'd missed.

One of the torpedomen shot another flare into the sky ahead of them. Dawn was starting to break.

With it, Chavez's best hope of escaping under cover of darkness. They only had so many flares, but with daylight…

The coastline was curving unpleasantly. Sandy beaches within a mile on either side. An inlet with a fishing village and a flagpole. Reiner couldn't see whose flag.

Sooner or later he'll run out of friendly ground to beach on.

Calina turned for a moment. A grin on his face.

"You wanna take a chance?" he asked.

"What?"

"There might be a shortcut. Saw it on the charts. It's high tide. We might make it."

"We're not gaining ground on them," Reiner said. He thought for a moment.

We might lose him completely. If Calina misjudges. He said he doesn't know these waters.

These engines won't last forever. They've been redlined for the last half an hour and they're going to blow sooner or later.

Surprised they haven't already.

His are fresh. The PNA doesn't have supply issues like we have.

"Do it," he said.

"Flares," Calina snapped. "Need to see better."

"Flares," Reiner yelled.

Three or four of them went up. Lighting the path. On the coast a few hundred yards ahead was a narrow inlet. It disappeared into the jungle, no more than thirty or thirty-five feet wide.

"Heard there was a mine here. They dredged the channel to bring barges out," Calina said.

That was before the war. Months ago.

We don't have a choice.

"Go," Reiner ordered.

As they approached, Calina swerved hard to starboard.

Jungle surrounded them.

"We lost another of the bastards!" Munoz cried.

That last one's probably Reiner.

The searchlight, and the shape of the boat, was a mile and a half behind. Steadily losing ground.

"I think we've made it," said Chavez.

"Go to Angle. We can continue with the original mission from here. We're two thirds of the way down Upham anyway," said Munoz.

Albertino nodded.

Sudden movement on their eleven. Blazing searchlight through the gloomy early dawn. For a second its blinding glare hit the *Rubina*.

Machine-guns blazing, the *Isabella* burst out of a small bay three hundred yards ahead of them.

"Take the red eyes first," Reiner ordered. It was two against one – the *Krantz* hadn't taken the shortcut and was still a mile and a half behind.

Didn't matter. Chavez seemed bent on running. That was a weakness.

"It's two on one and we don't have an option," Chavez snarled to Munoz. "We engage them."

A shell blasted from the *Isabella*. Machine-gun fire briefly raked the *Rubina*'s stern.

The *Charlina* turned in a tight evasive maneuver, her machine-guns opening up on the *Isabella*.

Scccrreeeeeee!

Salina's boat tore in half along its length. Men were thrown into the water. Something in the engine compartment began to burn.

"It's one on one now," Reiner muttered, as Calina drove on a hard intercept. Pulli was slashing machine-gun fire at the *Rubina*, which was no more than two hundred yards away and getting closer with every second.

The PNA boat's own fore gun didn't have the turning radius to get them.

Tex fired.

A fireball bloomed on the stern of the *Rubina*, over the engine compartment. It subsided a fraction and then no more. Fire.

Reiner pumped his fist into the air as the *Rubina* coasted to a dead stop. "We *got* him!"

There was a cold smile on his face.

"Move in for the kill," he ordered Calina.

"Engines gone. Everything's dead," said Albertino. Munoz had vanished below deck.

"Maybe he'll come around our bow," said Calina. The cockpit MG was worthless – Zedilla had been wounded, badly, by a fragment from the shell that'd taken out their engines.

Munoz and one of his Brotherhood men came out, holding heavy black suitcases – one in each hand. They pulled strings on them, then threw them into the water. The suitcases sank fast.

Machine-gun fire raked back and forth along the length of the *Rubina*'s starboard side. Men were throwing themselves into the water.

"I have detonation charges," Munoz said. "Timed to forty-five seconds."

"We'd better ditch," said Albertino. He was already getting up, moving away from the cockpit.

"We can't surrender," Chavez snarled. Impotent. Furious. "Not to *him*."

"We're not obliged to die unnecessarily for the Revolution," Munoz reminded him.

Boom, under their feet. The *Rubina* began to sink fast.

Munoz and Albertino were already in the water. So were Munoz's nine Brotherhood buddies – *one hell of an escort for a lousy insubordinate junior lieutenant*, Chavez realized for the first time through his frustration.

Well, the Brotherhoods knew what was best. Not as though it mattered any more.

Chavez drew his pistol. Raised it toward his mouth. He *couldn't* lose. He *couldn't* surrender.

Not to the man who'd killed Castro and done uncountable other atrocities to the Revolution.

The voice of President Ramirez, over one of the radio addresses, came into his mind.

'It is a great honor to die for the Revolution. It is a still greater honor to be allowed to live for it.'

The prisoner-of-war camps would need good organizers. The Accords said that it was his duty to escape, and the USC had to obey rules in that regard. And the way things were going in the Uphams, unless they moved the prisoners to the USC proper, he'd be liberated within a few weeks anyway.

To fight again. Rather than to die pointlessly.

He dropped the pistol, threw himself overboard.

A moment later, a three-inch shell blasted the cockpit. The *Isabella* nosed closer.

"Give me that gun," Reiner told Ricks.

The gangly blond PFC stepped away from the rail-mounted thirty-caliber machine-gun. What was left of the *Rubina* was dimly visible through perhaps ten feet of muddy water.

Two dozen PNA men were treading water above it. Under Reiner's gun. He recognized Lieutenant-Commander Chavez's chiseled face from intelligence photos. The man was soaked and desperate-looking.

Just like D Company was, off Rienfuegos, thought Reiner.

Only now the gun is on my end, you filthy murdering son of a bitch.

He moved the machine-gun over to point directly at Chavez. Savoring the moment.

"How does it feel, you murderer?" he muttered. Realized the safety was still on.

Thumbed it off with a heavy *click*. His finger clenched on the trigger.

This is for Lucas and Voetjans and Schneider and Thompson and Mitchell and all the others, you fucker.

Chavez raised his hands. Looking up into Reiner's thirty-caliber.

"I surrender," he said in English.

"Their hands are in the air," said Tex, coughing loudly. The other PNA men in the water had caught on. Cries of "me entrego" and "I surrender" echoed through the dawn water.

Reiner shook his head.

"I don't care," he said. His finger tightened on the trigger.

"This is friendly water. We control both sides of it," said Tex.

"You *know* what this bastard did to my company."

"Sir, look to your right. Please," the New Texan said.

Reiner didn't want to. He'd dreamed of this moment. Chavez was *exactly* where he'd prayed for him to be. For months.

Who says there's no poetic justice?

"Sir," Tex repeated. "Before you shoot. There are protocols. That man can get a war crimes trial and hang. He's guilty as sin and you have the evidence to prove it."

I'm going to blow him away myself, Reiner thought.

But there was something in the man's tone that made him turn anyway.

Five feet away, Turner stood watching. The Centralian observer's notebook was out and a pencil poised.

Oh, God. If he sees a highly-regarded USC officer killing prisoners in the water.

It could be the data point that brings Centralia in on the PNA's side.

And opens a continental front against us.

His finger loosened on the trigger, then tensed again.

"I don't care," he muttered under his breath.

Except that a continental front would give the PNA exactly what it wanted. It would give *Chavez,* posthumously, exactly what *he* wanted.

He heard more engines. The *Krantz* drew into his peripheral vision.

"Fuck it," Reiner said, and pressed down on the gun's handles, swinging the barrel upwards.

"Get on board," Tex ordered in crude Spanish. Pieter threw down a rope ladder. "And no goddamned funny business, you hear?"